Harl

They did
So how could one night in the *wrong* bed—with
the absolute wrong person—feel oh-so-right?
Or so confusing? Now the burning question is
what comes next?

Blind hands in a dark room, an innocent night
gone deliciously too far, an unexpected knock
on a bedroom door—however these couples
started out together, one thing is for certain…
they can't wait to do it again. And soon!

Our conflicted heroes and heroines know they
are completely mismatched, but their desire
to jump back in bed with each other tells
another story. Now if they can only get over
their differences and get on with the romance,
everyone can have their happily-ever-after!

If you enjoy these two classic stories, be sure
to check out more The Wrong Bed books in
Harlequin Blaze.

Kate Hoffmann has written over seventy books for Harlequin, most of them for the Harlequin Temptation and Harlequin Blaze lines. She spent time as a music teacher, a retail assistant buyer and an advertising exec before she settled into a career as a full-time writer. She continues to pursue her interests in music, theater and musical theater, working with local schools in various productions. She lives in southeastern Wisconsin with her cat, Chloe. Visit her online at katehoffmann.com.

Look for other books by Kate Hoffmann in Harlequin Blaze—the ultimate destination for red-hot romance! There are four new Harlequin Blaze titles available every month. Check one out today!

Kate Hoffmann
and
Joanne Rock

THE RIGHT MOVES

If you purchased this book without a cover you should be aware that this book is stolen property. It was reported as "unsold and destroyed" to the publisher, and neither the author nor the publisher has received any payment for this "stripped book."

Recycling programs for this product may not exist in your area.

ISBN-13: 978-0-373-60123-3

The Right Moves

Copyright © 2015 by Harlequin Books S.A.

The publisher acknowledges the copyright holders of the individual works as follows:

Your Bed or Mine?
Copyright © 2008 by Peggy A. Hoffmann

Double Play
Copyright © 2010 by Joanne Rock

All rights reserved. Except for use in any review, the reproduction or utilization of this work in whole or in part in any form by any electronic, mechanical or other means, now known or hereinafter invented, including xerography, photocopying and recording, or in any information storage or retrieval system, is forbidden without the written permission of the publisher, Harlequin Enterprises Limited, 225 Duncan Mill Road, Don Mills, Ontario, Canada, M3B 3K9.

This is a work of fiction. Names, characters, places and incidents are either the product of the author's imagination or are used fictitiously, and any resemblance to actual persons, living or dead, business establishments, events or locales is entirely coincidental.

This edition published by arrangement with Harlequin Books S.A.

For questions and comments about the quality of this book, please contact us at CustomerService@Harlequin.com.

® and TM are trademarks of the publisher. Trademarks indicated with ® are registered in the United States Patent and Trademark Office, the Canadian Intellectual Property Office and in other countries.

Printed in U.S.A.

CONTENTS

YOUR BED OR MINE? 7
Kate Hoffmann

DOUBLE PLAY 215
Joanne Rock

YOUR BED OR MINE?
Kate Hoffmann

1

HUGE SNOWFLAKES DRIFTED down through the night sky, spattering against the windshield of Caley Lambert's rental car. She watched through tired eyes as the wipers slapped them away, the rhythmic sound lulling her toward complete exhaustion. Her eyelids fluttered and she felt herself drifting, then reached down and opened the window.

The chilly night air was a slap to the face and Caley drew a deep breath. The flight from New York had been late getting into Chicago and by the time she'd arrived, the airport hotel had given away her room. Left with nowhere to sleep, she'd decided to drive the two hours to her parents' lake house rather than waste time searching for a room.

It wasn't so much an urge to get home that sent her into the midst of a snowstorm, but the fact that Caley just hated wasting time. After eleven years of living in Manhattan and seven years of working the cutthroat world of public relations, she'd learned to be very efficient with every minute of her day. She didn't waste time on anything that couldn't get her ahead in the world professionally. She worked out because the gym was a good place to network. She belonged to seven different professional organizations because all those names looked good on her résumé. And she had worked sixteen-hour days for seven years because that was the way to get herself a partnership.

"So what am I doing in North Lake, Wisconsin?" she muttered.

Her younger sister, Emma, had called a few weeks ago, insisting that Caley come home for the week before Valentine's Day. Emma had a very special event planned at the lake house, but she refused to give any details, only that every one of the Lamberts should be in attendance. Caley's parents had been married on Valentine's Day thirty years ago, so it hadn't been difficult to guess at the purpose of her sister's plans.

An electronic version of Mozart's "Eine Kleine Nachtmusik" interrupted Caley's thoughts and she glanced over at her cell phone sitting on the passenger seat. Snatching it up, she looked at the caller ID, then tossed it back onto the seat. Brian. He'd called at least twenty times since she'd left New York for a business trip in San Francisco a few days ago. So far she'd avoided answering.

She and Brian had been exclusive for nearly two years and he'd planned to come to North Lake with her and meet the family. But at the last minute, he'd canceled, begging off because of work commitments. It was at that moment Caley realized her relationship with Brian had become a waste of time. Between out-of-town business trips and busy schedules, they'd spent three nights together in the past month—not much considering they lived in the same apartment.

She squinted through the snow, searching for the sign pointing to West Shore Road. There was a time when she'd known every inch of the tiny town of North Lake. She'd spent every summer of her life here until she'd gone to college.

Even after years of being away from this place, and in the midst of a chilly winter night, she felt a familiar sense of excitement course through her. She remembered the frantic packing the day after school let out for the summer. And then came the ride from Chicago to the lake in an overstuffed minivan, her mother behind the wheel. Her older brother, Evan, always sat in the front and controlled the radio while Caley sat between her younger siblings Emma and Adam. The youngest, Teddy, was wedged into the far backseat between the suitcases and the boxes of kitchen supplies. Her younger siblings had always worn their swimming suits on the ride up so they could jump out of the car and into the lake without having to change.

But Caley had always had other things on her mind. With each mile that passed, she'd grown more excited, the anticipation building, the nerves fraying. What would he look like? Would he be exactly as she remembered or would he have changed? Had she changed? Would he see her differently? Would this summer finally be the summer when she'd kiss him?

Year after year, drive after drive, her every thought had always been focused on him. Even now, Caley found herself falling back into old habits. Jake Burton. He'd been her fairy-tale prince, her knight in shining armor, her schoolgirl crush and her first love, all wrapped up into one incredibly hot boy.

His family had the summerhouse next door. They'd

all summered together for years: the five Lamberts and the five Burtons, an unruly tribe of kids known around North Lake as the Burtberts. For years she'd looked at Jake like her older brother, Evan—an icky, gross, burping and spitting cad who had more cooties than she cared to count.

Then, one day they were swimming out to the raft and Jake dunked her under. She'd gone under as an eleven-year-old girl and surfaced a teenager with her first crush. He'd been thirteen that summer and a handsome boy. Even now she recalled his pale blue eyes and his perfect teeth. How little droplets of water had clung to his dark eyelashes as he smiled at her and how his face was so smooth and tanned she felt compelled to reach out and touch his cheek.

When she had, Jake had slapped her hand away, a confused frown wrinkling his forehead. But from that moment on, she'd been in love. It was only later that her hormones had turned chaste puppy love to teenage lust. And later still to feelings that bordered on obsession and finally, ended in humiliation.

She drew in a deep breath and sighed. Over the past eleven years, she'd managed to visit the lake house only when Jake was certain to be elsewhere. Yet, with each visit she'd secretly hoped that maybe she'd run into him again, maybe she'd have a chance to undo the mess she'd made the night of her eighteenth birthday.

Her phone rang again and Caley cursed as she picked it up. But this time, she didn't recognize the number, only the Manhattan area code. Now that she'd been named a partner, her boss was free to call her at any time, day or night, and John Walters had taken advantage of that fact more than once. Caley wondered what kind of emergency had come up at nearly 4:00 a.m. Manhattan time.

She flipped open the phone and held it to her ear. "Hello?"

"I figured you were screening so I was forced to call from the payphone on the corner."

Caley recognized Brian's voice and bit back another curse. "I really don't want to talk to you. I said everything I needed to say before I left. It's over."

"Caley, we can work this out. You can't just end it. Everything was going so well."

She laughed, shaking her head at his ability to spin the situation. Brian was one of the most successful young lawyers on Wall Street. Like her, he could put a positive spin on the worst disaster imaginable.

"How can you say that?" she asked. "We barely see each other. And when we do, we have nothing to say. We talk about work."

"What do you want? I can talk about other things."

"That's not the point," Caley said, growing more frustrated. Usually, she was able to express her views clearly and unemotionally. But this time she had no idea what she wanted. She just knew she didn't want to come home to Brian anymore. For a long time, her life had felt out of balance and this was the only way she could think to fix it.

"What *is* the point?" he asked.

"I—" she took a deep breath "—I'm not happy."

"When has that ever made a difference to you? You work nonstop, you never take a vacation, every minute of your life is planned. Of course you're not happy. Who would be? But, Caley, that's the way you like it."

"Not anymore," she said. "It just doesn't feel right."

Suddenly, she felt a panic grip her body. Was this the right thing to do? Was she really ready to give up? A buzzing in her ears made her dizzy and for a moment she thought she might pass out. "I—I have to go. I'll call you when I get back and we'll sort out all the details. Goodbye, Brian."

Caley quickly pulled over to the curb and rolled the window down, breathing deeply of the cold night air. For the past month, she'd been fighting these panic attacks. They'd become an almost-daily occurrence. She'd blamed them on the stress of being named a partner, on living in Manhattan, on her doubts about Brian. But Caley sensed that none of these factors were really the cause.

The sound of a siren startled her and Caley looked in the rearview mirror to find a police car pulling up behind her, lights flashing. She hadn't even been close to the speed limit! But when she'd pulled over to the curb, she might have swerved too suddenly in the snow. Caley watched in the side mirror as the police officer got out of his SUV and approached the car. A sudden shiver of fear raced through her. She'd seen the stories on the news. Rapists and serial killers posing as policemen. Caley brushed the thought aside. This was North Lake. Things like that happened in New York, not in Wisconsin.

When the officer reached her car, he tapped at the window with his flashlight. Caley pressed the button on the console and the window slid down an inch. "Show me your badge," she demanded. He held it out and Caley snatched it from him. It looked real enough. She opened the window a little more and handed it back.

"License and registration, please," he said.

"I-I'm not sure I have a registration," Caley said. "This is a rental." She pulled her license out of her wallet and handed it to him, then reached for the glove box. "The car comes from Speedy Rental at O'Hare. I have the rental agreement right here." She handed him the paperwork, then peered out at him. "I wasn't speeding."

"You were talking on a cell phone," he replied. "We have an ordinance against that in North Lake. Have you been drinking, ma'am?"

"No," Caley said, stunned by his question. "I just pulled over because I was tired. I needed some fresh air."

He paused as he examined her license. "Caroline Lenore Lambert," he muttered. "You're Caley Lambert?" He shone the flashlight in her face and Caley squinted.

"Yes."

"One of the Burtbert kids?"

"Yes," she replied.

He turned the flashlight off, then leaned down, sending her a friendly smile. "Well, don't you remember me?" He pointed to the name tag pinned to his jacket. "Jeff Winslow. We went out on a few dates the summer of…well, it doesn't really matter. I took you sailing. I ran the boat aground over near Raspberry Island and you called me an idiot and dumped a can of Coke on my head."

Caley did remember. It was the sailing equivalent of running out of gas on a deserted country road. She also remembered how Jeff Winslow had tried to kiss her and feel her up and how he'd chided her for acting like a priss. Most of the boys she'd dated that summer before college had served just one purpose for Caley—they were a feeble attempt to make Jake Burton jealous.

"Of course," Caley replied. "Jeff Winslow. My goodness, you're a policeman now? That's almost ironic considering all the trouble you used to cause."

"Yeah. A misspent youth. But I've reformed. I got a degree in criminal justice, then worked for the Chicago P.D.," he said. "Then I heard they were looking for a police chief here and I thought, what the hell. I'd been shot at four times in Chicago and figured my number was coming up. So I came home." He chuckled. "I guess you've caught yourself a lucky break."

"I have?"

He flipped his ticket book closed and tucked it back into his jacket. "I'm going to let you off with a warning." He returned her driver's license. "As long as you promise not to talk on your cell phone while you're driving. It's against the law in the entire county and it's a pretty big fine."

"Thank you," Caley said.

"So, what have you been up to? The last time I saw you in North Lake you were just out of high school."

"I work in New York," Caley said. "I don't get back much."

"Too bad," Jeff said. "Living in the city is great, but I never really appreciated this place until I left. There's something special about North Lake…something peaceful." He shrugged, then tapped her window with his finger. "You drive carefully, Caley. The roads are slick. And if I catch you talking on your cell phone again, I'm going to have to give you a ticket."

"I understand," Caley said.

"Good night, then."

For a moment, she sensed he might have something else to say. But then, he turned and walked back to his SUV. A few seconds later, the lights stopped flashing and Caley took that as her cue to pull out onto the street. Moments later, she spotted West Shore Road and made the turn, Officer Jeff following her at a distance.

The houses along the shore were dark, most of them unoccupied in the winter, and she squinted to see the mailboxes through the snow. She passed by the sign for the Burtons' driveway; the next one belonged to her parents' house. A small light glowed at the end of the drive and she turned in and steered the car down the steep slope through the leafless trees, holding her breath the entire way. The SUV continued past, Officer Jeff apparently satisfied that she'd made it to her destination.

She switched off the ignition and stared at the house through the icy car window. It was even more picturesque in the winter, the roof covered with snow, icicles hanging from the gutters on the white clapboard facade. Looking at the peaceful setting, Caley knew it would be impossible to get any work done while home with her family. And though she felt she needed a break from work, she knew she couldn't. So she had made a reservation, starting the next night, at the inn downtown. Between Evan's three kids and the usual craziness that occurred when her boisterous family was together, Caley was certain she'd need a place to hide out.

Caley stepped out of the car and grabbed her bags from the backseat. She couldn't help but glance over at the Burtons' house. There was a light on in the kitchen, but the rest of the house was dark. No doubt Ellis and

Fran Burton would be at the anniversary celebration. But there would be no reason for their children to be invited. Still, Caley had to wonder if there was a chance she'd see Jake. And if she did, what would it be like between them. Would he remember that night on the beach? Would he pretend as if nothing had happened?

It had been eleven years. Maybe it was time to let it go, Caley mused. She'd been a kid with a crush. She hadn't seen Jake since the night before she left for NYU. Until now, the memory of that night had always brought a surge of regret and utter humiliation.

They were adults now and if he wanted to rehash her silly teenage indiscretion, then she would simply refuse to discuss it. Certainly he'd made mistakes in his youth that he didn't want brought up around his family. Caley tried to think of one or two just in case she needed ammunition.

They had gotten into all sorts of trouble as kids. Even now, Caley was amazed that she'd managed to avoid a life as a juvenile delinquent. But she and Jake had been a pair and she'd been the only one of the Burtberts who ever accepted his dares.

She smiled. Once, they'd caught a squirrel in a live trap and let it go inside the police chief's cruiser. Then there had been the time she and Jake had stolen a bike from the town bully. The next morning, the kid found his bike bobbing up and down on the raft just off the public beach. That trick had gained them a lot of admirers, although they never admitted to it. And then, there had been all those times they'd broken into their "fortress," a deserted summerhouse on the east shore.

The house was dark and silent as she slipped inside. No one ever locked the door when the family was at home. She stood in the spacious foyer and took a deep breath, the familiar scent teasing at her nose—a mix of the lake and leaves, old wood and furniture polish and the vanilla candles her mother loved to burn to take the damp out of the air. Once, she'd known every inch of this house, every secret hiding place, every sun-drenched window. It had been her very own castle.

Caley slowly climbed the stairs then walked down the hall to her bedroom. But when she pushed the door open, she saw the room was already occupied—Evan's kids, two in the bed and the youngest in a portable crib.

She carefully closed the door and walked across the hall. Emma would probably have room in her bed. She slipped inside her sister's room and closed the door behind her. Caley set her bag down and walked to the bed. The room was chilly and Emma had found a down comforter and was buried beneath it, her pillow pulled over her head.

"Em?" Caley whispered as she stood over the bed. She shrugged out of her jacket and kicked off her shoes. Emma had always been a heavy sleeper. Caley sat on the edge of the bed. She could probably find an empty couch downstairs, but she was too exhausted to search. She'd catch a few hours' sleep and check into the inn for a long nap in the morning.

Caley slipped out of her jeans and crawled beneath the comforter, pulling it up to her chin. She closed her eyes, her mind drifting back to the last summer she'd spent at the lake house. Jake had been home from college that summer after his sophomore year. From the moment he'd arrived, Caley had been completely and thoroughly obsessed with him. He was gorgeous, lean and tanned and so incredibly sexy that Caley was sure she would die if she couldn't be with him.

The summer had passed, Caley trying anything and

everything to get him to notice her. Finally, on the night of her eighteenth birthday party, she had decided to make a bold move. College was just a few days away and she didn't want to leave for NYU a virgin. So she'd screwed up her courage, gotten Jake alone on the beach, torn off her shirt and asked him to make a woman out of her.

Caley groaned inwardly, pulling the comforter up to her nose. Even after all these years, the thought of her stupid offer was enough to bring a blush to her cheeks. She closed her eyes and said a silent prayer that Jake wouldn't show up in North Lake until she was gone.

He was probably miles away, Caley mused. Maybe even sleeping beside another woman. She frowned at the tiny sliver of jealousy that pricked at her thoughts. The torch she'd carried for Jake had been extinguished a long time ago. It wasn't jealousy. Closer to envy, Caley thought, for she had imagined Jake happy and settled and maybe even in love.

He probably had everything in life he'd ever wanted. And she was still trying to figure out what she needed to make herself happy. Caley thought she'd have all the answers by the time she was thirty. Now, her twenty-ninth birthday was just a few months away. There wasn't much time left.

Maybe a week away from New York and the life she'd built there would give her some perspective, a quiet moment to figure things out. Caley yawned, threw her arm over her eyes. She'd have plenty of time to think about all this tomorrow. Right now, she needed sleep.

THE SOUND OF A CELL PHONE ringing dragged Jake Burton out of a deep and comfortable sleep. He groaned softly, then realized that the electronic jingle didn't belong to his phone. It was only then that Jake felt the warm body beside him.

At first he thought he was dreaming, but the weight of her leg thrown across his thighs was real, as was the citrusy scent of her hair. He tried to move his arm and found her head nestled against his shoulder.

A name, he thought to himself. He was in bed with a woman and he couldn't remember her name. Though he'd indulged in a number of one-night stands in the past, he'd pretty much given that up as of late.

The phone continued to ring and then stopped suddenly. Where had they met? Where had he been last night? Jake waited for the signs of a raging hangover to seep into his consciousness, but strangely enough, he knew he hadn't been drinking. If that was the case, then why couldn't he remember the woman?

"Think," he whispered as he slowly opened his eyes. His surroundings were completely unfamiliar. But then, slowly, he realized where he was. The Lamberts' lake house. Emma's bedroom. But if that was where he was, then who the hell was in bed with him? Surely not his future sister-in-law!

He pushed up on his elbow and squinted at the clock. Six a.m. He looked down at his bedmate, then carefully brushed the wavy dark hair away from her face. "Oh, shit," he muttered, snatching his hand away. It had been years—eleven, to be exact—but there was no mistaking that beautiful profile, the upturned nose with the light dusting of freckles, the flawless skin and the long lashes.

She was exactly as he'd remembered her, only Caley Lambert was no longer a gawky teenage girl. She was a woman. His gaze drifted down to her lips, soft and full and slightly parted. A very sexy, soft, warm woman. But what the hell was she doing in his bed?

Jake fought the urge to bend closer and touch her face. God, he remembered those urges. Funny how they all came back so quickly. Just how many times had he thought about kissing Caley Lambert over the course of his life? A hundred, maybe two hundred?

The summer she'd turned eighteen it was all he could do to keep his hands off of her, from the moment he'd arrived at the lake house until the moment he'd left. He'd deliberately avoided her, just so he wouldn't have to think about it.

And now he had the chance. Why not take it? Why not see what he'd been missing all these years? He smoothed her hair away from her face and leaned over, then touched his lips to hers. As he drew back, she stirred and her eyes fluttered. A sigh slipped from her lips and she smiled.

Jake watched her warily. She obviously wanted something to happen between them or she wouldn't have crawled into bed with him. It was a pretty bold move, considering her parents were sleeping just down the hall. But Caley had been known for her bold moves and she obviously had become bolder since he'd last seen her. She lived in Manhattan. Hell, he'd seen *Sex and the City.* He knew what single women in New York were like.

"Do you want me to kiss you again?" he whispered.

"Umm." She snuggled closer, resting her hand on his bare chest.

"Umm" could be construed as a negative reply, but

Jake decided that, coupled with her sleepy smile, it indicated a positive response.

He stretched out beside her, furrowing his hands through her hair and gently covering her lips with his. She seemed to melt into him, her body pressing against his as another sigh slipped from her throat. In his youth, kissing Caley had been an obsession and now that it was a reality, Jake was stunned by the sensations that coursed through his body.

It was just a kiss! But it was as if all of the pent-up desire from his teenage years had suddenly been released. And now, he could actually imagine what might happen between them.

His reaction to the kiss was immediate and intense. It had been a while since he'd had a woman. During the past year, he'd found himself searching for something that had been difficult to find—a woman who was strong and independent and not afraid to be herself. He was through with women who were willing to remake themselves into whatever they thought he wanted.

Jake smiled. He'd known Caley for years and what you saw with her was what you got. Even now, he imagined that she was just as stubborn and opinionated and determined as she'd been as a kid. God, he'd always admired her. She was the only girl he'd ever met who challenged him.

Her hand moved down his back, her palm warm against his skin, then slipped beneath the waistband of his boxers. He held his breath as she moved her fingers forward, to his hip. Though he hadn't woken up to a morning erection, he'd managed to remedy that situation in quick order by kissing her.

He pulled her beneath him, his fingers still tangled in her hair and molding her mouth to his. Her hips rubbed against his, his shaft hot and hard between them. There was something so exciting about touching her, something almost forbidden.

"Jake," she whispered.

The sound of his name on her lips was like fuel on a fire. His desire surged and his kiss deepened, his tongue plunging into her mouth hungrily.

This was Caley, the girl he'd known all his life, the girl he'd so carefully avoided. But she could be his, here in this bed. There was nothing to stop them. In the past, the time had never seemed right, but now, every instinct in his body screamed that the time was perfect.

As he kissed her, he found himself caught up in a fantasy that he'd lived a thousand times in his dreams. He slipped his hand beneath her T-shirt and gently cupped her breast, rubbing his thumb across her nipple through the silky fabric of her bra.

She shuddered, then arched against him, but still her eyes were closed. An uneasy feeling came over him and for a moment, he thought she might be asleep and dreaming. Jake drew back and stared down at her face, watching her as he continued to caress her breast. "Caley?"

"Jake?" she murmured.

"Open your eyes."

Her lashes fluttered. She looked at him, at first with a blank stare and then with growing confusion.

"Morning," he murmured.

Caley frowned and rubbed her eyes with her fists. A cry of alarm slipped from her lips and then, in a rush, she pushed away from him, tumbling backward onto the floor, her bare legs tangling in the comforter. "Wh-what are you doing in my bed?"

"I think the more appropriate question would be, what are you doing in *my* bed?"

"Not your bed. This is Emma's room. It's her bed." She blinked, rubbing the sleep from her eyes. "And you're not her."

"Emma's staying at the inn in town so she can have a little peace and quiet. Our house was full, so your mother offered me the last empty bed."

Her phone rang again and Caley looked around the room, then crawled across the floor to retrieve her purse. She watched him warily as she flipped open the phone. "Hello?"

Jake grinned at her, letting his gaze take in her long, naked legs and the lacy black panties. Yes, the gangly teenager was gone, replaced by a long-limbed, incredibly sexy woman.

"Yes, John. I understand. No, I'll get right on it. You'll have it by the end of the day. All right. You, too. Goodbye." She closed the phone.

"Boyfriend?"

"Boss," she murmured. "You were in this bed last night. With me?"

Jake nodded. Oh, hell, she had been asleep. "Yes. But I wasn't with you. Not in the biblical sense. We were just next to each other. And then, well, then you woke up." The last thing he needed was Caley to go running downstairs, accusing him of being a pervert. "Hey, it was an honest mistake. It was dark. I looked like your sister. How could you have known?"

A frown wrinkled her forehead. "Then we weren't just... I wasn't... Nothing happened, right?"

Jake winced. "Well, there was a little something, but that was an honest mistake, as well. I just kind of assumed you'd crawled in bed with me for a reason, so—"

She touched her lips. "You kissed me?"

"But you kissed me back. And there was some localized touching going on, but only through the clothes. Except you did put your hand down my boxers."

Her phone rang again. Caley opened her mouth and snapped it shut, then looked at the caller ID. This time, she decided not to answer. Instead, she grabbed the corner of the comforter and pulled it off the bed to cover herself, leaving him in nothing but those boxers. She watched him warily, waiting for him to make the next move.

"Did you think I was someone else?" he asked.

"Yes," she snapped. But from the guilty look on her face, he could tell she was lying.

"Some other guy named Jake?"

"Yes. I happen to know three or four other Jakes."

He grabbed a corner of the comforter and pulled it over his lap. It would be hard to sell the "nothing happened" story with a raging hard-on pressing against the front of his boxers. Jake cleared his throat and forced a smile. "So, how have you been? It's been a while. How long? Eleven years?"

She nodded, clutching the comforter to her chest. Her cheeks were flushed and her breath was coming in quick gasps. And her hair, thick and wavy, was tumbled about her shoulders. She'd never looked more beautiful. Jake's gaze drifted down, stopping at the perfectly painted toes peeking out from under the blanket. She'd always had really pretty feet. He'd spent a lot of time looking at her feet when he was younger, simply to avoid looking at her breasts, which were also pretty incredible.

"Your mother said you wouldn't be arriving until this morning," he commented.

"I decided to drive directly from the airport. When did you get in?"

"Yesterday," he said. "So, what have you been up to?"

"Not much," she replied. "Just working. I'm still with that public relations firm that I joined right out of college. I was made partner last month. What about you?"

"I have my own design firm now. I'm doing mostly residential architecture. I kind of specialize in vacation homes based on classic camp designs."

"Interesting." She drew in a sharp breath, impatient with the idle chitchat. "What are you doing home? Why would you want to come to my parents' anniversary party?"

A slow realization dawned. Emma hadn't told her what was going on. Jake wondered if he ought to be the one to break the happy news or if she should hear it over the breakfast table. For now, it might prove a distraction from what had just happened. "This isn't an anniversary party," Jake said. "It's Emma and Sam."

She frowned at the mention of Jake's youngest brother. "Emma and Sam?"

"They're getting married."

At first she gasped, then regarded him with disbelief. This was the Caley he remembered. She always found a way to disagree with him, even if he was only claiming the sun rose in the east and set in the west. "Not funny."

"It's the truth," Jake said. "That's why we're all here. It's going to be a small wedding at the Episcopal Church in town on Valentine's evening. She's got the dress and they've got the license."

"They aren't even dating," Caley said.

"I guess they have been. They've been secretly seeing each other for the past three summers. They didn't want anyone to know. You know how our mothers are and how they've dreamed about making a match between the Lamberts and the Burtons. They got engaged on New Year's and decided to get married right away, before Fran and Jean could plan a big event."

"But they're only twenty-one," Caley said. "That's too young. What do they know about marriage?" She drew a ragged breath and stared at him, as if she were taking a moment to digest the news. Then, her eyes slowly dropped, first to his chest and then his legs. She pulled the comforter up beneath her chin. "Do you think maybe you could get dressed and—"

The door to the bedroom swung open and Caley's youngest brother, Teddy, stuck his head inside. "Hey, Jake. Are you going to want some—" His words died in his throat as he took in the scene in front of him. "Hey, Caley. You're home." He glanced over at Jake, then forced a smile. "Yeah, okay. Breakfast," he murmured as he closed the door.

"Oh, no," Caley moaned, scrambling to her feet. "No, no, no. Now he's going to go downstairs and this is going to be the subject of breakfast conversation. The two of us, in our underwear, in the same bedroom."

"And in the same bed," he said. "We could always

crawl back under the covers and really mess with their heads," Jake offered. She sent him a withering look and he held up his hands in mock surrender. "Bad joke. Sorry."

With a low growl, Caley scrambled to her feet and tossed the comforter aside. "You haven't changed at all, Jake Burton. Everything is always a joke to you. You never take anything seriously."

Jake watched as she searched for her pants. "Don't get your panties in a twist. I'll explain the mistake. Although I'm not going to give them all the details."

"The state of my panties is none of your business. And I don't remember any of the details. Why? Because I was asleep."

Jake laughed. To think he'd dreaded seeing her again, knowing how uncomfortable it might be. But they'd slipped right back into their normal dynamic. Jake swung his legs over the side of the bed, fighting the urge to grab her arm and pull her back on top of him, to remind her of her reaction to his kiss.

There had always been a heat between them, an attraction that he'd been reluctant to act upon. She'd always been too young, too naive. And he'd known she was in love with him, so it could only end badly. He'd thought he'd done the honorable thing that night so long ago, the night she'd offered up her virginity for his taking.

His rejection obviously still stung. If not that, what else could she possibly be angry about? "If you're still angry about—"

Caley gasped, then threw a shoe at him. "I'm not angry about that. Just forget about that. I was young and stupid and I've slept with plenty of men since then and all of them much better lovers than you could have possibly been. Some women might find you attractive, but not me."

Her phone rang for a fourth time. Jake jumped off the bed and caught her arm, then pulled her against him. Without a second thought, he brought his mouth down on hers and kissed her, deeply and thoroughly. He felt her soften in his arms and when her knees buckled, Jake grabbed her waist to steady her.

When he finally drew back, her face was flushed and her eyes closed. He felt his own reaction in his boxers, the desire returning immediately. This was going to be one helluva week if this was how they were starting, he mused. There had always been a sexual curiosity between them. Maybe it was time to satisfy it.

"Are you going to answer that?" he asked.

"It can wait," Caley replied breathlessly.

"Yeah," he murmured, "that's what I thought." Nothing had changed. He wanted her just as much as he always had.

Caley opened her eyes and stared at him, a sigh slipping from her lips. "I-I'd better get dressed. Everyone is going to be expecting us at breakfast." She quickly grabbed her overnight bag and rushed to the adjoining bathroom, then slammed the door behind her.

Jake sat down on the bed and smiled. This was a start and maybe that was all he could hope for. He glanced around the room, grabbed his jeans from the bedpost and tugged them on. He found a clean T-shirt in his duffel and pulled it over his head. He'd find a way to continue what they'd begun later in the day.

When he got downstairs, the huge kitchen was filled with people. Caley's mother, Jean, was busy at the stove, preparing pancakes for her family. Her eldest, Evan, was just a year older than Jake, but already had a wife and three children. After Caley came Adam and Emma, followed by Teddy, who would graduate from high school in June. Evan was reading the sports section and discussing the Bulls game with Jake's younger brother Brett.

"Good morning, everyone," Jake said, taking the first empty spot at the huge table.

"Sausage or bacon, dear?" Jean called.

"Bacon," Jake said. A moment later, a plate was dropped in front of him. He reached out for the lazy Susan, which held utensils, napkins, butter and syrup.

The Lambert house was so much like his own that he felt at home at their table. He couldn't remember the number of meals that he'd eaten in their kitchen, usually with several of his siblings. Jean and Jake's mother, Fran, never bothered to sort out their respective children at mealtime. Whoever was sitting at the table at the beginning of a meal got fed, no matter which family they belonged to.

Jake had just dug into his pancakes when Teddy walked in the back door, covered in snow and carrying an armload of firewood. He sent Jake a knowing smile, then dropped the wood next to the door. "Morning, Jake. How'd you sleep?"

"Teddy, I want you to take some firewood over to Ellis and Fran's house," Jean said. "Load a bunch in the back of your truck. We have plenty. Jake can help you load it."

Teddy grinned. "Oh, I think he might be too tired to load firewood, Ma. So didja get much sleep last night, Jake?"

"I've been meaning to get a new mattress for that bed," Jean said. "It wasn't too lumpy, was it?"

"Not lumpy," Teddy said. "Maybe a little crowded."

Caley's mother scowled. "Teddy, what are you talking about?"

The entire group turned to hear Teddy's response. "Caley was sleeping with Jake."

Jean gasped. "Caley's home? When did she get in?"

"At about three in the morning."

They all turned again, this time to Caley, who stood in the doorway of the kitchen. She was dressed in a bulky wool sweater a shade of blue that complemented her eyes. Faded jeans hugged her long legs and slender hips.

"I thought I was crawling into bed with Emma," she explained. "It was a mistake. And nothing happened."

"Emma's staying at the inn," Jean said, bustling over to give her daughter a huge hug. She stepped back. "That's right, you don't know the big news, do you?"

"Jake told me," Caley replied. "Sam and Emma. Who would have thought?" She cleared her throat and looked at the curious gazes of her siblings. "Nothing happened. It was a mistake."

"Of course nothing happened," Jean said. "You two are like oil and water." She kissed Caley's cheek and smiled at Jake. "How could you possibly mistake Jake for Emma?"

"He had the covers over his head," Caley explained.

"Well, since I don't have to worry about you two getting cozy, maybe I should just have you bunk together for the rest of the week," Jean teased. "Oh, and Emma is going to ask you to be her maid of honor, darling. I hope you'll say yes. Bacon or sausage?"

"I'll just have the pancakes," Caley said, glancing across the table at Jake. "And you don't have to worry about me. I booked a room at the inn." She paused. "I'll be able to help Emma out. Since I'm her maid of honor. And Jake can have Emma's room all to himself."

Caley searched for a spot at the table and Adam moved his seat to make a space between himself and Jake. Caley reluctantly retrieved a chair and sat down. Her mother put a plate down in front of her and Jake picked up the pitcher of orange juice and poured her a glass. He held it out and she hesitantly took it and set it beside her plate.

They ate in silence, the both of them pretending to listen to the conversation around them. Jake's foot brushed against hers and she coughed on the orange juice she was drinking.

It was so nice to be able to touch her, Jake mused.

He felt her hand push his leg away and he reached beneath the table to grab it, weaving his fingers through hers. Her eyes grew wide as his thumb rested on her wrist, just over her pulse point.

"What's the schedule for today?" Caley asked, her voice cracking slightly.

"Emma's chosen a dress for you at the bridal shop in town and you need to go try it on this morning. The snow is getting deep. Adam will take you in his truck."

"I'll take Caley into town," Jake volunteered, giving her hand a squeeze. "I have some errands to run anyway."

"I can drive myself," Caley said, tugging her hand from his.

Jean smiled at Jake. "Thank you, dear. I knew I could count on you." She folded her hands in front of her, then looked back and forth between Jake and Caley. "It's so nice to see you two together again. How long has it been?"

"Eleven years," Caley said. She grabbed her plate and stood up. "I've got to make some calls. And I can drive myself to town. I have to check in at the inn before I go to the fitting." She sent Jake a cool look, then stalked out of the room.

Jake stood and carried his plate to the sink. "Not much has changed. Come on, Teddy, let's get that firewood loaded."

As they grabbed their jackets and walked out the back door, Teddy chuckled softly. "Oh, I think a lot has changed."

"And I'm not so sure you need help with the firewood," Jake replied.

"Sorry," Teddy murmured.

Jake used to be able to hide his feelings for Caley. But from the moment he woke that morning to find her wrapped around his body, Jake knew he wanted to explore those feelings. He and Caley weren't teenagers anymore, they were adults. And there were no rules keeping them apart. Now that there was time to test their attraction to each other, he planned to take full advantage of it.

2

THE GENTLE SNOWFALL increased in intensity throughout the early morning. Caley watched it from the window seat in her father's den. She'd been trying to work, making calls back and forth to the office and trying to send a report via a dial-up modem. She decided to wait until she had better internet access at the inn and sent a text message to her assistant in the meantime.

Trying to concentrate on work had been impossible. Her mind kept returning to the bedroom upstairs and to the kiss that she and Jake had shared. A shiver skittered down her spine and she rubbed her arms to quell the goose bumps. It was usually so easy to focus on work and now just one silly kiss—two, really—had completely consumed her thoughts.

She closed her laptop and gathered up her things; she would check into the inn right after her fitting. But right now she had to concentrate on getting to her car, which was probably buried. She remembered Jake's offer of a ride, but thought it best not to tempt fate. It had been far too easy to kiss him. Given another chance, who knows what they might do?

Caley found a hodgepodge of winter outerwear in the hall closet and pulled on a jacket, boots, mittens and a cap. She tucked her phone into her pocket and trudged outside to shovel. She was glad for the distraction, for something productive to occupy her thoughts.

Other things had happened in that bed and she searched the haze of her memories for details. There had been a long, delicious dream in which Jake had finally succumbed to her charms. She'd spent most of her teenage years fantasizing about that moment when he'd pull her into his arms and kiss her, so it was no wonder that back in North Lake those thoughts had invaded her sleep again.

Yes, he'd kissed her. But the heavens hadn't opened and the angels hadn't sung. All right, a small chorus had made an appearance. After all, she'd have to be made of ice not to react.

As she started to shovel, she remembered the desire that had bubbled up inside of her the moment his lips touched hers. Caley had wanted him to continue, to make the kiss a beginning rather than an end. She'd longed for him to brush aside her clothes and kiss her naked skin, to pull her back to the bed and seduce her until she trembled at his touch.

She'd once fantasized that Jake was her Prince Charming, pure and noble. Now, she saw him as a man with a killer smile and an incredible body and a way of looking at her that made her tingle all over.

She stepped back from her task and drew a deep breath, trying to calm her racing pulse. It probably wouldn't be difficult to let nature take its course. Jake had clearly seemed interested that morning—more than interested, if what was going on beneath his boxers was any indication. And it wasn't as though she'd be seducing a complete stranger. She'd been so curious for so long, now why not enjoy Jake while she could?

She'd left New York with her life in turmoil, searching for the key to her happiness. Sleeping with Jake might make her happy for the short term. Though she'd insulted his prowess in bed, Caley suspected that she'd thoroughly enjoy being seduced by him. He was different now. A shiver skittered down her spine. He was definitely a man—a very sexy, handsome, powerful man.

She sighed, her breath clouding in front of her face. Her rational mind told her she didn't need to add any more complications to her life. But sleeping with Jake might not be complicated so much as exciting and dangerous and wildly satisfying. Closing her eyes, she took another deep breath. Was it really Jake that she wanted or just someone—anyone—who made her feel better about her life?

Caley had nearly cleared one wheel of the car when Jake pulled up in an SUV. He beeped the horn at her, then rolled down the window and grinned. "Get in," he said. "I'll take you to town. You'll never get that car dug out by yourself."

Caley held her breath as she stared at him. He'd looked handsome that morning, dressed in only his boxers, his hair mussed by sleep and a scruffy day-old beard darkening his jaw. Now, he looked almost irresistible. Her gaze dropped to his mouth and she wondered when she'd kiss him next. Caley turned back to her shoveling, afraid that she hadn't the power to resist him. "I—I can drive myself."

"Come on, Caley. You're not going to get the car out in any kind of reasonable time."

She glanced over her shoulder, ready to concede defeat on both the car and her immunity to his charm. Jake jumped out of the SUV, grabbed the shovel, stuck it into a snowdrift and held out his hand. "Come on."

Caley stared down at his fingers, long and tapered. A memory drifted through her mind, hazy but real. He'd touched her that morning. It hadn't been part of her dream. His fingers had danced over her skin and his touch had made her body come alive.

Hesitantly, she placed her hand in his and he led her to his SUV. He opened the passenger-side door and helped her inside, then circled around to get in behind the wheel. In the end, she really didn't want to drive into town on her own, especially along curvy West Shore Road. All it would take was a skid into the ditch and she'd have to listen to Jake's repeated "I told you so."

"Buckle up," he said.

Caley turned to him. "I think we need to get one thing clear. I'm not in love with you anymore. Any crush I might have had as a teenager is long gone. So don't act like you have me wrapped around your little finger, because you don't."

Caley turned to stare out the window, embarrassed by her sudden outburst. She was usually so careful about her choice of words. What was it about Jake that made her act like a petulant teenager? Why did he always have to challenge her?

Jake threw the truck into gear and headed up the hill to the end of the driveway. The SUV easily handled the deep drifts and the slippery conditions. But she wasn't about to give Jake the satisfaction of being right.

"You were in love with me?" he asked. "When exactly was that?"

"Years ago," she murmured. "For about a week. It's all a very vague memory."

"So you aren't even slightly attracted to me now?" A grin quirked at the corners of his mouth.

"No," she lied.

He considered her answer for a long moment. "Too bad. Because I'm still kind of attracted to you. Yeah, I know. Surprising, right?"

"Still?" Caley asked, stunned by his admission.

"Yeah, still. Hey, I always thought you were hot."

Caley laughed out loud at the audacity of his comment. "Please," she said.

"No, I did. I do. Come on, Caley, look at yourself. A guy would have to be crazy to think otherwise. You're beautiful and sophisticated and smart."

She wasn't sure whether he was teasing her or telling the truth. But it did make her feel better. Caley smiled.

"All the guys were madly in love with you that summer before you left for college."

"Now you *are* lying. But go on."

"I told them you were taken."

She frowned at him. "But I wasn't. Why would you tell them that?"

"They were only looking for one thing and I just didn't want them putting the moves on you. I didn't think you were ready for that. And maybe I felt a little possessive."

"You were the reason I left for college a virgin."

"Believe me, I would have loved to help you out on that one, but I wasn't sure I'd be the right guy for the job." He paused. "I'd assume you solved that problem a while ago."

Caley giggled. "Are you asking if I'm a virgin? I'm twenty-eight years old."

"I was talking about finding the right guy. Teddy mentioned that you're living with some lawyer."

Caley opened her mouth, ready to tell him that Brian was probably moving his stuff out of their apartment as they spoke. But admitting that would leave her with no defense against seduction. "Yeah. We've been together for a couple years. What about you?"

Caley didn't want to hear the answer. She wanted to believe that the only woman on his mind was her. But that would be unrealistic. Jake was an attractive, successful man.

"No one special," he said. "I guess I was saving myself for you."

She bit her bottom lip, focusing on the road ahead. Why did he say things like that? Was he testing her? Jake had always enjoyed teasing her, but this was different. It was as if he was daring her to take his words seriously.

They drove for a long while in silence. She took out her cell phone and began to text another message to her assistant.

"Do you take that thing with you everywhere?"

"I need to be available. People are counting on me."

"The rats would continue to race even if you weren't running alongside them. Take a break. You're supposed to be on vacation."

"Partners don't ever really go on vacation," she said. Still, she tucked the phone back into her pocket, leaving the message unfinished.

A question nagged at Caley's brain, a question she never thought she'd have the nerve or the opportunity to ask. But it needed to be answered. "If you were so attracted to me, then why did you turn me down that night?"

He smiled, but kept his gaze fixed on the road ahead. "You'd just turned eighteen. I was almost twenty. I didn't think it was the right time. It was your first time and I figured that should be perfect. I wasn't sure I would be able to do that for you." He glanced over at her. "I did you a big favor, Caley. I didn't want you to regret your first experience."

Caley sat back in the seat and stared out the window. Though his words did a bit to soothe the memory of her humiliation, she had a hard time believing Jake was that noble. "I was devastated," she said.

He reached over and slipped his hand around her nape. Her pulse quickened and Caley felt a rush of desire as his fingers tangled in her hair. "I'm sorry," he replied, gently forcing her to look at him. "But, if it will make you feel better, I'd be glad to do the job now."

She saw the wry grin on his face and Caley couldn't help but laugh. "I'll let you know."

"Hey, I've been told I do an admirable job in the sack."

"That's because all the women you sleep with are too blinded by your pretty face. They'd say anything to keep you in their beds."

Jake pulled the truck over to the edge of the road and threw it out of gear. "My charm worked pretty well on you this morning."

"I was asleep."

"You said my name."

She shrugged, trying to maintain a cool facade. It wasn't working. Her hands were trembling and she felt a little light-headed. "Well, it won't work anymore. Go ahead. Kiss me. You'll see, I won't have any reaction." It was a feeble challenge and she knew he could see right through it. But she didn't care. She wanted to kiss him again and she couldn't wait any longer.

To her surprise, he accepted her challenge. Before she could even take a breath, he grabbed her face between his hands and kissed her. At first, the kiss was full of frustration. But then, he softened his touch and slipped his tongue between her lips.

Caley grabbed the front of his jacket and pulled him toward her, until he was sprawled across the console, his hands furrowed through her hair. They couldn't seem to get close enough, tearing at each other's clothes, searching for something more to touch. Though she knew she ought to put a stop to it, the taste of him, the feel of his body against hers was exhilarating, like some crazy carnival ride that frightened her and thrilled her all at once.

He slipped his hand under the waist of her pants and clutched her backside, pulling her hips against his. He was aroused and Caley enjoyed the fact that he couldn't resist her any more than she could resist him.

"What the hell are you doing to me?" he murmured, his breath warm against her ear. "You have a boyfriend. You're living with him."

"We broke up," she murmured, nuzzling her face into the curve of his neck.

Jake grabbed her shoulders and pushed her back, staring down into her eyes. "Don't play games with me, Caley."

"I'm not. I swear, we broke up. It's over."

Jake dragged his thumb over her bottom lip. "Can we just stop pretending then? I'm man enough to admit that I want you. And I think you want me, right?"

"Maybe," Caley murmured.

"Not maybe," he said, shaking his head.

"All right. I'll admit that there is an interesting attraction between us."

"So what are we going to do about it?"

Caley frowned. "I don't know. It could be complicated."

He drew back, then grinned. "When you figure out what you want, you let me know," he said.

Caley gasped softly. Was that it? Wasn't he supposed to pull her into his arms and kiss away all her doubts? Or seduce her without any regard to her reservations? He wasn't supposed to drop the ball back in her court!

"I will," Caley said softly.

Jake straightened, sliding back behind the wheel. "We should probably get going."

When they reached the small bridal shop in the village, Jake parked, then hopped out and circled around the front to open her door. The Burton boys had always had impeccable manners.

"Watch out," he said, as he grabbed her waist. "It's slippery beneath this snow." His hands lingered on her hips as his gaze fell to her mouth.

They stood there for a long moment, frozen in place, their breath clouding between them. Then Caley pushed up on her toes and touched her lips to his. "I'm not playing games with you," she whispered. "I just felt like kissing you again."

"I know how that feels," he replied. His arms slipped

around her waist and he pulled her body against his. Jake brought his hands up to her face and gently cupped her cheeks as he returned the kiss. But the sound of laughter brought an end to their momentary pleasure. Caley turned to watch two teenage girls in the midst of a snowball fight.

"It's no one," he whispered, his breath warm against her ear.

"If we do this, we can't let anyone know," she said.

"I never kiss and tell," he said.

"I'm serious. It has to stay just between us. And it has to be just sex. Nothing more."

"Friends with benefits?" he asked.

She nodded. "I'll be right back," she said, glancing over at the bridal shop.

"I'll come in and wait," he said.

"Is that wise?" she asked.

"I'm not going to seduce you in a public place," he said. "And I don't think Miss Belle is going to go running to our parents to tell on us."

He followed her to the door, then pulled it open for her, placing his hand on the small of her back as she stepped inside. It was a simple gesture, but Caley realized that Jake was taking any opportunity offered to touch her.

The owner of the shop, Miss Belle, greeted them both, then drew Caley along to the fitting rooms in the back. She stopped and turned to Jake, motioning to him. "Are you coming, too?"

"Oh, no," Caley said. "He's not my—well, he's just a— I don't think he'd be interested."

"I'll come," Jake said, sending Caley a playful grin. "I'm very interested."

Caley took the dress into the fitting room and slipped out of her clothes. Though the dress didn't look like much on the hanger, when she put it on it was another story. The silky fabric clung to every curve of her body; the modest neckline plunged to a deep V in the back; the long sleeves fitted to her arms. She slipped out of her bra and then turned to examine the rear view. Emma had gotten the sizing perfect and had chosen a dress that would look stunning for an evening wedding.

Caley pulled open the fitting room door and stepped out. Jake had been sitting on a bench and the moment he saw her, he quickly stood, a tiny gasp slipping from his lips.

"Wow," he murmured. "That's some dress."

Caley smoothed her hands over her hips as she turned. "It is nice, isn't it?"

"Are you wearing underwear?"

She gave him a stern look. "It's too clingy."

"So, you're not going to wear underwear. Where the hell am I supposed to put my hands when we dance?" he asked. "This is going to be a problem."

"Are we going to dance?"

"You're the maid of honor and I'm the best man. I think it's a rule than we take at least one turn around the floor."

Miss Belle hurried up and studied Caley critically. "We'll bring the sleeves up a bit. I'd assume you plan to go…without?" She pointed to Caley's chest.

"Do I have a choice?" Caley asked.

"Well, we have the stick-ons."

"Can we see some of those?" Jake asked, a worried expression on his face.

Caley shook her head. "This will be fine."

Miss Belle held out a shoebox. "Try the shoes so I can check the hem."

Caley grabbed a shoe from the box and tried to put it on, but couldn't keep her balance in the long dress. Jake slipped his hands around her waist and steadied her as she put on the dyed-to-match pumps.

"Perfect," the shopkeeper said. "I'll be right back." Miss Belle hurried off to answer the phone, leaving Jake and Caley alone at the rear of the shop.

"Perfect," Jake repeated.

"Stop saying things like that to me," she murmured. "Sometimes I feel like you're playing with me."

He shook his head. "It's how we are, Caley. It's how we've always been."

She turned and walked back to the fitting room, and Jake followed close on her heels. When she stepped inside, Caley tried to close the door behind her, but Jake slipped inside, then leaned back against the door.

"In all the time that I've known you, have I ever lied to you?" Jake asked.

Caley stared at her fingernails. Until that night of her eighteenth birthday, Jake had been the one person she knew she could count on for unadulterated honesty. "I don't think so."

"Who told you to take the toilet paper out of your bra the night of the Fourth of July dance at the park? Who told you you looked like a giraffe when you started wearing those platform shoes? Who told you not to go out with Jeff Winslow because all he wanted to do was feel you up?"

"You did," Caley said. "But I went out with Jeff Winslow anyway. Of course, he did try to feel me up."

"See?"

"Just because you never lie to me doesn't mean that you don't have the capacity to hurt me."

He took a step toward her, then reached out and touched her cheek. "Does that hurt?"

Caley drew a shaky breath. It felt so good to have him touch her, his fingertips leaving a warm imprint on her skin. She shook her head. This time she wouldn't make it so easy for him. This time she'd resist him.

Jake took another step closer and kissed her softly on the forehead. "How about that? Tell me it feels good."

She swallowed hard, then sighed deeply as he kissed her temple. Did she have the strength? And was it wise to try and resist? It really didn't seem worth the effort. "Yes," she said. "It feels good."

He hooked his finger beneath her chin and tipped her gaze up to meet his. And then he kissed her, his tongue teasing at her lips before gently invading her mouth. But it wasn't like the kiss in the truck. This kiss was slow and sensuous, meant to melt all her resolve. Caley wrapped her arms around his neck and surrendered, enjoying the rush of heat that coursed through her body.

His hands slid down her waist to her hips, then circled to smooth over her back, left bare by the cut of the dress. Caley's mind whirled as she tried to remember every detail of the kiss, forcing herself not to slip into some hazy state of desire. But in the end, it was impossible to maintain her composure. Jake seemed determined to prove that he was quite possibly the best kisser in the entire world.

When his hand moved to her breast, she moaned softly. He grazed his thumb across her nipple, bringing it to a hard peak, sending a wild wave of pleasure coursing through her. When he finally drew back, Caley was dizzy with excitement. Her breath was coming in quick gasps and her pulse was pounding in her head.

"If that ever stops feeling good, you just let me know and I'll stop," Jake whispered. He kissed the tip of her nose, then walked out of the fitting room, closing the door behind him.

Caley stumbled back until she leaned against the mirrored wall for support. Her trembling fingers touched her lips and she felt a smile growing there. After all these years, it was hard to believe that all her fantasies about Jake might just come true.

There was something powerful pulsing between them and it didn't look like either one of them had the capacity—or the will—to stop it. And that made it all the more exciting—and dangerous.

"THE BURTBERT SNOW BOWL begins in fifteen minutes!" Brett called.

Jake and Sam looked over their shoulders at their brother and gave him a wave. "We'll be ready," Jake shouted.

They sat on the stairs that, in the summer, led down to the dock and the beach they shared with the Lamberts. The lake was frozen over and covered with snow, but Teddy Lambert had cleared an area big enough for skating or a pickup hockey game.

Jake stretched his legs out in front of him and watched the last of the snowflakes drift lazily through the air. The storm was over and everything was covered with a sparkly powder. "So you're getting married."

Sam smiled as he traced a pattern in the snow with a stick. "That's what I hear."

"I gotta tell you, Sam, I was surprised when I heard you were engaged to Emma. But then when I heard you were getting married so quickly, I was kinda shocked. A month and a half is a pretty short engagement, don't you think?"

"Maybe."

"How much time have you two really spent together?"

Sam shrugged. "Three summers, here at the lake house. And then I visited her in Boston over Thanksgiving and we got together during Christmas break in Chicago and we just decided we didn't want to be apart anymore."

"Why not live together then?" Jake asked. "Give yourself some more time."

"Because Emma wants to get married," Sam said.

"What do you want?"

"Why so many questions?" Sam asked, a hint of irritation creeping into his voice.

"That's my job as your best man. To be sure you're making the best choices."

"I want what Emma wants. I want to make her happy," Sam said.

Jake hadn't been thrilled when he heard about his little brother's plans to get married, but he chalked that up to surprise. But now that he had a chance to spend some time with Sam and talk to him, Jake realized that twenty-one was far too young to take such a giant step.

He'd spent the last ten years working his way through a variety of females, trying to figure out what made them tick, enjoying the full spectrum of pleasures in their beds. But it was only in the past year that he'd really come to understand what he needed in a relationship and the kind of woman he wanted to spend his life with. Sam hadn't even started on that journey and already he was tying himself down. How could anyone know they were in love at that age? Neither Sam nor Emma had experienced anything of the world yet.

"You're not even finished with college," Jake murmured.

"Emma graduates in the spring and she's just got a few independent study courses, so she'll be spending more time in Chicago. I'll finish at Northwestern at Christmas next year and then I'm thinking about law school. If we get married, we can start planning our lives together—and she can support me while I'm getting my law degree."

"You can do all that without getting married," Jake said.

Sam groaned, then leaned back on his elbows, staring out at the wide landscape of the lake. "Maybe I should have asked Brett to be my best man. Or Emma's brother Teddy."

"Marriage is a big step, Sam. You have to get married for the right reasons."

"What reasons would those be?"

"Because you can't imagine living without her. Because every time you look at her, you have to touch her, just to make sure she's real and she's yours. Because she's the first thing you think about in the morning when you get up and the last thing you think about before you go to sleep."

Jake drew a deep breath. This was the sum total of his knowledge about living happily ever after. It was what he'd decided it would take to tempt him into settling down for the rest of his life. And oddly enough, Caley seemed to meet all those requirements.

A shiver skittered down his spine. Women were supposed to confuse lust and love, not men. Still, Jake couldn't ignore his feelings. Things weren't the same as when they were kids. There was something deeper… something stronger drawing them together now.

He glanced over at Sam. "I'd hate to think you're doing this to please Mrs. Lambert and our mother. All that Burtbert shit is really silly. We can still be one big family, even if we aren't technically related."

"It's not about that," Sam said.

"What is it, then?"

"We just want to start our lives together."

"I know it seems like you'll never get enough of her, but that kind of desire doesn't last. It's not all about sex," Jake said. "There has to be something more."

"Oh, we haven't had sex," Sam said. "Emma wanted to wait until we got married."

Jake gasped. "You haven't— I mean, not even a little?"

"Well, a little. But not the whole way."

Jake groaned and buried his face in his hands. "How can you possibly make a decision about the rest of your life when you don't even know if you're compatible in the bedroom?"

"Lots of people wait," he said. "And it's not like I haven't done it. And Emma has, too. We just haven't done it together."

"Well, maybe you should," Jake said. "Just to make sure." Hell, he'd never even tried to regulate his own desires for women—and since Caley had arrived back in town, Jake didn't even feel in control of his libido. How did a guy just put those feelings on the back burner? Wasn't it scientifically proven that abstaining wasn't good for the male body?

He took a deep breath. "Why not just wait a little longer? It couldn't hurt."

"I love her," Sam said. "And she loves me."

"I love Emma, too," Jake said. "And Caley and Teddy and Adam and Evan. The Lamberts are like our family." Jake sighed softly, searching for another argument that made sense. Who was he to try to explain what went on between a man and a woman? Hell, he couldn't begin to fathom his obsessive attraction to Caley. All he knew was that it felt good when he was with her, so good that he never wanted to let her go.

He pushed to his feet and offered his little brother a hand. "Come on. If I know Brett, he's going to want to strategize before we get the game going. The last time we played football with the Lamberts, they beat us bad. They've got Evan's wife now and she's gone through natural childbirth three times. She's no wuss."

"And Caley plays like a guy," Sam said.

"Don't worry about Caley, I can handle her. You just take care of Emma."

Sam grinned. "Until we're married, she's still a Lambert. And the enemy."

They walked up to the lawn, now covered in a foot of powdery snow. After a few minutes, all the players were congregated at the center of the field. When Jake saw Caley, he gave her a wave and she returned his greeting with a hesitant smile. She looked so cute bundled up against the cold that it didn't take more than a moment for his mind to begin a fantasy of slowly peeling off all those layers of clothes. Jake drew a sharp breath and closed his eyes. Now was not the time to think about getting naked with Caley!

Once everyone was gathered, Brett raised his hand. "Welcome to the first, and possibly only, Burtbert Snow Bowl. In the tradition of our annual summer Toilet Bowl football game, we have decided to bring back the time-honored trophy." He pulled a toilet plunger from behind his back and everyone laughed and clapped, surprised to see the trophy after so long.

"The last time this was awarded was eleven years ago last summer and, according to the inscription, it was won by the Lamberts."

"On a touchdown run by Caley," Jake said. He looked at her. "Remember? Adam threw you the ball and you just took off down the field. No one could catch you."

She gave him an odd look. "I don't remember that."

Jake shrugged. "I do. It was a great play."

He slowly walked around the perimeter of the crowd as Brett went over the rules, stopping when he stood behind Caley. His gaze fixed on Sam and Emma. "They look happy," he murmured. "What do you think?"

Caley glanced over her shoulder at him. "Yes," she replied.

Brett pointed to the list of winners, written on the wooden handle with a marker. "Our captains today will be Sam and Emma. By my count, we've got even teams with Evan's wife, Marianne, and Ann's husband, John, so no one has to sit out."

Teddy disagreed. "We have three guys and three girls and you've got four guys and two girls. You call that even?"

"John just had knee surgery last year," Brett said. "And Marianne played college soccer. I'd say it's even."

The coin was flipped and the game began. Brett played quarterback for the Burton team and when he went out for a long pass to Ann, Caley stepped out in front of her and snagged an interception.

She started off down the sideline and Jake took off after her, making up the distance between them in a few seconds. He grabbed Caley around the waist and picked her up off her feet, then fell into the snow near the goal line, taking the impact with his body.

They'd played in this rough-and-tumble fashion when they were kids and back then it had been fun. But now, lying beneath Caley, her body stretched out on top of his, the game had taken on a sexual element.

"This is supposed to be touch football!" she cried.

"And I'm touching you," Jake murmured. "Although not the way I'd like to touch you." He rolled Caley beneath him, pinning her body to the ground with his. "We have to talk," he said softly.

She wriggled beneath him, trying to escape. "If you think you can convince me to throw this game," she whispered, "just because you kissed me then—"

"Later," he replied as he saw Brett approach. Jake rolled off her and helped her up and then brushed the snow off her backside, before sending her across the scrimmage line to her team. "Good catch," he shouted.

A change of possession put Jake on offense and he took a handoff from Brett and headed down the field. He saw Caley coming toward him and he knew she was prepared to hit him hard. That's what he liked about Caley. She never backed off from a challenge.

But instead of running away, he waited, slowing his run until she caught up.

Jake feinted to the left, then the right, but Caley surprised him by countering his moves. When Jake realized he wasn't going to shake her, he bent over, grabbed her around the waist and carried her toward the end zone with him. But Caley knocked the ball out of his hand as he ran.

"Fumble!" she shouted.

Teddy was right behind them and he picked up the ball and started toward the other end zone. Jake turned and dropped Caley into the snow, then ran after Teddy, but Caley grabbed his leg and pulled him down. When he was lying on his stomach in the snow, she crawled on top of him, straddling his hips, and watched as Teddy scored.

She bounced up and down as she cheered for her brother, the movement causing a definite reaction on his part. Cursing softly, Jake rolled over and dumped her into the snow, picking up a handful and rubbing it in her face.

"You are such a bad sport," Caley cried, grabbing a fistful of snow and throwing it at him. She wrestled him to his back, pinning his arms on either side of his head.

"Kiss me," he murmured.

Caley frowned. "Not here. Everyone will see."

Jake brushed the snow out of her hair. "Where? When?"

"Later," Caley said. "After dinner."

"Meet me at the boathouse," he said.

Caley shook her head, then got to her feet, running back to her team. She turned around and looked back at him once, smiling, teasingly taunting him. "You're gonna lo-ose," she sang. "You're gonna lo-ose."

She did a little dance, wiggling her backside, and Jake chuckled. God, she was sexy. As he watched her walk away, he thought about what it would be like to have an entire night alone with her. To have all the time in the world to seduce her. To slowly undress her and touch her body and make her moan with pleasure. She'd been the stuff of his adolescent fantasies. But now, the things he dreamed about doing with her—to her— weren't things he could have even imagined back then.

"Jake!"

He glanced up to see Brett staring at him. "Look alive," his brother shouted. "Keep your head in the game."

They played for exactly an hour and, in the end, the trophy went to the Lambert family on a last-minute touchdown pass from Evan to his wife, Marianne.

As they walked back up to the house, Jake lagged behind, his gaze fixed on Caley. He wondered how things might have been between them if he had accepted her offer that night eleven years ago. Would they be here, in the same place, still lusting after each other? Or might they look at each other with embarrassment or regret rather than anticipation and excitement?

Maybe things had worked out exactly as they were supposed to that summer. But what happened between them this week was still in the hands of fate. And it would either begin or end in the boathouse tonight.

DINNER WAS A BOISTEROUS EVENT with both families sharing chili and corn bread in the Burtons' huge family room. After dinner, Jake and Caley joined Sam and

Emma in a game of Monopoly, but Caley could barely concentrate. Jake had taken to playing a game of footsie beneath the table, running his stocking foot over hers in a very seductive manner.

Caley kept her gaze focused on the board, trying to control her wildly beating heart. There had been men in her life who had touched her in the most intimate of ways and she'd barely reacted. All Jake had to do was rub her foot and she felt like tearing his clothes off and jumping his bones.

"Park Place," Sam said as Emma landed on his property. "Let's see. That will be twelve hundred dollars, please."

Jake chuckled as he scrutinized Sam's stash of cash. "Looks like you almost have enough for that motorcycle you want to buy."

Sam shot his brother a cold look and Emma immediately frowned. "What motorcycle?"

"Sam's going to buy a motorcycle after you get married," Jake said as he straightened his property cards. "Our mother wouldn't let him, but once he's married, she can't say anything since you'd be in charge." He fixed Emma with an inquisitive gaze, waiting for her response.

Caley thought it was an odd turn in the conversation. She sent him a frown and he just smiled and began to count his money.

"You can't get a motorcycle," Emma said. "They're dangerous. I won't let you."

"But, Em, it would be practical. We can't afford two cars. And the gas would be cheap."

"No," Emma said stubbornly. "I won't allow it."

Sam straightened, his expression growing petulant.

"What is that supposed to mean, you won't allow it? You're not my mother."

"Sam should be able to make his own decisions," Jake murmured.

Caley gave him a swift kick beneath the table and he winced.

"Ow!" he cried. Sam and Emma looked at him and he forced a smile. "Cramp. Too much football in the snow." He snatched up his money and handed it to Caley. "I'm going to cash out now."

Caley looked back and forth between the glowering expressions on Sam's and Emma's faces to the smug smile on Jake's. He'd started this argument on purpose. "So am I," Caley said.

"Jake is right," Sam countered. "I'm an adult. I should be able to do what I want."

"Who's going to pay for this motorcycle?" Emma said. "Not me. And if you think you're going to use any of our wedding money, you'd better think again."

Caley quickly stood and followed Jake to the kitchen. He set his glass in the sink, then called out to his parents, who were playing cards with Caley's mother and father. "I'm going to go down to the boathouse and see if I can get the heat going. We're going to need the extra room."

"And I'm going to head back to the inn," Caley said. "I have to make some calls. I'll see you all tomorrow." Their mutual exit caused no undue interest. Jake helped her on with her jacket and they walked out the front door together.

When they got outside, he grabbed her hand and drew her along with him, toward the path down to the lake. "Jake, maybe we should— Where are we going?"

"The boathouse. I could use some help getting the heat going. You can hold my tools."

Caley laughed, then fell into step beside him. The crisp night air heightened her senses and she felt her heart skip, knowing what would happen once they were alone. Caley had never considered herself a very passionate woman. She'd always been able to control her desire. But with Jake, she seemed to be constantly fixated on sex.

Though she had good intentions of playing it cool, everything fell apart the moment he touched her. Her rational side could come up with an entire list of reasons why she shouldn't sleep with Jake. But then her pulse began pounding and she felt a tiny bit lightheaded and her brain stopped working entirely. It felt good to just let go, to feel something so strongly that it completely consumed her. She hadn't felt like this since that night with Jake on the beach eleven years ago.

But was she really ready to do this? For the past few months, she'd felt an emptiness inside her, as if her life had ceased to make her happy. It would be easy to fill that emptiness with Jake. And maybe she would feel better for a while. Still, Caley didn't want to believe that she needed a man to be happy. She probably just needed really good sex.

At least she was now old enough to know the difference between desire and love. If she did surrender to physical attraction, Caley would be able to control her emotions. Jake was the last person she would allow herself to love. In truth, he was the only man she'd known who had the capacity to break her heart. And that made him dangerous.

And yet, she wasn't afraid. Instead, she felt liberated. She could finally act on her desire for Jake and explore just how deep it ran. She didn't have to pretend anymore. He wanted her and she wanted him, and neither one of them had to deny it.

The shadow of the Burtons' boathouse, built into the slope of the shoreline, loomed at the edge of the lake. The lower level held the Burtons' small sailboat and their vintage motorboat, but the upper level was a small apartment that they often used for guests. It was fully furnished with a bed and a sofa and a small kitchen and bath. The windows had been shuttered for the winter, giving the place a cold and uninviting look.

Jake held her hand as she carefully climbed the snow-covered stairs. Caley glanced back over her shoulder to see the trail of their footprints in the moonlight. "They're going to know we were out here together," she said.

"I just asked you to give me a hand," Jake said. "It was a perfectly innocent request."

Caley took a ragged breath and clenched her fingers inside her jacket pocket. Just the thought of running her hands over his body, of having the freedom to touch him, to undress him, made her mind spin. She knew what would happen when they were alone and she wasn't afraid. All she could feel was an overwhelming anticipation.

When they reached the landing, Jake pushed the door open and then walked inside. She followed and heard the door shut behind her. The moment it did, Caley felt his hands on her face. His lips met hers and a heartbeat later they were lost in a deep and stirring kiss.

"I've been thinking about you all day," he murmured against her mouth.

"What were you thinking?" she asked, her breath coming in quick gasps.

"About what would happen once we were alone again."

"Tell me," she said. "What did you imagine?"

It was so dark inside the boathouse that they couldn't see anything, but she could feel his heat against her body, his warm breath against her cheek. The lack of sight seemed to heighten all her other senses and she shivered as she felt his lips brush across her cold cheek.

"I imagined that you'd stand in front of me and slowly take all your clothes off. And then, I'd finally be able to touch you. And I'd be able to see if it felt as good as I dreamed it would."

Caley unzipped her jacket and let it fall to the floor behind her. Then, she pulled her sweater over her head and tossed it aside. She wore a thin T-shirt beneath, barely enough to protect her from the cold. But strangely, she didn't notice the temperature. Her heart was beating so fast that her skin didn't even prickle into goose bumps.

Jake reached out and ran his hand down her bare arm, then grabbed her hand and kissed the center of her palm. "Wait here," he murmured. "The circuit box is in the closet."

He disappeared into the darkness and Caley leaned back against the door, her heart pounding. She heard him fumbling around on the far side of the room and a moment later, a match flared. The flame illuminated the interior of the boathouse, casting wavering shadows on the walls. Jake lit a lantern and set it down on the bedside table. Then he turned to her, motioning her closer.

Caley rubbed her arms, suddenly feeling the cold along with a rush of nerves. It was easier in the dark, like a dream, two bodies connected only by touch. But now that she could see the bed, could look into Jake's eyes, it had all become very real.

"Let me see if I can get the heat going," he said. He walked past her to the opposite wall and leaned inside the closet. A switch clicked. A moment later, he bent over the radiator and nodded. "It's working."

Jake moved back toward her, taking off his jacket along the way. He was the boy she'd always known, every feature still there—the dark lashes and brows, the penetrating pale blue eyes, the straight nose and sensuous mouth. But with age, his features had become even more captivating, more compelling. She couldn't take her eyes off of him.

When he stood in front of her, Caley reached up and unbuttoned his shirt, exposing his skin to her touch. "What are we doing here?" she murmured, pressing her lips to his chest.

"I have no idea," Jake replied, "but I don't want to stop."

He smoothed his hands up her back and Caley shivered at the sensation of his touch. "This is going to be impossible," she murmured, nuzzling her face into his neck.

"We're in the same state, living minutes apart. How is that impossible?" He pulled her along to the bed. "We have heat and light and a comfortable bed. What happens here is just us, no one else. I promise."

"This could change everything," Caley said as he kissed her neck.

Jake grabbed her waist and they tumbled onto the bed, the covers cold on her bare skin. "I'm counting on that," he said.

Caley reached up to run her fingers through his dark hair and smiled. "You know, I really don't think we should do this. You're not ready and it wouldn't be right and I just don't think of you in that way."

He frowned, pushing back. "You don't?"

"I just don't have *those* kinds of feelings for you, Jake," she murmured, deepening her voice to make the imitation more obvious.

She watched as a slow smile broke across his face. He'd said those same words to her that night on the beach. "I lied," Jake said. "Believe me, I did have those feelings."

His admission stunned her. "Really?"

"For a long time."

"How long?"

"Remember that red striped bikini you had? You were fourteen that summer."

Caley nodded.

"Since then. I remember I saw you in that bikini and later that night I was thinking about you and your body and how smooth your skin was and how perfect your breasts were and then I—well, you know."

"I do?"

"What? You want me to say it? I pleasured myself as teenage boys do on occasion. Hey, grown men do it, too." He chuckled softly. "All I remember is, from that summer on, being around you was pure torture."

Caley smiled, satisfied with the admission. So

the infatuation hadn't been unreciprocated. Oddly enough, that did make a difference. Why not make both of their fantasies come true? "So what else were you thinking about?" she asked as she dropped a line of kisses across his chest.

He pressed his mouth to her shoulder, gently biting as he kissed her. "I wasn't very experienced back then. I was still technically a virgin. But I thought about what you'd look like naked." Jake pulled up her T-shirt and trailed a line of kisses from her belly to a spot beneath her breasts.

Caley sat up and straddled his hips, then slowly pulled her T-shirt over her head. She remembered doing the same thing eleven years ago. But then, she'd been so nervous her heart nearly jumped out of her chest. Now, it seemed like the most natural thing in the world, to crave his touch, to offer him more.

Jake smiled as he reached out and cupped her breast in his hand, teasing at her nipple with his thumb. And then, in one easy motion, he sat up, wrapping his arms around her waist and pressing his mouth against her neck. He trailed kisses from her collarbone to her breasts as he unhooked her bra. Finally, he drew the hard nub of her nipple into his mouth.

She arched back, holding her breath as he pulled her back down with him. Caley remembered how fascinated she'd been with his body, watching it change from summer to summer as he slowly became a man. She was as desperate to touch it now as she had been then. Grabbing the front of his shirt, she worked at the remaining buttons, then brushed it off his shoulders until his chest was completely bare.

She drew back, staring at him as she tossed aside

her bra. Her fingers lazily following the line of hair that ran from his collarbone to his belly. Now he was fully formed, his shoulders broad, his body lean and hard, a body only a woman could appreciate.

Caley bent forward and pressed a kiss to his chest, then gently sucked on his nipple. What began as curiosity had now taken on a very intimate feeling. He groaned softly, then murmured her name. A shiver skittered over her exposed skin. Her breath caught in her throat.

"Are you cold?" he asked.

"No," she lied.

He chuckled softly, grabbing her by the waist and pulling their bodies together in a warm embrace. They kissed for a long time, hands touching, mouths tasting. It was everything she'd always thought it would be, yet more. It wasn't just about sex, it was about…trust.

He ran his hands through her hair, then pressed his forehead against hers. "Spend the night with me."

"Not here."

"Where then?"

"At the inn. We'll have more privacy there."

"What about Emma?"

"Her room is on the second floor and mine's on the third. There's a back stairway. I'll let you in and no one will know you're there."

Jake kissed her forehead, his lips warm and damp. "Have you talked to Emma yet? I mean, about the wedding."

Caley shook her head. "No. I told her I'd meet her for lunch tomorrow and I thought we'd have some time then."

"What do you think about this marriage? Do you think they're ready?"

"No!" Caley frowned, pushing up on her elbow. "Not at all. They're so young. I thought I was the only one who had concerns. Everyone is just so thrilled that our families will finally be related. But no one is even thinking about what will happen if the marriage doesn't work."

"I agree," Jake said. "I don't think they're ready."

Caley crossed her arms over his chest and stared into his eyes. "You started that fight between them on purpose, didn't you?"

"Someone has to shake some sense into them." He paused. "We need a plan. A coordinated effort between the two of us. If we go at it from both sides, maybe we'll be able to convince them to wait."

"I don't think they'll consider waiting. Everything is moving so fast and I'm sure they feel they'd be disappointing the families."

Jake reached out and brushed her hair away from her temple, his gaze skimming over her face. "I talked to Sam this afternoon and he's just going along with what Emma wants."

Caley gasped. "You think she talked him into this?"

"Maybe. I can't imagine he really wants to get married. What guy in his right mind would want a wife at twenty-one?"

"Well, he's the one who asked her," Caley said. "If he didn't want to get married, why did he ask?"

"She probably pressured him," Jake said.

Caley pulled out of his embrace and sat up, stunned by his comment and eager to defend her sister. "Emma wouldn't do that."

"I'm just saying that usually women are the ones who press for the wedding," Jake said.

"And you come by this knowledge how?" Caley asked. "Have you been manipulated into an engagement recently?"

"No, just the opposite. Every woman I've ever met has had marriage in the back of her mind. Come on, even you've thought about it. Wondered what it would be like if you and I...you know."

Caley scrambled off the bed. Marrying Jake was the last thing on her mind! And if he thought she had any designs on his future, he was sadly mistaken. "I think this was a mistake," she murmured, crawling off the bed. She searched the floor for her bra and T-shirt.

"Come on, Caley, don't be mad. I didn't mean to imply that—"

"No, I understand," she said as she pulled the shirt over her head. "You just assumed I wanted more than just...sex." She drew a ragged breath, shoving her bra in her back pocket. "See, that's why we shouldn't do this. Unless we're agreed on the reasons, it's bound to get very messy."

"Is it?" he asked.

She snatched up her sweater from the floor and tugged it back over her head. "I have to go."

Jake sat up and reached for her, but she avoided his grasp. "Caley, come on. I was just teasing. I didn't mean anything by it."

She shook her head. "I do agree about Emma and Sam. They're too young. You and I don't even know what we want. How would they?"

Jake grabbed her hand. "I know what I want," he said.

She stared down at their fingers, intertwined so tightly that she couldn't tell his from hers. Caley fought the temptation to strip off her clothes again and just forget her fears. But if she jumped into bed with Jake tonight, there would be no going back. "I'll talk to Emma."

"When will I see you again?" Jake asked.

"You're going to see me all week."

"You know what I mean."

Caley bit her lower lip. "I don't know. Maybe we ought to forget this. It just makes things too complicated."

"I'm not sure I can," he replied.

"Try, Jake," she murmured. Caley walked to the door, then turned back to look at him. "Try really hard."

3

Jake steered his SUV around a sharp curve on West Shore Road, his mother's grocery list clutched in his hand. He had an appointment for his tux fitting and then his mother wanted him to buy three "nice" chickens. He wasn't sure what qualified a chicken as nice, but he'd figure it out when he got to the grocery store.

The truck skidded and he took his foot off the accelerator, startled out of his thoughts. He'd gotten about two or three hours of sleep last night. The rest of his time in bed was spent trying to figure out just how he'd managed to screw things up with Caley.

Maybe the forces of the universe were sending him a message—don't mess with Caley Lambert. But though he'd considered heeding the message, his body didn't want to listen. Every time he came within ten feet of her, he found himself lost in another sexual fantasy.

This was his penance for keeping all his desire bottled up so long ago. It had increased over the years, like pressure in a simmering pot, until he was left with a need for Caley that threatened to boil over. He wanted to kiss her and touch her, to strip off her clothes and enjoy the pleasures of her body. He'd waited years and now that she was with him again, he wanted to make it happen.

But could it just be casual sex? Would he be able to enjoy the act and then walk away, no strings attached? From the moment he found her lying next to him in bed, he'd felt it. A deep-rooted connection, not diminished by time, but strengthened. She could never be just a physical release for him. Sex with Caley would have to mean something. But what?

Jake groaned, tightening his grip on the steering wheel. "It's just too complicated," he muttered, repeating her words. But it didn't seem at all complicated in his mind. In truth, seducing Caley felt like the most natural thing he'd ever done.

How long had he been searching for a woman just like her, a woman he could feel entirely comfortable with, a woman who didn't try to make herself into something she thought he wanted.

Jake had seen it all—the sexpot, the girl-next-door, the doting wife, the perfect mother of his children. They'd all tried to be something they weren't. He'd known Caley so long that she couldn't hide behind a facade. And if she tried, he would see right through it.

"Just take it slow," he told himself. He'd been able to resist her when he was younger and far less experienced with the opposite sex. It shouldn't be that difficult to bide his time.

His mind flashed back to an image of Caley, straddling his waist, tugging her T-shirt over her head. Jake's fingers twitched as he recalled the feel of her flesh beneath his hands, the taste of her skin, the scent of her hair. He drew a ragged breath and tried to banish the image from his mind and focus on something else.

He noticed a car ahead of him on the road and slowed, but the sedan wasn't moving. Instead, it was tilted at an odd angle. As he approached, Jake realized the car looked familiar—as did the figure standing at the front bumper. He carefully pulled over, then hopped out of the truck.

The moment Caley saw him, she turned away and shook her head. "Don't even say it," she muttered.

"Who taught you to drive?" he teased.

A reluctant smile broke across her face. "You did. Remember? You took me out in that old Cutlass you bought, then proceeded to yell at me for the entire lesson."

"You've forgotten everything I taught you, grasshopper," he teased, running his finger along her cheek. This time Jake fought the urge to kiss her and instead moved to the front of the car to examine the situation.

"We didn't cover ice and snow, if you recall."

"And how are you planning to get your car back on the road? By sheer force of will?"

"Maybe you could give me a push?"

"Not gonna work." Jake shoved his hands in his pockets. It took every ounce of his willpower just to keep from touching her. He never remembered her hold over him being this strong, but it must have been. How had he managed to say no the night of her eighteenth birthday? He shook his head. "It's going to take an hour of shoveling and two or three guys to get you out of this snowbank. I can go back home and get a chain and see if I can pull you out. Or I'll get Teddy and my brothers and we can shovel and push."

"My hero," Caley said with a mocking smile.

Jake's smile faded. He was short on sleep and tired of this game they played. Why did everything always have to be a challenge? "Am I? After last night, I thought you might not like me anymore."

Caley shrugged. "I like you. That's not going to change."

"I shouldn't have said those things about your sister."

She drew a deep breath and sighed, then reached out and touched his arm, as if to reassure herself that they were all right. "I'm as worried as you are. I'm having lunch with her later. I was hoping I'd get a better sense of what she's thinking."

"You know, they haven't had sex yet," Jake said.

Caley blinked, stunned by the revelation. "Really? They're both virgins?"

"No. They've both had sex, just not with each other. They're saving it for marriage."

"That changes everything," Caley said, her eyes wide. "I mean, I think it's an admirable concept, but it still worries me. Sex is an important part of a relationship. What if they aren't compatible in bed?"

"Exactly," Jake said. "Maybe we need to have one of those—what do you call them—interventions. We'll sit them both down and make sure they know what they're getting into and encourage them to do it."

"But we can't really speak with any authority," Caley said. "Neither one of us has been engaged or married so why would they listen to us?"

"And we haven't had sex," Jake said. "At least, not with each other."

"Well, we are older...and wiser. That should count for something."

Jake considered their dilemma. "You know, we grew up in the same household with our siblings. I guess if the sex was great between us, don't you think the sex would be great between Sam and Emma?"

"Are you suggesting we have sex so that we can use our experience to break up Sam and Emma's wedding? What if the sex were great?"

"Oh, it would be great," Jake said. "I know that for a fact."

"How?"

"By the way you touch me. And by the way you react to my touch. It would be great between us. Maybe Sam and Emma have that feeling, too. Maybe that's why they've been saving it."

He reached out and cupped her cheek in his hand, running his thumb over her lower lip. Caley closed her eyes and tipped her head back, waiting for his kiss. He held back, if only to prove a point. She wanted him and all he had to do was touch her to make her desire burn. He bent close and brushed his lips across hers.

"See," he murmured. "I just kiss you and you melt."

Caley smiled as she looked at him, then ran her hand down his chest to his waist. She brushed her knuckles against the zipper of his jeans. "And what about you?" she asked. "I just touch you and you do the opposite."

Jake groaned. "All I've been thinking about since last night is getting you back in my bed. If I thought I'd have to wait another day to touch you again, I think I'd cut a hole in the ice and jump in the lake."

"Don't do that," Caley teased. "That water is cold and the shrinkage would be horrible."

He laughed, the sound echoing off the trees. "The way you talk. Do you talk to the other men in your life like this?"

"Right now, you're the only man in my life. And it's easy to talk to you." She paused. "You're my oldest friend, Jake. I can say anything to you." She drew a deep breath. "I guess I didn't realize that until now. We haven't seen each other in eleven years and it seems as if nothing's changed. And yet everything has."

"I know," he said. "But it's not all bad." He kissed her again. "So we're okay. About last night?"

"I didn't sleep at all." Caley leaned back against the hood of the car.

"I didn't, either. I'm starting to think we'd do a lot better if we slept together." Jake rested his hands on her waist and stared down into her eyes. "You know you can't live without me."

"I know I can't get my car out of the snow without you," she countered.

He stepped back and carefully examined the task at hand. But the sound of an approaching car caught their attention and Jake watched as an SUV with police lights stopped on the opposite side of the road. The policeman jumped out of the truck and strolled across the road.

"I thought that was you," he said. "What's up, Caley?"

"Hey, Jeff," Caley called, giving the cop a friendly wave.

"If you tell me this happened while you were talking on your cell phone, you know I'm going to have to arrest you."

"I'm not used to the snow. I skidded on the curve and next thing I knew, I was in the snowbank."

"I've got a tow chain in the truck. I'll pull you out."

Jake watched as Caley gave the guy a dazzling smile. "Could you?" she asked. "That would really be great."

"I'm here to serve," he said with a crooked grin. He looked over at Jake and nodded. "Hey, buddy, you can be on your way. I'll help the lady with her problem."

Caley turned to Jake. "Well, that saves us both some time. Aren't we lucky he came along?"

Jake felt a surge of jealousy course through his body. The reaction stunned him. He remembered feeling that way when they'd been younger, when she'd turned her eyes toward other boys. But Jake had assumed he'd outgrown that particular emotion. "You know each other?"

"That's Jeff Winslow. You remember him. He used to work at the marina. He lived in town. He's the police chief now."

"That's Jeff Winslow?" As a teenager, Winslow considered himself the Casanova of the precollege crowd. He had girls falling at his feet and, according to rumor, he usually picked them up, seduced them and then tossed them aside for new conquests. The guys used to tease him that he'd have to take a second job in order to pay for the condoms he used. "Yeah, I remember him."

"He stopped me the night I got into town. I was talking on my cell phone. He let me off with a warning."

"You can't go out with him," Jake said.

Caley gasped. "He hasn't asked me out."

"He's planning to. I can tell by the look in his eyes. And you can't go out with him. He's a player."

"You know, you used to tell me who I could and

couldn't date when we were kids and I used to listen to you," Caley said. "But I'm a big girl now and I can run my own life."

"That's because you were too naive to see what guys really wanted."

"It's no wonder that I remained a virgin until I got to college. I was seriously beginning to develop a complex." She paused. "And I know exactly what *you* want. So see, I have learned a few things." Caley shook her head. "One moment, you're trying to talk me into bed and the next, you're acting like my big brother. No wonder I'm so mixed up."

"I don't want to be your big brother," Jake said.

"Then stop telling me how to run my life."

God, she could be so stubborn at times. Was she this way with all men or was it just him? "Well, I guess you don't need me or my advice. Officer Jeff can take care of all your needs. Automotive and otherwise."

Caley stared at him. "What is this? Are you jealous?"

The accusation stung, even though it was true. Jake trudged back up to the road and Caley trailed after him, stumbling in the deep drift that the plows had pushed aside. He grabbed her waist and helped her through the snow, then brushed off her pant legs when she reached the pavement. "I gotta go try on my tux. I'll see you later. Good luck with Emma."

"Jake, I—"

"I'll talk to you later," he repeated. He strode back to his truck and hopped inside, then skidded out on the road, heading towards town. There were moments when he wondered what he found so fascinating about Caley Lambert. She seemed to go out of her way to exasperate him. If she thought for even a moment that he was dictating to her, she'd dig in her heels and refuse to move.

No, he didn't want to act like her older brother! He had far more carnal interests than that. He looked at her as a woman, a beautiful, sexy, desirable woman. And he wanted her to see him as a man, not that guy who used to drive her crazy every summer.

How could he alter the dynamic of a relationship that seemed as if it were carved in stone? How could he make her see that they'd be so good together? He didn't want her to forget the past. That's what made things so easy between them. He just wanted her to see that they weren't kids anymore.

Things had changed. He'd changed. And he was ready to give her all she'd wanted all those years ago. Only this time, he could give her more than just one night of clumsy lovemaking and empty promises. This time, it could be a beginning.

"Where's he going in such a hurry?"

Caley stared at Jake's truck as it roared off down the snow-covered road. "He has an appointment in town," she murmured.

Jeff watched as he drove off, frowning. "He's speeding. Too fast for conditions. He's lucky I don't chase after him and slap him with a ticket." He walked around to the back of the car and hooked the chain to a metal plate beneath the back bumper. "So, are you and him—"

"Together? No," Caley said. "We're just…old friends."

"You know, he once threatened to beat the crap out of me if I did more than kiss you on our date."

"I guess you weren't too scared of him."

Jeff grinned. "Hey, I knew why you went out with me. It wasn't too hard to see what was going on between you two. He made things pretty clear."

"No," Caley said. "There was never anything. He was just…like an older brother."

"I don't think so," Jeff said as he walked back to his truck. "I'm pretty sure the guy was in love with you."

Caley stepped out onto the road, puzzled by Jeff's revelation. How could he have gotten all that from a simple warning? Still, Jake had admitted as much, only she thought he'd been teasing. What if it was true? What if his feelings had run much deeper than she ever suspected?

Jeff hooked the chain to his truck. He slowly pulled it taut. A moment later, her car began to move as it was gradually drawn back onto the road. "That's good!" she shouted.

Jeff parked the truck. He walked to the front of her rental car and examined it. "No damage," he said.

"Thanks." Caley reached for the door and Jeff quickly opened it for her. "I'm lucky you came along."

"Hey, there's a good band playing out at Tyler's tomorrow night. We could catch some dinner and then head out there. I mean, if you aren't busy with family stuff. And I promise I won't try any funny business."

Caley hesitated. There was absolutely no spark between her and Jeff, and she didn't want to lead him on. Besides, if she wanted sparks, she had the Fourth of July fireworks in Jake. "I'm trying to spend some time with my sister."

"Yeah, I heard she was getting married. Your mom told me when I saw her in town yesterday. That's a surprise. Little Emma Lambert and Sam Burton. Hard to believe they're old enough to get married."

"Maybe Emma and I will stop by and check it out," she said. A girl's night out might make her sister reconsider getting married. She had far too many oats to sow yet and Tyler's Roadhouse was known as a single girl's paradise.

"Well, then, I'll see you if I see you. I know the guy at the door. Just give him your name and he'll let you in without the cover charge. You drive careful now, Caley. I don't want to catch you in another snowbank. If I do, I might have to toss you in jail."

He opened her car door for her and she got inside. As Caley drove off, she glanced in the rearview mirror. Jeff Winslow was an attractive guy. And now that she was single again, she ought to have been flattered that he'd turned his attention to her.

Caley had never put much stock in sexual chemistry, but now she finally understood what it was all about. When she and Jeff sat in the same test tube, nothing happened. But when she got mixed up in a beaker of Jake, the combination erupted into heat and passion and uncontrolled need.

There was a strange connection between them, but she couldn't put her finger on what it was. Something was drawing them together, a power that was impossible to resist. And with every moment that passed, Caley wondered why she even bothered to try.

Her phone rang and Caley reached to get it out of her purse. But then she drew her hand away. For the first time in her professional life, she didn't want to think about work. She didn't want to answer some silly question or explain some figures on a report. She just wanted to be left alone for a day. Grabbing the phone, she switched it off, the Mozart tune ending prematurely. She'd deal with work later. And besides, the last thing she needed was a ticket courtesy of Jeff. She had more important things on her mind.

Her thoughts returned to Jake. There was one major fear holding her back, a fear that she would repeat past mistakes. What if they did have sex and what if it was the most wonderful experience of her life? And what if she fell in love with Jake all over again?

Those feelings had been buried so deep for so long that she'd thought they were gone. But the moment he'd kissed her, they'd floated back to the surface. Caley was much stronger now, but Jake had the capacity to sweep her off her feet, to make her lose touch with reality and reason.

She drew a ragged breath. Though it was frightening, this power he had over her, it was also liberating. When she was with him, she could let go and enjoy herself. For the first time since she was a teenager, she looked forward to getting up in the morning. While she was here with Jake, she didn't have to worry about all the public relations fires she'd have to put out in the course of a day, all the upset clients and curious reporters and skittish stockholders. She could relax and just be herself.

Why was it that Jake was always a factor in the choices she made? She'd gone to school at NYU because she thought it would impress Jake. She got a job in public relations because Jake had once told her she was good at solving problems. She'd worked herself ragged in the past seven years because, deep inside, she wanted to prove that she didn't need Jake in her life to be happy.

And where had it gotten her? Caley sighed softly. Right back to where she started, still chasing after Jake Burton. But this time, he was chasing after her, as well. And she now had control over what happened between them—until, of course, he touched her. Then all bets were off.

"That's the problem," Caley said. "I can control my attraction for Jake as long as we aren't close to each other. But I'm so attracted to him, I can't stay away. I'm damned if I do and damned if I don't."

BY THE TIME she got back to the inn it was nearly noon.

There was no one at the desk when she walked in, but Caley found her younger sister at a table in the dining room, a binder open in front of her. She munched on a breadstick as she flipped through the pages.

"Your maid of honor has arrived," Caley said, pulling out a chair across from Emma.

Her sister looked up and smiled. "Good. I need someone to distract me from all these details. My mind is so filled with minutiae that it's starting to leak out of my ears. Flowers, music, candles, dinner. I thought we were planning a small wedding, but it's starting to take on a life of its own."

Caley sat down, then reached out for the binder, scanning down her sister's "to do" list. She didn't understand why brides worried over such silly decisions. "This is the list of music? Go for the Pachelbel's "Canon" for the processional and "Ode to Joy" for the recessional. Red roses with my bridesmaid's dress would be too much. White would be better. And not the hybrid roses but the cabbage roses. Vanilla-scented tapers for the candles—you know how much Mom loves those. And surf and turf for dinner, that way you'll please everyone." Caley slammed the binder shut. "There, that was easy."

Emma blinked in surprise. "Caroline Lenore Lambert! You can't just decide so quickly. All of these things have to be discussed."

"With whom? Sam? He doesn't care. I've heard that brides often focus so much time and attention on the wedding that they forget there's a marriage that comes after it."

"That's why we wanted to keep this small," Emma said. "And more manageable. Between Mom and Mrs. Burton, we wouldn't have had a wedding, we would have had an event. But I don't want to make decisions just to get them out of the way. I want this wedding to be perfect. So does Sam."

"So you have to discuss everything with him?"

"No. He's leaving the details up to me."

Caley plucked a breadstick out of the basket and munched on the end. "That's odd. I mean, that he wouldn't even care. You know how those Burton boys are. They're so bossy. They have to run everything."

Caley could see Emma growing dizzy from the change in conversation. Tiny worry lines furrowed her brow and she kept glancing back down at her book, as if all the answers were contained within.

Caley couldn't help but feel a little guilty, but this marriage would be a life-altering event and if Emma wasn't prepared then Caley wasn't doing her job as a big sister or a maid of honor. "If it isn't perfect then the marriage will never succeed. It's like bad karma."

Emma frowned. "Yeah. I guess so." She paused. "Is it? Is that some superstition I haven't heard yet?"

"You're marrying the perfect guy so you have to be perfect in return. So did you solve your motorcycle dilemma? I'd stand firm on that one. Once you give in, he's going to take advantage and think he can run the show."

"He doesn't want to talk about it. He says it's his decision."

"Emma, things will only get worse after you're married. Marriage magnifies problems, it doesn't make them go away." It was armchair psychology and a deliberate manipulation but if it saved Emma from making the biggest mistake of her life, then Caley didn't care. If love couldn't withstand a bit of poking and prodding, then it would never last.

Caley winced inwardly. It almost pained her to say those words. But maybe that's why she wasn't happily married and living in the suburbs with 2.5 kids. Perhaps there was some truth in what she said. She reached out and took Emma's hand. "Are you really ready for this, Em?"

"I-I've thought about postponing," Emma admitted in a small voice. "But then, I just wrote it off to nerves. Everyone would be so disappointed."

"This is about you, not Mom and Dad," Caley said.

"But how am I supposed to know for sure? What am I supposed to feel?"

"Passion, contentment, anticipation. You're going to spend the rest of your life with this one man. You have to know that when you look at him over the breakfast table in thirty years, that he was and is the only man in the world for you." Caley sat back in her chair. "If you called it off, Emma, I would stand behind you. I'd help you explain it to Mom and Dad."

Emma drew a shaky breath and then forced a bright smile. "That's what you do for a living, right? Take disasters and put a pretty ribbon on them and pretend they never happened?"

"This wouldn't be a disaster," Caley insisted. But a divorce in two or three years would be. The families would be forced to take sides and that would destroy the lifelong friendship that they'd all enjoyed.

Emma shook her head. "Don't be silly. I'm not going to call it off. It's just prewedding jitters, that's all." She grabbed a menu from the center of the table and handed it to Caley. "Here. Why don't you order something for lunch. I'm going to run up to my room and get the folder from the florist and we'll discuss the bouquets. The florist needs to know by this afternoon so he can place the order."

Emma pushed back from the table and hurried out of the dining room. Caley slowly shook her head. The doubts she had before hadn't been dispelled. If anything, they were now magnified. Emma wasn't ready to get married, but she also wasn't strong enough to make the decision on her own. If the wedding were going to be called off, then Jake would have to talk Sam into doing it.

Caley grabbed Emma's binder and opened it again. It was filled with pictures torn from magazines and neatly scribbled notes. There was a whole section on bridesmaid's dresses and another on bridal gowns. It was obvious that Emma had been planning for this wedding for much longer than a month and a half. Some of the photos were at least five years old.

Caley groaned inwardly. Did Emma feel the same way about Sam as Caley had felt about Jake? Had she carried a secret crush around all these years? If she had, then trying to convince Emma to wait was going to be a much tougher job than she anticipated.

Motioning to the waitress, Caley stood up. "Can you let my sister know that I had to run an errand? I'll be back later this afternoon."

If she and Jake expected to have any effect at all, then they'd better coordinate their efforts. She reached for her cell phone before she realized she wasn't even sure Jake had a cell phone. How did a person exist in this world without one? Or without wireless computer access and a PDA and a fax machine?

Caley strode to her car, then remembered that Jake had an appointment to try on his tuxedo. The only place in town that rented men's formal wear was a shop two blocks down and around the corner. Caley glanced over at her car parked in front of the inn and decided it would be faster to walk.

When she arrived, she was out of breath. She walked to the rear of the store and the small section devoted to formal wear. An elderly man with a tape measure around his neck stood in front of a mirror. "Is Jake Burton here?" she asked.

"He's changing," the man said, pointing to a nearby fitting room. "He'll be out in a moment."

Caley strode over to the fitting room door, opened it and stepped inside. Jake stood in front of the mirror in his boxers and a formal shirt. He saw her reflection and smiled.

"You have a perfectly nice room at the inn and I'm staying out in the boathouse. Why do we keep meeting in fitting rooms?"

"We have to talk," Caley said. He slowly turned and her breath caught in her throat. His muscular chest was visible, his shirt half-unbuttoned, and Caley's fingers twitched as she imagined the feel of his skin beneath her hands.

Jake reached out and grabbed her wrist, then placed her palm on his chest. "So what is so important that it can't wait until I'm dressed?" He dragged her hand over his chest to his belly, then left it resting near the waistband of his boxers.

She traced her thumb along the deep cut of muscle that ran along his hip to somewhere beneath the blue-striped fabric. Caley wanted to follow it farther, to explore his body until she knew every plane and angle and curve and indentation. His body was flawless, a perfect specimen of male beauty.

She'd never paid much attention to physical beauty before, but then she'd never been with a truly beautiful man until now. Now, every detail, from the hard muscle of Jake's abdomen to the soft dusting of hair across his chest, intrigued her.

She ran her hands back over his chest, watching as his growing erection pressed against the front of his boxers. He pulled her toward him and kissed her, cupping her backside in his hands and moving his hips against her. Emboldened, Caley reached down and wrapped her fingers around his shaft, hot and hard through the soft fabric.

Jake's breath caught and then he moaned. "What are you doing?"

"I'm not sure," Caley said. And she wasn't. She was just following her instincts. It didn't make any sense and in the rational world, she might have been appalled at her daring. But when she and Jake were together, the normal rules didn't seem to apply.

"How does it fit?" the salesclerk called.

"It fits good," Jake replied, his eyes closed, his face a mask of pleasure. He wasn't talking about the clothes. They fit—her hand, his shaft, his hands, her backside. Everything seemed to fit perfectly.

"Can I see?"

"No!" they both said.

Jake looked down at her through passion-glazed eyes and smiled. "Is that why you came here? To torment me?"

"I—I came to talk about Emma," she admitted, realizing how far off track she'd wandered. She hesitantly drew her hand away.

"Don't," he whispered. "Touch me." Jake brushed his lips across hers. "I'm sorry I acted like such an ass earlier. I was out of line. Do you forgive me?"

"For what?"

"For what I said. For the way I acted. For being a jerk and leaving you out on the road with Winslow." He sucked in a sharp breath and moaned. "If you keep doing that, there will be consequences. Very messy consequences."

"Sorry," Caley said. "Maybe we should continue this later?"

"Maybe that would be best," he said. "I'm not sure I want our first time to be in a fitting room." He glanced down. "This is definitely going to affect the fit of my trousers."

Caley giggled. She sensed that sex with Jake would be amazing, heart-stopping, a powerful experience. But she also knew that it would be fun. And Caley had never really had a lot of fun in the bedroom. Sex had always been fraught with so many expectations, many of them never fulfilled. She was curious now, anxious to learn how it might be with Jake. "Maybe I should leave?"

"No, just give me a few minutes. I just have to focus on something else."

"Our plan," she said. "We need a plan. I talked to Emma and she's having doubts. I don't think she's ready, but she won't be the one to call it off."

Jake glanced around. "You know, this fitting room thing is pretty hot. It's like a public place but it's still private."

Caley gave him a soft punch on the arm. "We're talking about Emma and Sam."

"I don't want to talk about them. I'd rather talk about us. What are you doing this afternoon? I have something to show you."

Caley looked down, then rolled her eyes. "All you think about is sex."

"No. That's not true. And that's not what I was planning to show you." He grabbed her shoulders and turned her around. "Let me take care of this first." He opened the fitting room door and pushed her out.

The salesclerk was standing outside, a disapproving scowl on his face. "He'll be right out. I'm just going to wait up front. You have some very nice leather chairs." She forced a smile, but the man's expression didn't waver.

Ten minutes later, Jake joined her at the front of the

store. He took her hand and walked out with her and when they reached the street, Caley turned on him. "You have to stop making me do those things," she said.

"You used to be such a daredevil," he said. "What's happened?"

"I've grown up," Caley said.

"I dare you to kiss me, right here," Jake said. "In front of everyone." He looked around at the nearly empty street and then shrugged. "All right, in front of that woman with the poodle."

"Where are we going? You said you wanted to take me somewhere."

"I don't know if I should," Jake teased. "You've lost your nerve. I'm not sure this Caley would be up for what I have in mind."

She grinned, then threw her arms around his neck and kissed him deeply. Her tongue slipped between his lips and Caley used every ounce of her feminine wiles to arouse him again. "I'm just a little out of practice," she said. "The only daring thing I do is dodging cabs when crossing Fifth Avenue."

Jake grabbed another kiss, then pulled her along to his SUV. Caley really didn't care where they were going, as long as it was somewhere quiet and private where they might continue what they'd started in the fitting room.

4

"Where are we going?"

Jake glanced over at Caley and smiled.

After their rocky start that morning, Jake wondered whether he and Caley were doomed to spend their time revisiting the past.

They'd been such good friends growing up, doing everything together, climbing trees and exploring the lakeshore, fishing and swimming. But once they'd started to see each other as more than just good buddies, their relationship had grown strained. Though they'd still spent the majority of their time together, they had often been locked in a battle of wills, each of them trying to one-up the other.

Caley had used the stubborn determination he'd fostered and made a success of herself in a highly competitive field. He, in turn, had internalized her absolute confidence in him and used it to build his own business from scratch.

He'd never really thanked her for being such a good friend. But he didn't want to do that now. Instead, he wanted her to look at him as something more than a friend. He wanted to get back to that place, to that day right before they'd started looking at each other with teenage lust in their eyes. If he took them back, then maybe they'd be able to turn things in a different direction.

"I'd just like to know what this thing you're going to show me is."

"A surprise," Jake said. "Are you always this impatient? Or do you just hate surprises?"

"Both," Caley said.

"You're going to have to relax. You're not in the big city anymore. Take a breath, chill for a while. Enjoy the beautiful day."

Caley's phone rang and she pulled it out of her pocket, but before she could answer it, Jake grabbed it from her hands. "You can talk to them later," he said, taking a quick glance at the caller ID.

"I have responsibilities," Caley said. She took her cell phone back. "Don't you have a cell phone? Don't people from your office need to talk to you?"

"They don't have my number. I don't want anyone calling me so I don't give it out. When I leave the office, I'm done. Whatever they need can wait or they can figure it out for themselves. I'm not that important that I have all the answers. Are you?"

Caley frowned as if perplexed by his question. "Well, yes. That's how you get to be the boss. By having all the answers."

"Maybe you should trust the people you work with a little more. If you don't, you'll drive yourself crazy."

Jake knew from experience that it was best to take a more relaxed approach to work. When he first opened his own architectural firm in Chicago, he'd spent months of sleepless nights worrying about all the horrible things that might befall him professionally. And then, once he was sure they weren't going to come and repossess the office furniture, he stopped worrying. He didn't want to be a millionaire or appear on the cover of some glossy architecture magazine. He wasn't going to be the next I. M. Pei. He'd do his job well, he'd make a decent living and his clients would be happy with his work. That was enough.

"I work better when I'm crazy," Caley said. She flipped open the phone. "Give me your number. I might have an emergency sometime."

"I'll only give you my number if you promise that you'll use it," he said.

"For what? A booty call?"

"Maybe. Or a little bit of drunk dialing. Or when you get stuck in a snowbank on the side of the road." He reached in his jacket pocket and pulled out his own phone, then handed it to her. "Put your number on my memory dial. I might have an emergency of my own some night."

Jake carefully watched the side of the East Shore Road, looking for the weathered wooden sign that hung from an old maple tree. Havenwoods. When he saw it, he turned sharply into the woods, steering the truck down a snow-covered drive.

Caley looked around. "What is this? It said private property on that sign. We shouldn't drive down here."

"Relax," Jake said. "The owner hardly ever uses it in the winter. No one has been here for a while." Caley was silent and Jake looked over at her. "It'll be all right, I promise."

They wound through the woods and finally came

to a clearing in the trees. An old log house stood on the rise above the lake. A ramshackle porch, supported by a stone foundation, surrounded the house and three fieldstone chimneys broke up the roofline. Every time Jake saw it, he couldn't help but be amazed that it was finally his.

"Oh my God," Caley murmured, peering through the windshield. "It's the Fortress." She glanced over at Jake, a wide smile on her face. "I haven't been here in…years. It still looks exactly the same." She frowned. "But smaller."

"It's called Havenwoods," Jake said, "and I found out it was one of the first summerhouses built on this lake, back when the industrialists called their summer homes camps and North Lake was just a pretty fishing hole in the middle of a forest. It was built in 1885 by a railroad tycoon from Chicago who owned the entire lake and the surrounding property. It was designed by William West Durant," Jake continued. "Durant was the first to design in the Great Camp style in the Adirondacks."

"Someone is home," she said. "The porch lights are on in the middle of the day."

He shook his head. "The lighting is triggered by a sensor on the driveway. When you come from the lake side, the lights don't go on." He turned off the car. "You want to go inside?"

As kids, they used to come across the lake by boat and tie up at the rotting dock. They'd explored every inch of the property and had spent many rainy days inside the house, gaining entrance through a first-floor window with a broken sash lock.

"We can't go inside. That's trespassing. And breaking and entering."

"We used to do it all the time. No one will care," Jake said. "And I know where the key is so we won't have to break in." He jumped out of the truck and circled around, then helped her out. "If Officer Winslow catches us, you can just smile at him and he won't arrest us."

Caley's gaze was fixed on the facade as she walked closer. "You brought me here on my fifteenth birthday. And you gave me that arrowhead necklace. I wore that thing all year. My girlfriends in school thought it was the ugliest thing, but I thought…well, I thought it was special."

"Do you still have it?"

"I do. It's in my closet back in New York. The leather string broke, but I kept it. Along with everything else you gave me." Caley smiled. "I'll have to get that box and go through it."

"What else is in it?"

"Silly stuff. Mementos of our grand love affair. There's a piece of bubblegum you gave me. I was sure it meant that you wanted me. I used to take it out and touch it because I knew it had been in your pocket."

"That's a little scary," Jake teased.

"I know. I was a teenage girl hauling around a huge torch. Everything meant something."

They climbed the snow-covered steps and Caley walked to the window, peering inside, her hands around her eyes. "It looks the same. I'd imagine this was a beautiful place to visit in its day."

Jake walked along the outside wall until he reached the second set of windows, then bent down and pulled a stone from a spot beneath the sill. Beneath it, he found the keys.

"How did you know about that?"

"I was here alone one summer and the caretaker showed up. I saw him get the keys. After that, I could get in whenever I wanted." He grinned and grabbed Caley's hand and pulled her along to the corner of the house. "See this. These logs were hand-notched so they fit really tight. Durant always used materials from the surrounding forest."

Jake unlocked the three locks on the front door, then opened it. He stepped aside, waiting for Caley to enter. "It'll be all right. I promise."

They stood in the entry hall, an old deer-antler chandelier hanging above their head. The furniture was tattered and dusty, but he'd managed to clean up most of the mess left by the leaky roof and broken windows.

"Wow," Caley said. "This place needs a lot of work. It seemed like a palace when we were kids, but now I see it for what it is."

"Look beyond the surface," Jake said. "Can you see what it could be again?"

"I can," she said. She walked over to a low bench made of branches and twigs. "But it would take someone with a lot of time and a lot of money."

"I used to walk through this house and memorize all the details. This is why I decided to become an architect. I wanted to design houses like this. Summerhouses. Places where people relax and have fun."

Jake felt her take his hand and weave her fingers through his. It was a simple gesture, but he instantly knew she understood. He wasn't sure anyone else would. But Caley would. It seemed right that he share this with her again. "Come on, I'll show you around."

Though he hadn't kissed her or even touched her in an intimate way, Jake felt as though they'd suddenly become so much closer. This was who he was now, not the boy she'd known. And the woman standing beside him understood what it all meant.

They wandered aimlessly, Caley taking in all the details silently, as if caught in her memories of the past. Dust motes swirled around them in the light that filtered through the windows. When they passed through a shaft of sunlight, Jake gently pulled her into his arms and kissed her, his mouth searching for a familiar taste he'd come to crave.

"I need you," he murmured, his lips warm against hers.

Caley looked up at him, her gaze fixed on his mouth. "Show me the rest of the house," she murmured.

They walked slowly through each of the six bedrooms, Jake pointing out the architectural details that made Havenwoods so special. By the time they got back to the entry hall, Jake was almost desperate to kiss her. But he waited, hoping that this place would work its magic.

It was a great wreck of a house, but it was part of their history together, part of who he'd become. It deserved better than to be consumed by the elements and left for some errant campfire spark to take hold of and burn down.

He'd mortgaged his future to buy it, cashing in his investments, selling his sports car to buy a secondhand SUV. He'd even sold his house in Wicker Park and took up residence in a tiny one-bedroom in a seedy neighborhood, just so he could afford the mortgage and taxes.

It left little for renovations, but Jake felt it was worth the risk. Although, he still hadn't told a soul he owned it. His father would probably blow a gasket and his mother would never understand. But he had an ally in Caley.

"There are only two things I ever really wanted in my life. And this was one of them," Jake said.

"What was the other?" Caley asked.

"You," he said with a devilish grin.

JAKE LOCKED THE FRONT DOOR behind them and returned the key to its spot beneath the window. Caley watched him, her mind flooded with memories of their childhood. She couldn't count the number of days they'd spent at the Fortress. It had been a magical place, a place all their own.

It was sweet of him to remember, she mused. Even when things had been difficult between them, Caley had been able to count on Jake. As teenagers, they'd argue and pout, but he'd always be the first to come back with an apology—a gift of something he'd found in the forest or a plan for a brand-new adventure or just a silly joke that would make her laugh.

It wasn't difficult to understand why she'd been in love with him all those years ago. When she was with him, she felt as if she were the most important person in his world. And she felt that way now. There was an honesty between them, a respect that she'd never felt with any other man.

When he stepped back to her side, she wrapped

her arms around his waist and pushed up on her toes, dropping a soft kiss on his lips. "Thank you," she said.

"For what?"

"For bringing me back here."

Jake slipped his hands around her waist and drew her closer, his mouth covering hers. The kiss was quiet and gentle, his tongue caressing hers in a slow, seductive way.

It was as if they both finally knew that being together was inevitable. There was nothing stopping them anymore. All day she'd been thinking about this, about what even one kiss would do to her. If a kiss could devastate her defenses so easily, what would a night in bed do?

Suddenly, Caley wanted to find out. She didn't need to weigh the consequences of what she was about to do because she didn't care anymore about consequences. All she cared about was sharing herself, completely, with Jake.

"Would you like go back to the inn?" she asked.

"I thought we could walk down to the lake," Jake said. "There's something else I want to show you."

"I want to go back to the inn," Caley said. "With you."

He stared down into her eyes, an odd expression on his face. Then a slow smile curved the corners of his mouth. "We don't have to go back there," he murmured.

"We don't?"

He pulled her along the porch, circling the house until he'd reached the side that faced the lake. She saw the small log building about thirty yards from the house, connected by a covered walkway. They'd called it the Guardhouse when they were kids, but now

Caley knew what it really was—a summer kitchen. When they reached the front door, Jake pulled out his keys and unlocked the padlock.

"You have your own key?" she asked.

Jake opened the door. "Yeah. It comes in handy since I own the place," he murmured.

Caley gasped, not sure that she heard him right. "You own this cabin?"

"No, I own the whole thing. The house, the property, the rotting dock and the roofless guest cabins. The musty furniture and that old moose head over the fireplace. It's all mine."

Caley glanced around the small cabin. A drafting table was set up near the window and a small cot stood in front of the fireplace. She walked over to the table and stared down at the yellowed plans spread out there, recognizing the facade of the main house. They were covered with yellow sticky notes in Jake's handwriting.

Caley felt her heart warm, suddenly understanding the deeper reasons for their visit. This was his home. And he wanted her approval. "I can't believe this is all yours," she said. "How did you get it?"

"I was in New York for a seminar and I decided to look up the lady who owned it. I had the name from the tax records. We had tea and I told her about how much I loved the place and how I used to sneak in here. And she agreed to sell it to me, with the provision that I bring it back to what it was in her childhood. I made a promise and I intend to keep it. And when it's finished, she asked that I invite her grandchildren to stay now and then."

"Why did you bring me here?"

"It's our place," Jake said. "I thought you should

see it again. Because you're my oldest friend and you'd appreciate it."

Caley slowly unzipped her jacket. "I don't want to be your friend right now," she said, dropping the jacket on the rough plank floor.

He reached out and rubbed her arms through her shirt. "Maybe I should start a fire."

Caley sat on the edge of the cot and watched as he crumpled newspapers up beneath the grate in the old stone hearth. He tossed some smaller logs on top, then grabbed a match and started the fire. They both stared into the flames as they licked at the dry logs. Soon, a gentle heat was radiating through the room.

"Do you stay here often?" she asked.

"When I come out from the city," Jake said. "It's harder in the summer since my folks are in town. Then, I have to stay with them. In the winter, no one knows I'm here. I work on the house. It's quiet and I get some of my other work done, too."

"I'm used to having so many people around," she said. "I can't imagine getting anything done with all this silence."

"Sometimes silence is nice," he said, leaning forward to kiss her.

She reached for the buttons of her shirt, and Jake drew a ragged breath. Pressing her hand to his chest, she felt his heart pounding beneath her fingers. Caley was breathless, as if the anticipation itself was exhausting.

"Are you sure you want to do this here?" he asked. "Conditions are a little rough."

"This is perfect," Caley said. In truth, she'd always dreamed that it would happen this way with Jake, in some secret spot where no one would ever find them, in the backseat of his beat-up Cutlass or on a secluded beach in the middle of the night.

Jake reached into his jeans pocket and pulled out his wallet, then retrieved a condom. "I guess we'll need this," he said.

"Are you nervous?" Caley asked, reaching out to grab the front of his jacket and pull him down on top of her.

"No," he said with a grin. "Well, maybe a little. God, I feel as if we're in high school and this is my first time."

"I know. Me, too." She tugged on his jacket, drawing it down over his arms, then tossing it aside. "It makes it more exciting, don't you think?"

Caley got up on her knees and shoved her shirt off her arms, dropping it on top of his jacket. Jake rubbed his thumb over her nipple, bringing it to a peak beneath the silky fabric of her bra. "Sweetheart, getting naked with you would be just as exciting if we did it in the middle of Main Street with all of North Lake watching."

They tugged and tore at each other's clothes, their hands frantically skimming over each inch of naked skin. The air was still chilly and his touch raised goose bumps. But it only made each sensation more acute, exciting her so much that she trembled with each caress. Caley felt alive with anticipation, scared and nervous and aroused all at once.

When they were both down to their underwear, they stopped and stared at each other. Caley giggled softly. "Now what?"

"I'm the virgin here," Jake teased. "Maybe you should show me what to do."

Caley reached out and ran her finger over his lower lip. He was giving her control, letting her set the pace. This time, she would seduce him, like she'd tried to do all those years ago. And this time, she'd succeed.

She slid her hands along his body and hooked her fingers in the waistband of his boxers, then pulled them down. After that, she quickly took care of her own underwear. His body radiated heat, more than the fire burning on the hearth. He pulled her against him and his warmth became hers.

Stretched out on top of him, Caley reveled in the feel of their naked bodies pressed against each other. He ran his hands over her back, along her hips. She could feel his desire, hot and hard, between them.

She'd wanted to take everything slowly, to savor each moment. But she was impatient, desperate to experience it all at once. She'd waited for so long and now that she'd made the decision to have him, there would be nothing stopping her. She drew back, pressing a line of kisses to his chest, moving lower and lower until she reached the soft hair on his belly.

Caley knew the power of his touch on her body. Now, she wanted to test her power over him. She stroked him, wrapping her fingers around his hard shaft. Jake closed his eyes and groaned, his breath coming his short gasps. He arched into her touch and when she looked up again, his eyes were open and he was watching her every move.

"I don't think my first time felt this good."

Caley smiled, then dipped lower and took him into her mouth. Her touch was like shock to his body and he jerked, sucking in a sharp breath. "Am I doing it right?" she teased, smiling up at him.

"Oh, yeah. Oh, that's so nice."

Caley continued to caress him with her tongue and her lips, carefully gauging his reaction and drawing him away from the edge again and again. And when she suspected that he wouldn't last much longer, she moved back up along his body, until his swollen shaft rested between her legs.

She rocked above him, his erection sliding against her sex, the friction sending wonderful waves of pleasure through her body. In the past, sex had always been filled with nagging disappointments. She'd never really felt the kind of passion that she'd wanted to feel, that she knew she could feel.

This time, it would be different. Caley felt as if she could surrender by simply closing her eyes and letting herself go. She was so close already and he hadn't even touched her. An urgency drove her forward, toward something that she'd never experienced yet knew she wanted. Caley reached out and took the condom from Jake's hand, then unwrapped it.

"Wait," he murmured. "Slow down."

"I've been waiting eleven years," she said. "I can't wait any longer." She sheathed him, then straddled his hips, moving above him until he probed at her entrance. Then, with a deep sigh, she sank down on top of him.

The sensation of him filling her was a revelation. It was perfection and paradise, absolute intimacy. They were closer than they'd ever been before and yet it seemed so natural, as if their bodies had been made for this all along.

Jake began to move inside her, his gaze fixed on

hers, his fingers tangled in hers. Caley leaned forward and ran her tongue along the crease of his mouth. He reached out and drew her into a deep, desperate kiss, his lips and tongue communicating his need without words.

This was sex, but it was more than that, Caley thought to herself. It was passion and instinct, a need that had burned inside them for years. It was the past and the present, it was the two of them drowning in a world of pleasure. Now she understood why it hadn't happened all those years ago. She wasn't ready—they weren't ready—for the intensity of their joining.

Jake reached between them to touch her, but Caley grabbed his hand again and pinned it at his side. She was already just a heartbeat away and his touch would send her over. Instead, she increased her tempo, rocking faster and faster and feeling the tension tighten inside her. She ached to let go, but knew that if she waited just a bit longer, it would be all the more intense. She wanted to come, but she wanted it to be the most powerful release she'd ever experienced.

Jake wasn't content to play a passive role anymore. He sat up and wrapped her legs around his waist, impaling her until she could feel him deep inside her. When he began to move again, she knew she was lost. Every stroke was exquisite torture.

Caley felt herself reaching for ecstasy, her release so close she could almost touch it. And then it came down on her like a waterfall, washing over her until her whole body tingled with sensation. She cried out as spasm after spasm shook her, her body reacting uncontrollably.

And then, suddenly, Jake was there with her, driving into her one last time before joining her. He pressed his face between her breasts as he moaned, his hands clutching at her shoulders, driving her down onto him again and again until he was completely spent.

When their shudders had subsided, they collapsed into each other, Jake gathering her in his arms. It had happened so quickly and yet Caley felt complete and utter exhaustion. Her body, so tense just moments before, was almost boneless. "Oh, my," she murmured.

"Why did we wait so long?" he asked, pressing a kiss beneath her ear.

"It wouldn't have been this good eleven years ago," she said.

"I'm not talking about then. I'm talking about the past two days." He raked his hand through her tangled hair, then gently tugged back until she met his gaze. "This changes everything."

Caley frowned. "It does?"

"How am I supposed to be around you now? How can I keep from touching you and kissing you? I want you in my bed. Tonight. Tomorrow night. For as long as you want me."

"I guess this won't count as a one-night stand?"

"No," Jake said, shaking his head. "I don't think there's a chance of that. You can't resist me."

"And you can't resist me," she countered with a satisfied smile.

"Why should I even try?"

Caley snuggled up against his warm body. "We can stay here tonight. I know the guy who owns the place." She pressed her lips to his chest, then sighed.

"No one is expecting us back," Jake said.

"Except for Emma. But she can wait." Caley pushed

up on her elbow and brushed a lock of hair from his forehead. "So we could do it again?"

"Yeah," Jake replied. But then his smile faded and he cursed softly. "No. I only had one condom."

"There are other things we could do," Caley suggested.

"Really? I always loved your sense of adventure," he replied, grabbing her waist and pulling her beneath him.

His mouth came down on hers and Caley lost herself in his kiss. There were a lot things she'd never tried in the bedroom. But with Jake, all her inhibitions seemed to dissolve at his touch. She didn't feel vulnerable with him, she felt powerful. She didn't have to worry about what he wanted or needed because he wanted nothing more than to give her pleasure. She could let go and enjoy his body without sacrificing a part of herself.

They had been friends first and now they were lovers. There would be no going back.

"NO, DON'T GO," Jake said, pulling Caley back into his arms. "Not yet. Stay a little longer."

Caley glanced over her shoulder at him, snuggled beneath the covers of his bed in the boathouse. They'd officially been lovers for twenty-four hours and the sneaking around was already wearing thin.

After dinner at the Lamberts', Caley had offered up some silly story about working on their toasts for the wedding. They walked down to the boathouse and the moment the door closed behind them, they were tossing aside clothes and tumbling into Jake's bed.

Jake had spent last night in Caley's bed at the inn, sneaking out in the early morning hours so that he could get back to the boathouse before anyone noticed him missing. They were two adults and yet there were moments when Jake felt as if they were teenagers.

"Don't you think it's odd?"

"What?" Caley asked as she continued to dress.

"What we're doing is perfectly legal. Between consenting adults. And we have a variety of locations to choose from. We shouldn't have to worry about getting caught."

"It would complicate things," Caley explained. "There would be questions and speculation and expectations. I just want this to be about you and me and not our families, all right?"

Jake nodded. "So do you want me to sneak into your bed tonight?"

Caley grabbed her jacket and reached into the pocket, then withdrew a key, dangling it in front of his face. "I got you your own. Just don't let Emma see you come in. She's been going to bed early, so come over as soon as you can get away." She gave him a quick kiss, then pulled her boots on. "Are we agreed on our plan?"

Over the course of the past day, he and Caley had come up with a strategy to test Sam and Emma's commitment to each other. They'd discussed all the pitfalls and problems that couples encountered on the path to everlasting love and had put together an obstacle course for Sam and Emma to navigate. "Operation Wedding Trashers is ready to go."

"We're not trying to trash their wedding," Caley said. "We're just testing the depth of their feelings. Nothing more sinister than what a good marriage counselor would do."

"Except we have absolutely no professional qualifications or practical experience in marital matters."

"No. But we do have relationship experience," Caley said. "That should count for something." She sat down on the edge of the bed, now fully dressed in all her cold-weather clothes. "So tomorrow night I'm going to take Emma to Tyler's with me. There are always lots of single guys there to dance with and I'll make sure she drinks plenty of cocktails."

"And I'm taking Sam out for some fun. There's a strip club out on the interstate. I figured we'd go there."

Caley's eyes went wide. "Really? Is it one of those clubs where they take off all their clothes?"

"Almost," Jake said. "Just G-strings, shiny poles and lots of dollar bills."

"So you've been there before?"

Jake shook his head. "No. But I've heard about it. Brett and a bunch of his college buddies went there for his twenty-first birthday. Does it bother you that I'll be looking at naked women?"

"Of course not," Caley said.

"Because it would bother me if you were out looking at naked men."

"Maybe I should see if I can find a strip club for Emma and me to go to. There has to be one somewhere," Caley said.

"There's only one body I'm interested in seeing naked," Jake said. "And that would be yours. You don't have to worry. After what we've had together, a hundred naked women aren't going to get me excited."

"Good answer," Caley said. She lay down on top of him and gave him a more thorough kiss. "Later."

"I'm counting on it," he said.

She walked to the door, sending him a smile before she slipped out. Jake listened to her footsteps on the stairs. He crawled out of bed, wrapping the comforter around his naked body, then peered through the curtains to watch her run across the lawn toward the Lambert house.

The boathouse was now a cozy little haven. The heater had been running all day and though it was a bit chilly inside, it was comfortable. His mother had given him a down comforter and Brett had turned on the water so the bathroom was functioning. The accommodations were almost perfect, and almost completely private.

Jake flopped back down on the bed and closed his eyes. He'd made love to his fair share of beautiful women and each time he'd searched for that connection, that spark that might prove he'd found the right one. In the past twenty-four hours he'd realized that it was there with Caley. Maybe it had always been there.

But what did that mean? They lived in different worlds, lived different lives. Though he wanted to believe that love would conquer all, Jake certainly knew the realities of a relationship. Caley had made it clear that their affair would end when she went back to New York. Though he planned to do everything in his power to convince her otherwise, Jake had to prepare himself for the probability that it would be over at the end of the week.

He had known it would be difficult before, but now that they'd become lovers, it would be impossible. Surely, it wouldn't be easy for her, either. Her desire for him ran just as deep and Jake sensed that with every touch, every kiss, the bond between them grew stronger.

And if Caley left him, if things between them ended, he didn't think there would ever be another woman to take her place. In the back of his mind he'd always compared the women he met to Caley. He hadn't been aware of that fact until now. They'd been smart, but Caley had been smarter. They'd been beautiful, but she had beauty they'd never possess. He'd grown up wanting her and only her. Now that he'd had her, he was left to deal with the fear of losing her.

Jake threw his arm over his eyes and cursed softly. A knock sounded on the door and he sat up, surprised that she'd returned so quickly. He waited for her to come in, but she knocked again. Jake grabbed his boxers and pulled them on, then crossed the room and opened the door. But Caley wasn't standing outside. Sam was.

His brother peered inside. "Can I come in?"

"Sure," Jake said, stepping back to allow Sam to pass. "What's up? It's late."

Sam began to pace the width of the room, his shoulders tense, his expression grim. Then, he sat down on the edge of the bed and nervously twisted his fingers together. "I did like you told me. When I drove Emma back to the inn tonight, I told her it was time we were honest with each other. I said we needed to have sex before we got married."

"And she refused?"

"No," Sam said. "No, we had sex." He shook his head. "And it was pretty bad."

Jake frowned. "Bad? Like how bad?"

Sam flopped back and covered his face with his

hands. "About as bad as it could get. She was so excited and so was I—at first. I wanted it to be romantic and special, but everything I did seemed so forced. And then, I—I couldn't—you know."

"Get it up?"

"More like, keep it up," Sam said. He turned and looked at Jake. "You don't think I need Viagra, do you?"

Jake chuckled softly. "You haven't had any problems before, have you?"

"No! Never. But I was never marrying any of those other girls. What if this is the way it is with Emma? What if I can't…perform?"

"This happens occasionally. To every guy."

"Did it ever happen to you?"

"Well, no. But I was never under the kind of pressure you are. When I encouraged you to have sex with her, I didn't mean that you should do it just to get it done. It's not like mowing the lawn or changing the oil in your car. There's more to it than that."

"Like foreplay," Sam said. "I know, I tried that, but she was in such a hurry. I started out thinking I'd have to convince her, but she was completely on board. I guess Caley told her it was important to be sexually compatible with your husband." Sam paused. "I think Emma said *crucial*. That was the word. Or maybe it was *critical*. And that's when I started to get really nervous."

"Yeah, I can see how that could happen," Jake said.

Still, he couldn't really relate. With Caley, there was a need there that seemed to overwhelm all rational thought. When they were intimate, he didn't worry about the mechanics, it just happened. It was raw, primal instinct that aroused him. And the fact that it always ended with incredible pleasure was nature at work.

Jake sat down beside his brother and patted him on the back. "This doesn't mean it will happen that way every time."

"What if it does? I wouldn't want to marry me."

"It's just a temporary thing," Jake said. "Believe me. The next time, you'll be fine."

"It's not like I didn't want to," Sam said. "I mean, Emma is hot. She's got this great body and the way she kisses me just gets me going. You know what that's like, right?"

Jake bit his bottom lip and forced a smile, his mind rewinding back to the afternoon he'd spent with Caley. "Yeah, I know what that's like," he muttered.

"She and Caley are going out tomorrow night," Sam said. "Girl's night out. I know I don't have to worry about that. If Caley is there, nothing is going to happen to Emma. But what if Emma starts looking around for a guy who can...do it?"

"Maybe we should go out," Jake suggested. "Take your mind off of your troubles. Just the best man and the groom, some male bonding."

"Yeah," Sam said. "I'm twenty-one now. I can get into any bar."

"And I've got just the place." Jake stood and grabbed his jeans from the floor. "Listen, you can hang out here tonight. There's sheets and blankets for the sofa bed in the closet. I'm just going to run back up to the house and get us something to drink and then we can talk. We'll get this all sorted out."

"Thanks," Sam said. "I don't know what I'd do without you. Maybe, someday, when you get married, I can return the favor."

Jake slipped into his shirt, then pulled on his socks and boots. "I'll be back," he said as he headed for the door. "Just relax."

He jogged down the stairs, then walked across the lawn toward his parents' house. Jake pulled his cell phone from his pocket and dialed Caley's number. She didn't answer, her voice message picking up at four rings.

"Hey, there, it's me. Listen, I'm not going to be able to make it tonight. Sam stopped by the boathouse after you left and he needs some company. Man problems. So, I guess I'll see you tomorrow." He paused, holding back the next words he wanted to say. "Sleep tight," Jake finished.

The sentiment had almost come out without a second thought. Love you. That's what he'd wanted to say, what he'd meant to say. But at the last moment, Jake had censored himself, wondering if it was too much too soon. The words didn't always have to have such a serious meaning, did they? He did love Caley, but those feelings had changed and the words had now taken on a much deeper significance.

Being with Caley again had brought back a piece of his life that had been missing. She made him believe it was possible to find a best friend and a lover in one person. And it wasn't a stretch to add wife to that list.

Jake shook his head. He'd never thought much about marriage. Maybe he always knew in some secret corner of his mind that there was only one woman for him. He stopped, then cursed softly. Was it supposed to be this easy? He'd always assumed that it would take forever to fall in love and even longer to figure out whether that love could survive marriage. But suddenly, it all seemed so simple.

Jake's phone rang and he pulled it out of his pocket and squinted at the caller ID. He smiled when he recognized Caley's number.

"Hey," he said. "Did you get my message?"

"Yes. What's going on? What are man problems?"

"A couple days ago, I told Sam if he wanted to have sex before he and Emma were married, he should just tell Emma and they should do it. I guess it didn't go so well."

"How did it not go well? Did Emma refuse?"

"No. She jumped at the chance. She agreed and then they tried and Sam couldn't perform."

"Oh," Caley said. "That's got to be a little scary. I mean, she was holding out, hoping it would be the most wonderful thing in the world and then…" She drew a deep breath. "Thank God this didn't happen on their wedding night. Can you imagine what a disappointment that would have been?"

"So I guess this plays into our plan," Jake said. "They're obviously both having doubts right about now."

A long silence came from the other end of the line and for a moment, Jake thought the call had been dropped. "So we should continue?" she finally asked.

"I guess so," Jake said. "What do we know about their relationship? Hell, we can't even figure out what's going on between us."

"Sex," Caley said. "Lust. Curiosity."

"And that's all?"

"What else would there be?" she replied.

He cursed the fact that they were discussing this over the phone instead of face-to-face. He couldn't read her expression, couldn't look into her eyes for the truth of her words. "You tell me."

"I don't know. What do you want me to say? I don't know what's going on any more than you do. When the week is over, I guess we'll have to figure it all out."

"Right," Jake said. He glanced over his shoulder. "I should go back to Sam. He's going to want to talk and I told him I was going to grab some beer from the house."

"Emma and I are driving into Chicago tomorrow morning," Caley said. "She wants to check on the cake and some friends of hers are throwing a wedding shower. So I guess I'll see you sometime tomorrow night. Enjoy the strip club."

"Are you jealous, Caley?"

"No! I don't care if you look at naked women. Why would that bother me?"

"Because it would be nice if you were a little jealous. I'd like to think that you care enough about me to be worried."

"Maybe I'll have to give you a lap dance the next time I see you," she said in a teasing voice.

"Thanks for the image," he murmured. "Now I'm never going to get to sleep."

"Good night, Jake."

"Good night, Caley." He waited until she hung up before he switched off his phone. This was a strange, new feeling, Jake mused. They were almost acting like a…a couple. And even more surprising was that Jake didn't mind it at all. He wanted Caley to feel possessive and jealous and worried. Whether she was willing to admit it, she cared about him, maybe loved him a little bit. And maybe he loved her a little bit, too.

5

"I don't see why we had to leave. I was having a good time," Sam complained, his words slurred by all the beer he'd drunk.

Jake glanced over at his little brother. He'd never expected Sam to enjoy himself as much as he had. In truth, Jake had thought they'd spend an hour at the club and then head over to Tyler's to find the girls. Jake had finally convinced Sam to drag himself away from the dazzling charms of Tiffany Diamond and check up on his fiancée.

Though Caley might be worried about his night with naked women, Jake had much more cause to worry about her. He knew how he felt. She was the one who'd just dumped her boyfriend and tumbled into bed with the first man who tried to seduce her. Although Jake would like to believe Caley only had eyes for him, a few fruity drinks and some male attention could do a lot to a girl's memory.

"You know those girls were only being friendly to you because you were buying them champagne. They get a cut of everything you spend on them."

"But they were nice," Sam said. "Especially that Tiffany. She's going to meet us at Tyler's."

"You invited a stripper to meet us?" Jake shook his head. This was in addition to the Wedding Trasher plan. Stripper and fiancée meet. Jake wasn't sure any relationship could weather that particular event.

"Tiffany Diamond. Do you think that's her real name?"

He was actually beginning to feel a bit guilty about the evening, but this was ridiculous. If his little brother was this naive about strippers, then he had absolutely no business getting married. There were certain things a guy needed to know and Sam's education had obviously fallen woefully short. "Have you ever been to a strip club?" Jake asked.

"Sure," Sam mumbled, resting his head on the cold window. "But never one where the strippers were so nice. Do you think Emma would mind if I invited Tiffany to the wedding?"

"No," Jake said. "I'm sure she wouldn't mind. And Mom would be thrilled to meet her, too. Maybe she could wear that little outfit that she danced in."

"You know, she doesn't want to be a stripper all her life," Sam said. "She actually wants to be a professional cheerleader. Or a dancer in Vegas."

"Please tell me it's the liquor talking," Jake murmured.

"Yeah, it's the liquor talking," Sam said. "But I'm moving my own lips."

The next time Jake glanced over at Sam, he was asleep, his face smashed against the frosty window, his breath creating a tiny clear spot. Jake had to wonder about the sense of this plan that he and Caley had set in motion. When booze was mixed into the equation, there was every chance that things could go bad very quickly. Add a stripper to the mix and disaster was guaranteed. Were he and Caley really ready to deal with the fallout from this evening? Jake wondered. And would this be a true test of the commitment between Sam and Emma or just a blatant manipulation?

When he reached Tyler's Roadhouse, Jake pulled into a far corner of the parking lot. But instead of waking Sam up, he decided to go inside and find Caley and call this whole thing off. They'd gone far enough and it was time to put this wedding back in Sam and Emma's hands. He didn't want to spend the rest of their week together thinking about Sam and Emma. He wanted to focus on Caley.

Jake quietly slipped out of the truck and locked the door behind him. Though it was cold out, Sam could survive for the five minutes it would take to grab Caley and Emma and convince them to go home.

Jake paid the cover charge at the door, then pushed through the crowd, squinting in the dark to locate the Lambert sisters. He immediately saw Emma on the dance floor, dressed in a shockingly sexy outfit of skin-tight jeans, a sheer blouse and some kind of underwear beneath it.

She was dancing with a scruffy-looking young man in a backward baseball cap, the two of them laughing and waving their arms along with a Bruce Springsteen song. Jake's gaze continued to skim the crowd and he saw Caley standing near the edge of the dance floor. He cursed softly when he saw Jeff Winslow standing next to her.

Jake felt his fingers clench into a fist. Why did that guy get on his nerves so much? It was obvious from the way they were standing that there was nothing going on between them. But still, he'd never liked competing for Caley's attention, even when they were kids. And he liked it a lot less now that they were adults.

He wove through the patrons until he stepped up beside her. "Caley," he shouted. She jumped at first at the sound of his voice, but when she turned and saw him, Caley gave him a smile of relief. "Hey, Winslow," he said, giving the cop a nod.

Jeff smiled. "You two better take that girl home," he said, pointing at Emma with the neck of his beer bottle. "I think she's had enough."

"Where is Sam?" Caley shouted.

"In the car. Drunk and asleep." He took her hand and pulled her along toward the door. When they got there, he glanced back at Jeff Winslow. The guy didn't look happy, but he hadn't tried to stop Caley from leaving. Then he looked at Emma. "She looks like she's having a little too much fun."

Caley nodded. "That's because she's had a little too much tequila. It won't seem like fun in the morning. She's dancing with some guy named Robert. He seems harmless enough."

They stepped outside into the chilly night air and walked around the corner of the building. The moment they reached a private spot, Jake grabbed Caley, pressed her back against the wall and kissed her. It wasn't an expression of lust or even affection. He needed reassurance that nothing had changed in the hours that they'd been apart. When she responded, Jake felt an overwhelming sense of relief.

"That's better," he murmured. His hand slipped beneath her jacket and slowly searched for bare skin. When he found it, he splayed his hand across the small of her back. "You're so warm."

Caley shivered, her teeth chattering. "Not for long. My car is parked over there. Let's get out of the cold." She handed Jake the keys and they hurried over to the spot where she'd left the rental. Jake let her in the passenger side and then hopped behind the wheel. He started the engine and turned on the heater. "It'll take a while to warm up."

"I'm starting to think this whole thing was a really bad idea," Caley said, rubbing her hands together.

Jake took her fingers between his and blew on them. "Me, too."

"What ever made us think this was the right thing to do?"

"Maybe we're transferring our own fears about commitment to Sam and Emma. I mean, they seem to know what they're doing and we haven't had much success in that department."

"Well, a little success," Caley murmured, staring at her fingers as he kissed each one. "Just since we came home."

Jake smiled and pressed her hands to his chest. "Yeah. A little. More than a little, I'd say." He reached out and slipped his hand around her waist, pulled her closer. He'd spent the evening looking at naked women and he hadn't been the slightest bit affected. But the moment he touched Caley, his desire warmed and his pulse raced.

"Do you think if we crawled in the backseat and took all our clothes off anyone would notice?" Jake murmured. "People make love in roadhouse parking lots all the time."

Caley laughed. "Don't you think it would be easier if we just went back to the inn?"

"Only if you do that lap dance you promised me," he said.

"All right," Caley replied. "I think I can do that."

"We'll go inside, get Emma, then dump them both in Emma's room at the inn and let them figure this out for themselves."

"Good plan."

They both jumped out of the car and hurried back to the front door, but a small crowd had gathered outside. "What's going on?" Jake asked.

"There's a fight," one of the girls said. "Some guy and his fiancée and a stripper."

Jake groaned. "Oh, hell." He turned to Caley. "You stay here. I'll be right back." An instant later, the sounds of a siren could be heard in the distance.

"Get Emma," Caley cried. "Before she gets hurt."

Jake pressed through the crush of people leaving the bar and when he finally got inside, the place was lit up and emptied of half the patrons. The band was lounging around the stage and a small group was gathered in the middle of the dance floor. Emma and Sam were sitting on the floor, Tiffany was holding her nose and arguing with Jeff Winslow and a guy that Jake recognized as Emma's dance partner was laid out flat in front of them all, his hands clutching his crotch.

Jake strode up to group. "What's going on here?"

"Just step back," Winslow warned. "Everything is under control."

"This is my brother and my future sister-in-law. I want to take them home."

Winslow glanced over his shoulder at Jake and shook his head. "I'm going to have to take your brother and his fiancée in. They started this brawl. Assault, public intoxication—"

"They're in a bar," Jake said. "Everyone is intoxicated."

"You can meet them down at the station. We'll get things sorted out there."

"Come on," Jake said. "Don't be a hard-ass, Winslow. No one was seriously hurt here."

"She hit me in the nose!" Tiffany cried.

"She ran into my elbow," Emma countered. "I was trying to help Robert up after Sam kicked him in the crotch. And she got in the way."

"I didn't kick him," Sam said.

"Yeah, you did, man," Robert groaned from the floor.

Sam shrugged. "It was a knee to the crotch, not a kick."

"Isn't there just a fine I can pay right away and we can take care of this mess without wasting any more time?" Jake asked.

"What's going on here?" They all turned to look at Caley as she joined the group, a worried expression furrowing her brow.

"I'm breaking up with Sam," Emma announced. "We're not getting married."

"You can't break up with me," Sam countered, "because I already broke up with you."

Emma sent him a withering glare. "You have no reason to break up with me. I was just dancing with

Robert. I wasn't dancing *on* him like that stripper was doing to you."

"I'm not a stripper," Tiffany said. "I prefer exotic dancer."

"You invited her to our wedding!" Emma cried. "Sometimes, I wonder if you even have a brain in your head."

"And sometimes I wonder if you have a heart," Sam shot back.

"Enough!" Winslow shouted. "There will be no more talking. Or I'll throw all of you behind bars."

"Can I go now?" Robert asked. "I've got to start packing up the van. I'm with the band." He slowly got to his feet, wincing slightly as he straightened. "I'm not going to press charges."

"Neither am I," Tiffany said. She wandered over to Robert and smiled coyly. "So you're with the band? I love musicians."

The pair wandered off toward the stage and Officer Winslow started after them. Then he turned and pointed to Emma and Sam. "Don't move," he ordered.

Jake glanced over at Caley and shrugged. "Maybe you can talk to him. He seems to like you more than he likes me." He watched as Caley tried to plead their case. Though he hated sending her back to Winslow, he was certain there'd be no chance she'd be leaving with him.

A few seconds later, Caley returned, a satisfied smile on her face. "We can take them home," she murmured. "He's letting them off, but only if they agree to stay out of trouble for the rest of their time here."

"What did you have to promise him in return?" Jake asked.

"Nothing. He's doing it as a favor to me."

Jake cursed softly and looked down at Sam and Emma. "It would probably do them some good to spend a night in jail."

Caley shook her head and held out her hand to her sister. "Come on. Let's get out of here. I'll take Emma back to the inn and you bring Sam."

Sam also stumbled to his feet and brushed his jeans off. "This is all your fault," he muttered to Jake. "We should have just stayed at the strip club. I was having fun there."

They walked out to the parking lot together, Sam and Emma silent and sullen with Jake and Caley standing between them. As Caley started toward her car, Jake grabbed her hand. "I'll see you later?" he asked.

Caley nodded then walked away, slipping her arm around Emma's shoulders as they walked off. Sam stared after them, an enigmatic expression on his face.

"You're not really going to call off the wedding, are you?" Jake asked.

"I think we are," he murmured, before he turned in the opposite direction.

They didn't speak during the ride home, Sam lost in his thoughts and Jake unwilling to meddle even further. Though he and Caley had achieved their goal, now that the wedding was off, Jake wondered whether they'd gone too far.

While his feelings for Caley ran deep, he knew that they were also very fragile; would they suffer at the first test or would they endure? He knew how he felt, but he still couldn't be sure of Caley's feelings. Now that he'd fallen, Jake was wondering if the risk was worth the reward. Losing Caley would be much more difficult the second time around.

When Caley finally returned to her room at the inn, Jake was asleep in her bed, his naked body twisted in the sheets, his hair falling in waves across his forehead. Caley stripped off her clothes and tossed them against the wall, crinkling her nose at the scent of stale beer and cigarette smoke.

She glanced over at the clock on the nightstand and sighed softly. It was nearly 3:00 a.m. She'd spent the past three hours with Emma, trying to convince her to reconsider canceling the wedding and listing all of Sam's good qualities over and over again.

She couldn't believe Emma was so quick to dismiss her engagement. Caley realized that emotions ran much higher with all the alcohol that had been consumed, but Emma seemed perfectly lucid and determined to leave Sam and her wedding plans behind. She'd even called the airline to buy a ticket back to Boston on the first flight out in the morning.

Did anyone ever find a lasting love? Or was it all just an illusion, as shiny and clear as glass until something came along to shatter it? Did people stay in relationships only because they were too stubborn to admit defeat?

Caley knew her parents loved each other. They'd been together almost thirty years. And Jake's parents often acted like newlyweds. So why was it so hard for her to believe in love?

She walked to the bathroom and closed the door behind her, then turned on the shower, ignoring the urge to crawl into bed with Jake. It would be so easy to find comfort in his arms. She felt safe with him. But were her feelings real or were they just part of a fantasy that she was only now having the chance to live out?

There was no doubt in her mind that everything between them had changed. He'd become a part of her life and not a part she could easily excise. In truth, she couldn't imagine living without him. Yet, she couldn't quite figure out how she could live with him.

How would it work? Would they call it an affair? A relationship? An arrangement? Friends with benefits, she mused. That's what they had now, wasn't it? But for them to continue, they'd have to give it a name.

A soft knock sounded on the bathroom door before it slowly opened. Jake stepped inside, his naked body beautiful in even the harsh fluorescent light. He slipped his arms around her waist and kissed her forehead.

"Is everything all right?"

"I just needed to take a shower. I smell like smoke."

"How's Emma?"

"Still drunk, still furious with Sam and ready to go back to Boston in the morning."

Jake took her hand and pulled her along to the shower stall, then opened the glass door. He stepped inside, the water hitting his naked body and sluicing over his skin. Caley followed him, stepping right into his embrace.

His fingers furrowed through her hair and he kissed her, his tongue slipping between her lips to taste her mouth. The moment their bodies touched, every doubt and insecurity seemed to vanish. Why was it so easy to believe in love when they were making love and so hard to understand it when they were apart?

Jake drew back and stared down into her eyes, then

reached out to touch her breast. He cupped her warm flesh gently, running his thumb over her nipple until it became a stiff peak. Then he smoothed his hand along her hip, his fingers soft and teasing.

Caley reached out and brushed her fingers against his hard shaft. It had taken only a moment for him to become aroused and she found her power over him satisfying. Jake moaned softly as she wrapped her fingers around his heat.

Already, his body was so familiar to her. She knew how he'd react to her touch, the way his breath would catch in his throat, the sound of his voice whispering her name, the feel of his body tensing just before he reached his release.

Jake grabbed her waist and slowly backed her up against the tile wall of the shower. He kissed the curve of her neck and then moved lower, teasing at her nipple with his tongue. "Tell me what you want," he murmured as he gently caressed her nipple.

"You," she said. "Inside me."

He dropped his hand to the soft curve of her backside and gently squeezed. "Tell me how."

"First, you have to kiss me in just the right way."

Jake gave it his best effort, kissing her gently at first and then with growing urgency, dragging his tongue along the crease of her mouth until she surrendered completely. Her knees went soft and she felt herself melt in his arms, the warm water rushing over them both.

"That's a start," she murmured.

Jake slowly trailed kisses over her shoulder and down her arm. When he knelt in front of her, Caley raked her fingers through his wet hair, pulling him away when his tongue tickled.

He was so beautiful, so incredibly sexy. She couldn't imagine ever feeling this attracted to another man. There seemed to be electricity that crackled between them every time they were together. Just one touch of his fingers to her bare skin was all it took for the attraction to overwhelm them both.

Jake's lips trailed lower, until he found the dampness between her legs. She was already aroused and the moment he touched her there, her body jerked in response. "I love that I can touch you like this," he murmured. "That there's nothing left to stop us." He gently parted her legs, tasting her until she writhed against him.

"Oh," she breathed. "Oh, right there."

As he brought her closer and closer to her release, Caley murmured his name urgently, her fingers twisted tightly in his hair. Jake followed her cues, dragging her back from the edge when she got too close. It wasn't enough. She didn't want to experience this pleasure by herself.

She drew him back to his feet, tugging gently on his hair until he stood in front of her. Jake knew what she wanted without her even needing to tell him. He stepped back and gave her a crooked smile. "I have to go get a condom."

Caley grabbed his hand and shook her head. "It's all right," she said. "You don't have to worry."

"Are you sure?"

Caley nodded. She'd been on the pill for years and it had always seemed like such a practical thing. But now, it was liberating. She trusted Jake and he trusted her. She wanted to experience him without any barriers between them. And if they had this one night together, this chance to possess each other completely, then it would be enough. Caley didn't care what came later as long as this came now.

She turned off the shower, then pulled him along to the bed, their bodies dripping water on the carpet. She lay back on the mattress and Jake braced himself above her. Gently, she guided him to her entrance and he closed his eyes the moment they touched.

Slowly, exquisitely, he pushed inside of her, filling her inch by inch until he was buried deep. Caley felt the muscles in his body tense, but he didn't give in. Instead, he began to move.

She closed her eyes and focused on the sensations that washed over her body. She was already so close, but this seemed to take her to a higher level, the need growing more intense with each stroke. This was paradise, she thought. There was nothing more perfect. Every year that had passed since that night of her eighteenth birthday had led them to this moment.

"I want you," he murmured. "Come for me."

He increased his pace and Caley felt herself dancing on the edge. And when her release came, it came so fast that it caught her by surprise. She cried out and the pleasure shook her body, stealing her ability to think.

It was enough to send him over the edge and Jake surrendered a moment later. It was simple, uncomplicated and pure, the two of them searching for release and finding it with each other.

He was like an addiction, a craving that she could only satisfy for a short time. Though she felt sated now, Caley knew she'd want more, each time searching for that certainty, that knowledge that this was something that might last. He rolled over, gathering her in his arms and nuzzling into the curve of her neck. "Can we stay here forever?" he murmured.

"I think the maid will probably discover us when she comes to make the bed and do the vacuuming," Caley joked.

Jake pushed up on his elbow. "You're supposed to say yes," he teased. "Or I'll feel as if you weren't well satisfied."

"I was," she said.

They lay together, wrapped in each other's arms, for a long time. Caley listened to his breathing. He wasn't asleep and she wondered what he was thinking. But she was afraid to ask. They'd so carefully avoided the subject of the future, but it was coming at them quickly.

"What are we going to do about Emma and Sam?" she asked. "We're going to have to figure out a way to get them back together."

"I know."

Caley nodded. "I think they might actually love each other. And if it weren't for our meddling, this wouldn't have happened. So we have to fix it." She drew a ragged breath. "We have to."

"All right," Jake said, his hand slowly caressing her breast. "How are we going to do that?"

"I don't know. We have to make them want each other, the way we want each other."

"I don't think there's another man on the planet who wants a woman the way I want you," Jake murmured.

"Don't you wonder?" Caley said. "Is this unusual? Are we an…aberration?"

Jake answered before he even considered her question. "This is the way it was meant to be with us," he said.

"What are we going to do when this is over?"

The question seemed to take him by surprise and this time, he didn't have a quick and easy answer. "I don't know, Caley," he said. "I don't want to think about that."

"Promise me this," she said. "Promise me that before either one of us begins a life with someone else, that we'll meet back here and be together, just to be sure."

"I promise," he said. "We can come every summer and we can stay at Havenwoods. No one will know we're here. And it'll be just us. For as long as we're both...free."

Caley snuggled up against his body, pressing her face into his warm skin. It was enough for now, she thought to herself. She would have time to figure out how she felt, time to see if this need for Jake would fade with time and distance between them. And if it didn't, then Jake would be there for her. He'd promised.

JAKE AWOKE WITH A START. Caley shook him again and he turned to look at her. "What?" he murmured, rubbing his eyes.

"Wake up. It's nine in the morning. We overslept."

Jake rolled over on his stomach and snuggled into the pillows on Caley's bed. "I'm going to sleep in. I had a late night last night."

"And what are you going to tell your mother when she finds you missing?"

"I'm going to tell her that I drove into Chicago early to check up on things at the office and then stopped for breakfast on the way home. So we actually have the entire morning to spend in bed. It's a two-hour drive each way plus an hour at the office and another hour at breakfast."

Caley smiled. "And what if they see your truck in the parking lot?"

"I parked in back," Jake said.

"All right. I give up," Caley said. "We can spend the morning in bed."

Jake grinned and dropped a kiss on each naked breast. "Good. I knew you wouldn't need a lot of convincing."

She curled back up beside him, wrapping her arms around her waist. Suddenly, she drew in a sharp breath. "We can't stay in bed. We have to fix Emma and Sam." Throwing aside the covers, she stumbled to her feet, then searched the room for her clothes.

Caley's hair was wild around her face. She'd gone to bed with it wet and it had dried into a mass of waves and curls. "Emma said she was going to leave this morning. She may already be gone. And Sam has probably spilled the beans to the family. We have to fix that first, then we'll deal with us later."

Jake closed his eyes, his mind skipping back to the events of the previous evening. He wondered how long it would take for news of the canceled wedding to work its way through the Burtbert grapevine. Sam was probably sleeping off his hangover, but once he got up, he'd inform everyone of the details—including the roles Jake and Caley had played in the breakup.

Jake tossed back the covers. "What do you suggest we do?"

"I was hoping you'd have an idea. We don't have a lot of time left," Caley said.

Jake smoothed his hand over her thigh, then moved higher, wondering if he might tempt her just a little bit. Caley closed her eyes and moaned softly. "Don't," she whispered.

"I have to," Jake replied.

"You have to go talk to Sam," she said.

He slid his fingers into her dampness. "I will, as soon as I take care of this."

"We'll have time for this later," she whispered. "I promise."

Jake was well aware of how much time they had left. A week had seemed like forever when he'd first found her in bed with him. But the days seemed to dissolve in front of him until he was faced with the fact that there would be an end to this fantasy.

"Not later," he said. "Now." He grabbed her waist and pulled her on top of him, then caught her wrists behind her back. "Tell me you want me." Jake pulled her down into a long, deep kiss. "Say it and I'll let you go."

"I do want you," Caley murmured. She shifted above him, his hard shaft pressed between her legs. "I do."

Jake released her wrists, but Caley didn't move away. Instead, she raked her hands through his hair and returned his kiss, her tongue teasing at his. It was as if she'd sensed his desperation, heard the clock ticking on their time together. It was the end of the summer again, Jake thought to himself. It had happened every year, the waning season stealing her away from him once again. But this time would be different. This time, he could ask her to stay.

Jake cupped her face in his hands and looked into

her sleepy gaze. "What are we going to do about this?" he murmured. "Tell me."

Caley reached for him and a moment later he was inside her. "We can do anything we want," she said as she lowered herself on top of him. "We're not kids anymore."

They made love slowly, building the passion between them with soft kisses and gentle caresses. As he touched her, Jake memorized the feel of her body, the sound of her voice. After she was gone, he wanted to recall every detail. And when they finally surrendered to each other, it was as it had been from the start—perfect.

As she snuggled against his chest, Jake buried his face in Caley's hair, breathing in the scent of her shampoo. There were so many things he had to say to her, but he just couldn't seem to put them into coherent sentences. He wanted to tell her how much she meant to him. He wanted to promise her that they'd be together forever, no matter what happened. But he was afraid that saying too much too soon might scare her away rather than bring her closer.

"If only Emma and Sam were doing what we are right now," Caley murmured. "We wouldn't need to fix anything."

"Maybe there's a way to get them there," Jake said, toying with a strand of her hair. "If you wanted to plan the perfect seduction, what would you need?"

"You'd have to have a location where you'd be completely alone with nothing to disturb you," Caley began.

"We have that. Havenwoods. What else?"

"Champagne, good things to eat, a fireplace." Caley giggled. "Whipped cream, honey, chocolate syrup."

"You've got to have sexy underwear," Jake said. "I love those, what do you call them, they hold up stockings?"

"Garter belts," Caley said. "All men love those."

"Is there anyplace in town where you can get those? And black fishnet stockings. And one of those push-up bras. And a thong."

"I can see your evening at the strip club has made you an expert. Most women think those things are trashy. They want something pretty, feminine...but sexy."

Jake crawled out of bed, then grabbed his boxers and pulled them on. If he didn't get dressed, he'd never get out of Caley's bed. "I'll buy the champagne and the groceries. You find the lingerie. Then you get Emma and I'll grab Sam and I'll meet you at noon at Havenwoods. We'll lock them in and we won't let them out until they work out all their issues."

"And what will we do?"

"We'll sit back and wait," Jake said, "and hope that at least some of our sexual DNA is pumping through their veins."

A knock sounded on her room door and Caley bolted upright, her eyes wide. "Yes?"

"Caley? It's Emma. I'm packed and I'm ready to leave. I was hoping you might take me to the airport."

"What time is your flight?"

"It's later this afternoon. But I want to go. I don't want to see Sam."

"Just give me a minute," Caley said. "I'll meet you downstairs. We'll have some breakfast."

"All right," Emma said.

Caley threw on her clothes, then raked her fingers

through her tangled hair. "All right. I think I can stall her. But you're going to have to do the shopping. Don't get fishnets or a thong. Just get a pretty camisole and some sexy panties. There's a bath store just a few doors down from that restaurant with the cinnamon buns. They'll be open in an hour. I'll call and tell them what you need. Then, I'll bring Emma out to Havenwoods at noon."

Jake grabbed her around the waist and gave her a long, lingering kiss. "Noon," he said. "Once we get them settled, then you and I are going to spend the rest of the afternoon together."

Caley drew a deep breath and moved toward the door. But Jake caught her fingers in his and she turned to look at him. "What?"

"I'm glad we didn't do it that night on the beach," he said.

"You are?"

"It wouldn't have been like this," he said.

"Nothing has ever been quite like this," she admitted.

Jake drew his thumb across her lower lip, then kissed her again. "Sometimes I wonder, though. I wonder if we would have done it, maybe we would have been the two getting married instead of Sam and Emma. Maybe it would have been the start of something for us." He chuckled softly. "Maybe we were supposed to be together and we just got it all wrong."

"Or maybe we'd be the ones having doubts," Caley said.

Jake smiled, then waited as she walked out. It was

no longer possible to separate his life from Caley's. Every thought of the future, whether it was a day away or years away, always came back to her.

6

"I THINK THEY'LL BE ALL RIGHT," Emma said. "Mama seemed upset, but I don't think she'd want me to get married just so she won't have to waste all that lobster we ordered."

Caley glanced both ways, then pulled the car out onto the road into North Lake. She'd agreed to drive Emma to the airport to catch her flight back to Boston under the condition that Emma go to the lake house first and explain what had happened to the family. Now that she'd completed that task, there would be one more little detour.

"Don't you think you're being a bit hasty about this, Emma? You were drunk last night and you and Sam haven't even tried to work this out."

"Sam is an idiot," Emma said. "And I need to get back to Boston. I don't know what ever made me think we were meant for each other. I'm young. I should be out there exploring my options, not tying myself down with a guy who socializes with strippers."

"Sam had a little too much to drink. And I think it would be silly to throw your relationship away over one little indiscretion." Caley paused. "He didn't cheat, he was just being friendly. Instead of running away from your problems, you and Sam need to put some serious thought into what you both expect from marriage. But that takes discussion, not a drunken brawl at a roadhouse and you running off to Boston."

"I don't want to talk to him," Emma said stubbornly.

"Do you still love him?"

Emma turned her head away and stared out the window. "I don't know."

They drove through town in silence and headed out on the East Shore Road, Caley watching for the sign for Havenwoods. It was only a few minutes before Emma realized that they weren't traveling toward the interstate. "Where are we going?"

"I want to show you something," Caley said. "Jake showed it to me a few days ago." She turned into the drive and carefully navigated the curves down to the main house.

"What is this?"

"You'll see," Caley said.

She stopped the car in front of the house. Jake emerged from the house, stepping out onto the wide porch. A few moments later, Sam appeared in the doorway. Emma glanced over at Caley then looked out the window at her former fiancé. "What's going on?"

"You and Sam need to talk. Jake and I thought it would be best if you had a place where you could be completely alone and undisturbed."

"I have a plane to catch," Emma insisted.

"That can wait."

"What is this place? Some kind of haunted house?"

"It's not as bad as it looks. It's quiet and secluded.

And kind of romantic." Caley got out of the car, giving Emma no choice but to follow. When she joined Jake on the porch, he handed her the bag from the lingerie shop.

"I couldn't resist the garter belt," he murmured.

Emma joined them on the porch and Caley passed the bag to her. "You might need this," she said.

Emma peered inside, then withdrew a sexy black camisole and panties, followed by the garter belt and black stockings. "I thought you said we were supposed to talk."

"This is meant to help the conversation along."

"Hello, Emma," Sam said, stepping out of the doorway onto the porch. His gaze searched her face, but she refused to look at him.

"Hello, idiot," she muttered.

"Rule number one," Jake said. "No name-calling." He started down the length of the porch, then motioned Sam and Emma to follow. When they reached the lake side of the house, they walked down the snow-packed path to the summer kitchen. "All right. You'll stay here until you've worked things out. When you've both come to a rational decision about your future together, you can leave a lantern burning in the window and we'll come and get you. There's food and firewood inside. There's a bathroom through the small door near the fireplace. I want you both to go inside, take off your jackets, your shoes and the rest of your clothes and put them on the porch. I'll give them back to you when it's time to leave."

"What?" Sam said.

"I'm not giving you my clothes," Emma said.

"Do we really need their clothes?" Caley asked.

"They can't run away if we have their clothes," Jake

explained. "Unless they want to trudge through the snow in their bare feet, they won't be going anywhere."

"I'm not going to marry him," Emma said. "You could lock me up and throw away the key and I still wouldn't change my mind."

"I wouldn't marry her if she were the last person on earth," Sam countered.

"Fine," Jake said. "If that's what you decide. But you're going to come out of this with an understanding and a respect for each other. Our families have been friends for years and you're not going to mess this up because you both want to carry a grudge. You're the pair who started this and if you're going to end it, then do it right. Either you leave here as two friends or as two people about to be married, I don't care which."

"Where are we supposed to sleep?" Sam asked.

"There's a cot inside and warm blankets."

"I'll just call someone to come and get us."

"There's no phone inside," Jake said. "And I have your cell phone. You lent it to me earlier this morning. And Caley borrowed Emma's phone. You'll talk to each other and that's it. Now, Caley and I will be back to check up on you tomorrow morning."

"You can't do this," Sam said. "You're supposed to be on my side."

Jake shrugged. "Yeah, I can do this."

"Caley, you can't leave me here," Emma said.

"Maybe we should let them keep their clothes," Caley suggested. "The jackets and pants and shoes will be enough to keep them from running away."

"I wouldn't bet on it," Sam muttered. "You know, when the owner finds out that you kept us here, there'll be trouble. I could charge you with—with kidnapping. Or unlawful imprisonment. Or—or—"

"I know the owner and he won't mind," Jake said. "Now get inside and start undressing."

Grudgingly, Emma and Sam disappeared inside the summer kitchen and a few minutes later, they tossed their jackets, pants and shoes out onto the porch. Caley gave Jake an optimistic smile. "That didn't go so badly."

"Maybe we should wait around for a little while just to make sure they don't kill each other."

"Good idea."

Jake grabbed her hand and they walked back to the main house. He opened the front door and she walked inside. Caley looked at the house differently now that she knew it was Jake's home. She could imagine herself there on a warm summer day, all the windows thrown open to catch the breeze. The birds would sing from the trees and at night the leaves would rustle. She closed her eyes and inhaled the scent, determined to remember it.

"I love this place. I can just imagine what it was like years ago, without television and speedboats and electricity. It must have been so relaxing to live that way. To just slow down and let life happen."

"I've thought about restoring the place to its original state," Jake said, stepping behind her and slipping his arms around her waist.

His touch sent her pulse racing and she leaned back against him and smiled. "Really? You could live like that?"

"I wouldn't take out the electricity and the plumbing. I think the lack of conveniences might wear a little thin, especially in the middle of winter. I'd be chopping firewood twenty-four hours a day just to stay warm. But it would be all right to just turn it all off."

"Maybe for a day. But I really like a hot shower in the morning."

He rested his chin on her shoulder. "What happened to your sense of adventure? You've gotten to be very high maintenance, haven't you?"

Caley turned in his arms. "I'm still adventurous. And there are things you can do in a shower that you can't do washing up in the sink."

He growled softly, remembering their late-night lovemaking. "Yeah, I can see that. But skinny-dipping in the lake could be lots of fun, too."

"So what are we going to do here? We gave Sam and Emma the only bed."

Jake kissed her neck. "I was going to go up to the attic and look for the doors to the sun porch," he said. "Or we can find something more interesting to do. The grease trap in the sink needs to be cleaned. And I think there's a dead mouse in the linen closet."

"Let's go up in the attic," Caley said.

"There may be spiders. Or bats."

"It'll be an adventure," she teased.

Jake fetched a flashlight from the kitchen and they walked to the rear bedroom. He opened a door to reveal a stairway. They'd explored every inch of this house when they were kids, but Caley didn't remember ever venturing into the attic. "Have you been up here?"

"A couple of times," he said. "Watch out. The stairs are steep. You go first."

Caley stared up into the dark attic and shook her head. "You go first."

"You're the adventurous one."

"It's your house."

"I'll give you a hundred dollars if you go first."

Caley rolled her eyes. "What a baby you are." She squinted up into the darkness. "What are you looking for?"

"Doors. There should be two doors that used to hang in the entrances to the solarium. The doors that are there are too new. They have beveled glass windows, which isn't something that Durant would have chosen. I'm hoping the originals are up there."

The attic wasn't nearly as bad as Caley thought it would be. Though everything was covered with a thick coating of dust, it was tidy and snug. "I wonder what's in these trunks."

Jake shrugged. "Probably something creepy."

"Like what? A dead body?" Caley knelt down on the floor. "Hold the flashlight on this latch," she said.

"The doors won't be in there. They're huge."

"I know. But aren't you curious as to what's in here? It might be something interesting." Caley tugged at the latch and it flipped open. "If there's a skeleton in here, I'm going to scream."

"So am I," Jake said.

But when Caley opened the trunk, she found it filled with bundles of letters and greeting cards, old gramophone records and books. She pulled out one of the books and flipped through it. "It's a journal," she said. She grabbed a bigger book and found photographs inside. Caley handed it to Jake, then glanced around the attic. "Is there a gramophone up here?"

Jake scanned the room with the flashlight, letting

it come to rest on a covered silhouette on a table. "I think that's it. Can we look for my doors?"

"This is more interesting than your doors," she said. Caley pointed to the far wall. "Is that them?"

Jake grinned. "I think so. Come on, let's see if we can get them downstairs."

"Forget the doors right now." She walked around the chest. "If you pick up that end, I bet we could get it downstairs."

They wrestled the trunk to the stairway and maneuvered it around the old wooden banister. But as they began to take it down the steep stairs, Caley lost her grip. The leather handle had deteriorated with age and it broke; the trunk slammed down on her toes.

"Ow! Oh, that hurts. Pull it down."

Jake let the trunk slide to the bottom of the stairs, then climbed up to where she stood. "What's wrong?"

"It smashed my toe. Ow." Her eyes watered and she wriggled on her good foot, afraid to put weight on the other.

Jake stared at the toe of her boot with the flashlight, then cursed softly. "Come on. I think I have some first-aid stuff in the kitchen."

He helped her down the stairs, Caley limping and wincing against the pain. Then Jake scooped her up in his arms and carried her the rest of the way, setting her down on the counter in the kitchen. "I'd forgotten what a klutz you could be."

"I'm not," she said. "I'm very graceful."

"I remember the time you were walking down the dock in that little flowered dress and those high-heeled shoes." He pulled off her boot and tossed it aside. "You got your heel caught in between the boards and went over the edge into the water. I had to jump in and fish you out."

"I was mortified," Caley said. "I wanted you to look at me and think I was hot. Instead, I looked like a drowned rat."

"Maybe so, but when that dress got wet, you could see right through it. And you weren't wearing a bra. I did think you looked really hot."

She pulled her foot out of his hand and tugged off her sock. Her toenail had already begun to turn black. "Kiss it," she said, wiggling her toes in front of him.

Jake smiled, taking her foot in his hand and slowly massaging it. "Will that make it feel better?"

"Maybe. I've always wanted you to kiss my feet," she said, daring him to do as she asked.

Jake knelt down in front of her and pressed his lips to her ankle. It didn't take long for Caley to realize that he was turning her little game into a full-out seduction. He kissed each toe, then ran his tongue along her instep.

When he began to suck on her toes, Caley closed her eyes and leaned back. No man had ever done this for her. She hadn't realized that the foot was an erogenous zone. "Oh," she said.

"Do you like that?" he asked.

"Yes," she murmured.

"Does it feel better?"

Caley nodded. "Much."

Jake stood and ran his thumb along her lower lip. He bent close and kissed her. "Is there anything else that hurts?"

"Are you trying to seduce me?" she asked.

"Maybe. Do you want to be seduced?"

"Yes," Caley said with a smile. "See, isn't that easy? Just think of what might have happened if you'd said yes the first time I asked."

"I was tempted," he said, pulling her hand up to kiss her palm. "So tempted. You looked so beautiful that night. You were wearing that little lace blouse with blue flowers on the collar."

"You remember that?"

"I remember everything about that night. For the next five years, I'd sit on that spot on the beach and wonder if I'd ever get a chance again."

"I guess you did," Caley said.

"I just assumed you'd always be around. When you didn't come back that next summer, I thought I'd messed up bad. Now that I have you again, it's going to be hard to let you go."

It was as close to a profession of love as Jake had ever come and the sentiment made her heart ache. When she was young, she used to read all sorts of meanings into the words he spoke to her. But his meaning was clear now. The only problem was, Caley wasn't sure what she could do about it.

"I've got a sleeping bag in the back of my truck. We could put it in front of the fireplace. It's almost as good as a bed."

"I'll meet you there," Caley said. As he walked out of the room, she drew a deep breath. "I'm not going to be able to let you go, either," she murmured.

JAKE STOOD IN THE DOORWAY of the great room, his hands braced on the doorjamb. Caley sat in front of a crackling fire, her naked body wrapped in the sleeping bag. They'd made love twice in front of the fire, first with a frantic passion and then later slowly and playfully, the two of them teasing each other to completion.

The day was entirely theirs now that the wedding had been put on hold. Jake had felt so bad about her toe that he'd gone upstairs to retrieve the photo album and a few packets of letters from the trunk.

Though they'd enjoyed the sexual chemistry between them, the connection that afternoon had been more emotional than physical. Every time he looked at her, Jake realized how special she was. She was smart and funny. And she challenged him, forcing him to see her in a different light. She'd stolen a piece of his heart a long time ago and now Jake was certain that he never wanted it back. As long as Caley cared for him, he'd be a happy man.

"Are you warm enough?" he asked.

She turned and smiled, the light from the fire illuminating her pretty features. "I am. Come and look at this. I found a photo of the summer kitchen."

Jake crossed the room and squatted down next to her, taking the photo from her fingers. "Look at that stove. No wonder they had to put the kitchen in a separate building. One spark from that and this whole place would have been kindling." He stared at the ceiling. "I should probably put some kind of sprinkler system in here. I wouldn't want this place to burn down before I had a chance to pay for it."

"You should really send this stuff back to the family," she said.

"I don't think the owner realized there was anything left in the attic. I think I'll make an inventory and then see what she wants me to send back to her."

"What is her first name?" Caley asked. "Is it Arlene?"

"Yeah," Jake said.

"I've been reading these letters. They're from a boy she met at a summer dance. They had a romance. He was from town. And she lived in Chicago. It looks like they wrote to each other for years." Caley frowned. "There are some here from when he was in the war. And then they just stop. Are there more letters in the trunk?"

"I can go look," Jake said.

"You don't think he died, do you?"

"No," Jake said. "They're probably still in the trunk. I'll go get them."

Jake wandered back to the bedroom, grabbing the flashlight along the way. It felt good to have Caley in his house. It felt right. He could imagine them here together, spending their summers on the lake. Everything would be so much more interesting if she were a part of his life. They'd begin and end each day together and in between, they would swim and cook and make love by the light of the moon.

Jake rummaged through the papers and then found one more packet of letters, this one much smaller and tied with a black ribbon. He brought them back to Caley and sat down beside her.

"See, it's all right."

She stared at the packet as she slowly untied the ribbon. As she read the first letter, Caley slowly shook her head. "No," she murmured. She glanced over at Jake and he saw tears in her eyes. "This one is from his mother. He died in France in 1944." She flipped through the rest of the letters. "These are all from his mother."

Jake reached out and wrapped his arm around her shoulders. "It's all right. Why are you crying?"

"I don't know. It's so sad. They were in love and then they lost their chance to be together."

He kissed the top of her head, unable to soothe her distress. "I guess you have to just appreciate the time you have," he murmured.

Caley nodded, wiping her eyes on the corner of the sleeping bag. "I do appreciate it." She looked at him. "I do."

Smiling, Jake dropped a soft kiss on her lips. "Why don't we get dressed and I'll take you back to the inn. You can have a nice hot bath. We'll pick up a pizza on the way back and we'll spend the night watching movies."

Caley put the letter back in the envelope and retied the ribbon. He pulled her to her feet and helped her get dressed, wiping away the tears that continued to trickle down from the corners of her eyes.

Jake was sure she wasn't crying about the letter anymore. But he couldn't figure out what the tears were for. Had she realized that they wouldn't have much time left? Was she already contemplating leaving? Or was it something else?

"You should probably check on Sam and Emma before we leave."

"They'll be fine," Jake said.

He held her jacket out for her and as she pulled it on, she looked around the great room. "I really like this place, Jake. It doesn't matter how much you paid for it or how much it will cost to fix it. It was worth every penny."

Caley followed Jake back into town. He pulled into the parking lot of a small Italian restaurant next to the post office downtown and waited for her to pull in next to him. Jake had survived on their take-out pizza when he had visited North Lake in the winter. As they stood at the bar perusing the menu, he glanced at a waitress standing near the end. She smiled at him and gave him a little wave.

"Hey, Jasmine," he murmured as she approached.

"Jake," she said, smiling brightly. "You're back in town."

"My brother's getting married," Jake explained. He turned to Caley. "This is Caley Lambert. My brother is marrying her sister, Emma. She's the maid of honor."

Jasmine nodded. "It's nice to meet you." She turned all her attention back to Jake. "So why didn't you call me when you got in? I still have your jacket at my place. And that fancy corkscrew of yours. You should really come over and pick them up. And bring a bottle of wine along."

Jake had decided to forfeit the jacket and the corkscrew just so he wouldn't have to see Jasmine again. She was one of those women who looked good on first meeting but grew more demanding with each successive date. Jake had dated her for three months, off and on, and when she'd begun talking about kids and marriage, he'd decided to stop.

He'd never had the heart to lead a girl on, to make her believe that he felt something more than he actually did. When it got to that point with Jasmine, he'd stopped calling. But it appeared that she didn't think it was completely over. "What do you want on your pizza?" Jake asked.

"Everything," Caley said. "But no meat."

"Then that's not everything," he said.

"It's all the vegetables," Caley said.

"Are olives vegetables? What about anchovies?"

"No anchovies—anchovies are fish. Green and black olives, green peppers, roasted red peppers, mushrooms and spinach."

Jake wrinkled his nose, then repeated the order to Jasmine. "And then I'd like another pizza with pepperoni and mushrooms."

"Are you going to eat that here?" Jasmine asked.

"Can you have them deliver it?" Jake asked.

Her smiled dissolved. "Sure. Where to?"

"Northlake Inn. Room 312," Jake said. He pulled out his wallet and handed her enough for the bill and a nice tip, then took Caley's hand and headed back toward the door. Jake could feel Jasmine's eyes on him as they left, but he didn't care. He was with Caley now and, as far as he was concerned, he was off the market.

"So, obviously you two dated."

"We did. Last summer. And into the fall for a while. But she lives here and I was in Chicago, so we didn't see much of each other."

"She seems nice," Caley said.

Jake smiled. "I don't want to see her. I like seeing you."

"But I don't live here."

"Maybe we'll have to find a way to work around that," Jake suggested. He knew he was taking a risk, but it was time for her to know where he stood. He'd grown too attached to Caley to not wonder if she felt the same way.

When they reached the street, Caley turned to him. "Jake, we both know how this is supposed to end. I have a job in New York. I have people who depend on me. I can't move back here. If I did, I'd lose everything I worked so hard to build."

"I know," Jake said, nodding. He glanced down at her hands, her fingers so small and delicate in his. So now he knew. He'd suspected when it came down to choices, she'd choose her life on the East Coast. But the last few days, he'd felt they'd come close to considering a future together. And it was silly to think that she was the one who would have to relocate. He could work out of New York just as easily as Chicago.

But Jake wouldn't make that offer until he knew for sure what the future held. "Why don't you head back to the inn," he said. "I'm going to pick up some beer and a bottle of wine. I'll meet you there."

As he watched her leave, he felt the distance between them growing—not just physically but emotionally. She'd begun to pull away now, as if she were preparing herself to leave. He'd seen her do it time and time again in the past, when she'd been hurt or afraid of her feelings for him. Her offense had always been a stubborn defense, choosing to stand back and shut him out rather than admit she might feel something deeper.

But this time, Jake saw her retreat as a good sign. She was fighting her feelings for him and that must mean that she felt something. It wasn't much to go on, but Jake was satisfied that it was enough.

CALEY MUNCHED ON A PIECE OF PIZZA as she flipped through the channels. She stopped at a *Star Trek* rerun and frowned. She didn't watch much television and she couldn't believe that they were still showing *Star Trek*. The program had to be fifteen years old. "This is still on? Remember how you used to make me watch this? I hated this show."

"You loved this show," Jake said, popping open a can of beer and pointing to the screen.

She shook her head. "No, I didn't. It was too confusing. And that Captain Picard was so…bald."

"Then why did you come over and watch it with me every day?"

Caley picked a mushroom off her pizza, then threw it at him. "Duh. Why do you think? Because I was hoping that one day you might be overcome with desire for me and throw me down on the sofa and kiss me." She took another bite of her pizza. "I had a very active fantasy life."

"Did you ever see us together?" Jake asked.

"All the time," she replied.

"No, I mean together. For good. Forever."

Caley had felt his unease all evening. She sensed he had questions to ask but she'd tried to keep the conversation from getting too serious. In truth, she was as confused today as she had been on the day she arrived back in North Lake. Only, she was confused about different things.

Over the past few days, she'd realized that Jeff Winslow had been right. There was a certain charm to living a small-town life. And she hadn't missed the stress of work at all. The panic attacks that had been plaguing her had disappeared and she was finally sleeping through the night without waking up in a cold sweat, wondering what she might have forgotten to do at work. The only time she felt them return was when her cell phone rang. Like Pavlov's dog, she responded to the sound of the Mozart ditty. She even reprogrammed the ring to see if a new tune might be easier to take. But it didn't matter. The moment she saw a work number come up on the caller ID, she started to get queasy and fluttery and a little woozy.

She'd been happy here with Jake and though she didn't want it to end, Caley knew that, for all practical purposes, a future with him would be difficult. They had both built careers in big cities. Those cities just happened to be seven hundred miles apart. It seemed like a long way. But then, it was only a few hours by plane. She flew back and forth to L.A. at least once a month to see a client there and thought nothing of it.

Conceivably, if she wanted to see him, she could call Jake at lunchtime and be in Chicago by supper. It was possible and with every minute that passed, Caley was thinking more and more about what could be instead of what might have been.

"I should probably go check on Sam and Emma," Jake said. "Do you want to stay here or come with me?"

"I can come with you. I do want to see how Emma is doing. I feel a little guilty leaving her out there all alone. I mean, she's with Sam, but I think she might be pretty angry that we just left them there."

She picked up the pizza box and set it on the table near the window, then turned to Jake. He was stretched out on the bed, wearing just his jeans and boxers. His feet were bare, as was his chest, and he looked so completely at home, as if they'd been together for years and this was just an ordinary night.

"What?" he said, glancing over at her.

"Nothing," Caley said. She grabbed her sweater and tugged it on over her head. Then she looked at him again. Slowly, she crossed the room and ran her hand through his messy hair. "I like this. It doesn't have to be all passion and excitement," she said. "Although I do enjoy that."

"You want passion and excitement?" Jake asked. "I can do that. I just thought you were hungry."

"No," Caley said. "I mean, I love it when we…you know."

"Yeah, I know."

"But this is nice, too. It's comfortable. I've never really had this with a man. It feels real. We can be together and there's no pressure."

"Now you're starting to make me feel bad," Jake teased. "I don't want to be boring."

"You're not."

Jake got to his feet and grabbed his shirt, pulling it on. "You're right. I'm not. Come on, I'll show you some excitement."

"We're not having sex in a public place," Caley warned.

"No. We'll save that for later. I'm going to show you some real small-town fun."

Five minutes later, they pulled on their jackets and were headed back to Jake's car. It had grown colder, the temperature dipping toward the teens, and Caley pulled her hood up around her face. When she got inside the truck, Jake flipped on the heater full blast and then headed down Lake Street to the boat landing.

"Are we going to watch the submarine races?" she asked.

"Nope," he said. "We're going out on the lake."

Caley felt a rush of panic. "In this truck? Oh, no we're not."

"Don't worry. It's safe. The ice is really thick this year. We just have to watch out for ice-fishing holes."

Caley screamed as they drove from the landing onto the ice, expecting the truck to fall through the moment it got over the water. When it didn't, she glanced over at Jake. "Are you sure we're safe?"

Jake turned to her. "I would never do anything to hurt you." He'd expressed the sentiment before but Caley hadn't realized until now how strongly he felt it.

"All right. I taught you how to drive, now I'm going to teach you how to spin doughnuts. In the time-honored tradition of high school drivers, these are things you'll need to know. Number one, turn off the four-wheel drive. Number two, make sure your seat belt is buckled. Number three, don't steer into the skid. Got it?"

"I don't really want to do this," she said.

"It'll be fun," Jake assured her. With that, he hit the accelerator and the truck took off. A moment later, he made a sharp turn and they began to spin on the ice. Caley screamed, clutching at the door handle. At first, she was terrified that they were going to break through at any minute. But as the fear wore off, Caley found that the danger was exhilarating.

When Jake finally pulled the truck to a stop in the middle of the lake, she was breathless, her pulse racing. "That was amazing. Almost better than sex," she said with a giggle.

Jake pulled the truck out of gear and then crawled over the console, pressing Caley up against the door.

"I think we ought to make a comparison right here and now. A little experiment."

"You want to have sex in the middle of a frozen lake?"

Jake nodded. "I intend to seduce you in other memorable spots. That way, when you go back home, you won't forget me."

Caley heard the teasing tone in his voice, but the humor didn't extend to his eyes. She reached out and smoothed her palm over his cheek. "I'll never forget this," she murmured. She touched her lips to his and a moment later, they were caught in a passionate kiss.

She felt all the longing and the need between them. But she also felt a bittersweet resignation that from now on, every moment counted. As they slowly began to undress each other, Caley wondered how she'd ever be able to do without this. Passion had never been a big part of her sex life, but now that she'd experienced it with Jake, she couldn't imagine doing without it—or him. Would it even be possible to go a week without touching him or kissing him or feeling him move inside her?

"Are you sure we should be doing this?" she asked, running her fingers through his hair. "If we fall through, they're going to find our frozen bodies in a very compromising position."

Jake worked at the buttons of her blouse. "But at least they'll know we died happy."

"And since we'll be frozen together, they'll have to bury us together."

Jake groaned. "Now that's just morbid."

A loud pop shattered the silence outside the truck

and Caley jumped, startled by the sound. "What was that?"

"The ice," Jake said. "It creaks and pops. But it won't break."

Caley struggled to sit up and then rebuttoned her blouse. "Although this would be a lovely little story to tell friends and neighbors, I'm not sure that I'll be able to summon up the needed concentration to truly enjoy myself here."

"You wanna go back?" Jake asked.

"Yes, please," she replied. "If you get me off this ice, then I promise you can have your way with me."

"And if I hum, will you do a striptease?" Jake asked.

Caley thought about his request for a few seconds, then realized there were all kinds of fantasies left for them to explore. "Yes. But then I get to hum and you have to strip."

Jake quickly straightened up and began to put his clothes back in order. Then he got behind the wheel and put the truck back into gear. "Would you like to see how fast we can go on the ice?"

"No," she said.

Jake hit the accelerator and they took off again. "The only thing you have to remember is that it takes a lot longer to stop."

He drove the SUV off the ice at the boat landing in town. When he reached the intersection for East Shore Road, he turned. A few minutes later, they were bumping back down the drive at Havenwoods. Jake jumped out of the truck. "I'll be right back," he said.

As promised, he returned a few minutes later, a smile on his face.

"How were they?" she asked.

"Good, as far as I could see through the window. I think they might be asleep. I left Sam's cell phone on the porch. If they need it, they'll find it."

Caley nodded, then reached over and furrowed her fingers through the hair at Jake's nape. "Sometimes it feels like we've lived years in these few days. Back when we were kids, everything moved so slowly. And now, I can barely keep up."

"It's because we have a clock ticking," Jake said. He glanced over at her. "You know, we could just shut the clock off. The wedding is scheduled for Thursday night. If it happens, then we're done with our duties. We could grab a couple plane tickets to some warm spot and spend the weekend together. Or the next week, if you can take off work."

The idea was intriguing. Caley had plans to fly back to New York early Friday morning, hoping to have the weekend to catch up on the work she'd missed. But she was the boss now. If she couldn't let a little work slide, then what was the point of being in charge?

"We could do that," Caley said, surprised at how her attitude had changed.

"Mexico?" Jake suggested.

"Or the Caribbean. Someplace warm with pretty beaches and lots of fruity drinks. And luxurious rooms with big bathtubs. And a soft bed covered by one of those mosquito nets."

He grabbed her hand and pressed his lips against her wrist. "That sounds nice," he said. "Hey, if Sam and Emma don't get married, we could go on their honeymoon."

Caley gave him a disapproving look. "Don't even

say that. I want to believe that they'll work things out, don't you?"

Jake nodded. "I know. Me, too. I'll make the plans. We can leave right after the reception."

When they got back to the inn, Jake steered the car into a parking spot behind the building. Then he helped Caley out, grabbing her waist and setting her down in front of him. He kissed her deeply, his hands skimming over her body, searching through the layers of clothes she wore.

"Leave it to fate to put us together in the middle of winter," he muttered as he pulled up her sweater and rubbed his cold hands on her belly. "Too many clothes."

Caley giggled, pushing him away. "I'm sure we'll figure out a way to remedy that." She reached down and threw a handful of snow at his face. "Maybe we should find a vacation spot where they don't require clothes at all."

Jake gasped. "Are you serious?"

She nodded. "Why not? I'd like that, spending my entire day naked instead of bundled up like this."

Jake shook his head. "I don't think so."

"What? Are you a prude? You shouldn't be embarrassed. You're very well represented down there."

Jake chuckled. "Am I?"

Caley nodded. "Yes. Though I haven't a big sample to compare you to, I'd say that most women would find you more than adequate."

"Oh, lovely," he murmured. "More than adequate. That makes me feel good."

"Look at me!" She pointed to her breasts. "I should be the one feeling inferior."

"You have the most beautiful breasts in the world,"

he said. "I can't imagine how they could be more perfect."

Caley grinned. "So what's the problem then?"

"Oh, there are several I can think of. First of all, if you're running around naked, then I'm going to be running around sporting major wood. That's just a fact. And I don't think the public needs to be seeing that. And I also don't think strange men should be looking at your body the way that I do. I like being the only one to enjoy that pleasure."

"I like your body," Caley said. "And I'd like showing it off to other women."

"How about if I promise to flash an old lady at the airport? Would that satisfy you?"

Caley held out her hand to him. "I suppose it will have to do. And you were the one questioning my daring. You're all talk and no action, Jake."

Jake picked her up and tossed her over his shoulder. "You want action. I'll show you action." He carried her through the lobby, much to the interest of the front-desk clerk. Caley giggled as they stepped onto the elevator and she made Jake turn around so she could push the button for the third floor.

If she wasn't already in love with Jake, then she was falling awfully fast. And right now, Caley had no intentions of doing anything about it.

7

Jake skated in a slow circle, moving the hockey puck along the ice with his stick. Then, sprinting across the ice, he took a shot at the plastic crate he was using for a goal. The puck popped up and then disappeared into glittering snow just beyond the rink.

He skated to the edge and searched for the puck. When he finally found it, Jake tossed it back onto the ice and plodded through the snow in his skates. Glancing up, he saw Caley standing on the stairs leading down to the lake's shore. He stopped and watched her for a long moment, drawing in a deep breath and letting it go.

He'd barely seen Caley all day and when he'd tried to talk to her at the inn early that afternoon, she'd been preoccupied and irritated. They'd made plans for an early dinner and she promised to meet him at the boathouse. But she was three hours late and Jake ended up eating with his parents and siblings.

Everything had been going so well. Maybe this was bound to happen. If it was going to come to an end, then better with a bang than a whimper, he thought.

Yet, he wasn't willing to concede defeat just yet. He still had two more days, the rehearsal tomorrow and the wedding the next day. He turned away from her and returned to skating, moving around the perimeter of the homemade hockey rink.

"I'm sorry I'm late," Caley shouted.

"No problem."

She watched him skate for a while. "I'd like to explain."

"You want to talk, get a pair of skates and a stick," he said. "I'm playing hockey right now."

"Come on, Jake. Don't be mad. I had to work. There was a big crisis and they needed me on a conference call. Then I had to write up a strategy report and send that in. And I haven't been answering my messages, so my boss had a few choice words to say about the responsibilities of a partner at John Walters."

"Do you even like your job?" Jake asked. He faced her, skating backward, until he reached the edge of the cleared ice. He skidded to a stop and rested his hands on his hockey stick.

"Of course I do."

"Do you?"

"It's a job. I get paid a lot of money. I like the money."

"So, that's what it's all about then?"

"No. I suppose there's some satisfaction in it. Although I spend most of my time making my clients look good when they do bad things. It's not the most noble job on the planet. But I'm good at it. It's what I do."

"Maybe you should try something new," he suggested. He skated toward the goal again and took another shot. This time, the puck hit the inside of the crate and knocked it backward. When he turned back around, Caley was trudging back up to the house.

He skated to the other end of the pond, watching her retreat. He felt an empty ache tighten in his gut and Jake cursed softly. Maybe it had been a little too perfect to last. He'd managed to convince himself that he and Caley had something special, that they were meant for each other. But the more he pushed, the more she drew away. He'd begun to think that maybe there were other reasons why she was so anxious to get back to New York.

"At least I didn't love her," he murmured to himself. "Not the way I could have."

But even as he said the words, Jake knew that they weren't entirely true. What he felt for Caley was more than he'd ever felt for any other woman, more than he could imagine feeling for another. He didn't want to think of the two of them in finite terms, a relationship with a beginning and an end. Caley was the kind of woman who could keep him fascinated for a lifetime, the kind of woman he wanted to love.

Hell, if she was going back to patch things up with her old boyfriend, then he didn't stand much of a chance. Jake drew a sharp breath as a sudden realization struck. Was this her way of evening the score? He'd rejected her years ago and now she'd reject him. It certainly would put her back on top, Jake mused. And that was always the game between them, who could best the other.

Jake continued to skate along the edge of the rink, moving fast enough to make his lungs burn and his heart pound. He turned the notion over in his head, but it was hard to reconcile it with the woman he'd come to know over the past week.

Though Caley might want to balance the scales, she'd done that in many other ways. He had fallen hard and hadn't done much to hide his feelings from her. In truth, he'd done everything in his power to make her see how much he cared.

"Will you talk to me now?"

Jake turned the corner and saw Caley standing at the end of the rink, using a hockey stick to balance herself on her skates.

"Play," he said.

"I can't keep up with you."

"Try," he muttered.

When he came around the rink again, Caley skated after him, grabbing him around the waist and hanging on until they both fell to the ice. She hit hard, slamming down on her shoulder and crying out in pain. Jake quickly knelt down next to her.

"What the hell are you doing?"

"Trying to talk to you. But you don't want to listen."

Jake helped her sit up and gently rubbed her shoulder. "All right. Talk. What do you want from me? I've pretty much put everything on the line here and for a while, things were good between us. Now it seems that everything is moving backward."

"I don't know what you expect," Caley said. "Until a week ago, I was seeing another man. I'm not sure I'm ready to jump back into a serious relationship, especially with someone who lives halfway across the country."

"It's not halfway," Jake insisted. "It's about a third."

"All right, tell me how it would work, Jake," she

said. "How would we do it? Would we spend every weekend together? Or would we see each other once a month? Would we talk on the phone every day? Would you go out with other women? Would I be free to date other men?"

"I don't know," Jake said. "We'd have to figure that all out."

"I had a relationship with a man I never saw," Caley said. "It didn't work. And we lived in the same apartment."

"I'm not him," Jake said.

"I know. But that doesn't make a lot of difference. You still have the capacity to hurt me the same way he did."

Jake turned away, staring off into the distance, fixing his gaze in the direction of Havenwoods as he wondered at the wounds that ran so deep. Was he the cause of her insecurities about men? She was such a confident woman, yet she refused to risk her heart. He'd wounded her so deeply that she was still trying to recover.

Maybe he was the only one who could heal that hurt. Jake took a deep breath. "I'm in love with you," he said, struggling to his feet. He pulled her up beside him, handing her her hockey stick. "Maybe I've always been in love with you. I don't know. But I figured you should probably know. This is the last time I'm going to say it and whatever you decide to do with it, I'll be all right."

She opened her mouth to speak, then forced a smile, as she considered his admission. "I—I don't know what to say," she murmured. "There was a time when that's all I wanted to hear. But back then, it was just a fantasy. Now it's—"

They'd so carefully avoided any talk of the future, choosing to keep their relationship simple, sexual. And now he'd put all his cards on the table. Maybe he'd always known they'd be together. Perhaps that's why he'd turned her down all those years before. Because, deep inside, he knew they'd be together again—they'd have a second chance.

"How do you know you love me?" she asked.

Jake shrugged. "I don't know. I mean, I don't know how. I just feel it."

"Maybe you just need me," she said. "There's a difference, you know."

Jake sucked in a sharp breath, the cold air clearing his head. "No," he murmured. "That's not it." He grabbed her hands. "It's more than that."

"Don't do this," Caley murmured, forcing a smile. "It will only make things difficult in the end."

Jake cursed beneath his breath. "So what? I don't care. Maybe things should be difficult. Maybe it should be hard for us to leave each other. What's so wrong about that? At least I can admit I have feelings for you."

"I can admit that," Caley said. "We've known each other for years. Of course we'd care."

"It's more than that," Jake said.

Caley tugged her hands from his and shoved them in her jacket pockets. "I should get back up to the house. My mother is going crazy trying to figure out what's happening with this wedding."

"And I should go check on Sam and Emma. I'm going to spend the night out at Havenwoods."

"I—I thought we could—"

Jake shook his head. "You're right. We need to step back. I need some space."

She stared at him for a long moment, her expression unreadable. Then she nodded. "I understand. It's all right." Caley turned and skated over to the edge of the ice, then carefully climbed up onto the shore, maneuvering along the small path cut through the snow. When she reached the spot where she'd left her boots, she plopped down and began to unlace her skates.

She slipped her feet into her boots, then stood and hung her skates over her shoulder. "I'll talk to you later," she said.

"Later," he repeated.

It should be easy to rationalize the end of their time together, Jake mused. He'd walked away from any number of women with whom he'd shared longer relationships. But it wasn't just the physical uncoupling that he found difficult. He'd always been attached to Caley emotionally and that bond had strengthened over the past week.

Even now, the thought of letting her go caused an ache deep inside him, an emptiness that couldn't be filled. Maybe this was what he'd done to her all those years ago. He found it impossible to imagine being with another woman. The kind of pleasure that he'd experienced with Caley had been unique and perfect and it would be hard to find with anyone else.

Jake closed his eyes and drew a deep breath of the chilly night air. He would get over her and he'd learn to live without her. It was just a matter of letting go.

WHEN CALEY ARRIVED at the lake house the next morning for breakfast, the house was noisy with excitement. She walked into the kitchen to find the entire family, including Emma, gathered around the table eating pancakes. Her mother turned to smile at her.

"The wedding is back on," Emma cried, her eyes bright and her smile wide. "We have to go over the final plans with the caterer and then I want to decorate the room we're using for the reception. And you have to pick up your dress and I have to pick up Sam's tux." She jumped out of her chair and threw her arms around Caley's neck. "Thank you," she whispered. "For everything."

Emma glanced around at her family. "I have to go!" she said. "I'll see you all later. I can't believe I'm getting married tomorrow." She hurried out of the room, leaving them all breathless.

Caley breathed a silent sigh of relief. It had worked. She and Jake had managed to fix the mess they'd created. She returned her mother's smile. "I'm so happy for them." She drew a ragged breath. It was almost over, she mused. But she wasn't thinking about the wedding. She was thinking about her time with Jake.

It hit her hard, like a punch to the stomach. Once the wedding was done, she and Jake would go their separate ways. Though they'd talked about a vacation, Caley knew it wouldn't be the wisest choice for them.

"I'm just going to go get dressed," she said.

"No, sit down and have something to eat," her mother insisted. "You look a little pale."

"I-I'm really not hungry. I'll grab some coffee at the inn. It's going to be a busy day."

She hurried back out of the kitchen and walked to the front door. She hadn't slept more than a few hours last night. Instead, she'd stared at the ceiling and tried to convince herself that she didn't need to drive over to

Havenwoods and crawl into bed with Jake. She didn't need to feel his naked body against hers or enjoy the touch of his hands on her skin. She didn't need any of that!

But the more she tried to talk herself out of Jake, the more Caley realized she'd gotten herself so tangled up in him there'd be no way out. She'd done it again, only this time she'd known better. She was an adult and should have been able to control her feelings. But from the moment they'd first made love, she'd been lost.

All her talk about keeping things simple between them had been part of the wall she'd tried to build. But faced with the reality of their situation, that wall had crumbled in front of her. Her body belonged to him, along with her heart and her soul, and Caley knew that was all her fault. She'd fallen in love with Jake all over again, and this time, it was going to hurt a lot worse.

Caley opened the car door and slid inside, then stared out the windshield at the snowy landscape. Tears pressed at the corners of her eyes, but she refused to surrender to them. She had two nights left and if she could bear that, then everything else would get easier. Maybe that was all she needed to set herself back on the right course.

It was the wedding and all that silly romantic stuff that went along with it. That was her problem. She saw Emma and Sam ready to make a lifelong commitment and she felt left behind. After all, she was the elder sister and she should be setting the example, shouldn't she?

Instead, she had opted for lust and passion, instant gratification with no strings attached. They'd shared the best sex she'd ever had and it had left her aching for more. But she'd learned a long time ago that lust wasn't love.

Caley closed her eyes and ran her hands through her hair, trying to recall his touch. He was so gentle, yet there was a silent danger to the way he caressed her, as if he held the key to her body and its pleasure. Only he knew how to make her hunger for his touch, to crave the feel of him inside her.

She groaned and reached for the ignition, letting her hair fall back into her face. "Tell him," she whispered to herself. "Take a chance. Once you say it, maybe it will be true."

It wasn't so hard to imagine them together. They were such good friends that life with Jake would be easy. Loving him could be the most natural thing in the world. She stared at her reflection in the rearview mirror. She'd always run her life with such single-minded determination. And now, she couldn't even make a simple decision about her happiness.

The drive to the inn was quick and uneventful. She was getting used to navigating in the snow and ice now and wasn't afraid to drive a bit faster. When she arrived, she pulled the car into the parking lot and glanced around for Jake's SUV. But it wasn't where she'd hoped it would be. He'd spent the night at Havenwoods—was he still there?

Caley threw the car into Reverse and backed out, then turned toward East Shore Road. She had to trust her feelings and, ultimately, trust him. He wasn't a boy anymore. Jake knew what he wanted. He wanted her.

As she steered down the narrow drive through the trees, Caley felt her nerves begin to get the better of her. But she tried to marshal the same courage she'd found that night of her eighteenth birthday.

Though a long-distance relationship wasn't a perfect option, they could make it work. Seeing each other once a month was far better than never being together again. There'd be frequent-flier miles and meetings in cities in between New York and Chicago. As long as the passion was there, they could make it work.

When she reached the bottom of the drive, Caley looked around, but didn't see Jake's truck. She hopped out of the rental car, then walked back to the summer kitchen. To her surprise the door was ajar. It creaked as it swung back and Caley stepped inside.

The last embers of a fire still burned in the hearth. Sam and Emma had left a few hours before, but they'd tidied up the place first. The blankets were pulled neatly over the cot and the towels in the bathroom were folded on the rack. Caley closed the door behind her, then wandered through the room, her heart pounding in her chest.

When she reached the bathroom, she stared into the mirror for a long time, noting the color in her cheeks and the nervous look in her eyes. Reaching out, Caley opened the medicine cabinet and scanned the contents.

Though she'd made love to Jake in the most intimate ways possible, she really didn't know much about his day-to-day life. She pulled out his razor and examined it closely, then sniffed at the can of shaving cream, recognizing the scent. A row of aftershave bottles intrigued her and she tested each one until she found her favorite. Caley slipped it into her jacket pocket with a smile.

Wandering back into the main room, Caley stared at

the strange collection of things that Jake found important enough to keep—a bird's nest, a huge pine cone, a pretty pink granite stone that had been worn smooth by water. When she sat down at the drafting table, she noticed the bag from the lingerie store sitting beside it.

Caley reached down and opened it. The items he'd purchased were inside, the tags still attached. She shrugged out of her jacket, then stripped out of the rest of her clothes. After she'd pulled on the sexy camisole and little boy shorts, she searched for a mirror. But the only mirror available was in the bathroom.

Caley stood on the toilet and examined the fit, admiring her backside in the tight-fitting panties. Then she jumped down and went back to the fireplace, holding out her hands to the warmth. She'd never noticed the photos propped up on the mantle.

Reaching out, she grabbed one, then realized that it was a photo of her and Jake taken years ago. They both stood on the old raft that had floated just offshore from their beach. Jake's arms were curled up in a strongman pose and Caley was pointing to him with a wide grin on her face. How simple their life had been back then. Love had been so uncomplicated. Why couldn't it still be easy?

The sound of the door creaking startled Caley out of her thoughts. She turned to find Jake standing in the doorway, the cold wind blowing in around him, his arms filled with firewood. He stepped inside and closed the door.

"Wow," he murmured. "I thought these things only happened in my fantasies."

Caley smiled. "Emma didn't use the gift and you can't return underwear, so I was just trying it on."

"I like it," Jake said as he dropped the wood near the fireplace. "Maybe you should take it off and try it on again. Just so I can get the full effect." He crossed the room, then slipped his hands around her waist and dropped a kiss on her lips.

"I think you just want me to get naked," Caley said.

"I could get naked if you don't want to," Jake said. He shrugged out of his jacket, then began to work on the buttons of his shirt.

Caley reached out to stop him. "I came here to talk to you," she said.

"Dressed like that?"

She bent down and picked up her jacket, then slipped into it. Caley sat down on the edge of the cot and patted the spot beside her. But Jake refused her invitation and continued to stare down at her. "Don't do this," he murmured.

"You don't know what I'm going to say," she replied.

"Yes, I do. You're going to tell me that I shouldn't think about the future. That sooner or later we're going to go our separate ways and that I need to accept that fact." He paused and smiled ruefully. "I can deal. When we got into this, we knew that it would end. I'd just rather it end after our vacation than before."

Caley swallowed hard, pushing back the lump of emotion in her throat. That wasn't at all what she was planning to say. She wanted to tell him to give her a chance, to give her time to get over her doubts and fears about commitment. But he was giving up so easily. "You can 'deal'?" she asked.

Jake shrugged. "You were right, Caley. I got all caught up in this. I should have seen it for what it really was, just an affair. A good time. I know that now.

If we try to force it, we'll both end up unhappy and full of regrets."

Caley swallowed hard, trying to keep the emotion from clogging her throat. "That's exactly what I was going to say," she murmured. "I'm glad we're both on the same page."

That was it, then, Caley mused, ignoring the urge to confess her true feelings. She wasn't a teenager anymore and blurting out her love for him would have only caused more problems than it solved. This time, she'd made the right decision. If she'd learned anything in the past eleven years it was that she couldn't make Jake do or be or feel anything that he didn't want to.

Caley looked at him, her gaze taking in the features that had become so familiar to her…and so dear. For a long time, she'd carried an image of him as a twenty-year-old, but now that she'd come to know the man, she could accept him for who he really was.

"I should get dressed," she murmured. "Emma needs some help with the wedding arrangements."

"She and Sam are fine," Jake said. "You know there's a fresh bottle of chocolate syrup over there."

She knew what he was asking, but Caley wasn't sure she ought to agree. He wanted her, needed her body, just one more time. And though she didn't want to admit it, she needed him, too. "Are you planning to make me a cup of hot cocoa? Or a hot-fudge sundae?"

"Yes, I'm planning on making *you* a hot-fudge sundae," he said.

"We don't have any ice cream," Caley said.

"Where we're going, we don't need ice cream." Jake turned and retrieved the bottle of chocolate syrup from the table, then held up the can of whipped cream. "If you don't want to get your new underwear all sticky, I'd suggest you take it off."

Caley crossed the room and grabbed the can of whipped cream from his hand, then tossed aside the cap. She reached up and applied a thin stripe of it to his lower lip. "You're the one wearing too many clothes." Pushing up on her toes, she licked the sweet cream off with the tip of her tongue.

Jake groaned softly. "Maybe this was a mistake."

Caley sprayed a bit of whipped cream on his chin and proceeded to lick it off. She'd make him remember the last days he spent with her. From now on, every minute would be one that he'd recall again and again when he was alone, memories that would stir his desire and make him ache with need. He'd never find another woman who could arouse him the way she could and he'd always be left wondering if he'd made the right choice in letting her go.

Grabbing his hand, Caley placed a dot of cream on each fingertip, then slowly sucked it off, drawing his finger in and out of her mouth playfully. "Would you like to try?" she asked, holding out the can to him.

Jake sprayed a line from her shoulder to her wrist. With exquisite ease, he worked his way up until he pressed a kiss beneath her ear. And then, as if he'd already tired of the game, he tossed the can aside, grabbed her waist and picked her up off her feet. Wrapping her legs around his hips, he kissed her mouth, his tongue tangling with hers, the sweet taste of the whipped cream passing between them.

He carried her to the cot near the fireplace and sat down, Caley on his lap. For a long time, they kissed, exploring each other's mouths until they'd perfected their kisses.

If she could spend the rest of her life kissing Jake, Caley knew it would never become routine. Every kiss sparked her passion and elevated her need until she was frantic for a more intimate connection. But she wouldn't have the rest of her life. She'd have today and tomorrow and that was all.

She slowly undressed him and then drew him back down on the narrow cot, his body sinking down on top of hers, his hips settling between her legs. But as he brought her closer and closer to her release, Caley realized that what they were doing was wrong.

They were both trying to act as if it were just passion and lust driving them forward, as if what they were doing was sex and nothing more. But she knew it wasn't true. The emotional connection was still there, the force that had brought them together in the first place. No matter how much they both tried to ignore it, it wasn't going to go away.

And when it was over and she lay sated in his arms, Caley knew that they hadn't had sex. They'd made love.

8

Jake stared at Caley across the vestibule of the church. She stood next to Emma, standing so still and quiet that Jake wondered what was going through her mind.

He knew what was going through his. Images of her naked body, arching beneath him in pleasure, her face filled with the rapture of her release, her lips swollen from his kisses. They'd spent three hours making love that afternoon and it still hadn't seemed like enough.

In bed, Caley was adventurous and uninhibited, driven by her desire until he had no choice but to be swept along. The way she touched him was so tantalizing that it made him hard just thinking about it. In just a week she'd come to know his body so well that she could sense his pleasure before he fully felt it.

She glanced over at him and smiled and he licked his bottom lip. A pretty blush stained her cheeks and Jake felt a bit sinful trying to tempt her in church. But at this point, he was willing to take any opportunity offered.

He listened distractedly as Emma went over the directions for the processional. Jake had never been a best man and was surprised that his future sister-in-law knew so much about the mechanics of a wedding. When she told him to stand at the front of the church next to Sam, he dutifully followed orders and walked down the side aisle, having no idea what his next instruction would be.

A few minutes later, the organ started playing and Caley began her march toward the altar, her hands folded in front of her. He held his breath as their gazes locked and a flood of emotion passed between them. Suddenly, he felt as if this was his wedding and she was walking to him.

Jake looked away, unable to control his feelings. He'd never put much stock in the whole idea of *happily ever after.* But he needed to believe it was possible. If there was one woman who could make him happy for the rest of his life, it had to be Caley. There was no other choice for him.

Desire was a powerful narcotic, a drug that could muddle a man's brain. But this wasn't about desire. He would feel the same in a week or a month or lifetime from now. He knew that in his heart and yet she couldn't see it.

As Caley reached the front of the church, Jake noticed an odd expression on her face, as if she were about to be sick. Dark circles smudged the skin beneath her eyes and she seemed to be breathing in quick little gasps. When her knees nearly buckled, Jake moved to her side and took her arm.

"No!" Emma corrected from the back of the church. "You stay in that spot next to Sam. You don't take her arm until the recessional."

"Are you all right?" he asked softly.

Caley shook her head. "I-I'm a little dizzy."

"Can we take a break?" Jake asked. "I have to use the bathroom."

"And I—I need to get a drink of water. I'm—thirsty. Excuse me." Caley shoved her little ribbon bouquet into the minister's hands, then headed for the door. Jake followed her, ignoring the curious glances of their parents.

When she reached the vestibule, she shoved the front door open and stepped out into the cold. Bending over at the waist, Caley drew a deep breath and let it go, her sigh visible in the freezing temperatures.

Jake put his hand on her back and slowly rubbed. "Are you going to be sick?"

"I—I don't know," she said.

"Tell me if you are because I'm really no good with that. If I see you get sick, then I'll get sick. And I don't want them to find us out here puking on each other's shoes." That brought a small giggle and Jake was pleased that he'd been able to distract her. "What's wrong?"

"Nothing," Caley said, waving him away. "My stomach is just all tied up."

"Because of the wedding?"

She glanced up at him. "I get these panic attacks. I haven't had one lately and this one is really bad. Everything is happening so fast. I haven't had time to think. I just need some time to think."

"Caley, you do realize that we're not the ones getting married here, don't you? That's Sam and Emma. The best man and maid of honor aren't supposed to get cold feet before the wedding."

She slowly straightened, taking another deep breath. "I'm sorry."

Jake noticed the damp on her cheeks, then realized she was crying. He reached up and brushed a tear away with his thumb. "What's wrong? Tell me."

"I'm tired," she said. "And a little emotional. Emma is getting married. She's all grown-up and moving forward with her life and I feel like I don't have any idea where I'm going."

"What do you want, Caley?" He heard the frustration in his voice, but Jake couldn't help himself. Why couldn't she realize how rare it was to find something as special as what they shared?

"I don't know. I just don't want to feel like this, all confused and uncertain. I want my life to make sense. And it used to, a long time ago." She stared up at him. "I was happy once. I know I was."

"And you're not happy now?"

"No!" She paused. "Yes! Maybe."

"Which is it?"

"We've had a wonderful week together. I've had a chance to live out a teenage fantasy. And that should be enough."

Jake knew there was something more she had to say. "What do you want?" he repeated.

A weak smile curled the corners of her mouth and she took another deep breath. "I want you to tell me to stop being such a baby," she said. Caley ran her fingers through her hair and pasted a calm expression her face. "Sorry. I haven't been getting a lot of sleep lately. It's hard to survive on sex and whipped cream alone."

"We've been giving it a valiant try, though," Jake murmured.

"I could have used that vacation," she said.

"We can still go. You just say the word and I'll take you away from all this."

"I know you would."

"Come on," Jake said. "Let's go back in and do our duties and then we'll have dinner with the family and go back to Havenwoods. I'll make a big fire and we'll curl up on the cot and just sleep."

She looked up at him through damp eyes. "I can't. I promised Emma that I'd stay with her tonight at the inn."

"Then maybe we'll both get some sleep," he said. Jake took her hand and tucked it in the crook of his arm and led her back inside the church. Emma was waiting to walk up the aisle again and she waved Caley over. Jake gave her fingers a squeeze, then let her go before he moved up the side aisle to stand next to Sam.

"What is going on with you two?" Sam asked.

"Nothing," Jake said. "She just got a little emotional waiting for Emma to come up the aisle. It's a sister thing."

"Are you sure?" his brother prodded.

Jake nodded. He was sure. It was nothing.

This time, as Caley did her march, he grinned at her, trying to lighten her mood. She was right. They hadn't had much sleep and with everything they'd done over the past six days, it was a wonder one of them hadn't gone round the bend. It was also a testament to how well they got along.

"The perfect woman," Jake murmured.

"What?" Sam said, glancing over his shoulder.

"She's the perfect woman. Emma. Don't you think?"

Sam smiled and nodded. "Yeah, for me she is."

"And when you find the perfect woman, you don't let her go," Jake continued.

Sam frowned at him. "I'm marrying her."

The rest of the rehearsal passed without a hitch. Jake listened carefully to the directions that the minister gave him, but his mind was occupied with thoughts that he wasn't sure he ought to be having. He *could* get Caley to stay, to live here with him. All he had to do was ask her to marry him. She'd have to believe he loved her if he did that.

But though the plan sounded simple, Jake knew it was filled with danger. What if she said no? He almost preferred not knowing how she felt to knowing that she didn't want him. He thought back to her offer on the beach that night. How much courage had it taken her to approach him, her emotions laid bare? Couldn't he summon the same courage for her?

When all the details had been worked out for the service, Sam and Emma walked back down the aisle, Emma clutching her bouquet of ribbons and looking like a radiant bride. Jake and Caley met at the head of the aisle and he took her hand again and walked with her to the back of the church.

The family gathered again in the vestibule before splitting up to drive to the restaurant for the rehearsal dinner. Jake waited around until nearly everyone had left before cornering Caley in the shadows of a stairway. "I have to see you tonight," he murmured, raking his fingers through her thick hair.

"I can't. I promised Emma."

"I'll wait in your room at the inn. As soon as she's asleep, meet me."

"What if she wakes up? Or what if she never goes to sleep?"

"I don't want to spend a night without you," Jake said. "That's going to happen soon enough. It doesn't have to happen now, when we're in the same town."

He hadn't realized until now how strong his need was. He'd do anything to be with her—anything. And he'd ask her to stay, even if it meant getting rejected. The risk was well worth the reward.

Jake had to believe Caley just hadn't figured it all out yet. She was still fighting her feelings and when she finally reconciled herself to the fact that she might be in love with him, too, then everything would be clear. There was only one thing standing in their way, Jake mused, and that was their physical relationship.

Sex gave Caley an excuse to think of them in only those terms—lust and release, naked bodies lost in incredible pleasure. The kind of desire they shared would distract anyone—including him. He had to try a different approach. And for that to work, he'd have to keep his clothes on and his hands off her body.

JAKE GLANCED AT HIS WATCH, squinting in the dim light from the lamp beside the bed. He'd assumed Emma would be so exhausted after the rehearsal dinner and the six glasses of champagne she'd downed that she'd nod off well before midnight. But it was nearly two a.m. and still no sign of Caley. He looked over at the phone, wondering if he ought to call. But she knew he was waiting.

He closed his eyes for just a moment, letting himself relax. She'd been right. They hadn't had much sleep over the past week and it was starting to take its toll. He drew a deep breath and then another; sleep was inevitable.

When he woke up, Jake wasn't sure how much time had passed. But the bedside lamp had been turned off and there was someone in bed beside him. She'd unbuttoned his shirt and unzipped his khakis and was slowly kissing her way down to his belly.

"Caley?" he murmured.

"Were you expecting someone else?"

Jake chuckled as she slid her hand beneath the waistband of his boxers. "No," he said. "You're the one who always crawls into the wrong bed."

"Maybe it was the right bed all along," she whispered.

She took his shaft in her hand and slowly began to stroke, her tongue teasing at the tip of his cock. He was already so hard, but he couldn't recall getting that way. He remembered that he'd wanted to talk, but it was already too late for that. Closing his eyes, Jake gave himself over to the pleasures she offered. They could talk later, he thought as her warm mouth surrounded him.

Each sensation was heightened, made more intense by the lack of light around them. She'd already removed her own clothes, and he slid his hands over her silken limbs, recognizing each curve and swell of flesh that her body offered. Even in the dark, she was the most beautiful woman he'd ever known.

Slowly, she pushed aside his clothes to kiss and caress him. His shoulders, his nipples and the trail of hair that led down to his erection, it was all hers to enjoy and Jake didn't try to stop her. Caley was intent on seducing him and he wasn't about to question her motives.

As she worked her way over his body, Jake let the desire wash over him in waves. Though he wasn't trying to exert any kind of control, she seemed to sense when he was close to losing it and she slowed her seduction for just a moment.

Her lips continued to return to his shaft again and again, edging him closer to release and then leaving him just shy of orgasm. He'd never ceded so much control to her, but Caley seemed to need it tonight. There was a quiet desperation to her lovemaking. Whenever he made a move to touch her, she gently drew his hand from the damp spot between her legs. And in the end, Jake didn't fight her. He gave her exactly what she wanted—his body.

Yet as she sank down on top of him, Jake wondered if she'd take more. Did she want his soul and his heart and the rest of his life? If he offered, would she accept? He needed to believe that this feeling would never end, that he'd have eternity to explore it and enjoy it.

But Jake also knew that love could be fickle and fleeting, and even if they stayed together now, they might not be together later. He was willing to try, willing to give her whatever she needed to make it work.

He reached up and cupped her face in his hands, drawing her down into a long, deep kiss, tasting her sweet mouth. He couldn't seem to get enough and when she tried to pull away, Jake held tight, refusing to let her go.

He'd never felt this way before, this frantic need to possess a woman. Where did it come from? Why was it so important for him to claim her? She was his, whether she cared to admit it or not. Her body belonged to him. No man could make her ache the way that he could.

"I love you," he murmured against her lips.

The words came so naturally now, without even a second thought, that Jake knew they were real and not just imagined. He couldn't regret saying them. He did love Caley and nothing would change that.

"I love you, too," she said.

At that moment, Jake knew it would be all right. It may take weeks or months, but there would come a day that she would believe in what she felt. Grabbing her waist, he rolled her over on the wide bed and pulled her legs up alongside his hips. He began to move, slowly at first, his arms braced on either side of her head. He knew exactly how to make her come without his touch and with every other stroke, he withdrew and rubbed against her sex.

Her breathing grew shallow and quick and she moaned softly, grasping at his hips with her hands, raking her nails over his buttocks. He was close to his own release, but Jake ignored the signs and waited for Caley. Their coupling grew in intensity and became wild and uncontrolled. They spoke to each other in ragged fragments, the words disappearing into the darkness as they both lost touch with reality.

And then she was there, arching beneath him and crying out his name. Jake felt her convulse around him and then dissolve into powerful shudders. He let himself go, tumbling over the edge in a free fall of pleasure. He drove into her again and again, burying himself to the hilt until he was completely spent.

Jake had thought he knew what they were together, but suddenly, they'd broken through a wall and reached an entirely different level of pleasure. He hadn't been driven solely by physical desire this time. Their bodies had touched in the most intimate fashion possible, but this time, so had their souls.

Jake lay down beside her, pulling Caley into the curve of his body and slipping his leg between hers. "I meant what I said," he whispered. "I do love you."

"I know. And I love you."

A long silence grew between them and Jake knew there was more to say. "What does that mean?"

Caley snuggled closer and kissed his chest. "I don't know."

He could sense the bittersweet emotion in her words. Jake reached over and turned on the bedside lamp, determined to look into her face as they spoke. Her eyes were wide, watching him warily. "It has to mean something, Caley. I've never said those words to a woman before and I'm pretty certain you're the last woman I'll say them to."

"Jake, we've known each other for a week."

"We've known each other our whole lives," he countered.

"But that doesn't count."

Jake laughed sharply. "Why the hell not? It should count for a lot. You know me, Caley, and you know that I'll do everything in my power to make this work."

Jake rolled out of bed and snatched up his jeans, then pulled them on. It was difficult enough talking about such serious matters; he wasn't about to do it naked. "I'm not going to push you. If you want me, you know where to find me."

Caley sat up, pulling the bedcovers up around her naked body. Jake watched her, waiting for a reply, some sign that she was thinking about what this meant. "I'm leaving tomorrow right after the wedding reception. I got a call from the office and they need me back in New York on Friday morning. We have a client presentation that got moved up in the schedule and I have to be there to help prepare."

"You don't have to go," Jake said. "You can stay with me. I'll take care of you."

"Don't do this. Don't make me choose. People are depending on me. I can't take that lightly."

"And what about you? Don't you deserve something for yourself?"

In the end, Jake knew she wouldn't change her mind. She wasn't ready. But he also knew there would be another time. What had happened between them couldn't be put aside. Sooner or later, Caley would realize what they'd had and she'd come back to him.

"You should probably get back to Emma," he said. "You wouldn't want her to wake up and wonder where you are." He raked his hand through his hair. "I guess this is goodbye." He smiled and shook his head. "Goodbye, Caley. It's been fun."

"It has," Caley replied.

Jake nodded, fighting the urge to drag her into his arms and kiss some sense into her. But instead he walked to the door and opened it. He looked back once to see her still sitting on the bed, her gaze fixed on him. Then he stepped into the hallway, into a life without her.

He stood, staring at the closed door, for a long time, wondering whether this truly was the end. He'd always thought falling in love was supposed to solve every problem. Instead, it had just compounded the confusion.

He had to believe, to have faith in what he knew to be true. She loved him. And she couldn't live without him.

9

THE PHOTOS of Sam and Emma's wedding had arrived in yesterday's mail but Caley hadn't the courage to open them. She'd tossed them into her bag as she'd left her apartment that morning and now they sat on her desk, inside their padded manila envelope.

She knew what she'd find—happy pictures with smiling faces, everyone looking as if they were having the time of their lives at the wedding and the reception. She thought back to that night. Though it had been a beautiful, romantic wedding, it had also been one of the worst nights of her life, even worse than the night that Jake had turned down her offer.

After making love to Jake, Caley had returned to Emma's room and crawled into bed, determined to finally get a few hours' sleep. But instead she'd stared at the ceiling, thinking about what had passed between them.

The words had changed everything. The first time he'd said them, she'd brushed them off as an expression of his affection. But the second time, it had been more. It had been a promise, one she wanted desperately to return.

Until that moment, Caley had tried to put their relationship in its proper perspective. It had been just a momentary fling, an affair that had a beginning and end. But then Jake had to mess it all up. And worse yet was what she'd done in returning the sentiment. Now it was just dangling out there, unresolved.

She'd finally found a way to close the books on that night eleven years ago. She'd had sex with Jake, it had been wonderful. That part of her life could now be forgotten.

"Closure," she murmured, picking up the envelope. That's all she'd ever expected to get. But now, she'd have to put closure on her closure. Their affair hadn't been an ending but a whole new beginning. Caley had found herself imagining a future with him. Not just a weekend here or there, or a vacation together when they both had time. She'd thought about something permanent, something that might last a lifetime. The only way to get closure on that was to marry Jake.

Caley carefully opened the envelope and set the stack of photos in front of her. Three months had passed, but she could recall every moment of that week as if it were yesterday. There were nights when she lay in bed imagining Jake beside her…above her…inside her. She wondered if he was thinking about her, too, caught up in an arousing dream.

She'd reached for the phone countless times, ready to call him and put an end to the silence. But then, she'd remember his behavior at the wedding—polite, aloof yet properly attentive. He was giving her an out and she'd been a coward and taken it.

Caley flipped through the pictures until she found a photo of her and Emma, sitting at a table. Jake was standing nearby, looking at them both, a tiny smile curling his lips. She found another photo where he was watching her and then another. Caley hadn't realized, but in nearly every photo he was looking at her with an odd expression of…what was it?

She shook her head and set the photos down, then glanced over at a photo of her parents that she kept on her desk. There it was. The same expression on her father's face. He was sitting next to her mother at a picnic and she was smiling at the camera and he was smiling at her. It was love, adoration and respect all mixed into one simple look.

Caley took a deep breath and turned back to her computer screen, the media release blurring in front of her eyes. She'd been working on the copy for the entire day and had only managed to put together the first paragraph. It was due by the end of the day and she couldn't seem to come up with a creative way to announce the merger of two newspapers.

"Who cares?" she murmured to herself, sliding her mouse over the paragraph to delete it. "Yes, people are going to be upset because they'll only have one newspaper instead of two. But they'll get over it. A few months from now, no one will care."

Since the moment she'd arrived back in New York, she'd had a very difficult time settling into work. She'd become increasingly annoyed by what she was asked to do, her boss acting as if the world would end if the public didn't know that the French fries at a popular fast-food restaurant were made with a new blend of spices.

She delegated everything she could to her assistants

and spent her day browsing the online real-estate ads in Chicago. She wasn't sure why, but it seemed to make her feel as if she were accomplishing something. She'd also taken to flipping through some old photos she'd found from her childhood, trying to piece together when it was she'd fallen in love with Jake.

Caley reached up and fingered the arrowhead necklace she wore. She'd felt silly putting it on again after all these years, but it was something else that made her feel better, that gave her a measure of contentment.

Summer was approaching and the ice would be gone on the lake. The trees would be green and the shallows would soon be warm enough to swim in. As if by instinct, she started to get that trembling feeling of anticipation, the same feeling she'd had as a teenager. The entire summer seemed to stretch out in front of her, filled with excitement and promise. Filled with Jake Burton.

So why not go home? She could afford to take another week once she got this project done. Jake would most likely be there, working on Havenwoods. She'd fantasized about the moment they'd see each other again. And in every one of her fantasies, they'd fall into each other's arms and the world would suddenly make sense.

Caley had used her job as an excuse all along. In truth, it had been something to hide behind, a convenient reason to avoid commitment. Her career didn't matter anymore. If she wanted to work, she could find a job anywhere. She was talented and intelligent and knew the public relations business better than ninety percent of her peers.

Why not just do it? She could walk into John Walters's office right now and quit. She could clean out her desk, take a cab home and pack up her things. In less than a day, she could make a complete turn in her life and start all over. There had been a time when a thought like that would have terrified her. But now, the idea was infinitely appealing.

The buzzer on her intercom rang, startling her out of her thoughts. She picked up her phone. "Yes?" she said.

"Caley? There's someone here to see you."

"Who is it?" Caley asked.

"I'm not supposed to say," her assistant replied. "It's a surprise. Can I send him in?"

"Him?" Caley swallowed hard.

"Him. Tall, dark and handsome. Says he's related to you."

"Kind of a crooked smile? Pale blue eyes?"

"That's right, Miss Lambert."

She drew a quick breath. "Give me two minutes, then send him in."

Caley jumped up from her desk and grabbed her purse, then hurried to the mirror on the back of her office door. This wasn't how this was supposed to happen! She needed more time, a different haircut, a prettier dress, nicer underwear.

Jake had mentioned that he sometimes got out to the East Coast on business. But why wouldn't he have called first? Caley grabbed her lipstick and dabbed it sparingly on her lips. No need to look too obvious. Maybe he was afraid she'd refuse to see him. She pulled the rubber band out of her hair, then moaned. She hadn't been sleeping well lately, which meant she usually did the minimum to get ready for work in the morning. Oh God, what was she going to say to him?

Would he kiss her? Or would it be uncomfortable between them?

A knock sounded on the door and Caley jumped back, dropping her lipstick in front of her. She quickly kicked it aside, then tossed her purse onto a nearby chair. "All right," she whispered. "I can do this. He doesn't know I've been thinking about him for the past three months. For all he knows, I've moved on."

She reached for the door, steeling herself for the impact of that first glance. Caley wasn't so silly as to think it would be anything but devastating. But when she opened the door, a flood of disappointment washed over her.

"Sam," she said, forcing a smile.

Jake's brother grinned at her and held up his hands. "Surprised?"

"Of course. What are you doing here?"

"I'm on my way to see Emma in Boston. I've got a law school interview at Columbia."

"Law school? Here in New York?"

"I thought, since I was here, I'd stop and see my favorite sister-in-law." He stepped inside, taking in the luxury of her office. "Nice digs. So this is what a partner's office looks like. Maybe I should consider PR instead of law."

"It's all for show," Caley said.

Her gaze fixed on him as he walked around the office. Caley hadn't realized until this very moment how much Sam looked like Jake. Just staring at him made her ache for the sight of Jake's face, for the warmth of his smile and the teasing humor that sparkled in his eyes. She shook herself out of her thoughts and stepped back from the door. "Sit down."

"I thought we might go out for some dinner," Sam suggested as he glanced at his watch. "It's nearly seven. Aren't you hungry?"

"I have this project that we have to get done and people are in and out with questions. I really can't leave. But stay awhile and talk. I'll have my assistant go out and get us some sandwiches." She paused and smiled at Sam as he sat down. "You seem so grown-up with that suit on. All settled and married."

He held up his hand with the wedding ring. "Thanks to you and Jake," Sam said. "If it hadn't been for you two, I'm not sure we would have made it through the first three months of marriage."

Caley felt a blush rise on her cheeks. "How can you say that? We almost ruined your wedding."

"You did us a favor. Emma and I were going into it all naive and wide-eyed. You made us stop and think about what we were doing. You were better than any marriage counselors we could have seen."

"You're only saying that because everything turned out right."

Sam stretched his legs out in front of him and linked his hands behind his head. "Aren't you going to ask me?" he finally said.

"I'm sorry," Caley murmured. "How is Emma?"

"Not Emma," Sam said, meeting her gaze. "Jake. Aren't you going to ask me about Jake?"

"All right. How is Jake?"

"Not so great since you left," Sam said. "He misses you."

"I miss him," Caley admitted. "We're good friends. And it was nice to see him again after such a long time apart."

"You're more than good friends," Sam said.

"What do you mean?"

"Jake and I got drunk one night watching a Bulls game and he told me everything."

"Everything?"

"Can I give you some advice?" Sam asked. "I mean, you don't have to take it. You know what you want more than I do. But I think you and Jake belong together. It's always been that way. You're like a team. You're the reason why Emma and I fell in love."

"How is that?"

"We used to watch you two and you always had such a great friendship. You were equals. We both wanted something like that and when we started dating, we found it." He paused. "Plus, Emma was really hot. Oh, and smart and funny, too. But it was the friendship that sealed the deal. A relationship like that takes years to build and you two already have it. You're ahead of the game."

"But friendship doesn't always turn into love."

"Jake loves you," Sam said. "And I think you love him. And you're both letting it slip away."

"I'm not."

"Caley, I know my brother. And I know the only person who is going to make him happy is you. If you don't feel the same way about him, then you have to tell him straight out so he can get on with his life."

"I do love him."

"I'm throwing a graduation party for Emma on Memorial Day weekend. I'm inviting you and I expect you to come. Jake is going to be there. Maybe you two can…talk." Sam stood up and smiled. "That's really all I came to say. Dinner was just an excuse. So, how far is Chinatown from here?"

Caley walked Sam to the elevator and gave him a hug before sending him on his way with a list of recommendations for his evening in Manhattan. Though she thought about going with him, it was difficult to look at Sam and not think about Jake.

When she returned to the office, she sat down in her chair and reached for her calendar. She had two weeks to decide whether to go home for Emma's party or to put her relationship with Jake permanently behind her. A few days, if she hoped to get a decent airfare.

She reached for the phone and punched in the three-digit number to reach John Walters's assistant. There were other decisions to be made, as well, decisions that would be much more difficult than which flight to take to Chicago. "Alice Ann? It's Caley. Is he still in?" She drew a shaky breath. "I need to see him. I'll be right down."

Caley stared at the phone for a long time, her hand resting on the receiver. She was contemplating changing the course of her life—and all for a man. Was she really ready to do this? Or was she still trying to fulfill some stupid schoolgirl fantasy?

She glanced down at the photos and smiled. "For a man who loves me," she said.

JAKE STOOD IN THIGH-HIGH WATER, near the rotting pier at Havenwoods. "It's got to be at least fifty years old," he shouted to Sam.

"How can you tell?"

"It looks old." He stared down at the rusted motorcycle submerged in three feet of water. Jake had decided to start work on the beach so that he could at least swim when the weather turned hot. But there was so much trash in the lake that he had to do a major cleanup first.

"Can you get your truck down here?" Sam asked. "Maybe you can drag it out."

Jake raked his hand through his hair and stared up at the shore. "No. Maybe we can winch it out. Once we get it on shore, we can probably break it apart. It's pretty rusted."

"Or we can bring Dad's boat over and we can tow it out into the center of the lake."

Jake gave Sam a disapproving look. "That would not be very environmentally sound."

"But it would be easy," Sam countered.

"Go up to the summer kitchen and get that rope that I bought. We'll try to drag it closer to shore and then lift it out."

Jake stared down at the water, then bent over and tried to dig the back wheel out of the mud and sand with his hands. But he couldn't reach without going under. Grabbing a deep breath, he ducked his head beneath the surface and began to tug on the back wheel.

When he ran out of breath, he popped out of the water, shoving his hair out of his face. He looked up on shore for Sam, but instead, saw someone else walking down the path. "Emma," he murmured, wondering how much she'd be able to help.

Over the past few months since Caley had left, he'd been reminded of her on a fairly regular basis each time he'd seen Emma. Emma laughed like Caley, she moved like Caley, she even looked a bit like her older sister, especially in the eyes and around the mouth. Jake had caught himself staring on occasion, picking out that one feature that brought back all the memories of Caley.

He'd done his best to forget her, to move on with his life. But Emma was a constant reminder. This was what he'd have to look forward to for the entire summer, and at Thanksgiving and Christmas and every other major holiday that the Burtons and the Lamberts would now spend together.

Jake knew he ought to be grateful that Caley would probably choose to stay in New York, though he expected he'd probably have to face her once or twice at Christmas. That was nearly seven months away. By that time, he ought to be able to see her without lapsing into some intense sexual fantasy involving condiments.

"Emma, tell Sam to hurry up. I'm not going to stand in this water all day waiting for him."

Emma stood on the shore, her hand shading her eyes, watching him. Her hair was pulled back, but when she turned, he saw a glint of auburn and a curly ponytail. Jake's breath caught in his throat. "Caley?" he called.

She took another step closer and in that moment, he knew it was her. Hell, he'd wondered exactly how he'd feel the next time he saw her and now he knew. His reaction was powerful, like a punch to the stomach, and he could barely grab a breath.

As she walked closer, he could see her face. Her gaze watched him warily and Jake realized that she was as nervous as he was. It had only been three months, time that had crawled by at a snail's pace. But now, it seemed as if time had stopped dead in its tracks. Jake reminded himself to breathe, then waded slowly to the shore.

"I'm here for Emma's party," Caley said.

Jake took some satisfaction that their meeting was affecting her as strongly as him, that she couldn't think of anything more interesting to say. "I figured that."

"I thought it would be better if we saw each other first. I—I didn't want to surprise you and just—be there."

He nodded, his gaze skimming along her beautiful body. He felt a pulsing warmth rush through his bloodstream and pool in his lap. He hadn't had sex since she'd left and for the first time in three months, he felt it. Thankfully, he was wearing baggy board shorts that hid his reaction. "Good idea," Jake murmured. "So, how have you been?"

"Good," Caley said. "Busy. I've meant to call but..."

He waited for a long moment, wondering if she planned to finish the thought. When she didn't, he gave it a try. "But you were stranded on the top of a mountain without a phone? But you were in the hospital unconscious in a coma? Or you were on assignment for the CIA? Because that's where I was."

A tiny smile quirked the corners of her lips. "But I wasn't sure what I wanted to say," Caley finished. "I'm still not sure."

"You could tell me that you missed me," Jake suggested. "That would be a start."

"All right. I missed you. A lot."

Jake took that as his cue and he stepped out of the water and walked up to her spot on the shore. "When two people meet after being away for a long time, they usually kiss. Especially if they've missed each other. It's kind of a tradition, I guess." He leaned forward and brushed his mouth against hers.

He'd intended the kiss to be simple, almost platonic. But the moment their mouths touched, a current of desire passed between them. It was as palpable as heat lightning on a humid summer night, startling and intense.

Jake grabbed her waist and pulled her against him, kissing her again, this time more deeply. She immediately opened to his assault, as if she were desperate to taste him, too.

His hands skimmed over her body, feeling the familiar curves. She was dressed in a thin cotton shirt and a skirt that hugged her hips and her backside and it wasn't difficult to imagine her body beneath, all soft skin and naked flesh. Without speaking, he grabbed her hand and drew her along to the summer kitchen, the two of them climbing the rise from the water's edge to the cabin.

When they got inside, Jake walked to the bathroom and grabbed a towel, drying his hair and chest. Then, he kicked off his wet shoes and rinsed his feet in the tub. She was standing in the middle of the room when he returned, looking even more beautiful than he'd remembered.

"It's strange," he said. "I feel like I used to on that first day of summer vacation, when I'd see you after all that time apart. I was never sure of what I should say. Every summer, I'd spend hours thinking of a clever opening line."

"You should have tried kissing me," Caley murmured.

"I can see that now." Jake walked across the room and slipped his hands around her waist. "How have you been? And don't tell me about work."

"I've been…confused," Caley said. "I guess that's the best word for it. But I've begun to simplify my life."

"I've missed you, Caley. I'm not afraid to admit that."

"I'm glad," she murmured. With a trembling hand, she reached out and smoothed her palm over his chest. Her fingers raked through the trail of hair between his collarbone and his belly and Jake closed his eyes and enjoyed the feel of her touch.

He wanted to strip off her clothes and take her to bed, to prove that the desire they'd once shared still pulsed between them. Jake gazed into her eyes, knowing that she couldn't refuse him. But sex, however pleasurable between them, wouldn't solve their problems. They had to find a way to be together, and not just physically.

"How long are you staying?"

Caley shrugged. "I haven't decided. I wasn't sure how things would go." She took a ragged breath. "I need to be back by Thursday. So, five or six days."

"We can get into a lot of trouble in five or six days," he said.

"If we want to get in trouble," Caley replied. "Maybe we should just take things a little slower." She stepped back, out of his reach, then smoothed her hands over her skirt. "I should go. I promised my mother I'd help her do some baking for Emma's party."

"I guess I'll see you tonight, then," Jake said.

Caley nodded. "Yeah. We'll see each other."

Jake wasn't about to let her go without just one more kiss. He grabbed her hand again and pulled her against his body. Kissing her had always been a wonderful prelude to other activities, but this time, Jake made sure that the kiss was enough to convey his feelings. He lingered over her mouth, softly drawing his tongue over her lower lip. When he finished, he walked outside with her and watched as she hiked back up to her car.

A few moments later, as if on cue, Sam reappeared from around the corner of the summer kitchen. He stared off in the direction of Caley and when she turned to wave, Sam waved back. "She looks good," he said.

"She does," Jake agreed.

"I'm glad she accepted my invitation to Emma's party."

Jake frowned. "You invited her?"

"Yeah. I saw her when I was in New York for that law school interview. I told her you missed her and that you couldn't live without her. I guess it worked, huh?"

A curse slipped from Jake's lips. "Why the hell did you tell her that?"

"Because it's the truth," Sam said, shaking his head. "Stop pretending you don't want each other." He chuckled. "Emma and I should lock you up and take away your clothes and shoes. Maybe you'd figure out you belong together."

"Taking away our clothes would not help the problem," Jake muttered. "We do really well without our clothes. It's when we're fully dressed that we can't figure things out." Jake grabbed the rope from Sam's hands and started toward the lake. "And just stay out of my business, will you? I can handle this on my own."

"Hey, you helped me and Emma. I'm just returning the favor."

Jake hefted the coil of rope over his shoulder. He wasn't really angry with Sam. His brother's intentions were good and right now he needed all the help he could get. He had no idea how to make things work with Caley, but he was going to try.

And if he couldn't make things work by the time she left for New York, then he'd be forced to sell all his stuff and move there.

MUSIC DRIFTED through the warm summer night, mixing with the rhythmic lapping of the water against the sandy shore. Caley sat on the beach, staring out across the water at the lights from the homes on the east shore. She tried to find a light from Havenwoods, wondering exactly where the house sat on the shoreline.

She hadn't visited the lake in the summer months since that summer before college and she'd forgotten how calm and peaceful it was at night. In the distance, a motorboat crawled across the water and the sound sent a pair of ducks into flight, their wings fluttering as they skimmed along the surface of the lake.

She used to believe New York City was the most wonderful place in the world to live. But after coming back to North Lake, she'd learned to appreciate its charms. It was quiet and pretty, a world away from the hustle and bustle of the city. And Jake was here, at least for a few days a week.

They'd circled around each other all night, chatting every now and then, before wandering away to talk to other party guests. Caley was grateful for the time and the buffer that her family provided. Though she'd been sorely tempted to jump back into bed with Jake, there were reasons not to.

"I thought I'd find you down here."

Caley jumped, startled by the sound of his voice. A moment later, Jake plopped down beside her on the sand, kicking off his sandals and setting them beside him. "I like this place a lot more in the summer," he said.

Caley took a deep breath, then slowly let it out. Her heart pounded in her chest and her throat had gone dry. She'd come all this way to tell him and now was the perfect time. "Jake, I need to say something."

"So do I," he said. "I've been wanting to—"

"No," Caley interrupted. "Me first. When I made my offer that evening of my eighteenth birthday, I thought I was grown-up enough to accept the consequences. You were right to refuse me. I've been hurt and angry with you ever since but for no good reason." She drew in another deep breath. "I'm going to make you another offer and this time, I promise I won't be angry if you refuse."

"You know what's really great about summer?" Jake asked.

Caley turned to look at him. Didn't he want to hear what she had to say? "Jake, I'm trying to—"

"Swimming. The water's pretty warm already. Especially on the other side of the lake at Havenwoods. You see, the wind usually blows from the west and it blows all the warm surface water over to that side. It's probably five or ten degrees warmer on the east shore." He stood up beside her and began to unbutton his shirt. "I don't think it's too cold for skinny-dipping, though."

Caley gasped as Jake continued to strip off his clothes. His body was gorgeous in the moonlight, all hard muscle and lean limbs. A tiny shiver skittered down her spine and her fingers clenched with the need to reach out and touch him.

When he was completely naked, he stood next to

her and waited. "Skinny-dipping doesn't work with clothes on," he said.

"I'm not jumping in that water," Caley said.

"Come on. We can talk while we swim."

She shook her head, laughing at his audacious request. "No. I'll freeze."

A moment later, Jake ran in, executing a perfect shallow dive, his body slicing into the water with barely a sound. He surfaced ten feet from the shore, standing on his tiptoes on the bottom. "Come on, Caley. I'll keep you warm."

"There are guests still up at the house. What if they walk down here?"

"We can hide under the pier," he said.

"It sounds like you've done this before."

Jake laughed, then swam up to the pier. "No. But I used to think about it all the time. It was the stuff of my teenage fantasies. I used to think about you and me, doing this. Taking off all our clothes and playing around in the water. And then, we'd just swim together and I'd be able to touch you. I loved that fantasy. I still do." He dunked his head under the water, then slicked his hair back. "Come on, Caley. You can say everything you want to say once we're in the water."

"You're crazy," she said.

"I'm in love with this smart, sexy woman," Jake countered. "I'm supposed to be crazy. What about you?"

Caley smiled, then shook her head. "Is it really cold?"

"No." He paused. "Well, maybe a little. But if you keep moving it's not bad. Come on, Caley Lambert.

You used to rise to any challenge, accept any dare. You're turning into a wimp."

She got to her feet, staring out as he bobbed in the water. Then, Caley reached for the hem of her shirt and tugged it over her head. She kicked off her sandals and then skimmed her skirt down over her hips. When she stood in her underwear, Jake swam backward. But instead of running into the water, she walked slowly across the beach.

"It's not skinny-dipping unless you take everything off."

Groaning softly, she reached back and unhooked her bra, letting it fall off her shoulders. "Satisfied?"

"Not quite."

Grudgingly, Caley slid her panties down and kicked them aside. Then, holding her breath, she stepped in. She wasn't prepared for the temperature of the water. It wasn't cold, it was frigid, stealing her breath from her chest. When the water reached her knees, she pushed forward, submerging for a second before she surfaced, gasping and sputtering.

A moment later, his hands were on her body, holding on to her waist and pulling her farther from the shore until she could just barely touch the bottom. "Oh my God. A few degrees colder and we could play hockey."

They bobbed around for a while and to Caley's surprise, she did adjust. Before long, the air seemed colder than the water.

"See, it's not so bad," Jake said. She wrapped her arms around his neck and Jake slid his hands over her hips to cup her backside. "This is much better. Now, tell me what you wanted to say."

"Why did I have to come in the water to do that?"

"Because you can't tell me that you never want to see me again while we're swimming around naked together."

Caley kicked away from him, then splashed water in his face. "I want to see you," she said. "I don't want to be apart anymore." She shivered, her teeth chattering. "I quit my job. And sublet my apartment. In a few days, I'm not going to have anywhere to live. I was thinking, maybe you might need a roommate at Havenwoods. I could help you out with the renovation."

"Are we talking about forever here?"

"Yes. I think that might be nice."

"I could do forever," Jake said.

"Really?" Caley asked. "You're sure?"

"I haven't been happy since you left. And I was getting ready to move to New York."

"Don't do that." She stared up at the stars. "This is where we belong."

Jake pulled her body against his, wrapping her legs around his waist and rubbing her back. "So, I guess we're going to be together," he murmured, brushing his lips against hers.

"We are," Caley said. Raking her fingers through his hair, she pulled him into a long, deep kiss, their warm mouths meeting and melding.

Suddenly, she wasn't afraid anymore. Loving Jake was the most natural thing in the world. It always had been from the time she'd first really seen him as the boy of her dreams. Whether it was fate or circumstance or just good luck, she'd found a man whom she could love. He'd been standing in front of her for so long that all she'd had to do was reach out and touch him.

"How much longer do we have to stay in this water?" she asked, her teeth still chattering.

"We could make a run for the boathouse. No one would find us there."

Caley thought about the warm blankets and the soft bed in the boathouse, then nodded. She wanted to crawl beneath the covers with Jake and to let him warm her body and arouse her desire. "I suppose it would be all right if someone did find us. We're going to have to tell our families sometime, don't you think?"

"Maybe we should do what Sam and Emma did. Just get married."

Caley kissed him again. "If we tell our mothers, you know they're going to want to plan a big wedding. They missed out with Sam and Emma. They're not going to take this well."

"I could always fly back to New York with you. We could get married there, spend our honeymoon in some fancy hotel and rent a truck and move your things back."

She smiled. "I like that idea."

This was the beginning of their life together, here where it nearly ended eleven years ago. It was better this way, Caley mused. It was meant to be this way. And years from now, when they stood on this same shore and looked out over the water, they'd remember the night of her eighteenth birthday. But they'd also remember the night they went skinny-dipping and decided that they might love each other forever.

* * * * *

Three-time RITA® Award nominee **Joanne Rock** never met a romance subgenre she didn't enjoy. The author of over sixty romances from contemporary to medieval historical, Joanne dreams of one day penning a book for every Harlequin series. A former Golden Heart Award recipient, she has won numerous awards for her stories. Learn more about Joanne's imaginative muse by visiting her website, joannerock.com, or @JoanneRock6 on Twitter.

Look for other books by Joanne Rock in Harlequin Blaze—the ultimate destination for red-hot romance! There are four new Harlequin Blaze titles available every month. Check one out today!

DOUBLE PLAY
Joanne Rock

For Dean, who doesn't suffer baseball mistakes lightly—even in fiction. Thank you for helping me with my logistics!

Prologue

IF EVER THERE WAS an ideal man for a fling, it would be the hot baseball player next door.

Amber Nichols recalled her best friend's words, blaring in her ear like an iPod on full blast, as the male in question emerged from the surface of Nantucket Sound like a modern-day Poseidon. Amber watched him from the deck of Rochelle's home on Great Point, overlooking the water. Her former college roommate had generously offered her the beach house more than once during their decade-long friendship, an offer Amber had only accepted now that her life was imploding.

In the course of two months, she'd weathered a wretched breakup and major cutbacks at the newspaper where she worked as a book reviewer. While the breakup had torn at her heart, the cutbacks left her overworked and fearing for her job, leading to stress, exhaustion and shaken confidence all the way around.

Here, she could regroup and relax. Open a new chapter in her life that didn't involve playing it safe and overthinking every decision.

Of course, Rochelle had given Amber plenty of dating advice along with the keys to the place, convinced a wild affair would cure what ailed her. She had never understood Amber's penchant for practical, methodical men who approached life with the same sense of caution that Amber did. But then, Rochelle had never met Amber's perpetually heartbroken mom who had taught Amber the wisdom of holding something of yourself back. Amber simply made dating choices that reflected that.

Dating choices that still seemed to backfire just as surely as her mother's had, although for entirely different reasons. Obviously, something wasn't working with her approach. But Amber wasn't sure she was ready to take Rochelle's advice during her week of transformation and rest.

Rochelle had been particularly effusive in her description of the studly third baseman for the Boston Aces staying next door. Apparently the club's manager owned the house and frequently let various team members stay there as a perk.

The sleekly muscled male was living up to Rochelle's hype. The setting sun caught the rivulets streaming along his skin, making his bronzed body glisten. No slow-motion movie sequence had ever been more flattering to the masculine physique. His square, powerful shoulders were even more mouthwatering as he lifted his arms to wipe his hair from his face. Even from the front of him, she could see the muscles that would form the V of his back.

Her gaze followed that enticing stretch of sinew as she straightened, moving closer to the wooden railing of the raised deck as if drawn by a magnet. Taut abs flexed as he walked, each slab clearly delineated. A trail of dark hair disappearing into the waistband of low-slung cutoffs.

Wow.

Yes, Amber could see why Rochelle would think the Aces slugger would make the ideal fling. Not only did he exude animal sex appeal, he would also probably be on a plane in a day or two, safely gone from her life without doing any major damage. But the man was pure fantasy material and way out of Amber's league. She needed someone a bit more obtainable to help her regain her mojo.

She did want to put to rest her ex-boyfriend's damning accusation that she had Freon running through her veins when they were in bed together. She'd halfway believed him, knowing she'd always made safe and practical choices in her love life.

No more. She'd recalled an interesting book she reviewed about understanding sexual attraction and had promptly ordered a copy as a personal guide this week. As a longtime book lover, she remained convinced the answers to all the world's problems could be found in books if one had the patience to research. Armed with *The Mating Season,* Amber would make her first foray into living more passionately. And, thanks to the delectable man toweling off fifty yards away on their shared stretch of beach, Amber didn't have to worry about any ice in her veins. Sure, she had as much chance of snagging a guy like that as she had of roping the moon, but her two-minute fantasy reel of the baseball phenom had done her a big favor. For the first time in months, she felt sexy. And sexually interested.

As she headed back inside the house with a secret

smile on her face and a new swing in her hips, Amber thought she just might have the guts to leave the safety of the beach house for a night on the town after all.

1

THE LAST THING Heath Donovan wanted was to leave the house tonight.

He cursed the need as he parked his motorcycle among the thirty-odd mopeds the tourists favored outside The Lighthouse, a local tavern that still served food at this hour. Too bad it also functioned as a big-time watering hole that was packed every night of the week with people who might recognize him.

Locking up the bike, a 1961 Velocette Venom that he kept on Nantucket so he wouldn't be tempted to rack up the mileage, he bypassed the main entrance. Instead, he headed for the door that led to the take-out kitchen, hoping he could get in and out without anyone noticing him. He had hobnobbed enough in his years as a player. As the Boston Aces' new manager, he preferred a lower profile, especially the day after a highly publicized game where he'd gotten tossed for supporting his catcher in a spat with the home plate ump.

Lowering the brim of his Patriots hat to help hide his well-known mug, Heath opened the door to the building. The scent of barbecue and eighties rock music spilled out along with the dull glow of neon lights. The converted saltbox house was covered in gray cedar and perched at the water's edge near a decorative miniature lighthouse. But the picturesque New England vibe ended there. The place had been gutted to fit pool tables and jukeboxes, picnic tables and a dance floor. Tonight, the party overflowed onto the beach where the weekend bonfire would culminate in a midnight clambake.

He took his place in the waiting area—a backroom where they'd installed an extra bar and big-screen TVs for the take-out crowd. Heath wondered if the brunette he'd seen on his next-door neighbor's balcony would be here tonight. Unlike the downtown area of Nantucket, Great Point didn't have many choices for a night out. Would he catch sight of her white sundress in the crush?

Not that he planned to act on the rogue attraction that had washed over him like a wave off the sound. Right now, he needed to focus on plotting his way back into the administration's good graces if he wanted to keep the manager gig he'd worked his ass off to snag.

"Takeout for Jones." Heath called out the fake name to the woman behind the counter, the multipierced, purple-haired daughter of the guy who ran the place. He'd seen her here plenty of times before and knew she wouldn't recognize him—or the alias—since her eyes were always glued to the bouncer in the main bar.

The lady bartender gave Heath a nod, never glancing twice at his face and making it easy for him to keep his cover. Leaving him to stare at the TV just in time to see highlight film of his ejection from last night's game.

He cursed under his breath, pissed all over again to see the pitch that extended the outside corner by two city blocks. And even more pissed to remember that if he wanted to stay in the majors as a manager, he couldn't champion all his players' causes. He backed away from the bar to wait until they called him, sticking to the shadows at the back of the room.

He didn't see the woman with her nose buried in a paperback book until he almost flattened her.

"Whoa!" She stumbled sideways, her hand reaching for him reflexively to regain her balance.

"Sorry," he muttered, keeping his head down, trying to stay out of the lights to avoid the hoopla that public recognition caused these days. He'd told the front office he would stay out of sight on his forced two-day leave from the ballpark—a bonus slap from the team's powers that be following the one-game suspension.

But the sight of a white sundress grazing tanned knees forced his head up in spite of himself.

It was the woman who'd been watching him from his neighbor's balcony. The image of the setting sun piercing her thin skirt to outline the shape of her legs had been the solitary high point in the past twenty-four hours from hell.

Not so long ago, he would have welcomed feminine distraction. Hell, there'd been a time when he would have thought nothing of introducing himself then and there and letting his star power do the hard work for him. But he couldn't think like some airheaded celebrity slugger when he was back at the bottom in his career, fighting for a slot he wanted to keep more than anything.

"It's okay." She released him quickly and straightened the neck of her dress's halter top, a sweetly modest gesture that stoked an unwanted attraction. "My friends always tell me I need to read less and live more." She gave the book in her hand a rueful wave and stuffed it in her purse.

"The Mating Season?" Curiosity got the better of him as he spied the title on the volume. He tilted his head to one side to read the cover that remained visible in the top of her denim drawstring bag. "'The primal dance of ancient gender politics'?"

Not exactly your everyday average light reading material. But definitely intriguing. And unlike the women who'd collided with him on purpose in bars over the years, he knew damn well that hadn't been this woman's intent. He'd been the one who'd run into her.

"This is by Madeline Watson-Turner. Great title, isn't it?" She seemed sincere, missing his cynicism as she passed him the volume. "The book came out a few years ago, but it's a great survey of human behavior. I find it interesting reading in light of, you know, the bar scene."

She gestured to the dance floor where couples now two-stepped to a country tune as a big, blue moon-shaped disco ball descended from the ceiling.

Heath didn't need to look around to know what she referred to, however. He'd been a player in the so-called mating season plenty of times. Women flirted and primped, circling the room for the men that appealed to them most. Guys flexed muscles while doing innocuous things such as carrying a round of beers or setting up a shot at the pool table. All around them, men and women sent a hundred signals to each other in pursuit of that basic human need for intimacy.

"I think I recognize you from the beach earlier today." He figured he would give her the chance to 'fess up if she knew his identity. If she was a groupie—

someone who'd put herself in his path on purpose because of his connection to baseball—he'd rather know now before he thought about her legs in a sundress any longer. "Any chance you're renting the house next to mine a few miles down the Point?"

Nodding, she peered over his shoulder as if looking for a way out of the conversation. What was up with that? She hadn't been nearly this distracted that afternoon when she'd been watching him from the porch of the house next door.

"That was me," she admitted. "I was long overdue for some R & R."

"Jones," the bartender called into the tinny public address system that alerted take-out customers when their orders were ready.

Damn. He wouldn't have minded standing here another minute or two to hear the brunette's name or find out why she was reading about the pickup scene while the rest of the bar-goers got on with the business of hooking up. Was she actively on the prowl tonight? A part of him really hated that idea. Something about her crisp white dress and bringing a book to a bar made her seem far too innocent to play that game.

"That's my order." He handed her book back as he nodded toward the front counter. "Guess my wings are ready."

She smiled as she again tucked the volume inside her bag.

"No sense letting good food get cold." She winked. "Enjoy your dinner."

Without another word, she disappeared into the crowd, weaving her way through the throng toward the back door that led outside.

Heading home? Or did she simply hope to find better light for reading at one of the outdoor picnic tables?

And had she recognized him and his connection to baseball? He seriously doubted it. If she had known who he was, she did a damn good job of acting as if his fame were no big deal—as if *he* were no big deal.

Because she wasn't the least bit impressed by fame? Or because she'd never opened the local sports section? He had to admit she had him curious. And not just because he remembered the exact shape of her legs from that sunset illumination of her dress earlier. In spite of his self-imposed moratorium on dating—or maybe because of it—he found himself drawn to the book-reading brunette.

"Jones, your order is ready." The voice on the PA system sounded more impatient now.

Between the woman at the counter's surly attitude and the sundress siren blowing him off without a backward glance, Heath realized he felt like a normal guy for a change. He blended into the background, just like he'd wanted.

As his eyes followed the path the brunette had taken, he found the idea of taking his wings home to devour in silence didn't hold quite the same appeal as it had an hour ago.

Stalking through the crowd toward the bar, he picked up his food. But by the time he had the bag in hand, he'd already made up his mind that he couldn't leave the bar until he satisfied his curiosity about the woman. When was the last time any female had conversed about a book with him? Hell, it'd been a long time since anyone had talked to him as if he knew anything about a topic outside of baseball. Besides, she was staying in the house next to his.

Even if he didn't have any intention of hitting on her, the least he could do was offer her a ride home.

AMBER WAS MORE THAN a little surprised to see her big league third baseman headed her way. After all, she rarely ever attracted anyone but sweetly nerdy types. A celebrated athlete pulling down millions a year was not even a remote possibility. But he approached her now, winding through the throng of beach volleyball players and couples staking out places around a bonfire near the water.

She had headed out here to snag some fresh air before she made her first-ever move on some hapless study type as part of her plan to be more emotionally daring. Well, that and she also hoped the darkness outside the bar would help ease her nervousness about approaching a stranger strictly to hit on him. Somehow the dark lent a sense of anonymity to the whole nerve-racking business. She'd found a spot at a picnic table at the edge of the action where she could people-watch and plot her next move.

But the sight of Rochelle's megahot neighbor walking toward her saved her from having to flirt with some random stranger for a little while longer. Which was not only utterly unexpected, it was welcome news. She'd felt an odd connection with the star player when he'd bumped into her, when he'd held her steady with strong, warm hands. Crazy, yes. Improbable, definitely.

That didn't stop the way her eyes found his in a crowd while the rest of the world faded to insignificance.

Of course, that only meant *he* was magnetic as hell. She had no reason to feel as if the moment was full of destiny as he ambled his gorgeous self closer to her. She purposely hadn't tried to hone her flirting skills on him because he must be highly sought after by women who were a whole lot better than her at this dating business. Maybe she was just damned glad to see him because now she could relax.

Since the ballplayer wasn't a dating prospect, she could let her guard down and be herself around him.

"According to my book—" she patted the volume resting in her purse pocket "—you should move closer to the center of action if you're hoping to meet people."

Not that she necessarily wanted to watch him hooking up with any of the endlessly tall, cool blondes that seemed to populate Nantucket this weekend. But it was second nature to share the tidbits she'd picked up about dating from the book.

As a book reviewer, she frequently read about life instead of living it. At first, the tactic had been a brilliant way to save herself from a tumultuous childhood, holding her mom's hand between husbands who let her down. But at the age of twenty-eight, Amber knew her old standby of finding life's answers in a library wasn't exactly a healthy practice.

The ballplayer paused in front of her picnic table, empty save her. Most of the bar patrons were dancing—either inside or out—or playing beach games such as bocce and horseshoes near the water. Torches ringed the property, while a few strands of Christmas lights illuminated walkways and the gazebo down by a small pier.

He deposited a paper take-out bag on the end of the table and then—surprise—*two* bottles of beer.

"What makes you think I need tips from a book?" He sat down, uninvited but not unwelcome.

It gave her the chance to peruse him at length close-up. And, man, what a treat it was to ogle a handsome male from such an intimate distance. His knee brushed hers under the table, the denim rough against her bare leg.

She appreciated the casualness that kept her from getting nervous around him. Or worse, prickly. Sometimes when she liked a guy, her defenses turned into force fields worthy of a Starfleet ship.

"Oh, I don't know. I guess because you barrel through the place knocking women down before they know what hit them—"

"I hardly knocked you down." He set a longneck closer to her and moved his aside so he could open the box full of chicken wings with a side of ribs. "But in an effort to make it up to you, I've brought you dinner."

He picked up his beer bottle and clinked the side gently against hers where the brew still sat on the table.

"To chance encounters that don't have a damn thing to do with the mating season," he offered as a toast.

Charmed, she lifted the cold bottle and clinked it back.

"Cheers." Tipping the glass to her lips, she watched him do the same, her heartbeat stuttering at his warm regard.

She knew better than to pay attention to good looks—she'd trained that instinct out of herself at an early age, realizing even in high school that she had more fun hanging out with guys who could look beneath the surface. Still, here was the baseball hero, looking her right in the eye and seeming to like what he saw just fine.

"I'm Heath, by the way." He slid a paper plate across the table with a half-dozen wings. "Dig in."

Heath? Amber couldn't recall the name of the ballplayer, but she'd thought it was something more Hispanic sounding than Heath. She wasn't sure if Heath was part of the alias—as "Jones" so obviously had been—or if she'd gotten mixed up about the name Rochelle had mentioned. She'd never paid any attention to professional sports.

"Amber Nichols, book reviewer extraordinaire," she returned, telling herself it didn't matter either way since she hadn't expected him to be honest with her. Men in bars lied all the time. Even *The Mating Season* said so. "I've already eaten, but thanks for the beer."

She took another sip, savoring the icy flavor of a Boston microbrew while she watched him devour his first two wings.

"I figured if I bought you a drink maybe you'd fill me in on why you brought a book to a bar on a Friday night. But I guess I have my answer. You're writing a book review?"

The outdoor speakers blared a reggae tune while a new volleyball game got under way and the previous rivals paired off to walk on the beach. Amber realized her pool of dating prospects was dwindling, but with Heath sitting across from her, it was hard to care. He could seriously turn a woman's head.

"It's a long overdue case of reading for pleasure." She hadn't picked up a book of her own choosing in months.

He paused in his methodical demolishing of the food.

"If you're hanging out in a meat market like this, it seems like you could observe all you need to about—what was it?—the 'ancient dance of gender politics' from a firsthand perspective. Why be here and use the time to read?"

"Great question," she admitted, drawn to the natural inquisitiveness in his eyes that didn't seem like a put-on. "And I'm honestly not sure if it's because I'm too much of a chicken to face a bar crowd while I'm alone, or because I need a great deal of remedial help playing the pickup game."

She'd decided to be sincere with him since he was just being friendly.

A chicken wing fell from his fingers and he appeared surprised for a moment before he grinned and shook his head.

"It was a serious question."

Confused, she frowned.

"It was a serious answer."

He leaned back in his seat and angled his head to see under the table. Then, straightening, he looked her in the eye again.

"With legs like that, I find it tough to believe you don't rake in your fair share of male attention." He turned his gaze back to his dinner.

Flustered and half wishing she could consult her book for advice on what a guy like Heath might want from this kind of conversation with a woman of her tepid outward charm, Amber tensed.

"Now who's not being serious?" She knew very well her legs were nothing to write home about. The temptation to open up *The Mating Season* and reread the chapter "Liars, Posers and Pickup Artists" made her fingers itch. "I'm only here because I need to force myself to be more social."

His eyebrows lifted in unison, perhaps reacting to the surliness that had crept into her tone.

"Okay, *that* I believe. Are you always this defensive?"

"Actually, I'm being amazingly friendly toward you." When was the last time she'd let a stranger buy her a drink, let alone sit down and make himself at home at her table at an overcrowded nightclub? "I think it's because I'm certain you have no interest in me."

Heath balled up the paper plate and stuffed it inside the empty sack before sending the bag sailing in a neat hook shot into a nearby trash can.

"Well, Amber, I guess that just proves you can't learn everything you need to know from books because I'm more than interested." He lowered his voice and the brim of his ball cap as a group of women sat down at a table right next to theirs. "I'm flat-out attracted and hoping you'll let me take you home."

2

AMBER'S JAW DROPPED in an expression that was downright priceless. Had the male population become so blinded by a generation of silicone-enhanced females that they didn't recognize a truly hot version of the real thing?

He couldn't think of any other reason why Amber Nichols would have gotten this far in life without having a better awareness of her own appeal.

"Isn't that moving a little fast?" Her hand strayed to her purse, where that book of hers stuck out of an outside pocket. She ran an unvarnished nail along the closed pages, creating a soft zipping noise.

Heath couldn't remember ever having a conversation like this one. He'd been on the receiving end of big-time female attention from the time he was an All-State baseball player as a ninth grader on the varsity team. As a major leaguer, he'd had women stalk him, flash him and bribe the elevator guy in his building to get close to him. Not once in all that time had a woman questioned his technique.

"I don't know," he deadpanned. "Should we check the book?"

For a moment, she bit her lip and he wondered if she was honestly tempted. He half regretted teasing her.

"Make fun if you want, but I'm a little out of my element here." She stood abruptly, putting her purse strap over her shoulder and leaving the beer on the table. "Thanks for the drink, but I think I'll be heading home."

Strike. Out.

She couldn't have made the call any more clearly if she'd been sporting a blue shirt and a chest protector. Her long, dark braid whipped over her shoulder to trail obediently behind her as she walked away from him for the second time that night.

And for the second time, he realized he didn't want her to go.

Something about uptight, blind-to-her-own-appeal Amber Nichols made him want to turn her around and show her the time of her life. It seemed like a truly ill-timed impulse given the state of his slipping career status and his well-under-.500 ball club.

But look where all his intense focus on the team had gotten him. Booted out of the ballpark for two days until he could rein in his mouth and his temper on the field.

What if Ms. Serious who didn't know his famous name was just the ticket to a major attitude adjustment for him? He'd been so determined to set women aside this year. What if all the pent-up anger and stress stemmed from a lack of that basic release? Maybe he really needed the mood-altering benefits of a rollicking good time with a woman who was about as far from a clingy groupie as he could possibly get.

His feet were already making tracks to follow her while his brain slowly caught up. This was a good idea.

Instead of two days of reinventing his losing team, he'd have two days of Amber. Two days of mouthwatering legs. Two days of teasing her about her choice of reading material while showing her how sexy she really was.

Assuming he had any idea how to seduce a woman. The very real possibility that he'd only ever gotten laid because of his bat speed gave him pause.

"Amber." He caught up with her in the parking lot as she searched the long row of mopeds. "Sorry to give you such a hard time back there. I'm a wiseass, but sometimes it strays more toward pain in the ass."

She nodded, hardly looking at him.

"It's okay. I'm very uppity," she admitted, not sounding overly concerned about it. "Apparently I'm also very forgetful as I have no idea which one of these is my rental."

His eyes followed hers down the row of scooters, half of which were the exact same make, model and color. Even the helmets were identical since the local dealership issued the same basic gear to everyone.

"Well, I offered to drive you home earlier since you're staying at the beach house right next to mine. The offer still stands."

She straightened from her examination of the vehicles.

"You said you wanted to take me *home*." She pursed her mouth in a thoughtful little frown and he wondered what her lips would taste like if he nibbled on one. They looked slick and glossy, and he bet they smelled good, too. "I thought you meant you wanted to..."

He wondered if she was blushing as her words trailed off. He almost wouldn't be surprised. She was an interesting mix of fresh honesty and disarming sweetness. He all around liked Amber Nichols.

"I do. That is, you didn't misunderstand." He closed the distance between them, the scent of the ocean and the bonfire filling the air. "I issued a purposely ambiguous invitation, thinking I'd be happy if you took me up on it no matter how you interpreted it."

Her fist tightened on the key in her hand, her dark braid slithering over one bare shoulder as she straightened.

"So you *did* proposition me?" She sounded surprised.

"I did." He gestured toward his classic British motorcycle parked between the scooters and the Jeeps. "But you deserve a much better proposition than that. You can listen to my pitch on the way home and if you don't like it, I'll drop you at your doorstep—no harm, no foul."

"I don't think I'm going to be able to hear a proposition if I ride on that thing." She lifted one eyebrow, her expression skeptical.

He thought of all the women he'd known who would slither suggestively all over that bike for the chance to ride with him. And damn, but wasn't it different to be the one doing the convincing for a change?

"So technically, you might have to hear the pros and cons on your front porch instead of on the highway." He snagged a generic helmet off the nearest scooter and handed it to her. "Here. Put this on. No matter whose it is, there are enough here for everyone since you wore one."

She hesitated, peering back over her shoulder at the beach party kicking into high gear with the scent of the clambake and a vintage Lynyrd Skynyrd tune drifting on the breeze.

Heath dug for the last bit of persuasive ammo he could think of without touching her.

"I thought you wanted to read less and live more?" He parroted her words from earlier when he'd run into her.

Apparently, she was committed to that bit of wisdom because the prompt worked like a charm. She snatched the helmet from him and strapped it in place.

"You're on."

He didn't bother to hide a grin as he secured his own helmet and fired up the engine. She never hesitated when it came time to straddle the bike in her dress. With modesty and determination, she managed the trick without flashing him.

A damn shame.

"Ready?" he asked, looking forward to the moment when she realized she'd need to wrap herself around him.

As it was, she sat with her knees grazing his thighs, but the fun stopped there.

"I think so?" The rising inflection suggested she'd quite possibly never ridden a motorcycle.

"Hold on to me." The words came out rougher than he'd intended. Not that he was frustrated. If anything, he was more eager than he would have imagined to have her touch him.

There was a light brush of fingertips along his upper back.

"Uh, lower." His skin tightened with the myriad of implications in that one simple word.

Her touch vanished briefly, then reappeared at his waist. She slid her arms around him, her breasts pressed against his back.

"I'm beginning to think you had an ulterior motive in wanting to give me a ride."

He blinked to clear his mind of the wicked double entendres he'd begun to hear in their every exchange. She had his pulse fired up so hard he couldn't think straight.

"Is that right?"

She tucked her chin against his shoulder as he backed out of the parking spot and pulled onto the highway.

"I think you knew all along the persuasive measures were going to start on the way home, even if we weren't speaking."

She'd seen straight through him. But fortunately, she didn't sound annoyed about it. If anything, she just might be warming up to the idea of spending the night with him if the pebble-hard peaks of her breasts against his back were any indication.

No matter that his ball club was at the bottom of their division and the team owner was gunning for his ass. At this moment, everything felt right in his world.

AMBER WORRIED THAT HER brain had shut off right about the time her libido kicked into high gear.

Maybe that was why she'd always avoided situations like this.

She could never remember feeling so sexually edgy that she was about to come out of her skin.

Was it because of the element of daring involved with flirting with a stranger? The frank masculine appeal of a man who'd turned her on physically with just one look even before she'd arrived at the bar that night?

Or could it be the raw stimulation of having her thighs wrapped around Heath with nothing but a layer of cotton sundress and whisper-thin silk panties to separate her from the rough denim of his jeans?

No doubt it was a potent combination of all of the above. He revved the engine faster on a straightaway that cut through a patch of trees, casting them in even more shadows without the glow of the moon. She tightened her hold on his waist, her hands splayed against the rigid muscles of his abs.

And, heaven help her, she couldn't even think about words such as *rigid* without getting all hot and bothered. Which brought her to yet another reason for her turned-on condition. Heath had put the whole notion of sleeping together into her brain, the possibility teasing her thoughts at every turn until she could barely think at all. She could only feel.

The motor hummed a conspiratorial vibration between her legs, a ridiculously erotic stimulation that reminded her of sex. Well, right now, everything seemed to remind her of sex.

She closed her eyes to shut out the inviting sight of Heath's V-shaped back tapering into narrow hips. But that only made the scent of his skin beneath his shirt more tempting. Amazing how as soon as you deprived one of your senses, the others all became more acute.

What am I doing?

It was quite possibly the last rational plea of her reasonable mind, so accustomed to being in total control.

She didn't want to be the half-witted woman whose body was washed up on the beach the next morning because she went home with a stranger.

But Heath wasn't a stranger. He was a well-known public figure who would be risking his million-dollar contract if he got into trouble with the law. Plus, Rochelle knew Heath and knew Amber was with him. Amber had texted her friend while Heath was starting up the bike before she left.

Besides, he'd never once flaunted his star status to impress her. He could have used that to try to woo her in some smarmy pickup, but he hadn't even mentioned it. He seemed like a regular guy. A really hot regular guy.

Bottom line, Amber had come to the beach for just this kind of thing—to prove she could have a passionate, hot encounter without overthinking the whole thing. She wasn't a cold fish. She didn't have to plan every second of her life, which had been another one of Brent's accusations before he left.

It would be okay to let go of reason for a few hours. Maybe even all night. Heath was charming. Forthright. Sexy. Best of all, he was only interested in the here and now. She didn't have to worry about confusing, emotionally draining entanglements.

He might even be gone before she woke up in the morning.

What could one night with him possibly hurt?

She'd thought so long about it that she didn't realize they were home until Heath rolled the bike to a stop and flicked off the engine.

Suddenly, she sat in the dark chill of the cooling

night air, clinging to his back for dear life for no other reason than that he felt so good.

So warm. So fiercely masculine.

"Amber?"

His voice scratched over her senses, satisfying an itch and somehow heightening them at the same time.

"Mmm?" She told herself to let go of him, but her hands wouldn't obey.

The only response she got from her fingers was a slight flex against his abs, raking gently along the hard muscle there.

"We're home." He placed a warm palm against the outside of her bare thigh where her dress had hiked up to straddle the bike.

Ooh.

The broad splay of his fingers awakened her senses to even more sensual possibilities. What might those hands accomplish if given free rein over her body tonight?

She felt her nipples bead even harder against his back. The impulse to rub herself against him like a cat gripped her so forcefully she could barely resist it.

"I'm aware of that." With an effort, she unlinked her hands from his waist and reached up to unfasten her helmet. "Guess I got a little too comfortable."

Hooking the helmet on the back of the bike, she stood. Her body protested the loss of his and she wondered if her reaction to him was so fierce because she'd denied herself this kind of outlet her whole life.

Wasn't she the woman who chose her dates intellectually? Based on common interests? That had always seemed so smart and so much safer than dating random guys just because they looked good. But maybe she really had missed some important dating knowledge by denying herself the occasional—er—booty call?

"Comfortable?" Heath was off the bike and standing inches in front of her before she could catch her breath. "Is that what we were feeling the whole way home?"

She wondered how he knew what she felt. His dark, intent stare sure looked as if he had full knowledge of her riotous impulses. Could he honestly be feeling all those same things?

Her legs wobbled unsteadily beneath her. She hadn't felt so boy-crazy since her first high-school dance.

"Maybe *comfortable* wasn't quite the word I was looking for. Thank you for the ride."

She had no idea how to go about inviting him inside, probably because she'd never tried to make a move on a guy so early in a relationship. But damn it, she didn't want a relationship. She wanted mindless forgetting.

She wanted to feel hot and sexy and passionate. And her every tingling feminine instinct told her she could feel that way with Heath.

"You sound so formal," he teased, smiling. "I thought we got past that stage on the ride home."

Amen. But she didn't say that. Clearing her throat, Amber called up all her courage.

"Would you like to come in?" At some point during the asking she realized she was shaking inside—and a little on the outside, too.

Damn Brent for stealing her confidence and making her doubt herself.

Heath peered over one shoulder toward Rochelle's beach house.

"Actually, I'm afraid I won't be able to keep my hands off you once I cross that threshold." He made it a friendly warning, but the tense set to his shoulders told her he might not be kidding. "I'd rather not go in unless I'm sure I'll be staying all night."

In the old days—her pre-Brent days—she would have thought Heath's statement was coming on too strong. Right now, she liked the idea that he wanted her.

"I'm not sure—" she started, licking her lips since the words had dried up in her throat.

The breeze off the water blew her skirt lightly against her legs; the scent of the sea and Heath's aftershave wove around her.

"That's where the conversation comes in, remember?" He slipped a hand around her elbow and guided her toward the balcony where she'd stood a few hours earlier and ogled him shamelessly.

Back then, she'd been content to simply let the sight of a handsome man rev her snoozing libido. She'd never thought she would actually be returning here with him tonight.

"You're really going to try to sell me on spending the night with you?" She couldn't imagine he did that very often. Major League Baseball players had their pick of women at all times, right?

Her small kitten heels sank in the sand with each step as she followed him across the driveway and up the steps to the balcony. Once there, he wasted no time backing her onto the fat green cushions of the porch glider. He dropped down to the seat beside her, close but no longer touching.

He seemed respectful like that, despite his frank way of speaking. Amber thought Rochelle had said he was a young player, but Heath had a definite maturity about him. He obviously knew not to crowd her.

Now, he studied her in the moonlight, the soft white glow surrounding them in a bubble of privacy while the ocean waves rolled a relentless rhythm nearby. Cool sea spray carried on the breeze, coating her skin in a mist that made her shiver.

"Amber, I'm going to be honest with you." He angled his body between hers and the sea, effectively sheltering her from both the wind and the mist.

"I would hope so." She smoothed her skirt over her legs, the hem just barely reaching her knee. "I'm contemplating a fun fling, not a smarmy affair based on lies." Even as she said it, a horrible thought formed. "You're not married, are you?"

She figured Rochelle would have known, but what if her friend hadn't been aware of all the facts?

"Divorced for three years, actually," Heath clarified. "I'm not marriage material by a long stretch. In fact, I'm not even good dating material."

"I'm not looking for dating," she said. "God, that sounds tawdry, doesn't it? I'm sure this is supposed to be a lot less awkward. But I've never considered sleeping with someone just for—you know—fun."

Heath shook his head, a slow grin stealing over his mouth. What would it feel like to have those lips on hers?

"You're too much, Amber." He brushed his fingers along the side of her cheek, his thumb straying beneath her lower lip. "It's a good thing I got you out of The Lighthouse before you tried out your *Mating Season* techniques on the unsuspecting male population."

"You think I would have been a colossal failure, don't you?" She marveled at the way his light stroke could elicit a swirl of pleasure deep inside her, far from the point of contact.

How did he do that?

"I'm glad you weren't wasted on someone who wouldn't have appreciated you as much as I will." He lifted his thumb a millimeter or two, just enough to land on the plump center of her lower lip.

Somehow, he'd turned the most gentle of touches into something wildly erotic. Or had she built it into something carnal with her wayward imaginings?

"It's nice to be appreciated," she admitted, straining to maintain eye contact when her lids wanted to fall closed.

What would happen if she just gave in to what she wanted?

"I can do a lot better than this," he promised, his voice soft next to her ear, making her realize her eyes must have closed long enough that she hadn't seen him lean near.

His whisper made the back of her neck tingle.

"I'd like to see you try." She couldn't begin to imagine what pleasurable havoc he might wreak if she committed herself to this night with him.

"Then what's stopping you from saying yes?" His hand strayed lower, his fingers dipping beneath her hair while his thumb tipped her chin up.

Their eyes met for a long moment and she wondered which of her many fears to list. That things would be awkward between them in the morning? That her relationship instincts would kick in tomorrow and she'd mess up the fling by falling for him? She knew he was a wildly inappropriate choice for her heart.

But she didn't say any of that. Without thinking, she voiced her biggest worry.

"I'm afraid of being a sexual disappointment."

3

OF ALL THE THINGS Heath thought he might hear regarding Amber's reservation, a fear of disappointing him never would have crossed his radar.

He had to stop himself from saying "What?" emphasized with a raised voice and a few audible exclamation marks, even though that was his internal reaction. From the tentative note in her tone the first time, he guessed she wouldn't want to repeat the declaration.

So, smothering the urge to express disbelief and a healthy amount of outrage at whoever had put that kind of notion in her head, he managed to keep his tone neutral.

"Any man who claims to be disappointed in you is an idiot who's too scared to admit he only disappoints himself." He knew he might be condemning someone she'd once cared for, but how could he let her worry about something like that? He had a quick image of the kind of guy who would take advantage of a relatively inexperienced woman by making her think crap sex was *her* fault. The mental picture forced him to take his hands off her since his fingers flexed into automatic fists.

"You think so?" She wrapped her arms around herself, her expression dubious.

"I know so with a thousand percent certainty." The urge to gather her up in his arms and take her inside pulled at him with new ferocity.

Before, he'd wanted her because she made him feel like a regular guy, as if his wealth and fame didn't matter one bit. They'd just been two people attracted at the most basic level.

Now, he also wanted to prove to her beyond all doubt that she had the power to turn a man inside out with wanting her.

"There's no such thing as thousand percent certainty." The worry had faded from her voice as she flicked at the hem of her dress.

"There is in this case." He unclenched his fists now, determined that the best way to take revenge on the jerk who'd hurt her was to provide her with the most excellent sex of her life. Laying his palm over her hand where it sat on her knee, he let his touch speak for him. "Why don't you let me prove it to you?"

Her big, dark eyes, guarded but curious, met his in the moonlight. They definitely had a connection and he was more than happy to exploit it for their mutual benefit. She might not know how good it could be between them, but he did.

So, operating on instinct, he allowed two fingers to stray off the fabric of her skirt to brush her bare knee.

Higher.

He remembered how responsive she'd been on the back of his bike. How she'd pressed herself against him once she'd given in and put her arms around him.

He used that knowledge now to shamelessly coax the answer he wanted to hear.

"You're very persuasive," she admitted, her voice catching on a breathy note that teased his senses like a caress.

"Is that a yes?" Taking no chances, he pressed his advantage by lowering his mouth to hers.

Gently, he kissed her. Carefully, he kept the contact light so that he could walk away if she chose not to move forward.

He hadn't counted on her reaction.

She didn't sit still for the kiss. The tender meeting of mouths intended to seal the deal didn't remain chaste for long. Later, he would think to himself that the kiss had been like a spark in a dry forest. Instantly, everything took flame.

Amber's arms were around his neck, her soft skin and faint fragrance surrounding him. Her hips twisted toward his, her thigh pressed against his leg.

And her breasts…the sudden feel of her high, firm curves thrust to his chest brought on a blood rush that left him dizzy.

"That's a yes," he growled against her lips, breaking the kiss long enough to speak. "Where's the key to the house?"

"In my purse." She had sidled into his lap as if she belonged there, her fingers twining through his hair. "Hurry."

He was still reeling from the sensual onslaught. "We have all night," he assured her, needing to catch his breath before he untied the halter top of her dress while they were still outdoors. "There's no need to rush."

She wriggled and resituated herself on his lap, her

hip nudging him at a crucial juncture that damn near undid him.

"I didn't feel in a rush either until you started talking about thousand percent certainty and put your hand on my thigh." She let go of his neck to pick up the purse he hadn't been able to find in the dark. Emerging with a key, she dropped it in his hand. "Now I'm all kinds of curious and more than a little excited about how this is going to turn out."

Apparently satisfied she'd done her part to get them inside the house, she returned her attention to his mouth. Nipping his lip, she smoothed the spot with a quick dart of her tongue.

A groan ripped through him, the sound vibrating in his ears and humming along his skin as he rose to stand with her in his arms. Fumbling with the key and trying like hell to avoid the temptation of sliding a hand up her skirt, Heath plowed through the door of the beach house.

He dropped the key on a counter of some kind and toed the door shut with his boot. He walked slowly since he'd never been in the house before and he didn't want to ram into a piece of furniture with Amber in his arms.

"Which way?" he asked, arching away from her kiss long enough to obtain that vital piece of information.

"My room is at the top of the stairs. Through the living room on the right." She whispered even though they were alone in the darkened house. Moonlight poured in through a few windows where the shades hadn't been drawn, allowing him to make out the polished banister of a staircase. "But the living room is okay with me."

"Not a chance." He hastened his pace, hoping to hit

the steps before she kissed him again and his brainpower diminished. "I'm not going to let you get distracted by a sofa spring in your back or rug burn on the knees. I made you a promise that we're going to have the time of our lives tonight, and that damn well means a mattress."

"Rug burn?"

He took the steps faster than most of his rookie players could have, even with Amber in his arms. Then again, it was having Amber in his arms that drove him to find the bedroom so fast.

"Nothing you need to worry about now," he assured her, maneuvering her through the doorframe with care so he didn't bump into anything.

The room faced the ocean. Moonlight spilled in through the open French doors while the vast blackness stretched out on the other side. A white spread on an old iron four-poster bed, one of the few pieces of furniture on the sprawl of gently worn hardwood, welcomed them.

He hesitated before reaching the mattress.

"There." She pointed, as if he couldn't see the bed for himself.

"Not yet." He figured he was the one carrying her, so he could choose where they landed. Positioning her just in front of the French doors, he set her on her feet. "I've been remembering all night the way your legs looked with the setting sun shining through that skirt earlier. I'm thinking I can re-create the visual if the moon is bright enough."

He stepped back to admire the view, the moonlight giving her a back glow like an angel in her white dress. And how damn poetic was that?

"You're crazy," she admonished, fidgeting her way out of her shoes, clearly uncomfortable in the spotlight.

"Maybe." He reached for the long rope of hair snaking down one shoulder and caught the end. "Can I unfasten this?"

He pulled at the elastic.

"Um, sure. But this isn't some kind of Cinderella deal where I let my hair down and suddenly I'm gorgeous."

Pulling the hair tie free, he slipped a finger into one loop after another, methodically untwining the hair as silky waves slithered over his palms.

"No 'suddenly' about it." She was naturally beautiful either way.

The process was deliciously slow, and he took his time, enjoying the feel of her hair as it cloaked her shoulders.

She stepped closer, her eyes heavy-lidded.

"Only one knot left to unfasten," she whispered, pulling the long mane to one side of her neck and revealing the tie of her halter top.

His pulse stuttered and sped up. How had he gotten so fortunate as to run into this woman tonight? A woman who didn't know about his career and didn't care what he did for a living. She hadn't even asked.

Unable to keep his distance any longer, he hauled her up against him. Easing the knot in her dress, he undid the soft cotton until the triangles of fabric covering her breasts loosened and fell free.

But the feel of her pressed up against him didn't compare with the sexy gasp from her lips. The sound tripped down his spine like a lover's fingertip.

"No more knots." He smoothed his hands down her

bare shoulders, absorbing her shiver as he bent to kiss her neck.

"Good." She arched back enough to yank his shirt hem up and splay a hand along his bare stomach. "That means no more delays. No more waiting."

He had to admit it was tougher to be on the receiving end of sensual touches than to be the giver. Her fingers gliding just below the waist of his jeans couldn't have been more potent if she'd been stroking his shaft.

Heat blazed up his chest in spite of the cool breeze blowing in the window.

"I'd do a better job delivering on all those promises I made if you let me take my time." Even now, his hands shook with the need to hold back. It had been a hell of a long time since he'd been with a woman.

And ah damn, but he was feeling every one of those months—no, a year now—as Amber peeled off his shirt and stepped out of her dress.

Wow, she was an eyeful.

A barely there lace strapless bra matched white bikini bottoms. A thin silver chain looped around her waist and dangled three dark blue gemstones just beneath her belly button.

"It's because of those damn promises that I'm in a hurry," she argued with whispered urgency as she brushed kisses along his jaw. "I have bad memories to live down, remember?"

AMBER KNEW HEATH MUST have recalled her predicament, her wish to make sure she wasn't sexually deficient.

His touch went from reverent to mind-blowingly commanding. He lifted her off her feet and carried her to the bed, her unbound hair trapped between their bodies as he laid her on the chenille bedspread.

"Kiss me," he ordered, his tone warning that he wouldn't tolerate an argument.

Obediently, she arched against him, savoring the rough scrape of his whiskers against her cheek and the press of his thigh between hers. He was too good to be true. Too delicious for words.

She'd never imagined she could be the kind of woman who would find so much satisfaction in the physical, but right now she was a mass of throbbing want. How had she gone through life for twenty-eight years without ever seeking this kind of pleasure?

"Stop thinking," he muttered between kisses, breaking away from her mouth to lick his way down her neck.

His hot breath against her skin made her writhe against the mattress, which only succeeded in rubbing her thighs against his. She wondered if a woman could explode from desire.

"How do you know I'm thinking?" She hadn't been doing much of that. "I've mostly been panting and moaning and that sort of thing."

She tried to unfasten his jeans, but her fingers hummed with some kind of trembly energy as if she'd stuck her hand in a light socket.

"You weren't moaning," he assured her, circling a nipple with his tongue right through the lace of her bra. "I would have heard you."

She moaned. And not just for effect.

"That feels—" She couldn't explain it since she moaned again.

"That's more like it." He tugged down one lace

cup with his teeth. Then he unveiled the other the same way.

"What else can I do?" She didn't want to let him take the lead so much that tomorrow he would look back and think she'd been a failure in the sack. Not after what Brent had said to her. "How can I help?"

He lifted his gaze from her breasts for a moment, and the look she saw there sent a peculiar shiver along the back of her neck. Intense and determined, he didn't have the appearance of a young rookie sowing his wild oats with women far and wide. Just then, he had the hell-bent will of a man who could move mountains if he so chose.

"You can think about me." He took her hand in his and guided it to his shorts where an impressive bulge awaited her. "Only me. And how much I want you."

It was a sexy thing to say. It was also a beautiful thing to say to ease the last of her fears.

And just then, Amber had a taste of the dangers of sleeping with someone just for fun. Because with that simple statement, Heath had touched her heart no matter how much she wanted this to be uncomplicated.

But then, he palmed the throbbing place between her legs, applying sinfully delicious pressure where she wanted it most. Raw hunger edged out emotion and fears. She couldn't hold back the gasps and sighs as he worked the most sensitive places until she was slick with desire.

She had just enough sense to be sure he found a condom from somewhere before she allowed herself to become utterly mindless at his touch. Her panties disappeared around the same time he stripped off the rest of his clothes. The room became a sultry blur of body heat and ocean breeze, their limbs tangling in a teasing dance until at last he entered her.

Her nails bit into his skin at the same time her teeth nipped her lower lip. She'd never felt anything like what she felt with Heath. She lost herself in him, in this. Mindless with the sweetness of it all, she realized she shouldn't have to think so hard about sex. It could just happen. And be wonderful.

Her heartbeat thundered like a storm coming in off the water. An urgent fire built in her blood. She twisted her head back and forth against the pillow as he drove into her again and again. Slow, then fast. Slow again.

Her breaths came so quick she couldn't catch them. Her legs wound around him tight, clutching him hard and squeezing him to her as he found a spot that turned her into a crazy woman.

Release crashed through her so forcefully and for so long she thought it would never end. Waves of pleasure squeezed her insides, wringing every last sweet spasm from her until Heath joined her. Feeling his release was almost as gratifying as the amazing orgasm he'd given her. Knowing she'd satisfied him—this amazing, sexy, thoughtful man who could have his pick of women— made her glow with happiness, if only for a little while.

Tomorrow, she would think about how to say goodbye to him. How to forget the way he'd touched her heart even as he touched her body. But for tonight, she planned to cling to her third baseman for all he was worth, taking every ounce of pleasure she could find until the sun rose.

When she finally caught her breath, she kissed his shoulder and combed her hair off his chest.

"So tell me, slugger, how does it feel to hit one out of the park?"

4

THE WORDS KNIFED through Heath's euphoria like a one-hundred-mile-per-hour fastball coming at a man without a glove.

"What?" His hands slid away from Amber's shoulders, confusion fogging his brain.

Could it be a coincidence that she used a sports metaphor?

"You know." She gestured meaningfully toward their bodies where their legs were still entwined. "I don't know if you've got sexual superpowers or if that's normal for you, but...wow."

She smiled and his euphoria returned, relaxing his tense shoulders. He didn't doubt for a minute it had been fantastic between them.

"Right." Closing his eyes, he leaned deeper into the pillow, thinking he was comfortable enough he might spend the whole night here. "When you said 'hit it out of the park,' I—"

"You thought I was going to quiz you about your day job?" She reached behind her to tug a corner of the bedspread up over her shoulder.

Heath froze.

The blissed-out warmth he'd known a few moments ago dissipated.

"You knew who I was?" A lifetime of being sought after only for his wealth and fame gave the question more bite than he'd intended.

She must have heard it, because she quit tucking the spread around her and looked up at him. Her body tensed.

"Some big-deal third baseman, according to Rochelle. The friend who owns this house," she clarified. Then, as if to lighten the mood, she winked. "Why? Were you trying to keep it secret?"

He didn't know where to begin addressing that question. Had she targeted him from the minute she'd arrived? Or maybe she'd been content to meet some random player, clearly confusing him with Diego Estes. He didn't want to shuffle his view of her to accommodate that new information, far preferring his idea of her as sweet and awkward. Overtly brainy but quietly beautiful. But now, his whole perspective shifted.

"Oh, my God." Reaching for the bedspread again, she pulled it closer. "You really did want to keep it a secret."

The confusion in her voice didn't seem like an act. But damn. He'd been taken in by women who were only trying to get close to his job in the past. He wasn't in any position right now to read her motives.

He swiped his hand over his head, wishing he could wipe away the new ache that had started in his temples.

"It's no secret." Plenty of well-known personalities made trips to the islands off Cape Cod, so it was not as if he thought he was hiding. "But if you were trying to hook up with the third baseman, you got the wrong guy."

He was about as far from ladies' man Diego Estes as he could get. Grabbing his shirt, he got to his feet and pulled it on.

"I wasn't trying to *hook up* with anyone." Her voice was steely.

"What about *The Mating Season?*"

"Oh. Yes." That seemed to fluster her. "Well, I was trying to educate myself on the dating scene to help me meet people, but I certainly didn't set out to meet some big-deal ballplayer whose name means nothing to me anyway." She paused in the middle of the rant, sat up and yanked his socks out of his hand before he could put them on. "Wait a minute. Who are you if you don't play for the Aces?"

She looked so distressed at the idea he wasn't a major leaguer that it steeled any trace of regret at walking out on her. Memories of all the low-down tricks groupies had used to meet him came back with a vengeance—right down to the phone call a crazed lady fan had placed to his new wife, pretending to be his mistress. Anger burned hot in his gut as his brain lumped Amber into that category of tricksters.

Wrenching his socks back, he jammed them in his back pocket as he headed for the door.

"Instead of reading a book on how to meet guys, next time you ought to pick up a players' roster so you know who you're talking to." He paused to look at her, silhouetted against the bed with the moonlight as a backdrop. "I don't play for the Aces. I manage them."

Walking out of her bedroom, he didn't look back.

Heath had barely returned home when his cell phone started ringing.

He knew it couldn't be Amber since she didn't have his number. Furthermore, she probably didn't want to speak to him any more than he did to her. He'd been a little harsher than he'd intended.

Pulling the phone from his pants pocket, he saw the caller ID. Of all the freaking luck, it was Diego Estes, the Aces' third baseman that Amber had mistaken him for.

"Estes, dude, it's almost two in the morning."

"Is it that late already?" the kid shouted over music blaring in the background and the noise of a few hundred other hardcore partying types. "Sorry about that. I just wondered if you've seen my iPod. I think I left it at your beach house."

Heath had walked straight into the living room and turned on the television to distract him from thinking about Amber and how he'd rather be oblivious and in her bed than wise to her maneuvering and alone in his place.

"No sign of it, but I'll leave a note for the cleaning people and see if they find it when they come in."

"You okay, Skip?" The kid seemed to have found a quieter corner of the bar or party or wherever he was because the pulsing bass had decreased in the background.

It still made Heath feel a hundred years old to be called Skip, the traditional nickname for a team's manager in baseball. Wasn't he just the hotshot rookie a blink of an eye ago?

Having Amber mistake him for someone like Diego ticked him off, even though the guy was nice enough.

Estes had a world of problems of his own, and Heath was damn grateful to have escaped the worst of the groupie phase of his career unscathed.

"Yeah." Heath dropped onto a couch across from the TV, knowing he wouldn't be able to sleep for a while. "I just ran into a woman who thought I was you. Must be she knew you were staying here last week and somehow she got us confused. Too bad, because she seemed…"

He didn't finish the thought, knowing he shouldn't have this conversation with one of his players anyhow. Besides, how would he go about describing Amber? *Nice* didn't seem to cover it when she was sexy and straight-talking—or so he thought—and unexpectedly vulnerable.

"Was she hot?" In the background, Estes seemed to be waving off people who wanted to talk to him, their conversation interrupted by a muted "Not now." Then his attention seemed to return and he picked up where he left off. "You deserve someone totally hot, but someone with a good heart, too, Skip."

At twenty-three, Diego was older than a lot of rookies since they'd scouted him in the Caribbean where up-and-comers weren't involved in the baseball draft. Still, in the ways of the world, twenty-three was damn young, and in spite of the wise-sounding words Estes offered now, Heath knew the player had run aground in his own relationships.

"You think I'm taking dating advice from you, Estes?" Locker room gossip had it that Diego had been trying to get in touch with an ex-girlfriend back home in the Dominican Republic who'd dumped him before he came to the States a year and a half ago. Of course, there was a good chance she wouldn't want anything to do with a guy who had a huge female following and was frequently referred to as a ladies' man in the tabloids.

"Think what you want, but I know you shouldn't turn your back on the people who make you feel happy to be with them. That's too rare to give up for the insincere, fly-by-night types that surround us in this game."

Heath closed his eyes and pressed against the lids with his hands. His head hurt. And despite the anger he'd felt at Amber when he'd stomped out of her beach house full of righteous indignation, he felt regret flame to life.

"You there, Skip?" Estes prodded.

"I'm trying to decide if I'm just tired or if you're actually making sense." He was only giving the kid a hard time, since Heath hadn't been half as wise when he'd been twenty-three. Hell, he hadn't been half that smart when he'd gotten married and proved to be a supremely lousy husband.

The bark of laughter on the other end of the phone hinted at a dark bitterness.

"I had my heart gouged out with a spoon because I was too blind to recognize something good when I had it. Trust me when I tell you that I'm making sense." Estes muttered something about double-checking his car for his iPod and then he was gone—leaving Heath wondering what was going on between Diego and that ex-girlfriend of his to have the guy so turned around lately.

Diego's batting average had taken a nosedive in the last four games and Heath had hoped that the rest over the All-Star break combined with time at Heath's Nantucket place would straighten Estes out. But clearly, the player was still struggling with personal stuff.

Sad to think the twenty-three-year-old was giving *him* advice when it should be Heath helping his players wade through the challenges of playing in the big leagues. Was Estes right about not being so hard on people that made you happy? Heath flipped the channels on the television, thinking about how Amber hadn't really pursued him. Sure, she'd run into him at first, but then she'd disappeared into the crowd and had sought out privacy at a picnic table back at The Lighthouse. It wasn't as if she'd actively tried to hit on him.

He'd bought her the beer and invited himself to have a seat with her because she'd seemed down-to-earth. And yeah, maybe he'd kind of liked that she'd been totally unimpressed with him. So could he blame her now for not making a big deal about knowing his affiliation to baseball?

Thunking his head on the arm of the overstuffed sofa, he had the sinking sensation he'd been an ass to walk out on her earlier. He'd apologize tomorrow. Make it up to her somehow.

Because despite the fact that his career dreams were teetering on destruction as Estes's bat cooled off and the numbers in the loss column got higher, Heath had enjoyed himself tonight.

And that was the first time he could say that about any moment spent off the baseball field in a long, long time.

OF ALL THE NERVE.

Amber had repeated the phrase like a mantra to herself a few dozen times since Mr. Full of Himself had departed the night before. Now, she muttered it in between writing lines for the lone book review she'd promised to her editor during her vacation. A week off wasn't really a week off in her department these days.

She'd taken her laptop onto the patio of Rochelle's house, refusing to allow her conceited neighbor to think she was hiding from him after he'd walked out on her before the sheets were cold. Of course, the day's favorite phrase—*of all the nerve*—had the tendency to show up in her book review, insinuating itself into the text so that she had to keep going back and erasing it.

Honestly, where did the man get his arrogance? She'd refrained from calling Rochelle, preferring not to share the embarrassing details of her encounter with Heath. But part of her wanted to know more about him, if only to understand why he'd treated her the way he did.

He'd been kick-butt awesome one minute, making it his mission to prove to her she was a desirable woman worthy of sexual fulfillment. And when she remembered *that* Heath, she wanted to knock on his door and kiss him all over. But how could that same man turn so wretched the next moment, implying that she'd gone out hunting for a famous face?

"Amber?"

The sexy timbre of the familiar male voice rolled over her senses, making her aware of the new arrival on the other side of the patio railing.

She hadn't noticed his approach, but Heath stood there dripping wet from a morning swim, the rivulets of water running down washboard abs into soaking swim shorts.

"Amber?" she parroted, forcing her gaze back down

to her computer's screen. "Are you sure you know who I am? I could be hiding the fact that I'm a nuclear physicist or a genetics engineer. Oh, wait, those aren't superstars in your book. I'd only have to be subversive about my identity if I was a rock star or an athlete, right?"

She typed another line of her book review and ended up with *of all the nerve* in capital letters.

"I came to apologize if I was out of line last night." He leaned wet arms on the porch railing, putting his gorgeous, half-naked body far too close to hers.

"If?" She hit the delete key with too much force, pounding it over and over.

Too bad her life didn't come with a delete key. She'd have been tapping away at that sucker for months.

"I got to thinking about it last night after I got home and I realized I might have jumped to conclusions about your motivations."

Slamming her laptop closed, she gave him her full attention.

"You know, I purposely avoided you out here yesterday, not wanting to tangle with a man too far out of my league." The thought of it made her mad now. "As if your ability to hit a ball—or, I guess, tell someone *else* how to hit a ball—makes you any better than me. But I figured plenty of women come on to guys in your field so there was no sense in adding to your prodigious list of fans."

She stood, too irritated and—yes—hurt to have this conversation sitting still. Of course, hadn't she wanted to take a risk this week? To do something wild without considering every possible consequence?

She had to admit that Heath had helped her do just that. And he'd given her tremendous pleasure. Sure, the aftermath had stung. But at least she hadn't fallen for him first.

"You never mentioned that you knew who I was when I introduced myself." He seemed to have expected full disclosure on her part even though he'd waltzed into the bar last night throwing around an alias.

Didn't that seem just a touch hypocritical?

"It didn't occur to me you needed adulation for prancing around the baseball diamond in tight pants or sitting in a dugout spitting a wad of chew."

"I did already apologize," he reminded her, his jaw jutting forward with a stubborn tilt. "But I've been maneuvered and manipulated by groupies enough times that by now I—"

"You think I'm a *groupie?*" Any fear she had about growing tender feelings for this man vanished. She was so incensed she could hardly see straight.

"To be fair, you thought I was a Casanova young stud of a player." He stood toe to toe with her despite the railing in between them. "Maybe you thought I'd be an easy candidate for your full-court mating press."

His voice whispered along her senses despite the sting of the accusation. Incredibly, her body responded to his nearness, remembering all the ways he'd touched her the night before. All the ways he'd reassured her she was special. Worthy of his sole focus and attention to bring her to a place of total bliss.

"Looks like we both made some false assumptions." Her voice floated along on a breathless note, her skin tingling in spite of her brain's warning to bail.

"So why don't you let me make it up to you?" He edged his way around the railing to stand on the patio beside her. "I go back to work tonight now that my two-day suspension is over. We've got a home game against Chicago. Why don't you make use of my ticket allowance and see the game from behind home plate?"

She felt her jaw slide open, surprised at the offer.

"I don't know anything about baseball." Did he want to see her again? Or was he just trying to smooth over the fact that he'd sprinted from her bed?

"Obviously." He picked up the tail end of her braid and used the tip like a paintbrush to trail lightly over her shoulder. "Anyone who can't tell a manager from a player is clearly not a fan. But have you ever been to a game?"

Heath studied Amber's dark eyes, hoping for a clue about what was going on in her head. He wasn't sure why he'd invited her, knowing he couldn't afford distractions this season. But he'd been wrong to jump to conclusions about her and he honestly wanted to end this on a good note.

No matter that he wasn't in the market for a relationship, Amber Nichols was the most interesting woman to cross his path in a hell of long time. She deserved better than his disappearing act.

Especially given what he knew about her past—that some guy had tried to pass off his own shortcomings as hers. The notion still pissed him off.

"No. I've never set foot in a baseball stadium."

A fact that further demolished his theory that she was a groupie.

"So don't knock it until you've tried it."

She hugged her laptop to her chest, planting a bulky physical barrier between them.

"I don't know." Frowning, she turned to look out toward the water where a young couple played in the surf with a loping St. Bernard. "Wouldn't a groupie try to wrangle good seats out of you?"

"A good groupie would be too busy throwing herself at me to worry about tickets."

The tide crashed higher on the shore beside them, spraying a fine mist along her skin. She rolled her eyes, but couldn't stifle a grin.

"As enticing as it sounds, I'm afraid I'll have to pass. Rochelle was kind enough to share the beach house with me this week so I could stock up on R & R and I plan to do just that." She nodded toward a picnic basket teetering on the end of the patio table, a blanket and a bottle of wine poking out one side.

"What's more relaxing than a baseball game?" He couldn't imagine anybody turning down seats at one of the most fabled stadiums in the majors—except for a New York fan, maybe.

She bit her lip, and he felt a phantom brush of her teeth along his skin, half remembered from the night before. The sight sent a surge of longing through him.

"Come on," he urged, knowing now he'd been dead wrong about her only being interested in him for his money or his fame. He'd had to talk her into sleeping with him, for one thing. Now he had to talk her into a date. "Give me the chance to make it up to you for thinking you were a groupie."

Finally, she nodded.

"Okay," she agreed, though she sounded as wary as if he'd just invited her skydiving. "But I'm not sure how I can make it up to you for thinking you were a home-run-hitting superstar. Seems to me I was having more kind opinions of you than you were of me anyhow."

He knew she was teasing. She wouldn't have any

idea how tough it had been to leave his playing days behind and become a manager. Baseball had been the only thing that got him through the years after his mom died. The only thing that connected him to his father—a one-time pitcher for a west coast team who'd never married Heath's mother even after two kids together. Taking off the Aces' uniform after they'd had his last game had been a pain that didn't stop until he'd been hired back to manage the team. He'd only resigned himself to the gig since he was back in Boston blue and red.

Now he just needed to ensure this team played well enough to renew his contract. And with the pressure mounting from the higher-ups to turn the season around, that was going to be damn difficult.

"I'll figure out a way for you to make it up to me," he assured her, hiding how much the sport meant to him by distracting her with a quick kiss. Right over that plump lower lip that had taken his eye. "Game time is 7:00 p.m. and the tickets are at the Will Call window. If you stick around afterward, I'll give you the grand tour."

She looked dazed from the kiss, a thought that went a long way toward improving his mood. He didn't have any idea what he was doing by inviting her deeper into his world. All he knew was that after last night and the way she'd gotten under his skin, he wasn't ready to walk away yet.

5

"But I was supposed to walk away," Amber explained to Rochelle that night during the seventh-inning stretch at the Boston Aces' home game against the Chicago Flames.

Amber had coerced her friend into meeting at the stadium since Heath had left two tickets. Plus, Amber needed a cool-headed perspective on whatever was happening between her and the hot manager of the Boston team. Now, the former college roommates shared beers and a bag of peanuts after the Aces fell behind by a run. All around them, the crowd was on their feet singing about rooting for the home team. The night would have been really fun if she hadn't been a paranoid wreck about getting in over her head with a man who at this point was probably just being nice to her.

"I don't get it." Rochelle shook her head, long blond curls hopping around the shoulders of her shiny satin baseball jacket embroidered with the Aces logo from the seventies. "Why were you supposed to walk away? Who would ever suggest you ditch a hot guy like Heath?"

"Didn't I tell you about my plan for this week?" Amber hated throwing the peanut shells on the stadium floor, even though the rest of the fans seemed to. Instead, she balanced the box that had been their drink carrier on her lap and cracked them over the cardboard.

"I thought you wanted to meet someone." Rochelle cheered as the Aces came to bat and Diego Estes, the third baseman, warmed up his swing. She pointed to his photo as it flashed on the jumbo screen. "That's the guy who was staying at Heath's place when we were there last week."

Amber had to admit she never would have confused the young Latino with Heath if she kept track of the team at all. It was obvious the women went wild for Estes since the cheers took on a distinctly feminine sound.

"I did want to meet someone," Amber clarified, not wanting to talk about her mix-up the day before. "I also hoped to keep it uncomplicated and temporary. I don't need to romanticize every guy I get involved with, right?"

"You purposely sought out a one-night stand?" Rochelle's beer sloshed over the rim of the bottle as she whipped around to confront Amber.

"Well…" Hello, Awkwardness. "You encouraged me to have a wild affair, didn't you? I figured as long as the guy seemed game for a no-strings night, it wasn't a big deal."

Rochelle's eyes went as wide as her gold hoop earrings.

"You threw away your every cautious, careful instinct to have an affair just because that bozo Brent broke your heart?"

Amber appreciated her friend's concern—and her indignation on Amber's behalf. But she wasn't interested in bashing Brent so much as she wanted to move on. That meant figuring out what to do about Heath.

Shrugging, Amber washed down the last peanut just as the crack of a bat told her Diego had a hit. All around her, fans jumped to their feet and followed the progress of the ball toward the left field wall.

When the left fielder made a diving catch into that same wall, the fans fell back into their seats in unison with a communal wail of despair. As the next hitter came to the plate, Amber wondered how Heath was taking the catch in the dugout below. For now, however, she wanted to squeeze whatever wisdom she could from Rochelle about handling her upcoming sort-of date with Heath.

"I just want to see what it feels like to go out with someone without visions of happily-ever-after mucking it up for me. I've spent all my dating years either seriously involved or seriously single. I've never dated for fun."

"And you picked Heath Donovan for your 'fun' guy?" Rochelle toasted Amber with her beer. "He's hot, but he's also one of the most focused and intense coaches in the majors. Before that, he was one of the most focused and determined players. He's got a rep for being no-nonsense, even though my personal opinion is that he goes too easy on his veteran players."

The batter at the plate struck out, apparently, and the crowd erupted in booing at the umpire's call. Amber was more interested in what Rochelle had said about Heath being intense. It definitely might have been easier to keep things casual with a younger player—like she'd thought he'd been—but she wouldn't trade her night with Heath for one with another guy for anything in the world. She'd never felt anything close to the way he'd made her feel.

"Uh-oh." Rochelle clutched Amber's arm and pointed toward the home plate where Heath had made an appearance to speak to the umpire. "Heath got tossed from a game on the road three nights ago because he argued a strike three call too heatedly."

Amber watched him, the view from the front-row seats allowing her to see how good Heath looked in uniform. He wore a different jersey than his players—his shirt a navy V-neck with the team logo on one side as opposed to the buttoned vest over short sleeves that the team wore. But the gray baseball pants were just the same and—my—he sure wore them well.

"I've never dated a guy like that," Amber observed, as much to herself as to Rochelle. She really had no idea how to proceed.

No clue how to date just for fun, especially with a guy who was a no-B.S. straight shooter. He didn't seem to raise his voice with the ump, but he definitely got in the guy's face. Still, after he spoke his peace, he stalked back to the dugout without escalating the argument.

"Well, from where I'm sitting, he doesn't seem like the kind of guy who could do anything casually." Rochelle pulled out her phone to check an incoming text, probably an SOS from her husband who was home alone with their two small children. She popped the phone back in her bag and returned her attention to the game. "But maybe he'd be good for you since he's nothing like the guys you normally date."

"Nerdy professors?" Amber knew that was how Rochelle saw her taste in men. And Brent had taught a groundbreaking new style of psychotherapy at Yale.

"Cerebral types who spend too much time in their heads to know how to relate to people." Her friend zipped up her jacket and pulled her purse onto her shoulder. "I need to dash, Amber, but I think you'd be crazy not to at least see where this leads. Sometimes there's no predicting the people we're compatible with."

Or the people we lust after.

Amber couldn't help but acknowledge that with Heath, physical attraction came into play to a degree she wasn't used to. But she had no reason to think he was ready for anything more than a good time.

Amber kissed her friend's cheek and gave her a hug. "Thank you for coming and be careful heading home, okay?"

"You, too." Rochelle winked as she stood to leave. "But maybe you won't be heading home at all after the grand tour. Call me tomorrow, okay?"

Nodding, Amber waved goodbye and returned her attention to the eighth inning where the Aces' pitcher threw one strike after another to speed the game along. Nervousness set in about the night.

About Heath.

She had no idea what she was in for by spending more time with him. But as long as she kept her B.S. meter finely tuned and her heart out of the equation, she could afford to have a little fun. Couldn't she?

Getting into the spirit of the game as the Aces turned a double play, Amber congratulated herself on taking a risk. That had been one of her goals in this week all along. Now, the trick was not to get hurt.

"DID YOUR TWO-GAME suspension help you cool off, Donovan?" some snot-nosed young reporter asked Heath at the postgame press conference.

Heath had been fielding questions about his blow-up on the strike call throughout the conference, amazed at how many ways sports journalists could ask the same damn thing. He yanked his gaze off the young reporter who—honest to God—appeared to be texting his story notes into a phone the size of a postage stamp. Collecting his thoughts, Heath stared at the door at the back of the room while trying to formulate a spin-proof answer that communicated exactly nothing.

And who should walk through the rear exit but a slender brunette with a long braid snaking over one shoulder of a white blouse. A green and pink paisley skirt fit her narrow hips perfectly, calling attention to long, tanned legs.

He'd seen her in the stands during the game, but those brief glimpses hadn't been nearly enough to satisfy the hunger for her that had developed. He'd planned to meet her near the Aces' front office after the interview, but he'd forgotten that she would have media credentials as a book reviewer for Boston's biggest paper. She wouldn't have been admitted to the brief press meet and greet otherwise.

"I wouldn't say I cooled off during the two-game suspension," Heath answered finally, knowing his response wasn't watered down enough. But he had a tough time playing it safe when Amber was around. "I've always approached the game with fire and intensity, and that's what I bring to the dugout as a manager. I'm not going to apologize for how I run the team."

Amber's gaze met his over the heads of forty other journalists, her dark eyes registering an elemental response when he talked about fire and intensity. Even across a crowded room, he felt the connection to her, a connection that went beyond the physical and appealed to him on every level. He remembered how offended she'd been at the suggestion of being a groupie, her huffy denial as she'd banged the keys on her laptop.

"I'm afraid we've run out of time," Heath began his standard routine for retreat, ready to exit and see where tonight led with Amber. Had she come simply to smooth things over and part on good terms? Or was she feeling the same call to explore their attraction?

"But, Donovan," the young reporter with the cell phone piped up again, pressing forward in the crowd so that he was tougher to ignore, "with less than a full season remaining on your contract, are you at all concerned about what the message from the Aces' administration is when they told you not to come to the ballpark for the two games during the suspension?"

After almost twenty years in the majors in one capacity or another, Heath knew he ought to remember that sometimes a ball came in from left field when you were least expecting it. He'd thought he was sailing into home and *Bam!* he was dead at the plate thanks to a hell of an arm on this kid.

The room went silent. Even though every person present knew the kid was out of line, every last one of them couldn't wait to hear Heath's answer. Except for Amber, every damn one of the people in this room knew baseball was Heath's whole life. He'd never hid that fact.

"I want what the administration wants—to win games." Heath congratulated himself on the perfect blandness of the answer even though the kid had tapped into his biggest fear with a sledgehammer. "We will continue to work toward that shared goal."

Switching off the microphone, Heath stalked away from the platform as the room erupted in follow-up questions. Fortunately, a throng of shouted inquiries were easier to ignore than single, well-pointed questions in a quiet crowd.

Still, he had to walk through the reporters to get to Amber, and that made things a little stickier. By the time he reached her, she had the rear exit open and a paper plate full of pilfered munchies from the reception table in hand.

"Tough day at the office?" she whispered, offering him his choice of popcorn and peanuts.

"Damn vultures," he grumbled, keeping his head down to avoid any candid shots on his way out of the press room. "They circle and circle when they sniff out the least chance for blood." He took two cream puffs and steered her toward a bank of elevators, where he selected the last car. There, he inserted a key card to open the door.

"They are under a lot of pressure to produce stories that sell," Amber observed, taking in the Aces memorabilia on the walls all around them. "Their jobs depend on it."

He tugged her into the elevator cabin with him as a couple of reporters emerged from the press room.

"Don't tell me you're taking their side." He used his key card again inside to access their well-secured destination. "The media sharks are my mortal enemies."

"I thought that distinction was reserved for the New York Scrapers." She popped one last peanut in her mouth before taking a swig of cola and tossing the can.

"They're my enemy on the field. Off the field, it's the press." Heath couldn't avert his gaze from the glistening moisture on her lips. His finger gravitated to her mouth.

The softness of her beckoned, urging him to touch and taste, to linger and savor. But the doors slid open to reveal their destination, distracting them both.

"Oh!" Amber's eyes widened at the sight in front of them.

The owner's sky box was perched high in the Aces' state-of-the-art stadium, a sleek retreat with all the comforts of a five-star hotel room except that on one side, instead of a wall, there was floor-to-ceiling glass overlooking the field. Wide-screen televisions filled another wall, providing the room's occupants with additional views of the games in progress. But the most breathtaking feature was the live view from the best seats in the house.

"Come closer." He urged her forward, tugging her into the plush box situated to the right of home plate, just three stories up. "This is something to see."

"It's okay for us to be here?" She looked around as if fearing they'd be caught on security cameras or something.

"It's the team owner's box. He keeps it for his family and friends, but every now and then he gives me the green light to use it." Heath had gotten the idea of doling out his Nantucket beach house to players from seeing the way the team's owner—Bob Tarcher—shared the box with people he wanted to encourage or reward.

"Really?" She sounded surprised as she stepped deeper into the room, and approached the bank of glass. "Those reporters made it sound like the team wasn't very happy with you."

"Tarcher is in my court, but there are more opinions than his weighing in on whether or not I'll get to keep the managing job." He studied her face as she took in the view. "It's tough to coach in a city where you played, especially since I was a very visible, outspoken player."

"The prophet can't preach in his hometown?"

Not quite the metaphor he would have chosen. "I guess the locals know me a little too well. Or think they know me. I'm still paying for mistakes I made as a rookie player."

"The past definitely has a way of sticking with you," she mused, folding her arms as she tilted one shoulder into the glass wall and peered down.

"Speaking from experience?" He would be all too glad to deflect the talk from his precariously balanced career that could implode at any moment.

Besides, he realized he genuinely wanted to know more about her. He'd been so caught up in wanting her the night before that he hadn't really spent time delving deeper.

"Sort of." She pushed away from the glass to walk the perimeter of the room, her fingers gliding over the backs of plush gray couches. "I'm definitely pigeonholed in my job as the relentless fact-checker and hardcore book investigator."

"I thought you were a reviewer?" He watched as she admired the hardware on the kitchen cabinets.

"Me, too. But I uncovered a few holes in a celebrated writer's so-called autobiography and ever since my paper expects the same performance with every project I'm given. Authors hate it when they hear I'm reading their novel because they assume I'll be tearing it apart. And the sad thing is, I love books."

She rested a hip against the countertop and he couldn't help but remember what those same curves had felt like pressed against him.

"Are you under a lot of pressure at your job? Like the sports journalists?"

"I'm under a lot more pressure, actually. All the newspaper departments are struggling, but our readers love sports, so that section will always be a part of the paper. The books section isn't as much of a staple. So my job is a whole lot more dispensable." With one fingertip, she drew designs on the polished granite beside her. "In fact, half my department was cut six months ago. That's why I really needed the R & R this week. I've been doing the job of more than one person."

"It's impossible to keep up that kind of pace." He understood completely. "I tell my players that all the time. I send them to the beach house in Nantucket for the same reason you went. It's good to get away from everything."

He thought about her soaking up the sunshine on the patio the day before, slowly tanning those endlessly long legs. And it made him damn glad it had been him staying next door instead of any of his players.

"Maybe that's why your team wouldn't let you come to the ballpark for a couple of days," she suggested. "You needed to get away from it all, too."

He inched closer, needing to touch her.

"Well, if that's the case, it didn't work because I got too damn distracted along the way." Nearing her, he slowed his step, waiting to see how she responded.

"Too many groupies mobbing you wherever you go?" She arched an eyebrow, but there was no fire behind the question.

"No. Just one really interesting woman." He reached to stroke a finger along her chin, tilting her face to his. "But I'm thinking maybe we could take a little of that R & R together."

"I don't find you very relaxing," she admitted, though she didn't move away from his touch. "Exciting, maybe."

"I'd settle for being a welcome distraction." He threaded his fingers through the hair above her loose braid at the back of her neck.

He could feel the rapid beat of her heart there, and he liked knowing that she wanted him. She presented such a cool facade to the world, he might not have guessed that she responded to him this way without those cues.

"I'm not ready for anything serious." She blinked up at him with worried eyes, perhaps concerned that this would offend him. "I just want to be honest with you about that."

He sensed a wealth of nuance in her warning. A whole host of potential complications. But being with her had made him realize he needed a diversion this season more than ever. Amber Nichols could be the antidote to the intensity that had gotten him in hot water with the team before. She'd talk to him about book reviews instead of baseball.

And when they weren't talking? Even better.

"Sounds like a deal to me." Tugging gently on her braid, he tipped her head back. He sealed his mouth to hers in silent promise.

6

Heath had offered to fly them back to Nantucket tonight since he had access to a plane and a pilot's license.

It was one of many moments in the evening when Amber had been reminded she was in over her head. Heath had apparently already retired from one extremely lucrative career and now begun another. The spoils of that career were evident in everything from that vintage bike he'd driven on Nantucket to the splashy SUV he retrieved in the parking garage underneath the stadium. Instead of the private flight, she'd agreed to a late dinner at his place on the mainland.

They drove there now, south of Boston toward Cape Cod where he had a house on the water.

"So you have a home on the Cape *and* on Nantucket?" She couldn't imagine the cost. The brownstone she'd bought in Boston proper had nearly broke the bank, but she'd been so determined to own her own place, she'd managed. Then the economy tanked and she'd had to rent out half of it to keep up the mortgage payments. "You must really love the northeast. If I could afford two houses, I'd look at the Florida Keys or Costa Rica or something warmer."

He shifted gears as they exited the main road winding along the coast. Here, the scenery changed from T-shirt shops and big, family-style restaurants to more residential homes dotted with the occasional church or post office. An old-fashioned ice cream parlor was one of the few signs that resort towns lurked nearby. Cars still filled the big parking lot, and vacationers crowded around picnic tables even though it was shortly before midnight.

"Actually, the place on Nantucket has been in my family for a long time. It's a great spot because property is tough to come by on the island, but it's rare I make it out there. I'm usually at my apartment in Boston or the house on the Cape since they're both closer to the stadium."

"You had an apartment in town and yet you opted to drive all the way down here tonight?" She craned her neck to see the rest of a seaside mansion surrounded by trees.

There were no streetlamps now, only the occasional landscape lights around the looming homes.

"You'll like the house better." He pulled into a driveway and rolled down his window to punch in a security code for a tall, wrought-iron gate. "The condo is just a place to crash when I'm too tired to drive home."

As the gate slid open, Heath drove around a paved horseshoe to land in front of a sprawling white clapboard home perched on a bluff. On the side facing the driveway, two stories and a gabled roof presented a cozy exterior. But on either side of the home, stone steps led down to the shore side of the home, hinting at another level built into the hill. Already, Amber could hear the steady roll of waves off the Atlantic.

"Wow." She'd been to splashy publishing parties at places like this, but never as a private guest. "This is beautiful."

Not waiting for Heath to open the door, she let herself out of the SUV, ready to stretch her legs and get a closer peek at the house.

"Thanks." He joined her on the cobblestone path that snaked around the exterior, one hand landing in the middle of her back. "You want to check out the view?"

He led her toward the stone steps she spied, and she wondered if the home was so illuminated even when he was staying on Nantucket or traveling with the team. Lights dotted the flower beds of white hydrangeas and rhododendrons, making it easy to see her way down the wide, curving stairs to—

"Oh!" She gasped in delight as they reached the back courtyard where a table had been set outside on the cobblestones. Hurricane lamps sat on the table next to covered silver serving dishes. A filmy white canopy draped over a huge pergola, and purple lights filtered through the gossamer curtains, creating a magical setting for their dinner. Silver urns of fat white hydrangeas, alternating with large hurricane lamps, ringed the front of the bamboo table.

"I called a local caterer ahead of time," Heath explained, taking her hand and leading her to a seat. "I figured I owed you a nice dinner after I downed all the wings and ribs by myself last night."

In moments, he had the serving covers off the dishes and her plate filled with fresh seafood. Scallops and mussels, clams and a lobster tail competed for space alongside warm polenta and fat slices of tomato.

"It was delicious." Amber wrapped her fingers around the stem of her wineglass and tipped the dry pinot grigio to her lips.

She didn't mean just the food. The whole night had been perfect, from the scenic drive to the gorgeous house, to the ocean view. And while she appreciated every moment of an enchanted evening offered by a man who appealed to her senses even more than the opulent lifestyle, Amber couldn't imagine how she could keep things uncomplicated with this kind of treatment. Every facet of the night had been romantic. Sensual. The ocean air caressed her skin with teasing breezes while the wine hummed pleasantly through her veins. She would have to tread carefully.

"There's more where this came from." He shoved aside his plate to lean across the table, piercing her with a hot stare.

"I couldn't eat another bite," she protested, hating to waste so much as a single scallop.

"No. I mean, more of this." He gestured vaguely to everything around them. "More dinners. More skyboxes. More beautiful places."

Frowning, she set down the wine, needing to make sure she had a clear head for whatever he was suggesting.

"What do you mean?"

"Come on the road with me this week. We've got a series in L.A. starting the day after tomorrow and I'd like to have you with me."

CANDLELIGHT FLICKERED between them, the golden glow reflected in Amber's eyes as she struggled for words.

Clearly, he'd surprised the hell out of her. But what did it hurt to ask?

"Amber, I don't have a normal job. I'm all over the country most of the year. It's lonely. It's isolating. It'd be great to have some company for however long you're willing to travel."

"I have a job." She shook her head, leaning back from the table and out of the warm ring of candlelight. "I couldn't possibly tell my editor that I'm not coming in for another week after I've already taken a vacation."

"But your vacation isn't over yet, is it?" He could figure a way around her objections. After all, he'd courted some of the best new talent in the world, convincing talented players from all over to sign with the Aces instead of the other teams.

"No. But I only have three days left." She folded her arms, her white blouse a bright spot in the shadows.

"So come to L.A. for those three days and try out life on the road. I guarantee you the most relaxing, fun three days ever. But if you want to go back afterward, I'll be sure you're in town on time if I have to fly you myself."

"You have a team to coach. A position to protect. Won't it interfere with your work if I'm—"

Standing, he moved to her side of the table and drew her to her feet, needing to make his case with every weapon at his disposal. He slid his arms around her waist.

"I'm not connecting with some of the players on my team, and I'm beginning to think it's because I can only coach the way I played. Maybe I need to relax a little so they can, too. And bottom line, I can't relax thinking about winning most waking seconds." He palmed her back through the smooth cotton. "You have a way of making me think about other things."

She laid her hands on his shoulders, a light touch that reminded him he hadn't gotten to do half the things he wanted to with her last night.

"All I'm asking is for you to give it a try. And if you have as much fun as I think you might, well, we'll see where we stand after the three days are up."

"I could never stay longer than that with the demands of my job," she assured him, although he noticed she'd stepped closer and her hands had started to roam over his shoulders. His chest. "But if you can promise to have me back in time—"

He captured her words with a kiss, unable to hold back any longer. Besides, he wanted her to remember what he'd said, and this way, he'd punctuated the statement in a way she couldn't forget.

"I wanted to take you for a walk on the beach," he whispered between kisses, his fingers already untwining her braid. "Or for a swim."

He'd wanted their first real date to be unforgettable, so good that she couldn't ditch him at the end of her vacation. But he'd been patient for hours, inhaling the scent of her clean skin without touching her, listening to her hum with satisfaction while she ate. He couldn't wait to touch her another minute.

"I'd take this over the beach any day." She flexed her fingers against his chest, brushing her hand lower. Lower. "I was starting to think I only dreamed last night."

Drawing her backward, deeper into the courtyard toward the house, he fumbled in his pocket for the key, but found his caterer had left the doors unlocked.

"It was better than a dream." He turned away from her to flip on a light inside.

She closed the door behind them and stepped out of her shoes before she flung her arms around him.

"Last night was pretty amazing." She did some kind of dip and shimmy move with her hips that stroked him in all the right ways. By now, her hair had unraveled completely, the kinky waves spilling over both their shoulders.

"And that wasn't a fluke." He held her hand, stilling her long enough to ensure she got the message. "It's going to be like that every time between us."

She leaned into him.

"Prove it." Unmistakable challenge lit her eyes.

The fire inside him leaped higher. Hotter.

And Heath realized that in eight thousand square feet of house, there was no bedroom close enough.

With a growled oath, he backed her into the den off the kitchen. A sofa would have to suffice. Amber didn't seem to mind, her fingers raking off his shirt in record time. She rained kisses down his neck and over his shoulder, a soft shower of sweetness while her hands went to work on his belt.

Finally, they reached the couch and he lowered her onto the soft blue tapestry. The lights from the courtyard filtered in through the windows, allowing him to see how good she looked stretched out on his furniture. Her blouse had come partially unbuttoned, revealing a hint of a creamy lace cup hugging her breast. A gold necklace with three pearls slid into the vee of her cleavage. Her skirt hem dipped between her thighs, the line askew so that he could see more of one leg than the other.

"So beautiful." He dropped a kiss there, high on one thigh, just to make her think about it.

She shivered and made a sweet sound in the back of her throat, making him recalculate his whole approach. They had all night.

"Let me," she urged, reaching for the belt she hadn't finished removing.

Moving away so she couldn't complete the task, he unfastened the clasp himself.

"Close your eyes." He placed his palm over her eyelids. "Don't think. Just feel."

"I haven't had a thought in my head for hours," she assured him, her whole body wriggling and restless until he planted another kiss between her thighs.

A slow, thorough kiss.

Her breath caught. Held. Her legs tightened and braced against the couch. Then, within a few heartbeats, her limbs went limp and languid. He reached to unfasten the rest of the buttons on her blouse, easily popping open one after another while he inched higher up her body with his mouth.

He had just reached the hem of her skirt when the doorbell rang.

And rang.

Amber bolted upright, straightening clothes and tucking strands of hair.

"It's okay," he assured her, not in any mood to see who was on his front porch at one in the morning. "They'll go away when we don't answer."

Riiingg!

Whoever it was really laid on the bell, drawing out the chime for five times longer than normal.

"It sounds urgent." Amber skittered away from him

on the sofa. "I don't mind waiting while you see who it is."

As if he was in any condition to deal with company now.

"Shit." He indulged in the curse, feeling certain the situation warranted that and more. "I'll get rid of them, I promise."

If he only had a few days with Amber, he planned to make the most of them.

Riing!

"That's fine. Just, maybe, hurry." Amber handed him the shirt she'd torn off him earlier.

Grumbling and complaining all the while, he dragged his feet to give himself time to cool down. Heath elbowed his way into his shirt as he opened the door.

His third baseman, the notorious Diego Estes, stood on his front step. A black Mercedes coupe with a wrinkled front fender hissed in the driveway behind him.

"Thank God you're home, Skip." Diego ran a hand through hair that looked as if it had already been well raked. "I need a place to crash. I'm wrecked in more ways than one."

"Is anyone hurt?" A million ugly scenarios raced through his head.

"No." Estes shook his head, eyes widening briefly at the suggestion. "Of course not. I just forgot you had that damn security gate and I clipped the front of the thing before I put it in Reverse and punched in the code you gave me. As long as I don't have whiplash, no one's hurt."

Curses rose to Heath's lips as he thought about all the reasons why he should boot Estes off his team for pulling this kind of crap the night before the most important road trip of the season. Still, Heath reined it in because Estes was a five-tool player with an on-base percentage no one could deny.

"I have company, but if you just find a room and lock yourself in, I guess you can—"

"Hel-*lo*." Diego's eyes—even while under the influence and bleary from the demons that drove him—lit up at the sight of Amber.

Heath didn't need to turn around to feel her presence in the foyer behind him.

Just like that, he didn't feel so charitable toward his superstar guest, five-tool player or not. With Diego attempting a ludicrous once-over of Heath's woman, it made it damn easy to slam the door in his face.

"Forget it, Estes," Heath shouted through the oak barrier. "The pool house has a futon. You can crash there or I'll be on the phone to the cops so fast you can kiss your season goodbye."

Turning back to Amber, he was all too ready to take up where they'd left off. But the worried expression on her face suggested it wouldn't be as easy as returning to the den. For one, her concern nipped at his conscience, which informed him he needed to address this situation better.

"Shit." Opening the front door again, he let the third baseman in and hoped he could restrain from kicking his ass long enough to show Amber he wasn't such a bad guy.

No doubt about it, he was in for a crappy night.

7

"You're fortunate you didn't hurt anyone." Amber poured Diego a second cup of coffee the next morning, wondering how Heath coped with a team full of young guys with too much money, fame and opportunity to get into trouble. "Thank God the only thing damaged in all this is the car and Heath's gate."

After Heath had let Diego in last night, he'd admitted he had been drinking, but Amber didn't think he'd been over the legal limit. Still, riding around upset and nipping from a flask was idiotic and asking for trouble.

She'd retired early, finding a guest bedroom and giving Heath privacy to talk to his friend. Apparently, Diego had been in a tailspin after discovering his old girlfriend back in the Dominican Republic had given birth to his baby after their breakup. Amber hadn't figured out all the dynamics of that relationship, but she'd learned that much from Heath when he found her before dawn and carried her back to his bed. She'd been too tired to capitalize on his nearness, and they'd spend those few hours together sleeping.

Her wild affair wasn't exactly off to an auspicious start. But then, she still had the rest of her vacation and a trip to L.A. ahead.

Now, Diego hung his head over a heavy stoneware mug while he sat at the breakfast bar. His eyes were rimmed with red, and his thick, dark hair had seen better days. Even so, Diego Estes was a tremendously attractive sight. Not that she'd trade the raw sex appeal of Heath for an instant. But objectively speaking, she could see where Diego might earn a reputation as a ladies' man. She'd bet it hadn't required much effort on his part to gather flocks of female followers.

"Did Heath tell you what happened?" He didn't bother stirring in any sugar, but he clanged a spoon around the mug anyhow, clearly tired and out of sorts.

"He said you were upset because you found out that you missed the birth of your son." She found herself identifying with the jilted girlfriend back in his hometown and strove not to sound judgmental.

Amber's mother had been two-timed by her first husband for months. Amber hadn't even been more than eight or nine in the aftermath of that hellish time, but she recalled what it was like to see her mom's heart broken into a million little pieces.

"I didn't just miss his birth. I've missed—" He shook his head. "If I had known I was going to be a father, I would have been there," he vowed, pounding the counter with his fist. "My son is six weeks old, and I never even knew about him until I tried calling my ex-girlfriend and her mother picked up with a kid crying in the background. The mom told me about my son. Jasmine never even tried to let me know."

Amber slid the coffeepot back onto the hot plate, hoping Heath wouldn't mind that she'd made herself at home. Or at least started the java. His sleek granite and stainless steel kitchen wasn't exactly what she'd call homey. But Amber didn't have any way of getting home until Heath woke up. And Diego seemed as if he needed comfort. The guy sounded sincere. Hurt. She debated what to say as Heath entered the kitchen.

Hair slick from his shower and his jaw freshly shaven, he wore a suit without the jacket. Charcoal pants matched the coat he pitched onto a nearby chair. A blue silk tie had the Aces logo embroidered in the middle, accentuated by a silver tie clip.

Bearing little resemblance to the laid-back biker dude she'd met on Nantucket, Heath was all business today.

"Maybe Jasmine knew you would be there if she told you, and she didn't want you to walk away from baseball and resent her for it later." Heath skirted around the breakfast bar and came straight to her.

She caught a hint of spicy aftershave as he captured her waist and kissed her hard on the cheek.

Oh. Hormones flared to life. Thoughts of Diego's problems fled.

"Do you know that?" Diego was on his feet, apparently plenty interested in Heath's take on the situation. "Did you know about this kid when you recruited me?"

"Hell, no." Releasing her waist, Heath helped himself to coffee, not seeming to mind that she'd raided his cabinets to find the necessary items. "Just an educated guess. But I've been around athletes and their girlfriends long enough to have seen this happen before."

Amber would have never suspected that Heath spent his free time dealing with things like this and she wondered if other managers were a part of their players' lives this way. Or did he have a special relationship with Diego because he'd personally recruited him?

Slowly, Diego sank back into his chair. Amber collected the things she'd assembled to make eggs for the hungover Diego, but Heath shooed her away and passed his mug of coffee to her.

Nice. She smiled as she poured in the creamer, pleased to see her seriously rich new lover didn't need to have all his food catered.

"You have been in the game a long time, haven't you, Skip?" Diego used the nickname for a manager, she'd learned, though it sounded old-fashioned and quaint to Amber's ears. "And your dad played before you, right?"

Heath's father had been a ballplayer, too? Her mug hit the granite harder than she'd intended, sloshing a bit of coffee over the side as she contemplated what she was doing dating someone involved in a major league dynasty.

"Sorry," she murmured, hastily wiping up the excess with a napkin.

"Yes. My father pitched for the L.A. Stars." His words were clipped, but a hint of pride remained. "His jersey still hangs in the stadium. You'll see it tomorrow at the field."

"Really?" Amber wondered why Rochelle hadn't mentioned that. "Does that make you baseball royalty?"

She said it to tease him, but he didn't crack a smile as he broke the eggs over a frying pan.

"He didn't acknowledge me until after I was drafted. He never married my mom."

Heath tapped one shell after another until the pan was full, focusing all his attention on breakfast. But

Amber had been forced to share the story of her own family history enough times to know you didn't spill those details without an answering spear of pain.

Diego seemed oblivious, though, still stirring black coffee. "Maybe your mom was like Jasmine. She wanted your dad to have his career."

"Could be," Heath agreed easily enough, retrieving plates from an overhead cabinet. "Families make sacrifices all the time to see their own go pro. You can fly Jasmine and your son up here to spend time with them, but don't blow it for them and mess up the career. You've got a hell of a lot to be proud of, and so do they."

Amber soaked in the import of that advice while Diego accepted a plate full of eggs.

The two men moved on to discussing their chance of a win in L.A. and Amber used the time to think about what Heath had said. Did he speak from experience and a real desire to reassure Diego? Or was Heath's main goal just to retain a successful player on his roster? He certainly had reason to want the team's best hitter focused on his game.

But she hated to think Heath would ever suggest one of his players ignore a son in favor of making a name for himself in the big leagues.

Not that she planned on getting caught up in Heath's life. She was just here for the road trip and the fun. Relaxation and romance.

Right?

"Amber?"

Heath's voice filtered through the worries chasing around her brain.

"Yes?" She realized she hadn't touched the plate he'd put in front of her.

"When you're ready, I'll run you back home so you can pick up some things for the trip." He studied her curiously over his coffee cup.

"That would be great." It would give her a last chance to back out if she discovered Heath was the kind of manager who told his players whatever they needed to hear in order to show up at the park every day.

And if not? If Heath really walked the walk of a child left behind by a father too famous and important to be bothered by his own progeny? She would have far too much in common with her hot baseball manager lover.

She was screwed either way. So far, she was down in the count for keeping things light and uncomplicated.

HE'D BEEN AN IDIOT.

Diego dove into the pool behind his manager's house, taking advantage of the cold, clean water to clear out his head.

He hadn't just used poor judgment last night, when he'd been tipping a flask of Wild Turkey to drown the pain of discovering he had a son he'd never known about. That ranked high on the idiocy scale. Diego had been operating on diminished gray matter since he'd left Jasmine behind to pursue his career in the States. He'd been home once ten months ago, and there'd been that one time they'd caved to the heat that always flared between them. That must have been when she'd gotten pregnant.

He flipped underwater and pushed off the side of the pool, holding his breath while he swam the length of the in-ground monstrosity again.

He'd loved Jasmine. But they were young, and their

dreams were so different. She wanted to work with kids who'd grown up in at-risk communities—the places where they'd come from. He couldn't wait to get out of there and live the good life. Why couldn't she understand that with the money he pulled down here, he could buy her a whole damn center to take care of those kids? He wished Jasmine understood there were different ways to help out—that he wasn't turning his back on the people at home. Sure, she was trying to show kids how to have a better life—but so was he.

His lungs burned as he started his third lap of the pool, his oxygen-starved blood making him lightheaded. Enlightened. Because sure enough, he saw now he wasn't living the good life alone in the States, hounded by females who didn't care about him half as much as they cared about the houses, clothes and cars that his kind of income could buy.

He broke through the surface of the water, gasping and spluttering but never breaking pace as his arms pinwheeled around for one stroke after another. Jasmine had just been smarter than him. She hadn't dumped him a year ago because she was jealous of his soon-to-be fame or because she was trying to give him an ultimatum about staying with her. She'd simply known what she wanted and known that she didn't need a fat bank account to be happy.

Or to make their kid happy.

Hell, maybe Jasmine had saved their son from being raised by a loser who still kept a flask of Wild Turkey around like some kind of high-school kid.

Screw. That.

Diego pushed himself deep under the water again,

but this time he opened his eyes to see what was in front of him.

Baseball wouldn't be there for him if he kept up the hitting slump. But Jasmine and his kid—Alex, she'd named him—would be a part of him forever, no matter what.

He wasn't going to mess around with his life anymore, now that he knew what he had to do. He would call her tonight and ask for another chance.

"HOLY COW." Heath took two steps into Amber's Boston apartment and wondered what he was getting into. "Don't tell me you've read all these."

Books filled every conceivable inch of the space. Built-in shelves butted up against furniture racks so that the walls looked as if they were covered with spines for wallpaper. The whole place was bright, though. She must have covered her collection in paper jackets of her own making because all the spines were mostly white with brightly colored strips in the center where the title and author went. All the white books with red strips were grouped together. Then white with yellow. White with green. Between the books a few odds and ends were stashed to break up the marching rows—a striped hat box, a ceramic cow, a fat gold ship's bell.

"I've probably read about half from cover to cover. A quarter I've used for reference and the rest are all on a growing list of things I'd like to read."

Amber had already disappeared somewhere in the apartment, her voice raised enough for him to follow the direction of it. He wound around an old-fashioned tea cart to catch a glimpse of her in a room that looked like a bedroom with an office on one side. No, more like a library with a desk and a bed.

"I didn't fully appreciate what it meant to be a book reviewer." He ran a finger along a few of the titles, admiring the paper jackets, which were all pale yellow in this room. "Is there some significance to the color coding?"

"It's my nod to the Dewey Decimal System without having to broadcast the numbers." She pulled open a closet door and emerged with a suitcase. "I know the greens are bios. Yellow is history, and so on. But there aren't many books here that are related to my reviewing work. Sadly, this is the extent of my personal entertainment most days."

"Not this week, it's not." He'd been dying to get her alone ever since their date had been busted up by Diego's appearance the night before. He cornered her by the closet. "You've got me and you've got baseball to keep you entertained. Very much in that order."

He cupped her shoulders, slowing down her brisk movement around the room. Not until then—when it took her a long moment to say anything—did he realize she hadn't said much on the ride over here today.

"Can I ask you a question?" She didn't relax into his touch, putting him on guard.

"Have you changed your mind about this week?" He suddenly recognized that he wanted her to accompany him with a fierceness that surprised the hell out of him.

"No." The tension didn't leave her shoulders. "I just wondered about what you said to Diego at breakfast. That stuff about your dad."

In the same way one player's anxiety about a game could affect a whole locker room, Amber's tension was now his own. But he'd dodged this kind of thing from reporters for years. He had no intention of trotting out anything more than the status quo. His time with Amber was supposed to be about de-stressing, not confronting skeletons in the closet.

"Fire away." He forced his voice into that easy, trust-me octave that could convince the press—and his rivals—that a star player's injury was nothing serious.

Sometimes being a manager meant being a master of spin.

"Did you let Diego think you had something in common with him to make him feel better? Or do you honestly believe his playing career made it okay that you were ignored by your father?"

Heath blinked. Processing.

He was pretty sure his trust-me expression had frozen onto his features.

"Wow. I forgot what a straight shooter you are." He'd never met a woman like her. Direct. Forthcoming. No games.

Hell, he didn't know if he could match that uncompromising honesty. And he'd been worried about her playing him to get near a star? The idea had become so ludicrous to him in the past twenty-four hours that he wondered how he'd ever dreamed it up in the first place.

"I don't mean to pry." She backpedalled, no doubt sensing she'd stepped in over her head. "I was just blown away to think you could forgive a father for something like that, but then again I really hated to think you'd say that to Diego just to—"

"Don't even finish the thought." He lowered himself onto her bed beside the suitcase she'd placed there. "I would never concoct a story to manipulate my guys like that. I might hype up Boston to get them to play for me, and I might talk up east coast women like they're the hottest to ever walk the earth to tempt the holdouts. But I'd never be dishonest with them."

She moved toward a dresser tucked between two bookshelves and opened the drawers, top to bottom, pulling out shorts and tank tops. The sight cheered him, assuring him that he would have her all to himself tonight.

"I should have known." She tossed the assortment of cotton in the suitcase and stepped closer to him. "You were good to Diego last night, letting him have a place to stay. And you must have been trying to help him out last week by giving him some time at the Nantucket house."

"It's tough for the young guys. Everybody wants something from them. They don't know who to trust. Most of the people they meet only want access to a lifestyle. So they romanticize old relationships because at least before they made it big, they knew they were involved with people who genuinely cared about them."

"And you can relate because you've been there." Amber wrapped her hand around his.

He wanted to pull her into his lap and hold her there, but he knew the moment called for some nod to her original question about his father.

"Relating to the players is a big part of the job. But I don't bring up the topic of my dad too often since I don't like being compared to him. I still don't see him all that much, but I forgave him a long time ago for ditching the parenting role. There are some people who do more damage than good by hanging around."

She frowned and he sensed that comment only stirred up more questions on her part. Damn it. Maybe they weren't going to be able to keep things simple between them, after all.

But then her expression cleared and she nodded thoughtfully.

"Okay. One last question before I finish packing." She pinned him with a level stare and he wondered what she could fire his way next. Something about his screwed-up childhood? His failing career?

He steeled himself.

"What I really want to know is—and be honest—do you think it makes me less of a nerd if I told you I read wearing—" she dug into a drawer and shook out a tiny scrap of lace and satin that blew his mind "—nothing but this?"

8

Maybe Amber had been a coward to back down from the conversation that would have helped her understand Heath better.

But by the relief in his eyes when she'd let him off the hook made her feel as if she'd just given him a Christmas present. She enjoyed making him happy. She still couldn't believe she had that power over this sexy man.

He tugged her closer until she stood between his legs where he sat on her bed. His suntanned skin made him look like a swarthy, stubble-faced pirate on a sea of white chenille. He slipped the satin merry widow from her fingers and let it fall to the bed, all his focus on her.

"You'd be sexy wearing anything. And it's not the books that run the risk of making you nerdy." A grin teased his lips as he bracketed her waist in his hands. "It's the fact that you dressed them all up in matching outfits like paper dolls."

His fingers slid under her blouse to palm her bare spine. She liked fitting there, between his thighs, warm and safe and teasing. In fact, she liked everything about the man and the moment, including the knowledge that he seemed to want her as much as she really, really wanted him.

"I'll have you know that my volumes will last longer because of those book jackets." She steadied herself against him, bracing her hands on his shoulders as he tipped her forward, closer.

"Face it, Amber. Color coding your book covers is treading strongly into obsessive-compulsive terrain." His hands spanned her ribs and skimmed upward, higher, until he cupped her breasts in his palms.

Pleasurable shivers arced through her, heating her blood and reminding her what sex had been like with him the first time. How generous he'd been. How he'd made her feel special when she'd been flat-out afraid of failure.

"I'll stick with nerdy, thanks. And at least here we don't have third basemen ringing the doorbell to interrupt."

A fortunate thing, because she really wanted to see where this would lead. Her heart skipped and started a jerky rhythm as Heath eased the cups of her bra down. Capturing the taut peaks of her breasts between his fingers, he rolled the tips against his knuckles. His eyes never left her face, cataloging her expression and response.

Could he tell that he made her insides melt?

"You make a good point. Because if the phone rings or someone knocks on the door now, I'd really like to ignore them." He released her long enough to unhook the bra and tumble her down to the bed with him. Over him.

"Lucky for you, reviewing so many books every month seriously cuts into my social time. My friends don't ever come around to try to drag me out of the house anymore." She also didn't usually have a hot man in her bed that made her feel beautiful.

But this week was all about pushing out of her comfort zone.

"Lucky for you, I think book reviewers are really hot." He tugged her blouse off, whipping it across the room as if it had been a frustrating impediment to the breasts he now kissed and licked.

He didn't rush, even with a plane to catch in a couple of hours. Instead, he flipped her to her back and nudged her suitcase off the bed with his toes.

"It's a blast being lucky," she murmured, her eyelashes falling to half-mast with the instinct to shut out everything but what Heath made her feel. She couldn't close them completely, though, not with the temptation of peeking at Heath's hard, honed body.

What an incredible-looking man. She had never taken the time to salivate over athletes on television before. First, because she didn't really watch sports, or much TV for that matter. Second, because she'd unfairly stereotyped athletes as jocks who were more interested in bodies than brains.

And while that hadn't turned out to be true with Heath—clearly he appreciated her brain or he wouldn't have asked her to spend more time with him—she had to admit that she'd begun to see the appeal of raw male muscle.

It was so much more than the ability to swing a bat or run fast. It represented a dedication to excellence that she'd never thought about before. Plus, just the feel of that sinewy strength pressed against her body put her halfway to orgasmic.

Now, he unfastened her jeans and peered up at her with a dark, sexy stare that made her smolder.

"No more thinking," he reminded her, just the way he had the last time he sent her careening into sensual bliss.

For a woman who'd built a career on thought and words, she had to smile at the dictate. It warmed her heart that he would remember her hang-up and caution her to avoid it.

"My brain is blank." She closed her eyes now, settling the restless churn of thoughts so she could concentrate on just this moment.

He cradled her cheek and skimmed a thumb along her jaw.

"You can still look at me." His voice in her ear startled her eyes open as much as the words. "I like your eyes on me."

They connected in that moment. Amber felt the jolt as their gazes met. Locked. Whereas two nights ago had been all about want, need and desire, another element awakened just then to add to the mix of emotions.

Amber could not analyze it, though. Heath had succeeded in stripping her down to her panties, and he palmed the warmth between her legs through the white silk.

She gasped at the feel of him there, her mouth falling open while her pulse throbbed fast against his hand.

"That's better," he crooned, encouraging her with soft words as his fingers played over her sensitive flesh.

She clutched his shoulders, knowing if she could keep him there—right there—she would be spiraling off into bliss in no time.

HEATH LIKED THE BITE of Amber's short nails in his skin, the soft sting against his back telling him that she was long past thinking and ready to feel.

He'd remembered that part from the last time he'd been able to touch her. Take her. She'd been thoughtful and still for a while, and then something had hit a switch for her and she'd lost herself to the moment so fully that he'd hardly recognized his brainy, cerebral lover.

The nails in his shoulder told him she'd arrived at that place now, and he felt like a few million bucks to know he could do that for her. It made holding back so damn worthwhile. He'd been ready for her since the previous night, so ready that he would have gladly jumped her the second they'd walked through her apartment door. But he'd waited and—damn—payback was sweet.

The soft cries in his ear were like Morse code for what she wanted, the notes higher and sweeter when she was getting close to the edge. He could have brought her there quickly, her body hot and wet and very ready for him.

But he drew out the pleasure to make it last for her. When she teetered too close to that sensual precipice, he allowed his fingers to wander away and tug her panties off. Or trace a damp pattern with her wetness along the inside of her thigh.

"Heath." She flexed her fingers against his shoulder, her thigh hitching higher along the outside of his leg. "I'm so close. So—"

A low moan trembled through her. Everything remained suspended for a long moment. Then her cry filled the room, drowning out the soft whir of a ceiling fan overhead.

He held her tighter, absorbing the shock waves that rocked her body inside and out, anchoring her through the pleasure. He wanted his scent on her body and his voice in her ear when she came. If he only had these days with her, he would imprint himself on her so thoroughly she would never forget.

When the tremors eased, he released her enough to retrieve a condom from the pocket of his jacket that he'd tossed on the pillow.

"I'll do it." Amber surprised him by snatching the wrapper from his hand. Then, she seemed to second-guess herself. "Can I?"

Rolling onto his back, he gave her room to work. Her cheeks were still flushed from the orgasm, her dark hair slipping free from the tight braid so that she looked like a sweet, sexy mess.

"I'm yours to do with as you see fit." His blood ran hot and his cock had been stiff for hours. "But you might want to be, uh, no-nonsense in your approach. I'm loaded and ready."

Her gaze flashed to his and he could see the nervous excitement there.

"I'll try not to get too distracted." She had the wrapper off and prophylactic in hand. Her gaze dipped southward toward his boxers, erected like a damn circus tent. "But it might not be easy."

She might as well have stroked him with her tongue. His cock stirred and throbbed. Seeming to sense the urgency, she worked to free him from the boxers. Still, by the time she rolled the condom on, he had no choice but to take charge again before he lost it all over her.

He thrust deep, burying himself inside her. Then stayed there for a long moment to collect himself. Sweat popped along his forehead and his back, the effort of holding back rapidly catching up to him. He bracketed her shoulders with his hands in the bedspread, levering himself above her to find the right angle that would take her to that sensual ledge all over again. This time, she seemed to know what she wanted, wrapping her legs around his hips and lifting to meet each thrust.

As he followed the song of her gasps and moans, he didn't let go until he heard that high, keening note in her throat. Only then did he move as deep, as hard and as fast as he wanted, chasing that perfect pleasure until it steamrolled him.

Bliss filled his veins like an illicit drug, a heady rush that bowled him over and made his blood boil. It was a union as un-freaking-real as anything he'd ever felt in his life.

He had no business getting involved. No right to bring a woman on the most important road trip of his life.

Furthermore, the brainy reviewer and the driven athlete made no sense together.

But no matter that nothing added up. He couldn't wait to have this woman all to himself.

9

AMBER HANDED HER champagne glass to the flight attendant on her way off the plane with regret, thinking she could get used to flying first-class.

Hitching her bag on her shoulder, she followed a few men in suits who'd sat in front of her on the commercial flight, winding through the jetway and into the concourse. Heath had apologized for not being able to seat her on the team's chartered aircraft, explaining that he could only bring the team, the trainers and Aces' staffers on board. But he'd meet her at LAX as soon as her plane landed since they got in at the same time.

No skin off her nose. She'd never experienced the luxury of a seat on an airline that left her room to cross her legs and served her peanuts before anyone else even got on board. She couldn't imagine what a first-class seat reserved just hours in advance must have cost. Probably enough to pay her mortgage for a month. Possibly two.

Her cell phone buzzed in the pocket of her long linen shorts and she pulled it out to answer as she dodged two little boys chasing each other while engaged in a swordfight with paper straws.

"I'm never flying coach again," she answered,

knowing Heath would be on the other end, looking for her.

She stood on her toes to try to see him ahead of her as she rode the escalator down to the exits for ground transportation.

"Amber?" The voice in her ear was not the low, sexy growl she thought it would be.

In fact, just then she spotted Heath waiting for her by the doors, just as he'd promised. And he didn't have a cell phone in his hand.

"Brent?" Her forward progress slowed. Halted.

A woman behind her bumped into her and then went around with a muttered oath about cell phones being the work of the devil.

"Where are you?" her ex-boyfriend asked, not bothering to answer her question.

And well, duh, she recognized his voice just from hearing him say her name. How many weeks had she gone hoping he'd give her a call and see the error of his ways, if only so she could tell him to taking a flying leap off a short building?

"I just touched down in L.A." She didn't tell him to make her life sound exciting—it hadn't been until two days ago—but so he wouldn't fret. One thing she'd credit Brent with was that even if he thought she was an Arctic breeze in the bedroom, he would still worry about her if she refused to tell him where she was. "I'm meeting some friends."

Up ahead, Heath appeared concerned. He started toward her as she ducked out of the rush of humanity toward the exits. Her butt hit the wall of free phones for local hotels.

"You're in Los Angeles?" He didn't sound relieved

to know where she was. "Your paper is on hard times, your section might get scrapped, your job is in jeopardy and yet you found time to make a run for the Pacific? What the hell are you doing there?"

She straightened, not appreciating his tone one bit.

"I'm sure it's no concern of yours," she told him coolly, half wishing she'd told him she couldn't talk because she was in bed with her new lover. Her eyes went to Heath, who was only a few steps away now. "What did you want, Brent? I'm really busy."

"I'm sorry." His tone was conciliatory. "I emailed you a couple of days ago to see if you had time to talk. When I hadn't heard back—"

"You hoped to talk?" She wished that sentiment didn't make her feel like a wrung-out washcloth, but it did. "Doesn't that fall into the too-little-too-late category?"

She wanted to hang up on him. Truly, she did. Heath stood beside her with his overwhelming sexiness and his thoughtful concern for her, having paid a boatload to transport her here for a few days. But how could she cut Brent off at the knees when Heath would vacate her life and leave her with the Brents of the world?

As much as she resented Brent personally, she owed it to herself to try to recognize what went wrong with him. That way, she would do better the next time when she—inevitably—ended up with that same type of quiet, practical, steady guy.

"I just need to see you, okay? I need to explain about some of the things that happened. Will you call me when you get back in town?"

Her eyes slid to Heath, who tugged her rolling suitcase out of the path of pedestrians. He withdrew his cell and made a quick call of his own.

Damn it, she wouldn't waste Heath's time or hers talking to someone who'd already tossed her aside.

"I'll think about it. But I have to go now."

With a muttered goodbye, he was gone. Leaving Amber confused and a little off her game. She needed to relax. Play. Enjoy a man who only wanted a good time.

"Is everything okay?" Heath asked her, shoving his own phone back into his pocket. "I asked the cab to wait, but if you have things you need to take care of, I can let him go."

"No." Flustered, she gripped the handle of her suitcase and jammed her phone into an exterior pocket, not wanting to answer it again for a long time. "My flight was great and I'm ready to be with you."

Heath took her suitcase from her and nodded toward the double doors ahead to indicate they should get moving.

"Is that because you are totally enamored with me? Or because Brent was too little too late?"

"All of the above." She wasn't surprised he'd overheard. And she had nothing to hide.

"You want to talk about it?" He held the door for her even though he was the one with all the bags.

She had to admire the chivalry.

"There's not much to talk about. We dated for nine months and I thought we had carved out an intelligent, balanced relationship. He thought I had the emotional quotient of a computer. End of story."

She slid into the cab he indicated, waiting inside while he gave the bags to the driver. Palm trees and the pastel walls of a nearby parking tower told her they were in California. Otherwise, the airport hummed with the same kind of traffic as any other major hub. Hotel and rental car shuttles vied for the best position near the curb while airport security motioned cars and people to where they belonged.

Eighties tunes played on the cab's radio, but the young driver turned down the music when he got into the car. Heath directed him to a hotel and they were on their way, cocooned in semiprivacy with the plastic divider closed and cabbie singing along to The Bangles.

"I only picked up the phone, by the way, because I figured it would be you looking for me," she explained, feeling awkward about the whole business.

Brent had no right to butt into her life after he'd told her they needed time apart. No, after he'd dumped her.

"You don't believe in caller ID?" Heath asked, picking up her hand where it lay on the seat between them and folding it into his own.

She warmed to his touch. To him. How was it she found him so easy to talk to when she'd been reticent around guys her whole life? She made a mental note to try to find out if he had any secret nerdy tendencies—that might help explain her feeling more at home around him even though she didn't know about them.

"I was anxious to tell you how cool it was to fly first-class so I just answered the phone and blurted that out, thinking it had to be you on the other end."

He laughed as the cab pulled out of the final airport exit and out onto a highway that was massive even by Boston standards.

"I'm sorry that wasn't me on the phone. I would

have liked to have had that conversation with you." His eyes told her that he would like a lot of other things with her, too.

A flutter started in her chest, her breath catching. How did he make her think about getting horizontal with him without even trying?

"I don't act like myself around you," she admitted, having lost most of the filters that usually helped her navigate conversation with men. "Usually I check caller ID. I check email. I measure my words. I overthink things. With you I'm really shooting from the hip and I'm not sure why."

The cab wove through three lanes, dodging and darting around traffic so that she scooted closer to Heath. If they got into an accident, she'd prefer to have her body ejected near his.

"Vacation romance, maybe. That's why the kids have so much fun on spring break, I hear." He pointed out the Hollywood sign up on a hill.

"Maybe." She wasn't sure at all. "I would have never even considered a vacation fling until recently. Usually, my vacations in the past meant I read for pleasure instead of work."

"You're a real wild woman, Amber." He released her hand to tug on her braid.

"You see my point? I'm so totally not. I would have thought I'd be terrified to be with someone famous and accomplished—"

"Let me stop you right there." His hand fell to her thigh, and he nudged her whole body to face him. "I'm a divorced, washed-up player trying like hell to stay in the majors. There's a good chance they'll boot my butt out the door before the season even ends. I'm just trying to give it one last battle, all the while knowing I need to prepare myself somehow if it all falls apart."

Flashes of that intensity Rochelle had talked about glittered hard in his eyes. He really saw himself that way. *A washed-up player.*

"That's your secret nerdiness." She should have seen it all along.

"What?" He looked at her as if she'd sprouted an extra head.

"Sorry. I just had been thinking earlier that maybe I relate to you because you have some nerdiness of your own stashed away in that gorgeous exterior. You know how I'm a book dweeb with my matching dust jackets? Well, you're not exactly a devil-may-care, swing-for-the-fences kind of baseball player that saunters in for his five minutes of fame and retires on a fat salary to write a book. You're a baseball nerd. This sport means everything to you."

Heath told himself she was babbling. That her light-bulb moment in the back of the cab was cockamamy B.S. and the only reason they really related was hot sex.

But the longer the words rolled around in his head, the more he wondered if she had a point. Not that he could truly speak to the reason she liked him.

And she did—he could tell by the way she moved closer to him whenever he was near. The way her eyes would find him in a crowd with unerring speed, drawn to him as powerfully as his gaze was to her.

No, he wasn't sure what had made his brainy book reviewer notice him instead of some professor type who knew all about the ancient dance of gender politics and the assorted think-y stuff that interested her.

But he knew she had a point about his lifelong fascination with baseball. He'd never played the sport like a mere *game*. For him—corny as it sounded—baseball was poetry and a philosophy. An approach to life. It colored his perspective of everything from how he read the newspaper (box scores first) to how he interpreted the weather (rainy years in the Caribbean meant less practice for future prospects and possibly a worse crop of players).

Other guys played the game. They passed through the sport year in and year out, going on to do other things after they left the majors. Heath had adopted a way of life where the world only gave you so many strikeouts. A bad day at bat meant hours in the cage to straighten out your swing.

That was why he couldn't mess up his last stand as a manager. He had to stay in the sport because it was the only place where life made sense to him. He understood the rules. And somehow, being with Amber while he led his shaky team through a key series felt like the right thing to do. Before he'd met her, he'd gotten ejected from a game because he'd been so damn tense, and that wasn't serving the greater needs of an uneasy young team that needed leadership. His veteran players were letting him down in that department, so he probably needed to step up and be more of a hardass with the younger kids. Basically, he had to have his head together. And Amber made him feel more level than he'd been in a long time.

"I think we're here," she pointed out, nodding toward the old-school Beverly Hills hotel that would house the whole team for the next few days. "Sorry if I was out of line about the baseball thing. I'm sure you couldn't be nerdy if you tried."

She bit her lip and didn't try too hard to hide a smile. Ragging on him again.

God, she was a handful. He couldn't imagine what this wisecracking, honest, sexy woman had ever seen in the stodgy, idiotic Brent back home. She seemed to have opened her eyes, though. She was here with him in L.A. instead of listening to Mr. Intellectual catalog faults she didn't have.

If nothing else came of this road stand, Heath planned to make damn sure Amber Nichols knew her own worth. He was just the man to show her how irresistible she was.

10

"Oh, my God, that's Heath Donovan."

The same phrase, with minor adjustments, was whispered, squealed and hyperventilated throughout the upscale Beverly Hills hotel lobby. Amber must have heard it a dozen times already and they hadn't even hit the elevator bank yet.

She'd been so busy preparing herself for the new experience of vacationing with a hot guy just for fun—a wild and utterly new venture for her—that she hadn't thought to steel herself for the scores of female fans eyeing Heath.

As they wheeled bags toward the elevator banks, their room keys already in hand thanks to the advance legwork of the travel administrator, women of all ages paused to swoon. Amber knew they weren't just looking at Heath. Diego and the rest of the team caught a fair share of admiring stares. But Heath was still a star in his own right, his playing days not so far behind him that he didn't have a fan following in the lobby. One woman grabbed her girlfriend's arm and jumped up and down in high heels with the friend's shoulder for leverage, panting, "Heath, Heath, Heath, oh, my God, it's Heath," as they walked by. Amber tensed, debating ducking and running for cover, but Heath gave a terse nod and shouldered right through the crowd, letting one of the team's assistants deflect the attention.

When Amber and her famous companion entered the elevator, the doors closing them into semiprivacy with the catcher Brody Davis and pitching sensation Jay Cannon, she had to give herself a shake to call back reality.

"You guys have shown me what it means to be invisible," she announced to no one in particular, surprised not one of them mentioned the hubbub they'd caused. "You would think people in L.A., of all places, would be accustomed to seeing a few famous faces."

"My wife used to try to smuggle me through a back door when she traveled with me," the catcher admitted, grinning. "But somewhere along the line she decided she'd rather tattoo herself to my side and march me through the front to make sure the women of the world know I'm taken."

The gold band around his left ring finger glinted in the fluorescent light as he held the elevator door for someone hopping on the lift on the third floor.

"I don't even hear it," the pitcher joined in, pulling free the earbuds he wore, the sound of Metallica evident even four feet away from him. "My dad says to keep your head in the game, not in the fame."

He tucked the buds back in, and Heath nodded affirmation.

"Wise man."

He didn't say any more, however, leaving her in the dark about how he reacted to his apparent legions of admirers.

On the sixth floor, the players piled out with their

bags. Heath reminded them to be at the ballpark early the next day and then hit the button to put them up one floor higher. Amber remained silent in the interim since a teenage boy rode with them. At their floor, she stepped into the hall and a new wave of nerves assailed her as she took in the wide hallways of the elegant, Italian Renaissance-themed hotel.

What did she think she was doing with this famous, sought-after man whose career took him all over the country, where women threw themselves at him?

Up until now, she'd avoided those fears since she hadn't fully appreciated how much of a total woman-magnet he was. But old insecurities ran deep, tied up with fears of being abandoned, fears of letting anyone get too close.

She could simply not afford to grow attached to Heath. As long as she kept her head screwed on straight, she'd be okay.

She hoped she'd be okay.

Heath had opened the door by now and he held it for her, revealing a suite that had probably been featured in world-class travel magazines. The living area where they entered was big enough to host a basketball game. A wide, white stone chimney housed a giant flat-screen television above the hearth. A uniquely arranged bouquet of exotic flowers graced a coffee table near a basket of fruit.

"I'm panicking." She hated to be a downer, but she figured she might as well cop to the truth since they had a nice honesty thing going between them and she didn't want to blow it now for the sake of an ego that wasn't all that rock-solid anyway. "The women, the perks, the first-class… I didn't really comprehend the lifestyle even though I knew it intellectually."

Heath set down the suitcases and drew her purse off her arm to set it on a nearby stand. Divested of baggage, he took her shoulders in his hands and looked her in the eye. His Italian silk suit and understated tie bore little resemblance to the T-shirt and jeans he'd been wearing at the bar where they met. French cuffs bore links engraved with the Aces' logo and a number. His old player number?

Not in a million years would she have risked talking to him if he'd looked like this when they first met.

"We are overpaid and overprivileged," he told her. "It's not right that a man can make more than the Gross National Product of a Third World country just because he can throw a hundred-mile-an-hour fastball or hit off a left-handed pitcher. But that's the reality of the game and the value other people place on a narrow skill set. It doesn't make sense, and I know that."

"You do?" She hadn't expected him to tackle the issue head-on—and with such a self-deprecating perspective—but there it was. Groundedness. Maturity. "I can see why you make a really good manager. I'll bet it's healthy for your players to be reminded of that sometimes because this—" she gestured to the well-appointed room "—could go to people's heads."

"It can and does. And, yeah, I like to think I bring some hard-won wisdom to that dugout, but unfortunately, it takes a hell of a lot more than that to be a successful manager."

The panic eased, her worries seeming kind of superficial next to his. He really wanted this job to work, really needed it to, from what he'd explained in the cab. For him, baseball wasn't about the groupies—damn it, she of all people should know that. It meant everything to him.

"You really think you'll only get this one season to prove yourself?" She would have hated to work in a field where you had so little time to grow your talent.

"Most definitely." His hands smoothed over her shoulder and then moved lightly down her back, as if he could rub out the rest of her nervousness and transition her to another level, a tension deliciously different from the stress she'd been feeling. "The sport has the potential for big earnings, but it only rewards the smallest fraction of a percent who are at the top of their game."

"Sounds stressful."

"It takes a lot of competitive drive." His fingers rode down her spine in soft circles until she swayed closer. But then, his massage faltered and she felt him tense. "It cost me my marriage."

She straightened, curious. He'd mentioned being divorced that first night in the bar, but she hadn't been paying much attention. At the time, she'd just been relieved to know he wasn't married, given how they'd been flirting.

"What happened?" She didn't want to think about him caving to the temptations of the road. She could only imagine how aggressive the women would have been back in his playing days if they were this assertive now when he walked through a lobby with another female on his arm.

"Too much time apart. I had to be away for eighty-one games a year in twenty-six or twenty-seven different cities, give or take. Add to that the travel days to get there and back, plus sometimes heading straight from one city to another for a long stretch on the road." He shrugged and the helpless gesture made him look less like the slick manager and more like a normal guy just as confused as anyone else about how to hash out a relationship.

"She didn't want to travel with you?"

"It was too much time on the road for her. The season starts when pitchers and catchers report to spring training in the middle of February. Then, if you make the playoffs, you're playing into November. Basically, by the time I was done, she was so fed up we hardly talked over the holidays."

"That would wear on a relationship." And, not that Amber would dare to ever think about Heath in those terms, it would devastate someone like her who would always worry about infidelity and being left behind. Her own father had checked out on her, for crying out loud. What reason would she have to trust a boyfriend?

That was why she tended to go for men who approached relationships intellectually. She figured guys who looked at commitment through rational, practical eyes would be more likely to stay for the long haul.

"It did. Big-time." Heath shook his head and seemed to will away bad memories. "But I don't want to bring you down. That's been over for three years and I don't have feelings for her anymore other than regret. Besides, I brought you here to have fun."

She nodded, wondering how to separate the baggage from his past and his fame from their time together. Heck, she had a tough enough time untangling herself from Brent, apparently, since he was still calling. Not to mention, her feelings for Heath grew more complicated by the hour.

"It was all good while I was still operating under the champagne buzz from the airline service in first-class." She'd only been focused on the fun side of her impulsive decision to come with him then. Now, she felt her tendency to overthink things creeping back into her head.

"I'll bet you I can bring the buzz back." He brushed a kiss along her forehead, and the contact spurred several ideas for her.

She couldn't help but appreciate how easily he could make her whirlwind of thoughts grind to a feel-good stop. Her hands landed on the hard plank of his chest, the muscles honed from a lifetime of athleticism. She would take him at his word about what he wanted and not let anything else get in the way, damn it.

"I think I'm already humming pleasantly inside, now that you mention it."

"No more panic?" His lips hovered close to her face and she debated how best to put them in contact with her skin again.

"No. I think I hurdled past the panic to the realization that I'm alone in a hotel room with a man who holds the key to my orgasmic potential."

"Too bad I hadn't planned this better or I would have capitalized on that state of mind." He eased back, giving her time to process what his words meant.

"No quickie against the door?"

His eyes widened a fraction and she realized how much she enjoyed keeping him on his toes.

"I'm not saying no, but I did schedule a massage for you while I attend a meeting with the trainers." He checked his watch as if considering how long it would take to have her against the door.

And while she squirmed happily at the picture that painted, she was also intrigued by the alternative.

"A massage?"

"The hot stone workup is great here, but ask them for whatever you want. I figured it was the least I can do for hauling you across the country when you wanted to relax this week."

"You don't owe me anything," she protested, peering toward the window out onto a terrace with a view up Rodeo Drive. "I haven't taken a trip farther than Nantucket in years, so just being here is a treat. But tell me this—what's your meeting about?"

She was having a hard time envisioning the full scope of his responsibilities, and his work intrigued her. He wasn't just getting paid for hitting a ball with a bat, the way she'd teased him once. She'd seen him exchange words with some of his team members back in the lobby earlier, and it struck her that Heath must have his hands full keeping that many young hotshots on track. Besides the obvious problems inherent in dealing with rookies who might be away from home for the first time and suddenly raking in millions, Heath also had to cope with the logistics of the different languages spoken in the dugout. Besides English and a few different Spanish hybrids from the Dominicans, Mexicans and so on, there was a pitching ace from Japan who couldn't communicate with any of them. Had to be tough to build team chemistry, let alone give your basic pregame pep talk.

"We need to revisit the workouts for some of our guys on the disabled list and see if we can figure out a way to keep Diego in the training room instead of on the phone with Jasmine every day. I'm really worried about him—his batting average has taken a nosedive the past two weeks, and I know he's going to be in a tailspin if he gets cut from the team."

"It's that serious?" She remembered the fans whooping it up for the third baseman at the stadium and couldn't imagine him disappearing from the game. But maybe it wasn't so rare for someone to screw up the chance of a lifetime.

Heath picked up the room keys off the dresser and gave one to her while putting the other in his pocket.

"It's like a disease in the dugout and it's infecting more players every day. Diego's swing is off, and it throws off the guy behind him in the lineup who now needs a big hit and not just a single. We're down by a few hits each game, and the pitchers start getting antsy, thinking they have to win the games with defense because the offense isn't producing. But aside from the way one guy's problems play out in a game, the effects are worse in the locker room." Heath shook his head, clearly frustrated.

"How so?"

"Diego's girlfriend had a baby and the news gets passed around the players and their girlfriends and wives. There's some jealousy from the wives who have been wanting to start families but their men have put it off because of their careers. Other players see the hell Diego is going through and bust up with their girlfriends because they've been struggling to make their relationships work, and seeing Diego get the crap kicked out of him by life only makes them more wary about getting involved. None of them want to screw up their careers."

"You guys really live in each other's back pockets that much?" It sounded more like a dysfunctional family than a team. Although they did spend a lot of time together, Amber supposed. The bonds would be tight.

"We're like a travelling fraternity." Heath checked his watch and pulled her in for a kiss. "We spend more time together than we do apart. If you ever spent three hours in a rain delay before a four-hour game, you'd know that it makes you damn close to the people waiting out the storm in that dugout with you. Good or bad, you know each other's business."

The visual created a concrete image for her and Amber thought she understood a little better. This *was* Heath's family, maybe more than the real genetic deal had been. No wonder he didn't want Diego to lose his spot on the team. He was one of Heath's own. And—to take it a step further—how crappy would it feel to get booted from your own family?

It was the position Heath sat in as much as Diego. One more reason why Heath surely fought to keep the player in the game. Knowing that about him—that he would work hard to help someone who was struggling—touched her.

"Good luck at the meeting." Winding her arms around his neck, she leaned in for a last kiss. "I'll see you back here later and you can make up for the quickie against the door."

His muscles flexed in the most interesting places in response.

"You're on." He growled the words against her ear, his mouth dipping to the sensitive place just below there to brush a kiss. "Be thinking about me when you get that massage, okay? Know that I wish it could be my hands all over you."

She tilted her head to one side to give him full access to her neck, her breath catching at the idea of stripping down and letting Heath feel her everywhere…

"Amber? Will you do that for me? Picture my hands on your hips when you're getting touched here." His palms drifted down to the curve of her waist and then edged lower. Lower. "And here."

"Mmm," she agreed, ready to shed her clothes here and now. How could he ramp up the heat between them so fast? If she'd ever felt like this with Brent, she would have known she wasn't cold.

Then again, maybe the problem had been that Brent had left her cold and she'd been too stubbornly determined to make a rational match that she hadn't seen that.

With one final kiss on her hungry lips, Heath turned and sauntered out the door into the hallway. She was so hot and bothered she slumped into a boneless mass against the back of the sofa. Flustered and breathless, she hugged her arms about her waist, holding the feeling tight.

For the first time, she realized that saying goodbye to Heath at the end of the week would be more difficult than she'd ever guessed.

11

DIEGO ESTES KNEW BETTER than to hit the hotel bar.

Even as a rookie, he had an identifiable face and people tended to recognize him. Normally, he didn't mind the attention. Hell, he'd risen from the slums of the Dominican Republic to become a highly paid athlete. He still couldn't believe his good fortune to have a gift for baseball. He'd been a skinny, gawky kid with zero interest in sports, but his father had made him try out for a team when he was twelve.

Somewhere in between his old man shouting expletives from the stands and his new coach quietly explaining how to crank back his bat for the most power, Diego had fallen in love with the game. And not just because his father quit yelling for the few hours a week when Diego connected with one pitch after another. No, Diego liked baseball because it was a way he could stay out of the gangs, yet have a brotherhood all his own. The toughest gangs he'd ever run across in the D.R. still liked baseball. Being on a team had saved Diego in a lot of ways.

He sat in the juice bar at the hotel spa, a place where a few women might hit on him, but a place where he wouldn't be recognized. At least not at a hotel in L.A.

On the east coast, he might not get away with it, but in the Midwest or the west coast, the women who frequented the spa weren't expecting to meet a ballplayer downing carrot juice with ginseng. The spa towel partially draped over his head as if he were in between aromatherapy treatments helped, of course. Moving incognito through a spa was a cakewalk.

"Diego?"

The feminine voice behind him, therefore, surprised him.

Turning, he found Amber Nichols, the manager's new girlfriend. The skipper hadn't revealed much about the woman when Diego had shown up at his place the other night, but Diego had eyes. He knew Donovan was seriously hot for her.

"Hi." He gestured to the row of vacant chairs beside him and hoped the skip wouldn't castrate him if he bought her a drink. "Want to join me? I seem to be the only one in town feeling the carrot ginseng special."

"Actually—" she peered over her shoulder toward the reception desk just visible in the next room "—I do have a few minutes before my appointment."

She climbed onto the stool next to him, her long, dark braid swinging around her shoulder to brush against his. She was the kind of pretty you saw in a soap commercial. Nice skin. No makeup. A smile like she was happy inside and not trying to play head games with you.

Right now, he could really appreciate the appeal of that kind of woman.

"Any luck with Jasmine?" She pointed to the cell phone in his palm and he wondered what Donovan made of her pull-no-punches approach.

The Aces' manager wasn't exactly the kind of guy who spilled his guts for snickers and giggles.

"Nah." He couldn't even think about Jasmine without his heart going into a stop, drop and roll routine as if it sensed the need to protect itself. That shit hurt every time. "I think she's screening her calls for me. I tried from the hotel phone, too, but she must know the team is in L.A. this week." He ordered another carrot smoothie special for Amber from a spa employee who did double duty as the juice bartender and spa greeter.

Taking her drink, Amber thanked him and passed him her cell phone.

"Why don't you try calling her from mine?" She sipped the dark orange concoction experimentally. "I've got great international rates on my phone plan."

"She probably wouldn't pick up for any Boston-based number. Maybe she wouldn't pick up if I called from anywhere in the whole damn U.S."

Amber set down both the phone and her glass.

"Okay, that's way too defeatist of an attitude. First of all, she's got to talk to you sooner or later because you have a legal right to see your child." She tapped an unpolished fingernail against the smooth granite bar top. "Plus, she needs to know you want to see her and work this out, so you need to call her, her family and her friends until she gets that message. If she doesn't want anything to do with you after that, you can work out some custody with the courts, but at least you'll know you did everything you could."

She blinked at him with an earnest expression on her face and the sincerity in her voice made him feel that she knew what she was talking about. At least she had a better approach than he did, which had mostly been to drunk-dial Jasmine and tell her how much he missed her.

But maybe he didn't need to win her over to see his kid. Maybe, like Amber said, they could work out something for his son whether they were together or not.

"I don't know. I think she just flat-out hates my guts." He slumped on the juice bar, wondering where the hell his confidence had gone the past two weeks. But when even his baseball skills were in the crapper—the one thing he'd always counted on to pull him through whatever life doled out—he had to question himself.

"Get real. She had your child. She'll always be connected to you." Amber drummed her nails on the bar. "Think about it from her perspective. She's taking care of business back home while you're playing baseball for legions of adoring female fans and living it up in fancy hotels. All the groupies could give any woman a complex."

"You think?"

"Imagine how you would feel if you saw twenty guys swarm your woman for an autograph."

Diego pounded the bar and both their glasses rattled. Damn, he hated that picture.

"You talk some sense, you know that?" He took Amber's cell and dialed Jasmine's digits, thinking he could find her sister's number somewhere if she didn't answer. That sister had never liked him, but damn it, even she had to see the wisdom of letting a kid know his father.

Even if they thought he'd screw up the paternal thing, they'd have to appreciate the child care funds he wanted to contribute. His kid wasn't going to end up in a gang.

All his arguments and rationalizing disappeared, however, when Jasmine's voice answered on the other end.

"Diego, I know it's you. You can't call me every ten minutes. This phone ringing all night is going to make me lose my mind." She wasn't yelling, exactly. But it wasn't the warmest greeting he'd ever received.

Still, he enjoyed hearing the husky briskness of her voice, a voice that had whispered some really amazing things in his ear when they'd made love once upon a time. She'd always made him feel like a million bucks—long before baseball had ponied up the cash.

"Don't hang up. I need to talk to you." He tucked his head against the bar to shut out the sound of the smoothie machine mixing up a drink nearby; he didn't have to worry about Amber hearing anything because she'd already discreetly excused herself.

She hadn't even asked about getting her phone back.

For the first time in two weeks, Diego felt that he wasn't drowning in his own life. He knew he couldn't think about baseball until he had his personal stuff resolved.

On the other end of the phone, Jasmine hadn't said a word. For all he knew, she'd set the handset down and left him there to talk himself hoarse. But in the background, he heard the trill and coo of an infant and his heart puddled up inside.

"Jasmine, even if you don't want anything more to do with me, we need to at least work out something for our son's sake."

He held his breath, hoping she was there somewhere,

listening. The soft sigh he finally heard might have been heavy with resignation, but after weeks of silence, it seemed like sweet music in his ears.

"Okay. But I've only got a few minutes before Alex needs a bath."

THE HOTEL ROOM was dark when Heath returned.

He'd checked out of the training meeting early, hoping to catch a glimpse of Amber in a towel down in the spa. Visions of her half-naked in the middle of a rubdown had plagued him so bad he hadn't been able to focus. But when he'd arrived in the spa, the director said she'd already been there and left, skipping out on her scheduled appointment with profuse apologies.

She didn't seem to be lying in wait for him in the hotel room, either. He hoped she would leap out at him from a darkened corner to demand her quickie against the door, but she was nowhere to be found.

When his phone rang, he expected to see her number on his caller ID. Instead, the illuminated digits belonged to his boss back in Boston. Or at least, one of his bosses. Although the team was owned jointly by several companies and individuals, the guy with the controlling share had hired him and—should the need ever arise—would be the one tasked with firing him, as well. Heath's blood temperature dropped about twenty degrees in two seconds.

"Heath Donovan," he answered, knowing Bob Tarcher III rarely made his own calls anyhow. Usually an administrative assistant contacted Heath or, if Bob needed to talk to him, the assistant got Heath on the line first.

"Heath, this is Bob. You have a minute?"

Shit. The big kahuna dialing him directly. Heath's gut sank like a high fly ball dropping in centerfield.

"Sure. Just finishing up a meeting with the trainers to evaluate some workouts. We're working with the hitting coach to see if there's anything we can tweak in Estes's swing." Might as well be straightforward about the team weaknesses. They'd been obvious enough to fans and sportswriters around the country. Thankfully, no reporters had found out about Estes's problems back home. Media glare always made that stuff worse.

"Good, good." Bob cleared his throat. "I'm calling to—hell, I don't want to be making this call at all, Heath. You know I've been behind you ever since Jeff Rally retired. But you're taking over for one of the most storied managers in baseball history. Of course that's going to invite unfair comparisons."

Heath was pretty sure his knees buckled. Something damn well buckled, because he found himself holding on to the wall like a drunkard making his way to the bar bathroom. He shook his head to clear it.

"You're axing me?" He'd been an assistant coach for one season and the manager for less than that.

"Not today, Heath. But the board met earlier in the week and they're coming down on me hard about the recent losses. You know with your inexperience, you were a controversial pick. I can only fight for you for so long."

He so did not need this now.

"Look, I appreciate the warning. Really. But I can't play every game like the guillotine is about to fall or I'm not going to build a stable foundation here." He couldn't fix Estes's problems overnight any more than he could tell the rest of the clubhouse not to worry about them. "We're dealing with some personal stuff as a team and I'm trying to help these kids, but they're young and they're rough and they don't need instability. They need consistency and help navigating rough waters."

Pulling him out of the head slot would only send the guys reeling that much more. Not that he was such a great manager. But he was a known entity at a time when the club was really struggling to find their identity. Cohesiveness.

"Right. And I agree. I just wanted to let you know to do everything you can do to win this road stand. If you can win in L.A., I think it will buy us the rest of the season without the board breathing down our necks."

Heath shook his head. Clearly, Bob had already struck a bargain with the other owners—if the Aces won on the west coast Heath would have the team for the remainder of the season.

"Understood." Not that he liked it one damn bit. How much more pressure could he put on these guys? "But I guess I'd better get back to work if I'm going to make that happen."

They disconnected as Heath slumped down into the hotel couch, his brain turning backflips to try to figure out what he could do differently for tomorrow's game when his heart told him he shouldn't rattle the team any more. What he really wanted—needed—right now was to see Amber so he could quiet the useless second-guessing in his head. He'd never met anyone else who could divert him from baseball as well as she could. Sadly, that list included his ex-wife who had been so passionate about her job that she'd tended to get as thoroughly lost in her work as he did in his. Drawn together because they understood one another's drive, they'd quickly grown apart because their strong interests didn't leave enough time for each other.

Heath dialed Amber's cell phone, hoping that wherever she was, she could be here soon.

He damn near had a heart attack when a male voice answered her phone.

"Where's Amber?" he barked, heart slamming in his chest as if he was ready to break into a fist fight.

All that tension churning in his gut had just found an outlet.

"Skip?" the voice on the other end responded, sounding confused and appropriately wary.

He recognized the voice. The light accent.

Steam hissed from Heath's ears as he considered the implication of Diego Estes having Amber's phone. They were together? He told himself not to jump to conclusions, but life had been so damn adversarial with him lately, that proved tough to do.

"Yes," he answered tightly, slipping off his necktie before it strangled him. "Put her on the phone now."

"Whoa." Estes tried to take the laid-back approach. "Relax. Amber let me borrow her phone to call Jasmine, but your girlfriend took off before I could give it back. She left a message for me with the guy behind the juice counter at the spa before she left, though. She told him she was going to some college library. I guess she wanted me to let you know that if you called her phone."

A library? Frowning, Heath rose to his feet and strode back to the entryway of the suite. Turning on the light there, he saw a note on a stand near the basket of fresh fruit:

Had a lightbulb moment in regard to your team and went on a run to the college library on the UCLA campus, which stays open late. Come join me or else I'll be back when it closes.

P.S. I let Diego borrow my phone to call the mother of his child and apparent love of his life.

P.P.S. You're not off the hook with the quickie.

The storm inside him eased as he read the note. Amber wasn't having a secret tryst with the third baseman. Duh. Although that twist of momentary anxiety and fury made him better appreciate how hard it had been for his ex-wife to deal with his fame and all the women it brought across his path. Jealousy sucked.

"Right. Sorry, man," Heath replied lamely, knowing his fear had been obvious in his voice when he'd asked for Amber. But damn it, the call from the team owner had screwed with his head. "I'm going to find her. Just drop off her phone at the front desk, okay?"

"Sure thing, Skip. She really helped me out today, you know? I think I've got Jasmine actually considering making a trip up here."

Estes sounded happy. Excited. And somehow Amber had a hand in that. Was it possible that Estes's game would improve tomorrow because the guy had turned some kind of corner on his personal problems?

"I'm glad for you, man. Get to bed though, okay? Big game tomorrow and I'm counting on you."

"Right, boss. One thing, though. You ever have a girlfriend ditch you for a trip to the library before?" Estes cracked himself up with that one before he cackled out a goodbye and hung up.

Guy was in too damn a good mood, something that

hadn't happened in weeks. Heath, meanwhile, was already in the elevator and on his way down to the lobby to call a cab. He wasn't missing out on Amber for the sake of her books.

He'd been jealous to think of her with anyone else when Diego had picked up her phone. Now, all that possessiveness and the stress from the day needed an outlet.

But, oddly, he realized he wasn't just anxious to see her because he wanted to give her that massage she'd missed with his own two hands. He was also curious as hell about what she'd told Estes and what was so all-fired urgent that she needed to visit the local book mecca at nine o'clock at night.

Her note suggested she had a thought about the team.

Even though he couldn't imagine her books could provide the answers to his young team's myriad problems, he appreciated that she wanted to help save his career from going down in flames when this road trip ended.

12

A COPY MACHINE HUMMED in the background while Amber worked in the library on the UCLA campus. The sound blended with the soft whir of an excellent ventilation system that kept the books in the stacks in optimal condition. The murmur of muted study group conversations drifted occasionally to her ears. Now and then, these comforting sounds that were the same in libraries everywhere were interrupted by the high giggle or squeal of some female in the stacks.

Again, totally normal. Apparently the semiprivate nature of the floor-to-ceiling bookshelves provided enticing opportunities for grab-and-grope games on a universal basis.

It was the giggling that distracted her, reminding her that she could have stayed at the hotel and enjoyed even more private games with Heath. She only had him for such a short amount of time. What was she doing wasting precious hours with her nose in books, just like that night they'd met?

She knew the answer and didn't want to face the truth.

She was falling for Heath in spite of numerous reasons that told her it was a very bad idea. They'd only just met. He'd admitted to being bad long-term material by way of the marriage that didn't work out and his easy agreement to keep their relationship on a temporary basis. His work demanded so much from him that he had no time—or made no time—for anything else. Even if that hadn't been the case, his job would always present endless temptation in the form of female fans. How could she ever handle that with her deep-seated insecurity issues? She'd drive him away with worrying.

Then there was her job, which wasn't all that stable, either. The list went on so long she'd drive herself crazy thinking this to pieces—

"There you are."

Heath's voice sliced through the anxiety, scattering her thoughts and drawing her focus to the here and now. He strode down the aisle of tables tucked between the shelves of the biography section.

Eyes focused, jaw muscles flexed, he had looked just this same way that night she'd seen him stalk out to home plate to speak to an umpire. He appeared determined. Intense.

Ready to have his way.

A happy shiver trembled over her skin. Even knowing that being with him could be harmful to her heart, she couldn't fight the desire to take whatever happiness she could squeeze out of these few days.

"Hi." She felt breathless. Awkward.

Another muffled giggle that emanated from the rows of book nearby made heat suffuse her cheeks.

Heath didn't seem aware of the sound, however. His attention veered toward the books scattered around her. He turned two of the volumes so that the covers faced him.

"Red Auerbach. John Wooden." He turned more covers. "You've got coaching books from every sport here. Everything from NHL great Lester Patrick to baseball's own one-line king, Yogi Berra. Does this have to do with your lightbulb moment?"

"I—" She took a deep breath, willing away the strong attraction she now realized was rooted in more than the physical. As much as she'd like to hide in a hotel room with Heath for days on end, she also wanted to help him. "I could be way off base here, and you know my baseball knowledge is zilch. But I ran into Diego at the spa today."

She launched into a retelling of their conversation about the third baseman's girlfriend while Heath dropped into the seat next to her. His expression remained thoughtful, considering. Which seemed nice, given how far she'd tread out on a limb to offer an opinion on the baseball world.

"So, call me crazy," she continued, holding a high-school football coach's memoir close to her chest, "but I thought I'd go to the source for the best wisdom out there on how to develop team chemistry and motivate players. It seems like that can help win games when you've already got the necessary talent in place."

"You researched all this stuff for me?" He thumbed idly through a book of motivational quotes taken from coaches of every conceivable sport.

Amber couldn't tell if he thought she was simply being nerdy again, or if he was feeling that she'd stepped on his toes by trying to research something he'd devoted his life to. Then again, maybe he didn't think either of those things and he would see beyond the books to a depth of caring about him that she hadn't meant to reveal.

Hastily, she began stacking the resources to diminish the visual impact of the umpteen volumes scattered everywhere.

"I'm a bookworm. It's what I do." Too late, she realized her actions had uncovered a legal pad full of notes in longhand.

Amber Nichols, geek extraordinaire.

Heath's hand darted to hers, stilling her efforts to clean up the area.

"This is really great of you. I've meant to read a lot of these at different points in my career, but never made the time."

His eyes conveyed a sincerity that melted her heart and made her realize she was toast when it came to this man. How had she let this happen?

"It was nothing—"

He kissed her, staunching the flow of words with the tender barrier of his lips. Awareness flamed to life, flicking over her skin to tantalize every inch of her with wanting. Her eyelids drifted closed, her senses narrowing to focus on Heath's scent and touch. She breathed him in, letting the moment burn away the awkwardness, the worries and the burden of too many thoughts.

He pulled away from her so slightly that she did not even bother to open her eyes.

"It's *not* nothing," he whispered, his thumb roaming over the back of her hand in a sweet, subtle stroke. "It's something no one else would have thought to do for me and something I really needed tonight."

She forced her eyes open at the vehemence—the

pure conviction—in his voice. Happiness warmed her heart for a moment and then her attention snagged on the last part of what he'd just said.

"What do you mean? Did something happen?" She could tell something must have gone wrong.

"The team owner called after the meeting. He said they're giving me run of the team for this road series, but if I can't win in L.A., I'm done."

"You can't be serious." Her eyes were wide-open now, the electric hum in her skin short-circuiting at the news. "That's like my department editor saying I have to sell a few thousand more papers to keep writing my column."

How incredibly unfair.

Behind them, an assistant librarian strode through the floor announcing they would be closing shortly.

"Well, it's done." Heath squeezed her hand tighter. "I can't make any radical changes to my game plan at this point, but who knows? Maybe I can light a fire under these guys in the locker room thanks to your help."

He gestured toward her piles of notes and books. Never in her life had her academic approach felt as small as right at that moment. He was being unfairly railroaded, and there wasn't a damn thing she could do to help.

"I had so many ideas. I thought the players' wives and girlfriends would get together more. I thought you could get some more translators for a night out—"

"And maybe I'll have the chance to try all of that." Rising from the chair, he scooped up her bag and notes. "I'll sure as hell look over some of this before I hit the locker room tomorrow, but right now there's only one thing that will make this better."

"A breach of contract lawsuit."

"No." With his free hand, he tugged her toward the elevator. "Sex all night long. And the sooner the better."

Her heart tripped over itself even more than her suddenly stumbling feet.

"Oh." She looked back with longing at the high shelves of books that hid lovers among the stacks. "I know somewhere we could go just to, er, take the edge off."

He'd been tempted.

Amber had glanced toward the towering racks with a mischievous gleam in her eyes, twirling her braid between her fingers like a naughty co-ed bent on getting into trouble. It was the last thing he'd expected from her, and he'd bet his World Series ring that she'd never tried something like that before. Which, of course, had made him all the more eager to take her back there and fulfill every fantasy.

But a public indiscretion could have him booted out of the clubhouse before tomorrow's game even got under way, so he'd opted to pay the cab driver double to deliver them back to their hotel quickly.

Now, he sat beside her in the darkened backseat of a yellow taxi while the driver sped down Sunset Boulevard.

"I can't believe I missed out on a chance like that." Heath breathed in the scent of her shampoo where he'd already started to unwind the braid. The layers of hair inside were still slightly damp even though he'd bet she'd showered hours ago. "If I get fired tomorrow and my public image no longer matters, you have to promise me you'll go back to that library with me."

"No way." She ducked her head against his shoulder and rubbed her cheek against his chest. "I can't believe I proposed something so outrageous in the first place. It's just that I've heard couples fooling around in the stacks in libraries a million times. Maybe it's a rite of passage for academic types."

Other cars honked as their cab extricated itself from a knot of traffic.

"Damn it." Heath could picture her working diligently in nameless libraries around Boston, trying to ignore the sounds of couples sneaking a feel nearby. "I deprived you of something you could have thought about every time you're in a library for the rest of your life."

And knowing Amber's love of books, that would be a lot of times.

"Why don't you make it up to me by providing what I've *really* wanted all evening?"

As the cab drew to a stop in front of the hotel, he racked his brain to think what that would be.

"The massage?" He hated to give her up for that long, but this was supposed be her vacation.

One of the hotel valets opened the taxi's door while Heath paid the driver. Amber's half-undone hair slid forward over one shoulder as she stepped out of the cab and peered back at him.

"The quickie."

Hallelujah.

Heath turned to the valet still holding the cab door while Amber walked toward the hotel a few paces ahead of him.

"The front desk has my girlfriend's cell phone. Could you send it up to Room 5163 in about an hour?"

He passed the kid a ten. Then dug in his wallet for a second. "Actually, make that two hours, and could you tell room service to bring something then, too? Good red wine and a pizza?"

"Of course, Mr. Donovan." The kid nodded, hiding any smirk he might have had at overhearing Amber's mention of a quickie. "And I'll be rooting for you tomorrow. I'm from Hartford."

"Good man." Heath slapped him on the back. "We'll need some fans on our side."

He hurried to catch up to Amber, wanting to touch her so he wouldn't think about that damn game anymore. As much as he appreciated hearing from the Aces' fans, he couldn't worry about things he couldn't control. His best pitcher wouldn't be ready to pitch until the following game, so they had to go with a new guy they'd just pulled up from the minors. The bullpen had been struggling all year since they had no depth in that department— *No.* He shut down that line of thinking, jogged through the hotel doors that a bellhop held open for him and hurried past the front desk.

At the elevator bank, Amber stood inside an empty car, one finger pressing a button on the control panel.

"Going up?" A smile teased one side of her lips. She'd lost the tie in her hair somewhere between the cab and the hotel, so now the waves spilled free over the shoulders of her simple cotton dress.

"Hell, yes."

He barged in the elevator and dragged her finger away from the button that held the doors open. He didn't wait for them to close behind her, but backed her up against the rear wall, his hands on her waist.

She went willingly. Eagerly. Shrugging her purse

strap off her shoulder, she let it fall to the floor and then wrapped her arms around his neck. He pulled her hips to his, sealing them together.

"You forgot to hit the button for the fifth floor," she whispered, arching her neck as if she wanted a kiss there.

"I know exactly what to hit to take you where you want to go." He breathed the words along her skin before he took a sample taste.

Her soft whimper vibrated against his lips and hummed along his tongue. He could feel the thrum of her pulse at her throat and the need to have her naked seized him hard.

"Hurry," she urged, untwining an arm from his neck to reach for the elevator buttons.

Some part of his brain told him they were probably at the penthouse level by now. Thank God no one else had wanted a ride yet. He leaned back enough so she could reach the button for their floor.

Ding!

The elevator chimed as it slowed to a stop—on the sixth floor instead of the fifth.

"Stay in front of me." Heath moved Amber to stand between him and entrance, unable to gain control of himself before the sliding doors hissed open.

He kept his arms wrapped around her waist and ducked his chin to kiss her shoulder.

"Hey, Skip." The Aces' big-money closer, Chase Montoya, stepped into the cabin with star pitcher Jay Cannon.

Clearly dressed for a night on the town, Jay's black silk shirt and black pants made him look like stereotypical New York mafia while Montoya's baseball jersey and gold necklace as thick as a climbing rope were more suited to a rap video.

"You guys aren't setting a bad example for my rookies by blowing off curfew, are you?" Heath wished he could put Amber under his arm and hide her from view since these two gawked at her as if they'd never seen a woman before.

She did look hot as hell with her cheeks all flushed and her lips swollen from his kisses. And that hair—so long and wavy—made her look like some lush, mythical goddess.

"I'm not due on the mound tomorrow, boss," Jay clarified, though they all knew that Chase would be tapped for a save if the Aces got a lead. "Tonight, we figured we'd hit the bars for a celebrity hunt."

With Montoya a veteran earning the big bucks, Heath let it go. As a player, he'd never appreciated being told how to prepare for games. But damn it, these guys set a bad example for the new and impressionable types.

"Just stay away from fans with videophones, all right? I don't need to see you two on TMZ highlights tonight." Heath wondered if he'd even be employed by the team on Saturday when it was Jay's turn to pitch.

Ding!

The car arrived at their floor, and Amber wrapped her arms around him.

"Night!" she called to them as Heath escorted her out of the elevator and down the hall to his suite.

Nothing else was getting in the way of what he wanted now. No players. No meetings. No phone calls threatening his job.

"I'm bolting the door and throwing my phone across

the room," he warned her, inserting his key card into the lock. "No more interruptions. No more trips to the library."

"Really?" She crossed the threshold as he held open the door. "What if I have a sudden urge to consult a book?"

He followed her inside and slid the bolt into place. Blue lights from above the bar were the only illumination, except for the glow from the street below that filtered in under partially closed blinds. The lights from Rodeo Drive remained bright long after the stores closed.

He regretted that she hadn't gotten to see anything of the city so far, but that was what his life was like on the road—hotels and ball fields.

"I'm going to teach you everything you'll need to know. No books necessary." He stepped deeper into the room and shrugged off his suit jacket.

Loosened his tie.

Her eyes followed the movement of his hand on the knot before her gaze tracked back up to his face.

"But I like being an expert on things," she persisted, though she was already stepping out of her shoes. Her purse hit the bar with a thud.

"Guess I'll have to send you straight to the master class."

He reached for her, and she was in his arms in a heartbeat. Quick, clever fingers fluttered all over his chest, dipping between shirt buttons to unfasten them.

"Less talk. More naked." She yanked his shirt backward off his shoulders and nearly strangled him with his tie. "Oh!"

She reached to loosen it more, but he beat her to the knot.

"I've got it." He tossed the neckwear with all the power of a centerfielder going straight to the plate.

"I told you I need my reference manuals," she reminded him, placing a kiss on the hot skin of his chest.

The soft curve of her breasts teased him through the fabric of her cotton dress. She was so sexy in her classic, simple clothes and her practical braid. Not femme fatale heels and knock-him-out perfume. Amber was beautiful for not trying. And just what he needed to keep his mind off tomorrow's game. This was more than a good idea. It was a damn great idea.

"One day when we're not in a hurry, I'll give you a step-by-step tutorial," he assured her. "Right now, we're going to fast-forward through all that."

"No instructions?"

"No more fighting with the clothes. We can work around the rest." He picked her up and backed her against the door they'd just entered. He gripped her bare thighs beneath her dress, but she wrapped her legs so hard around him, he could have let go and she wouldn't have fallen.

A gasp rose from her lips. She clutched his shoulders and made sexy little sounds that drove him crazy.

"I've wanted this all day." His thumbs speared beneath the lace of her panties, claiming the new terrain of unbelievably soft skin.

Silky damp curls hid her slick heat, but he sifted his way through to touch the tender bud of her sex. Wet with wanting, her body wept for him in the sweetest sign of feminine desire.

Heat fired through him, his whole body a hot, hard

ache. He didn't just want Amber. He needed her with a fierceness that rocked him.

The drive to be inside her—to give and take, pleasure and possess—was so strong he unfastened his pants and nudged his boxers aside. He was beyond ready.

"Condom," a voice of reason murmured. Her voice. "Please say you restocked."

It took him a moment to realize she was digging through his pants pocket for a reason. A damn good one, at that. When had he ever lost control so badly that he never even thought about protection?

She emerged from the pocket with the necessary item and lost no time ripping open the packet with her teeth. Her one-handed effort to slide the condom on him was a teeth-clenching exercise in restraint, but he managed to hold back until she guided him toward the slick feminine heat between her legs.

The urge to explain himself—that he couldn't slow down because he'd never felt like this before—died in his throat. He gripped her thighs, drawing her closer to edge his way deeper.

Burying his face in the cascade of hair over her shoulder, he inhaled the scent of her. Soap and flowers. Sex and desire.

For a long moment, he just held her there, acclimating to the feel of her. Relishing the fact that he'd gotten lucky enough to find her that night at The Lighthouse.

"I'm so close," she whispered, her voice thin and sweet in the darkness broken only by the blue bar light. "It feels so good."

Heath thrust and watched her through half-opened eyes, her head tossing back and forth as if she were in the throes of a dream she didn't want to end. Raw masculine pride surged through him that he did that to her.

And suddenly, it was all too much.

He held her steady, burying himself inside her over and over again as his release blindsided him. Amber held on tight, her nails finding purchase in his shoulders for a moment before she shuddered and contracted all around him.

Nothing else mattered but her. This moment.

Their bodies slick with heat and sex, they dissolved together in a boneless heap and he was damn lucky he didn't drop her. Forcing one foot in front of the other, he stalked through the suite to the bedroom with her in his arms. They collapsed onto the pristine navy comforter, surrounded by pillows and bolsters.

For once, baseball didn't come rushing back to his brain in the quiet moment when his body was satiated. It was there in the background, but he could separate himself from it, and for that, he was damn glad.

"You're amazing." He couldn't begin to analyze the way she'd gotten into his head and stayed there.

She'd crashed into his life, not looking where she was going, and that had turned out to be the best accident that had ever happened to him.

"Maybe it should be me teaching the master class after all," she murmured, rubbing her cheek on his shoulder like a contented cat.

Like someone who cared about him.

The warmth of the moment fractured a little at the realization. Funny that it wasn't baseball that did it, but his own fear of hurting her. Of disappointing her.

His gut clenched at the thought.

Ruthlessly, he ignored the niggling concern, knowing he couldn't think about that now with her lying beside him. She'd come to him with too many old worries about sex for him to get wrapped up in his head now. She deserved to have him wax poetic about how fantastic she was.

"All those book smarts must be paying off," he agreed, vowing he would not let himself hurt her. Even if that meant he'd have to let her go sooner than what he wanted. Reaching for her, he rubbed her hip and realized he'd never undressed her. A fact which he would remedy immediately. "But I think we'll need to test your skills one more time before you're awarded that designation."

"Knute Rockne said we should build up our weaknesses until they become our strong points." She helped him untangle her bra straps from her clothes so he could reveal every smoking hot inch of creamy flesh.

"Bring it on, Professor," he replied.

It was going to be so damn hard not to fall for her.

13

"I CAN SEND A PLANE down there right now and you could be watching my game tonight." Diego cradled the hotel phone against his ear at one o'clock in the morning, grateful to have Jasmine on the other end of the line after so many failed attempts to reach her over the past two weeks.

"Forget it. I'm not some spoiled socialite who needs a private jet and a designer purse with a cross-breed dog the size of a rodent," she protested, stringing her words together in a whispered rant out of deference to their sleeping son.

Damn but she was a good mom.

He could picture her in the condo he'd helped her move into after college so she could be close enough to the local rec center to walk to her job. She'd worked hard to obtain a four-year degree as a counselor in three years. And he'd known she would be great at setting wayward kids straight since she was the most nonsense, get-your-act-together person he'd ever met. Jasmine had always been the practical problem solver. He'd been the dreamer.

"I would never try to make you into someone you're not. I respect you and the way you see the world. You encourage people to look beyond themselves to make it a better place." He hoped he'd said that right. He didn't want to waste his one chance. "But there's nothing wrong with wanting to be with you right now. And you've got to know I can't wait to meet Alex."

His throat burned if he thought about it too much—that he'd missed his son's first weeks. Diego punched the overstuffed hotel pillow next to his head to try to make a dent, but the thing exploded right back into shape.

"I *do* want him to know you." Jasmine's quiet admission surprised him. Up until now, she'd only defended her right to raise the child on her own since Diego had left, according to her, without a backward glance.

Which had been true. But damn it, he hadn't possessed all the facts.

"You have a damn funny way of showing it. You could have called me. Or told my mom." Diego had moved his mother to southern Florida after his father died last year. "You know my mom would have been so happy."

"Have you told her?" Jasmine diverted the underlying question, but he didn't mind.

As long as she came here, Diego didn't care about the rest.

"No." He flipped the pillow, hoping the other side would be more accommodating than the rest of his screwed-up life. "Can you imagine if I told her she had a grandson and the boy wasn't right there for her to kiss and hug and spoil? I'd never hear the end of it. When I tell her, it's going to be with you at my side and a kid in hand."

"I'll bet your mom has had a hard year with you being away all the time."

"She's living in the nicest house in Coral Gables." Did she think he wouldn't take care of his own mother?

"Mmm."

She didn't say anything about the house, but he could tell he'd somehow screwed that up, too, although how a guy could go wrong buying his mother a sweet-ass house with a hot tub and a security gate, he didn't know. He was about to ask, but she filled the quiet space with an observation of her own.

"She lost her husband right when she was trying to get used to you being in the States. And while I know you had good intentions moving her to Florida, I'm sure she's a little homesick for the Dominican Republic. She has so many friends here." Jasmine made sympathetic sort of noises that made him feel less as if she was blaming him. "What's all that noise on your end?"

He stilled in between the blows he delivered to the crappy piece of foam that had become his worst enemy. The damn thing wasn't like the ones back home, just like nothing else in his life was the same as it used to be.

"I can't get comfortable with these hotel pillows." It was a small thing, but damn.

Her squeal of laughter on the other end surprised him.

"Oh, God, I can picture that. You only like those squirrelly down pillows once there's no feathers left inside." More laughter. "Why don't you travel with yours in your suitcase? It wouldn't take up more room than a pair of jeans, knowing how you like a pillow."

He tossed the foam imposter onto the floor and

balled up the bedsheet to put under his head instead. He felt better—not just because of the sheet solution. But because he had Jasmine laughing that big, brassy laugh in his ear, keeping him real and solving problems in ways he wouldn't have thought of if he traveled for ten more years.

"Were you born knowing everything, woman?" He wasn't about to let her discover she could buy and sell his heart three times over. Not when she could still hang up the phone and shut him out of her life again.

"Not even close." Her sigh put him on alert. Something was bothering her.

"Why do you say that? What's wrong?" Diego might suck at fixing his own problems, but he would make sure hers went away.

She was a good person and she deserved life to be easier a whole lot more than he did. Too bad working with kids and keeping them out of harm's way in the inner city didn't pay nearly as much as baseball.

"There's a lot I don't have figured out, Diego. Starting with how I'd deal with the fame if I got involved in your life again."

She was actually considering it? That was the best freaking news he'd had in weeks. No. Honestly, it was the best news he'd had all year. He'd missed having her around to keep him grounded. To call him on it when he let success go to his head. To help him ward off false friends who only wanted to borrow money or cash in on his career. Beyond that, he missed the down-to-earth reality of a woman who was more concerned with living a happy life than keeping up appearances.

"Baby, the fame has some perks that can make your life easier."

"Like your mama's big house in Coral Gables? I don't want to be stashed away in some cold mansion and wait around for you to visit twice a year, thank you very much."

Damn. He remembered what Amber had said about the fame—well, actually, the abundance of available females—giving a woman a complex. Maybe that was part of what was bugging Jasmine.

"You and Alex could travel with me," Diego assured her, already picturing how different his hotel room would look if there was a playpen on one side of his bed and Jasmine lying right next to him. His heart hurt just thinking how much better he'd like that. "You both can be with me every minute I'm not on the field. And it's not like in the minors where we travel on buses and stay in crap places. We'd have the money for a nanny and direct flights first-class—anything that would make it easier for you."

"A nanny?" She sounded indignant, but amused at the same time. "Wait until you see this baby of yours. You won't ever want to give him up long enough to hand him over to anyone else."

His heart did that aching thing again.

"Let me see." His voice went all hoarse and he had to clear his throat before he could continue. "Go take a picture and send it to me on the phone."

"Okay." She made some rustling noises and he heard a door creak on her end. "It might be a little dark, but I can't turn on the light."

"It's okay." Diego lay back down, wondering if he could convince her to stay on the phone all night. He couldn't go back to that place he'd been the past two weeks—running around like a jackass, taking nips from a flask and hitting the skipper's security gate. What would she think of him if she knew about that?

"There," she whispered. The creaking noise returned and he pictured her leaving the nursery. "I'm sending it now. You can check your email in a second."

He listened to her messing with the phone buttons as he stared out the open blinds at the lights from Rodeo Drive below. Los Angeles held no appeal for him without her. Without his family.

"Jasmine, I need you to be here for tomorrow's game." So much was riding on it. Heath hadn't said as much, but Diego knew the higher-ups were breathing down his neck.

Diego also knew a lot of that was his fault. He had to pull himself out of this slump.

"I don't know, Diego. I don't want to be the woman who holds you back from achieving your dreams. That was the main reason I had to set you free the first time. I knew you were too big to stay here and I wasn't ready to leave home."

He digested her words and the idea of her "setting him free" so he could chase his dreams instead of her dumping him. Was that really how she saw it?

"My dreams aren't all that fun without you." He put the phone on speaker so he could tap his way through to his email.

"They say you're a ladies' man now." Her voice was formal, with no trace of the warmth or the laughter that had been there before.

"Jasmine." He wondered how to address that and figured the best response was the truth. "It hurt like hell when you broke up with me. I only dated a lot of women because I could tell after one dinner out that they didn't come close to you."

He heard a little sigh from her on the other end of the phone and he thought maybe he'd made some small amount of headway. God, he regretted hurting her. He'd make damn sure it didn't happen again.

"I'm a single mom, you know. I can't afford to get my heart broken, or worse, have you get close to our son and break his heart, too."

Just then, he found the email in his inbox. His gut clenched. He clicked it open.

"Oh, my God." Diego stared at the picture of the sleeping baby with a Spider-Man pajama top snapped on little red shorts that showed off chubby legs. Little Alex gripped the ear of a terry-cloth rabbit with one hand, while the other rested by his mouth, as if he'd just quit sucking a thumb. Diego felt his heart damn near burst out of his chest. "That's our boy."

"Yeah." Her voice went soft again and he could hear maternal pride radiating from eight thousand miles away. "He sure is."

A new, scary sense of responsibility made him a little light-headed. He was a father. He was responsible for that scrap of life. His hand gravitated toward the screen to stroke the swirls of dark curls on the boy's head. He knew being responsible called for more than just putting a roof over his head and teaching him how to throw a ball; Diego had to make sure that he had reasons to smile.

"I'm opening a bank account for him—for you both—tomorrow before the game." His son would have anything he needed. Diego's priorities had reshuffled so fast he could hardly process all the things he needed to take care of. "You're letting me help you out, Jasmine. I'm going to be down there to help you raise him every day that I have off. And I'm sending open-ended plane tickets so you can be here any time you want. I understand if you're not ready yet. But I'm willing to wait until you see that I'm not going anywhere and I'm not giving up on you or him."

"Okay." Her word was so soft he almost talked right over it.

"What?" He paused in the middle of zooming in on the baby's face. "Okay what?"

"Okay, go ahead and send your chartered flight down here tonight if it really won't break the bank. I can get tomorrow off from the center. Alex and I will come see you for a few days, and I'll see for myself how serious you are."

He nearly dropped his laptop as he sprang off the bed, instantly alert as if he'd chugged two Red Bulls.

"Seriously?"

"Call me a sucker for the father of my child." Her voice was a little breathless and he hoped like hell that meant she was excited to see him, too. "But yes. I can't wait for you to meet him. And we'll just…see what happens."

Happiness exploded in his chest like the fireworks after a grand slam for the home team. His hand was shaking like a rookie's in his first plate appearance as he reached for his laptop to set the wheels in motion.

"You won't regret this." He would be awake all night making arrangements, but he would ensure everything was perfect for her.

He just hoped he could put the bat on the ball tomorrow since he wouldn't get much sleep. But with his son and the woman he loved on their way to see him, he couldn't find it in his heart to care.

"I COULD GET USED to this." Amber chased her slice of wood-fired pizza with a sip of mellow Chianti from her perch against the pillows in the hotel bed. "The wine really goes with the red sauce."

Room service had delivered her phone along with the food, providing the perfect dinner in bed to cap off a really incredible night with Heath.

"Yeah, but what's with the goat cheese?" Heath eyed his third slice suspiciously, though the wariness didn't seem to diminish his appetite. "I'm a purist when it comes to pizza."

"Must be a west coast thing." She tipped her head against the smooth, polished headboard and admired the view out the partially opened blinds. Their hotel was taller than most of the nearby buildings, so there was little danger of anyone looking back at them.

Heath seemed very careful about protecting his privacy from camera lenses, which fit with what she'd learned about him after their very first night together. He would never be the kind of guy who sought the spotlight and that felt reassuring to a woman who occasionally grappled with insecurity.

"I can't believe I got you room service for dinner on your first night in Beverly Hills." He moved the box off the bed and swiped away the crumbs. "You deserved to see more of the city."

"Not just room service." She pointed to the advertisement on the pizza box. "It's the best pie in town. Besides, if you started to wine and dine me, I'd have major culture shock and might go running back home.

Midnight snacks during the late show are right up my alley."

She'd been out of her element at the spa today—no doubt that had been one of the reasons she'd followed her nose to the local library on the first excuse she'd found. She hadn't just been helping out Heath with her research about creating a healthy team psychology. She'd been running to a place of comfort in a world shifted far off-kilter.

"That's my world, too, most nights." He refilled his glass with the dark red wine, but she declined more. If the room started spinning tonight, she wanted it to be because she was seeing stars from the way Heath made her feel, and not because she'd gotten carried away on Chianti.

"So you said your ex-wife wasn't interested in traveling with you?" She wanted to know more about the marriage that hadn't worked out for him. Not because she was nosy but she couldn't imagine a woman giving up on him so fast. And maybe she secretly wondered if he still had feelings for her. "I'm surprised she didn't at least try that the next baseball season instead of walking away after just one year."

"She said my job shouldn't be more important than hers, and I could see her point." He shrugged, his shoulder brushing hers as he slumped back against the headboard with her, gazing out at the city lights and the low rooftops of the buildings nearby.

A few streets over, she spotted a hotel or maybe a nightclub with a pool on the roof surrounded by palm trees and late-night partiers.

"But marriage is about compromise." Or it should be. In her parents' marriage, her mother had done all the compromising, and it still hadn't been enough to keep her father faithful.

"That was her point exactly. She said she'd travel with me for half the year if I'd travel with her for half the year. But since baseball demands more like three-quarters of a year, I wasn't holding up my end."

"She must have known that when she met you."

"Well, if either of us had been planners or thinkers like you, we would have had that mapped out ahead of time." He clinked his glass next to hers and took a drink, as if toasting her worst trait—overthinking. "But since she was more like me with that 'I know what love is when I see it' kind of attitude, we flew into the unknown without really figuring out how it would all work. And it didn't."

So they gave up?

As much as the outcome of that story seemed frustrating from a romantic's standpoint, Amber appreciated the ending, given that his divorce had allowed her to meet him in the first place. Heath Donovan was so different from any other guy she'd ever dated. What had started out as a big risk for her was rewarding her many times over. Pizza and Chianti in bed was only the beginning.

"What about you? Didn't you plan for a future with Brent?" He set her empty glass aside along with his and then dragged her down to lie beside him, their heads sharing a pillow.

He even edged back a little to make sure she had enough room in a gesture that squeezed her heart.

"I did plan on a future, right down to where we would live and where we could vacation that would be halfway between my mother's house and his parents' place so that our families could spend quality time with us every year." She felt embarrassed thinking about it now—like a high-school girl coloring in her initials next to her boyfriend's on a notebook. "But you can't plan to fall in love with someone. And just because you'd like it to happen doesn't mean it will."

Heath was silent for a long moment. Then he leaned closer to brush a kiss along the top of her head.

"My father always tried to tell me I didn't plan enough—in life or in baseball. His big motto is See The Whole Field. But I never understood how you could plan for things when you never knew if the next pitch would be a curveball. You can only work with what you're given, and most of the time, you don't have any damned control over what that will be."

Amber knew he was right, but she hated to think she had so little input on her future.

"Will your dad come to the game tomorrow?" Idly kissing Heath's shoulder, she wondered how she'd ever go back home to the isolated nights in her apartment after the days and nights she'd known with him.

Would she ever get to meet Diego's girlfriend? Or enjoy being by Heath's side when his team was on a winning streak and his job was secure?

"Front and center. As a former L.A. star, he's able to command the best seats."

"Is that weird?" It was a vague question, but she was curious about the family dynamic.

Even though Heath said he'd forgiven his father for not being a part of his life—for not accepting him until he proved his worth on the baseball field—Amber sensed a strained relationship at best.

"Maybe. Yes." He stroked through her hair, twining

it around his fingers, back and forth. "It's tough to be your best in front of someone who only seems to see your shortcomings."

"Will I meet him?" She didn't know if that was pushy. After all, most guys didn't introduce their girlfriends to their parents unless it was serious.

But she was stuck to Heath's side while she was in L.A., so they might run into his dad whether or not Heath meant for it to happen.

"Probably. If you want to." He stopped weaving her hair and she peered up at him to see him frowning. "Amber?"

"Yes?" She tensed, reading some sort of reservation—a guardedness—in his expression.

"If we lose tomorrow, I'm not sticking around town to meet with the higher-ups and take the ax in person." The grim set to his mouth told her that he considered this a real possibility. "I don't want to ruin your vacation, but it will be a PR nightmare for the team and for me, too."

"Won't it be even worse for you in Boston?" She worked for a newspaper. She knew exactly how much interest a change in management for Boston's baseball team would generate. The guys in the sports department would work around the clock, literally, to exhaust the news value of that story online and in print.

Too soon, she'd be right back in the thick of that endless pressure herself, a thought she'd stuffed to the furthest recesses of her brain these past few days. It wasn't healthy to feel so much anxiety about a job—hers, or his, either.

"I don't think I'd return to Boston. At least not right away." His eyes were fixed on some distant, invisible point out the hotel window and she felt a gap a mile wide open up between them. "I couldn't even go to the beach house on Nantucket. Too many reporters know to look for me there."

"So..." She waited for him to spell out what that meant for her. When his brooding look never changed, she thought she'd better pin down some clarification. "You'd like me to return to Boston on my own, then."

She hoped that wasn't what he meant. And yet...he didn't answer very quickly.

His gaze flickered back to her, his hand still woven through her hair like a forgotten project.

"Only if we lose." Gently, he untangled his fingers. "I hope you know I never expected I'd receive this kind of ultimatum when I asked you to come here with me."

She felt a little shell-shocked at the realization that her time with him would be over—for good—if his team lost tomorrow. Intellectually, she knew he had to feel even more adrift than her since he'd put his whole life into baseball and he could lose it in the course of a game. Still, it was clear that Heath didn't have the sense of attachment to her that she'd developed for him over the past few days.

Months ago, Brent's defection and parting jab had made her question everything she thought she knew about love and dating. Sure it had hurt. But now, she understood that Brent had mainly wounded her pride— she hadn't really loved him.

Amber might not have realized that at the time. But now she knew for sure. What she'd felt for Brent was a pale facsimile of the emotions she'd experienced with Heath.

Emotions she would not name—even in the privacy

of her own head—to save herself from admitting to a feeling that would only devastate her.

"Amber?" Heath's voice prodded her for a response, reminding her that he was waiting for her to relinquish any claim to him this week so he could leave town if the need arose.

No muss. No fuss.

"Of course, I understand." It was the truth, since she was an expert at thinking through things and she could fully appreciate that Heath would have few professional options after tomorrow's game if he lost his job. "It makes sense to avoid the Aces' backyard for a while."

Her heart burned even more than her eyes as she said what he wanted to hear. Hadn't she promised herself to date for fun and not get caught up in romanticizing things? But damn it, Heath wasn't like the other guys she'd dated. She herself wasn't the same person she'd been the week before. Knowing him had opened up a new side of her that she hadn't known she possessed. Someone bolder and more adventurous. Someone who had a world of knowledge to share.

Her heart ached at the thought of all she'd lose tomorrow if the Aces lost.

And if they won?

She'd only be putting off the inevitable. Los Angeles had been her fairy-tale world where all things were possible. No matter when she returned to Boston, she would be alone once that plane touched the tarmac.

Heath couldn't have been any more clear.

"Right." He appeared relieved that she understood. "But I'd make sure you got back to Boston, first-class and whenever you want. I can make all the arrangements for you, even if I need to leave right from the ballpark."

The pizza that had tasted so good a few minutes ago churned uneasily in her gut. He would really do that? Jet right out of that ball field like a stranger to her and leave her on her own to pack and get to the airport?

The chill of that potential non-goodbye opened her eyes to what little held them together. Or, rather, what compelled *him* to stay with her.

Absolutely nothing beyond the physical.

A gaping hole opened up in her chest, and it was all she could do not to clutch the spot with both hands.

"Don't worry about it," she reassured him, her mouth on autopilot since her heart was currently six feet under and her brain had shut off in protest. "I can make my own plans to return home if that happens."

And damn it, either way now—win or lose—she would make her own travel plans home. Like him, she didn't want to stick around and wait for the ax to fall. She would help him get through the game tomorrow because—whether he knew it or not—he needed her. She had something to offer and if he was too thickheaded to recognize that, she wasn't about to chase after him to make him see the obvious.

Yes, her heart hurt like hell, but she deserved better.

"No, Amber, it's my fault you're here." He punctuated it with a kiss that failed to reassure her. "I'll take care of everything and make sure you return home safely. I'm not going to let my career ruin your week, as well."

Too late. It already had.

14

HEATH WAS OFF HIS GAME today and couldn't quite figure out why. Nerves, he could understand. But his brain was in some kind of mental fog that he couldn't shake.

He'd slid out of bed before dawn to seek coffee in a quiet corner of the hotel. Now he sat at a small table between the gift shop and a croissant cart, sucking down an espresso while trying to sift through the flotsam junking up his head.

Yes, he could be facing the end of his career. That would rattle anyone. But he also kept thinking about Amber back in the hotel room and how he'd pushed her away prematurely. He'd known the whole idea of not wanting to wreck her vacation had been B.S. Preparing her for the inevitable had felt wrong even though he had damn good reasons. At the start of the night, he'd been so grateful to be with her that he didn't think about his impending career doom. Then he'd robbed himself of that happiness, convinced he'd screw up with her the same way he'd messed up with the Aces.

"Heath?" A familiar gravelly voice cut into his thoughts.

He looked up to find a grizzled old baseball hero

peering down at him, still wearing an L.A. Stars jersey twenty-five years after he'd retired from the game.

"Dad." Heath used one foot to nudge forward the chair opposite him before he rose to clap his dad on the shoulder in a sorta-hug Heath reserved for him alone. "Have a seat."

The man frowned as he took off his cap and set it on the table before sliding into the chair.

"You don't look surprised to see me." Mark Donovan still worked out five days a week and maintained his athlete's build.

Fans of all ages frequently recognized him, and Heath's father seemed to like that quite a bit. Mark Donovan hadn't just been a player. He'd been a sports superstar, crushing fastballs into the third tier of baseball stadiums around the country before a knee injury had finished his playing days.

Even now, he seemed to expect a ticker tape parade wherever he went and, frankly, Heath wasn't up for it today.

"No, I'm not surprised to see you around." Heath had half expected his father to show up at the hotel yesterday since the Major League Baseball schedule was made public well in advance of the season and Mark knew where the Aces preferred to stay when they came to town. Besides, Mark shared Heath's habit of waking early to scout out caffeine. "I figured you'd have some words of wisdom before the curtain falls on my managing career."

Heath had just hoped he could have received them in a voice mail or a text message.

Across the table, his father signaled to the woman behind the croissant kiosk and asked for a latte. Heath didn't bother telling him this wasn't a sit-down restaurant since the lady hurried over with a tall cup and a wink for him.

"You don't really think they're serious about cutting you loose after less than one season?" At least his father did him the credit of sounding genuinely shocked.

"I've been put on notice that if we lose this road series, I'm out."

"Son of a—"

"Exactly. But right from the start it was apparent that anyone taking over for the legendary Jeff Rally in Boston would be screwed." Heath had weighed the consequences, knowing the Hall of Fame–bound coach who'd put twenty years into the team would be a tough act to follow. But maybe failure wasn't something he'd ever really seriously considered.

Now, it seemed as if he was facing defeat on every front, including his relationship with Amber.

What if today was the end of everything for him? Would she really fly back to Boston alone?

Around them, a few early-morning risers were whispering and pointing at the father-son baseball pair and while he didn't ever mind meeting with fans, it might have been nice if his dad had skipped the team jersey for their impromptu family breakfast.

"Any manager needs more time than that." Heath's father sipped his latte thoughtfully.

"It's not a one-man show in the owner's office anymore. Bob has to answer to a board." There didn't seem to be any way around that.

Mark nodded, his face a fast-forwarded version of what Heath would see in the mirror in twenty more years.

"How are you going into the game?" he asked, rubbing his hands together as if he were getting down to work. "What's your plan?"

Heath cleaned off the rest of the espresso and wondered if there was any statute of limitations on how long you had to explain yourself to a parent.

Although to be fair, the question might not bug him so much if Heath had a better strategy.

"I've gone into every game like it's just a game and it's served me well so far. I played the World Series the same way I played rec ball or a Triple A matchup during spring training." He'd been quoted on it before because his perspective was unique, but it had worked for him. "It keeps the nerves down, and it helps me focus on fundamentals."

Because at the end of the day, that was what baseball was about. Bat on the ball for offense. Glove on the ball for defense.

"Son." His father hunkered down in his chair and leaned closer. "You can't coach like you played. That mentality worked for you personally on the field as a player. That doesn't mean it's going to work for all your guys. See the big picture and think about what *they* need to hear. Think about each and every one of those guys in the locker room and ask yourself, what does this kid need to know before he goes out there?"

For a second, the message buzzed around Heath's head as if it might make some sense.

"You never coached." He didn't mean it as a slam. But it made him curious why his father would offer the advice. "How do you know what I should be doing?"

His father leaned back from the table.

"I don't." Picking up his Stars' cap, he put it back on

his head. "In fact, I think coaching isn't all that different from raising kids, and I effed that up, too. But there are lessons to be learned from mistakes, Heath. And I can tell you right now that sometimes you need to open your damn eyes and see what's in front of you. Before you lose it, you ought to ask yourself, what does that person need? Or, in your case, what does each member of the team need?"

Standing, Mark took his latte and slapped Heath on the back before Heath could begin to untangle what his father had just said.

"You're leaving?" Obviously he'd ticked off his dad, but he had too much on his mind today to figure out what he'd done wrong now.

"I'll let you get back to what you were doing." His cagey look said he knew that had been exactly nothing. "I'll see you at the game, son. Good luck out there."

Shit.

Another strikeout with the people around him. And Heath wasn't any closer to answers now than he had been before. He still felt edgy and uneasy.

Off.

He could go back up to the hotel room and look through Amber's notes to get some ideas for what he'd say to the guys before what could easily be the last game of his life. But something told Heath the discontent brewing inside him didn't have jack to do with his plans for the team or lack thereof, no matter what his father said.

He had his head on sideways today, and the reason had to do with the woman lying in his bed. A woman he wanted, even though he'd told himself she would be better off without the upheaval, the travel and the scrutiny that came with his life. He had good reasons for sending her safely back to Boston. For once, he wasn't being selfish and was thinking about what was best for someone else.

He just hadn't gotten used to how it felt to make the altruistic decision. Judging by the ache in his chest and the cluttered thoughts in his brain, he damn well didn't like it.

It was a hell of a way to go into the most important game of his career, and he couldn't help feeling a little superstitious, as if he'd somehow jinxed the outcome already.

"So you're dating the manager."

The catcher's wife, Naomi Benoit Davis, asked a simple enough question as she helped herself to the continental breakfast in a private room reserved for the Aces and their families.

Amber followed along behind the petite redhead, filling a plate with fresh fruit and carbs. The private suite was large, so even though there were ten other people having breakfast—coaches and travel staff, mostly—they weren't close enough to anyone else to be overheard.

Naomi had approached her in the hall outside the breakfast room, having apparently been briefed by her husband about Amber's relationship with Heath. Amber remembered they'd ridden up in the elevator with Brody Davis when they first arrived at the hotel. He'd been the one who joked about usually having his wife glued to his side when they traveled.

"It's complicated," Amber answered finally, unwilling to compromise Heath's privacy by kissing and telling.

The redhead stopped in the middle of slathering jelly on her toast. A heart-shaped amethyst barrette winked in the overhead lights as she turned.

"Isn't it always?" Naomi nodded toward a vacant table near a window overlooking the shopping district nearby. "Want to have a seat?"

For a moment, Amber considered making excuses. She wanted to email Rochelle, and she was curious if her editor had sent her any news about her department even though she was on vacation. But hadn't she committed to not overthinking? That ought to apply to hanging out with a potential new friend and not just her relationships with men. This week, she'd proven she could take risks.

Besides, she wasn't so sure she'd be returning to the book reviewing job when this vacation was over. Watching Heath's frustrations with his career made her think about her own. Was it worth sacrificing all her free time for the sake of job security? Maybe she could find another productive outlet for her skills that wouldn't make her feel so anxious all the time and rob her of a social life.

"That would be nice." Amber followed the other woman to the table and set down her dish and a cup of tea. "I'm keeping an eye out for Diego Estes's girlfriend, though. She should be easy to spot since she'll be with a baby."

Diego had called the hotel room this morning after Heath had left her to wake up alone. While she'd had half a mind to hop a plane back home since he had already checked out on her emotionally, Amber hadn't wanted to abandon the team, crazy as that sounded.

She wanted to see Diego hit one out of the park for his son. And she had to admit she was a little curious how Heath would handle the team today. Would he think about any of the research she'd done?

When the young third baseman had asked her to help his girlfriend, Jasmine, find her way to the ballpark, of course she'd said yes. As it turned out, she'd been more invested in Heath's player than Heath had been in her. And that hurt.

"I'm so glad you're doing this." Naomi reached across the table and squeezed Amber's wrist. "I've been telling Brody all season that the team would be a happier place for the guys if there was some more feminine influence. A manager's wife to coordinate some events for the players' wives every now and then."

Amber's spoon clattered into her dish, the word *wife* catching her off guard.

"We're not—that is, Heath and I just barely started dating." And from what she could tell, they were also just barely broken up.

The ache in her chest returned with a vengeance.

"Of course! Sorry to stick my foot in it so fast," Naomi hurried to reassure her. "Don't mind me. I don't mean to have you married already. I just think it's great that you're looking after Diego's girlfriend."

Naomi broke off in the middle of her sentence; her silver Celtic bracelets jingling as she suddenly lifted her hand to point. "This must be her."

Amber turned to see a young, dark-haired woman enter the room, cradling a sleeping infant in one arm. The woman wore jeans and a black blazer with a series of skinny gold chains to fill in the neckline. The baby's blanket was blue and gray, covered with the Aces' logo.

"Jasmine?" Amber rose at the same time as Naomi, the two of them descending on Diego's girlfriend to *ooh* and *ahh* over the tiny baby born just six weeks earlier.

Introductions were made over the child's sleeping head as Amber quizzed her about her flight and whether she'd had any rest.

"Come and sit with us," she urged, pointing out their table. "I can hold Alex if you'd like to grab a plate."

In no time, the infant was handed off to her and the new mom went with Naomi to secure some breakfast. As Amber stood there, holding the smallest baby anyone had ever entrusted her with, she felt her heart knot up in her chest. What would it be like to be part of a family like this, where women handed you their babies and trusted you to care for them? Where players looked to her for help with their personal lives so they could do what they did best out on the field?

Her book knowledge had served a bunch of strange purposes this week. Right now, she had the oddest sensation that she'd been studying up for a position she could have been perfect for if only things had been different between her and Heath.

"Amber?"

Behind her, a few more players had entered the breakfast room with Heath among them. He paused near the entrance, his eyes inscrutable as he studied her.

"Is that Diego's kid?" He peered down into the blanket at Alex's tawny skin and dark hair that formed a

V in the middle of his forehead, a handsome carbon copy of his father.

"Yes. Diego talked Jasmine into flying up last night and I told him I'd help look after her today until she gets settled with the other players' wives and girlfriends." She gestured toward Brody's wife as she steered Jasmine to the coffee bar. "I considered leaving this morning after what you said about going our separate ways once the team lost. But I realized I really wanted to be here to cheer on the team."

Frowning, Heath tugged on her sleeve, urging her deeper into the recesses of the room.

"You thought about taking off today? Before the game?" His brows knitted together, his forehead wrinkling in concern. "I told you I'd take care of everything. For that matter, if we win tonight, we can go out and celebrate anywhere you choose."

"No." She put her answer out there before she let herself think about how nice it would be to languish in Heath's arms, savoring all the feelings he inspired inside her. Logic told her that the longer she spent with him, the more painful it would be to walk away.

That wasn't overthinking. That was a truth it had come time to face.

"Why not?" At least he sounded as frustrated as she felt.

"Because relationships aren't just about being together when things are good—only if you win. That's not how it works."

Behind her, a few more players who called greetings to Heath as they entered and he nodded at them in return. Then, lowering his voice, he focused on her again.

"You promised me three days. Maybe it's a mistake to quit this—" he struggled for the right words "—*relationship* until we at least give it that much time."

Alex made a sleepy sigh and flexed a tiny fist, his warm body snuggled against her giving her courage to fight for the kind of happiness she deserved. Hadn't she entreated Diego to fight for Jasmine? She'd read enough of *The Mating Season* to know when a relationship was real and worth the effort.

"My feelings for you have changed." She found it difficult to admit, knowing her emotions were not returned. "I got into this thinking I could gain back some self-confidence and start taking a few chances in life. And I've had so much fun—"

"So have I." He reached for her, taking his shoulders in his hands and pouring all of that Heath-intensity into her as he met her gaze. "This week should have sucked, given the way my career is falling apart, but our time together in Nantucket and even here has been…incredible."

Her heart melted and she felt herself swaying. Thankfully, Naomi was marching into her range of vision, waving a cell phone to snag her attention.

"Excuse me." Brody's wife grinned at Heath and then turned to Amber. "I just wanted to see if you'd like to ride over to the game with all the players' wives?"

Another reminder of what she would have to leave behind tonight.

"That would be great. Thank you."

"And you're okay with the baby?" Naomi peeked into the blanket once more, an expression of maternal longing evident.

"I'm fine, unless you want to take him—"

Naomi had him scooped up and nestled under one arm before she finished the sentence.

"I'll take good care of the little guy," she assured Amber before she backed up a step. "Sorry to interrupt!"

Amber waited until she was certain they wouldn't be overheard.

"I know you're already making plans for what happens when you leave the team. But they need you right now and you're still in charge." She knew it wasn't her business, but damn it, she was making it her business. "And when I said that these past few days have been fun, I was only just beginning. It's been more than fun for me."

Her voice cracked and she knew that any attempt at maintaining her aloof and studious bookworm facade was long gone. The sensitive soul inside had broken through.

She had no idea if Heath could see that, however. He'd admired her for being forthright with him in the past, but maybe he only liked the side of her that could give as good as she got—a side that was more of a protective coating over the tenderhearted romantic she hid inside.

"I don't understand." Heath shook his head. "Isn't that a good thing? Doesn't that prove my point that we should spend more time together?"

"I don't want to spend more time running away from the team or the past or real life." What had started out as a way to thumb her nose at Brent had snowballed into something so much more profound. "I'm falling for you, Heath. And I can't pretend that it's just been a few days of fun."

He rocked back on his heels, so visibly surprised she would have had to laugh if she hadn't been utterly mortified.

"Yo, Skip!" One of Heath's players jogged over to them, his heavy necklace swinging around his neck. "The bench coach is looking for you, and one of the trainers said to let you know we can take some swings before the home team starts batting practice if we get to the field early enough."

"I'll be right there," Heath said without even looking up.

The player rubbed tired eyes. "Sure thing, Skip."

"I know you have to get ready." Amber was glad for the interruption, not sure she could have handled Heath's stunned silence any longer. "I just wanted you to know why it's best for me to make my own way home after the game."

"Amber, wait." He gripped her wrist to hold her in place.

"I'm sorry." She cut him off, knowing she'd put him in an awkward position. "You've got too much on your mind to deal with this now. Good luck today."

She flexed up on her toes to kiss him on the cheek, an awkward goodbye that wasn't helped by the many pairs of eyes studiously not looking their way.

It was the presence of all those eyes that saved her before she could cave to some compromise of a relationship that would leave her lonely and heartbroken in the end.

Determined to salvage what she could of this day, she hurried toward the gathering throng of players' wives and girlfriends and prepared to cheer on the team for the last time.

15

I'M FALLING FOR YOU.

Amber's words were all Heath could think about as game time neared. He'd had ten guys in his face after the end of his conversation with her at the team breakfast, all wanting a piece of him. Refusing to shove his foot any further in his mouth than he had after revealing his plan to cut and run if he got axed, Heath had let Amber go.

Now, sitting in a courtesy office outside the visiting team locker room an hour before the first pitch, he tried to figure out how to get through this game. His third baseman hadn't slept all night, his twelve-million-dollar-a-year reliever had been in the strip clubs until dawn, and the team as a whole was wired from tension Heath himself had undoubtedly passed along to them.

It wouldn't be news to anyone on the team that they were all underperforming—Heath included. But he didn't have a clue what to say to fire them up.

I'm falling for you.

Heath pounded the empty desk with his fist, knowing he was missing something here, but damned if he could figure out what. Amber told him she was falling for him and in the same breath she'd accused him of running out on the team. If that was the case, how could she fall for someone like that?

Out in the locker room, he could hear the guys talking and laughing. He had no doubt Chase Montoya was holding court in one corner, telling the rookies how many bottles of Veuve Clicquot and Cristal he'd wasted on exotic dancers who would have no doubt appreciated cash more than the alcohol.

Other than that predictable patter, the locker room was actually kind of quiet. Heath knew he'd been tagged as more of a "players' coach" since coming on board in Boston, letting the veteran guys take a leading role to help shape the team. Once a veteran himself, Heath had appreciated managers who weren't hard-asses about mindless hours of infield practice or forcing big hitters to bunt around a run in some peabrained excuse for strategy.

But hearing Montoya's guffaws in the other room made him wonder if he'd been too lenient. Too much of a player when he should have been more of a leader.

His hand went to his shirt pocket, where he'd tucked a few sheets of paper containing Amber's notes from the library last night. Her handwriting flowed neatly over the page, compact and graceful, each line dovetailing smoothly into the next.

From the middle of the page, a quote jumped out at him. A tidbit from famed Dodger coach, Tommy Lasorda. "About the only problem with success is that it does not teach you how to deal with failure."

Funny how sometimes an obvious truth could whack you upside the head with implications you'd never seen. Because that quote was all about him—Heath Donovan—in a nutshell.

Heath had been a success all his life. Some sports writers had termed it "phenomenal success," and if that didn't go to your head, what would? But maybe all the success in the world had been piss-poor preparation for this moment. He needed to reinvent the wheel, and he needed to do it today.

Standing, he clutched Amber's notes tighter in his hand, hoping there was something in there that would speak to his team as loudly as those words spoke to him. He didn't have a plan, per se. But he had his eyes open in a way they hadn't been all season.

His father's harping on him had helped. But Amber's generosity—both with her heart and with her time—had driven the message home.

He wasn't going to fail her or the team today. Because starting right now, he wouldn't just be another successful player at the helm. He was officially taking charge.

He was the leader. The manager. And right now, the Aces were still his team.

AMERICA'S PASTIME WOULD have seemed like a great way to spend a summer afternoon if Amber's heart hadn't been fractured at the seams. It didn't help that the Aces had played eight innings of baseball in the past three hours and were down by a run as they headed up to bat in the ninth.

The sun had slipped down in the sky but remained visible over the open-air stadium, throwing just the right amount of warmth on her bare arms and legs as she sat in her cargo shorts and navy blue Aces tank top. The shirt had been an unexpected gift from Naomi Davis, the catcher's wife. She'd decided Amber's arrival in their group deserved to be celebrated and she'd bought out the gift shop's small supply of visiting team apparel to give a matching shirt to all the players' significant others.

The glittery heart around the Aces' logo was decidedly girly and nothing Amber would have chosen, which made her love it all the more. She felt like a different person than the one she'd been just one short week ago, and her ultrafeminine tank top broadcast a new confidence to the world. She wasn't going to hole up in her apartment any longer, working hours on end for the sake of her job. The new Amber was all about balance.

Too bad the new and improved Amber didn't date guys who were only looking for a fling. Why couldn't Heath see they could handle something more?

"Get your peanuts! Get your popcorn!" A teenager carrying a tray full of snacks tromped through the stands, his red and white striped paper hat tilted over one eye.

Next to Amber, Diego's girlfriend twitched in her seat as the first Aces batter grounded out and the next popped up.

Two outs.

"We could still win this game." Jasmine had been optimistic from the start, even when Diego had struck out twice before getting a walk in the sixth. "You wait. My man won't leave this park without lighting up this pitcher."

Amber smiled, thinking Jasmine was as crazy about Diego as he obviously was about her. She could picture them together for the long haul—her toting around a cute clan of kids to his games, him doing anything in his power to make her happy. Amber had already overheard Jasmine asking around about the team's charity involvement and good works' projects. Apparently, the woman had a lot to give in that department. No doubt, the Aces would have some serious resources for her to sink her teeth into.

Why couldn't a future for Amber and Heath be just as possible?

She couldn't imagine going back to her walls of white books for company after being exposed to the riot of colors and people in Heath's world.

She could have a place here. It wasn't a big, splashy spot like Jasmine would undoubtedly make for herself. But Amber could easily envision a role where she coordinated some trips out with the women who normally only saw each other at games. This group would benefit from a few activities together to prevent them from feeling isolated.

Amber knew firsthand how isolation led to insecurity. If her mother had had more of a network around her, maybe she wouldn't have been so quick to fall apart when Amber's father had left. For that matter, if Amber hadn't allowed herself to become so isolated in her world of books—much as she enjoyed them—maybe she wouldn't have been so devastated by Brent's defection.

Damn it, this was what Rochelle had been telling her ever since college. If it had taken her ten years to see, maybe Amber shouldn't expect Heath to recognize something that was obvious to her in just a few days.

Regret nipped at her for piling more grief on his worries with the team. Could she have chosen worse timing? But she hadn't wanted to repeat the mistakes she'd made in the past, coasting along without committing her heart half so much as her head. Heath had touched her deeply and she'd wanted him to know it.

"Amber Nichols?" A fresh-faced bat boy with a baseball cap pulled way down to his eyebrows stood at the end of the seating reserved for the players' families.

"I'm Amber Nichols." She raised her hand to draw the boy's eye.

"This is for you." He passed her a piece of paper and then darted back toward the field where he slid through the bars next to the dugout.

An usher standing guard nearby didn't even raise an eyebrow.

Snap!

The crack of a bat made her look up. As one, all the players' wives and girlfriends leaned forward in their seats to watch the progress of a ball through the infield.

"Single." Naomi Davis let out a whoop followed by something that sounded like a war cry. "We'll take it, baby!"

Apparently her husband had been at bat as the catcher now stood on first base.

Still, one runner on base wasn't going to make up for a one-run deficit in the ninth when they already had two outs. Amber's time in L.A.—her time with Heath—was running out.

"Well?" Jasmine elbowed Amber. "Are you going to open it?"

She nodded pointedly at the paper in her hands, the paper Amber had half forgotten.

"Yes." Her heart pounded harder, knowing that only Heath would have sent her a note.

"The managers never like cell phones or texting in

the dugout," one of the other women in a seat behind her clarified.

Unfolding the paper that was actually a preprinted form for a player roster, Amber read the handwritten scrawl on the blank side.

I haven't been seeing the big picture—on the field or off. But that's changing starting right now. Win or lose, I want to be with you. Please meet me in the players' parking garage after the game. I'll be out as fast as I can.

Her hand shook. She knew because the paper trembled in her fingers. Did he really mean that about wanting to be with her? Or was he just hoping to slow her exit after the game so they could talk?

Either way, a small spark of hope flamed to life inside her, and the day took on new possibility.

"Yes!" the wives screamed all around her.

For a moment, the enthusiastic cries felt like a chorus cheering the good news.

Then, Naomi put an inside-out baseball hat on Amber's head.

"It's a two-out rally, girl. Get your rally cap on."

Her emotions were all knotted up, but she'd said she was here to cheer Heath's team on and she planned to do just that.

Did he really want to be with her, win or lose?

She wondered as Diego Estes came up to bat.

"He hasn't had a hit in three games," Jasmine reminded everyone around her before she kissed Alex's head. She stood up, baby in her arms, as if Diego would see her. "It's your turn, Diego! Go get yours!"

The batter never looked her way, but he took one hand off the bat before he settled into his stance, and pointed right at her in the stands as if he knew exactly where the mother of his child stood.

Amber's heart warmed to see that connection, a bond that twenty-four hours ago Diego had been scared he'd never feel again. If these two could overcome distance and hurt on both sides to support each other, Amber wanted to believe she and Heath could fight their way through whatever life threw at them.

Win or lose...

Diego fouled off one ball and then another. Two strikes.

They were one strike away from going home when Diego delivered on Jasmine's faith in him. He smacked a fastball so hard and so straight into centerfield, Amber feared for whoever was seated in those upper decks.

Screams erupted all around her. Even Alex woke up to make some noise while his mother hooted and hollered.

Amber was thrilled for the team and for Heath. But it wasn't over yet. The best of the Stars' batting order would still come up to the plate in the bottom of the ninth.

Unfortunately, the pitcher due up on the mound was the Aces' veteran closer, Chase Montoya, the same player who'd closed down the strip clubs the night before, according to rumor. If Heath was seeing the big picture right now, he had to know they were in one heck of a tight spot.

CLEARLY, HEATH'S commitment to a new coaching style was being tested.

He'd told Amber that "win or lose" he wanted to be with her, and he meant it with every fiber of his being. But he preferred to win, and fate had handed him a two-run inning after two outs. Normally, an Aces' lead meant one thing..."Money" Montoya. His star reliever had successfully closed out the first fifteen games of the year before losing momentum in midseason. The highly paid veteran had flat-out squandered leads in three consecutive games.

Still, conventional baseball wisdom said you went with your big-money closer.

But middle reliever Dave Bryant had just thrown a perfect one-two-three eighth, striking out two of three batters and retiring the other on a feeble tapper back to the mound. Bryant was in a groove. Furthermore, Montoya had opted to party all night and spread the culture of fast living to a bunch of neophyte players who looked up to him.

Stop being the players' coach. Be a leader, damn it.

He could almost picture that neat writing of Amber's on the folded paper in his pocket. "If you're in control, they're in control." He was pretty sure that one came from Tom Landry. Heath hoped like hell it was true when the dugout phone rang with the bullpen coach asking if he wanted Montoya.

"I'm sticking with Bryant."

Next to the phone on the bullpen monitor permanently fixed on the opposite side of the outfield wall, Donovan could see Montoya kick the dirt on his way back to the bench, that big rope of a chain swinging around his neck. No turning back now. Montoya was no longer in the mindset of closing out games, and would likely demand a trade as soon as this one ended. He was never a team-first player.

Still, two bad pitches and Heath could start thinking about a career after managing baseball. He half wished Amber knew what a monumental decision this was for him. For the team. Then again, if Naomi Davis still had her ear, she'd probably fill her in fast enough. The catcher's wife knew as much about the sport as him.

Fully committed now, Heath turned his attention to the mound. Bryant had dominated the competition as the saves leader at Triple A the previous season. Still, the lineup on deck—Robins, Sorilla and Kazan—was as formidable as any in the game.

"You gotta know the shit's gonna hit the fan after this, Skip," the bench coach observed between chews on his tobacco. Grizzled and gray, the Aces' second-in-command had been a coach when the elder Donovan had played, so that told Heath he had to be nearing retirement.

"It already has." Heath wasn't going to defend himself. There was a new era in this dugout if he stuck around the team past tonight, and it was just as well everyone knew it.

"Shane Robins is a slap hitter," the old bench coach, Butch Casey, observed. "More infield hits than anyone in baseball this season. A well-placed bunt along the third baseline and forget it, the leadoff hitter is on."

Heath sorely wished the old guy would focus on his chew. Ideally, a bench coach was more for bouncing around strategy ideas, not articulating a manager's worst fears. But there you had it. Heath's job hadn't come with the ability to pick his own coaches.

"Always a possibility," Heath agreed amiably, hungering for a view over the dugout to see Amber in the stands.

Turning back to the game, Bryant appeared determined to pitch the speedster inside. Donovan knew that although Montoya had better pitches than Bryant, Bryant's command was superior, as he could pinpoint his location in the strike zone. And that was exactly what he did, retiring Robins on a harmless grounder to the first baseman.

The dugout gave a cursory round of shouts and encouragement, the mood among the guys surprised. Confused. No doubt every one in there was second-guessing this new management style.

"I don't think you'll get off that easy with Jose Sorilla," Butch observed, standing at the fence and breathing his tobacco-scented words of doom in Heath's ear. "He's had thirty home runs and thirty stolen bases in the same season, a rare breed. And for a right-handed hitter, he's especially hard on lefties."

"Heard and understood, Butch." Heath knew if he was going to get second-guessed for his decision to not use the closer, Sorilla was the reason why.

However, catcher Brody Davis had a thorough understanding of Bryant's pitching capabilities as well as the batter's style. Once again, Bryant spotted the pitch exactly where the catcher set up—at the knees and on the outside corner.

Sorilla swung violently at the pitch, pulling a shot down the line that landed cleanly in Diego Estes's waiting glove. The home crowd cheers quickly turned into groans.

Then, silence.

Heath actually started to hope.

"It's not too late to send in Montoya," Butch told him in low, confidential tones. "Bryant still has to face Kevin Kazan."

Not even know-it-all Butch felt the need to give Kevin "Bam Bam" Kazan's stats. The guy was primarily an all-or-nothing batter, having homered or struck out in sixty-five percent of his at-bats. Kazan, who led the league in home runs, was not the guy to make a bad pitch to.

"I'm not yanking Bryant." He wasn't giving up on someone who was working hard and doing everything Heath could have asked of him.

It was a hell of a lot more than he could say for Montoya. And, as messages to the team went, this one decision was going to speak louder than any locker room speech or postgame pep talk he could have crafted.

Amber's quotes and research hadn't been meant for spouting to his players anyway, though he hadn't realized it at the time. They'd been the final ammunition to help him understand what his father had been telling him. See the whole field.

God, he couldn't wait to tell her how much she'd helped him today.

On the mound, Bryant went to work, firing one ball after another. The kid walked Kazan on four straight pitches, and putting the tying run on base in the process.

Heath could already hear the criticisms weakly veiled as questions in the postgame press conference... *Why stick with Bryant after he walked Kazan on four pitches? Why not bring in Montoya at that point? Wasn't it evident that Bryant was choking/ tiring/ill-suited for the closer role?*

Nonetheless, Heath was determined to stick with his newly appointed closer, a decision that grew even more questionable when he fired a wild pitch to the Stars' next hitter in the lineup and "Bam Bam" advanced to second. Now, a single could tie the game and effectively put the winning run on base.

"This one's a pesky hitter," Butch announced, pointing to Micah Bailey at the plate.

But before the old guy could start in on stats that Heath already knew, star pitcher Jay Cannon moved closer to Heath at the rail and whooped it up for the young gun on the mound.

Well, damn. Except for Amber's sighs in his ear, Heath couldn't dream up a sweeter sound at this moment in time.

Jay Cannon was probably the only guy on the team pulling down more dough than Montoya. His support told everyone in the dugout—loud and clear—that he supported Heath.

There were victories on this day, damn it, no matter what the final outcome.

Still, after two consecutive balls, it looked as if Bryant needed a pep talk. Just the kind of thing Heath sucked at.

He rubbed the paper in his pocket, thinking Amber would have something smart to say, even if she copped it out of a book. The woman knew to go to the experts, unlike stubborn former ballplayers who thought they knew everything. Heath walked as slowly as possible out to the pitching rubber, not quite sure what words to use.

Brody Davis jogged up to the mound, too, pulling up his catcher's mask, his face intent.

Heath took a second to glance up into the stands, knowing his dad was up there somewhere. Amber, too, although he knew she'd be sitting directly behind him right now.

"Davis, you got any ideas on pitches?" Heath figured he'd ask the experts. Just like Amber had showed him.

The catcher shrugged. "I thought maybe the changeup?"

"Sounds good."

Bryant didn't look one bit reassured by the talk. He wiped the sweat off his forehead with a corner of his shirt. "What's the scouting report on this guy? How does he do with the changeup?"

Heath shook his head. "This game isn't about what *he* can do, it's about what *you* can do. The ball is in your hands, tiger, and you wouldn't be my closer today if you couldn't get out of situations like this. Don't worry about him. Just let it fly and hit Brody's mitt."

He clapped the kid on the shoulder and let the pitcher and catcher get back to work. Walking away from the mound, Heath peered up into the stands above the dugout and spotted Amber with ease, as if his gaze was for her alone.

Thank God she was still sitting there, right in the middle of about twelve women—mostly wives but a couple of girlfriends—who frequently came to the games. She belonged here. With him.

He'd import books from all over the globe to keep her by his side. Hell, he'd hire a staffer to cover them all in white dust jackets, too.

She didn't give him a reassuring smile, but she didn't flip him off, either. And the fact that she was still here gave him more hope than his sorry ass deserved.

As he ducked back into the dugout, the game resumed.

The next pitch was a knee-high fastball that Bailey could only pound into the ground—right back at Bryant. He fielded the one-hopper and threw to first for the out.

Game over.

Heath's team had just won the single most important game of his career as a manager. He was so damn proud of his guys he choked up like a girl when Jay Cannon pounded him on the back. The dugout went wild, sensing a shift in momentum that was going to do them a whole lot of good.

But if Amber Nichols wouldn't give him another chance, this win wasn't going to mean jack in that big picture that Heath now saw all too clearly.

16

AMBER WATCHED A LIMOUSINE pull up to the curb in the players' parking lot just at the same moment Heath plowed through the doors into the underground garage.

He wore shorts and an Aces' T-shirt, his hair slick against his head as if he'd just stepped out of the shower. He looked just like he had that first day she'd seen him on the beach in Nantucket.

If ever there was an ideal man for a fling...

She remembered thinking that the first time she saw him. Her heart lodged in her throat now, however, since she wanted much more than a fling.

He spotted her and gave a nod toward the chauffeur hopping out of the limo, even though he never took his eyes off her.

"I dialed up a ride for you." Heath jogged to shorten the distance between them. The stark expression on his face would have never given away the fact that his team had won a significant game less than an hour earlier.

His job was safe. He'd proven his worth and more to the Aces' owners.

"A ride for me?" She hoped she hadn't misunderstood his note during the game. "You're not going with me?"

The players' garage was quiet on this side of the elevator bank since most of the players drove their own vehicles and used the valet service. A few taxis waited, but no fans thanks to excellent security.

It was so quiet, Amber's question echoed back to her off the concrete walls.

"More than anything, I want to go wherever you're going." He waved off the chauffeur who had just opened the door for them, probably so they could talk in private. "But I want you to have the option of kicking me to the curb for being too stubborn and blind to see that you weren't a groupie and that this wasn't just a temporary thing."

Her heart swelled that he would do something so incredibly thoughtful. It was also sweetly insightful to let her feel as if she had the decision-making power after Brent had made her feel so insignificant.

She drifted a step closer to Heath.

"It's been quite a few days since you thought I was a groupie." Their time together had been fast and intense. The most exciting days of her life. "I don't think I can keep holding that against you."

His eyes were so steady on her that her heart tripped up in its rhythm.

"Still, I want you to have the choice of taking this free ride wherever you choose, even if you want to head to the airport and back home. I've been so busy living in the moment—riding the wave of success I had as a player—that I didn't see I'm thirty-eight years old and it's past time to take a long view on my career, my life and the people in it."

Amber saw a few guys emerge from the elevators and she waved Heath into the backseat of the limo.

"Why don't we at least sit inside where it's private?" She hopped up into the back and then slid into one of the leather seats.

Her living room didn't have much more square footage than the vehicle's spacious interior. As Heath settled in next to her, however, the space shrank. She might as well have been tucked inside a broom closet with him since her whole body tingled with awareness.

His scent was familiar to her by now. His thigh rested mere inches from hers and she could imagine the heat they would generate if they closed that distance.

"Congratulations on keeping the team," she blurted, feeling guilty she hadn't mentioned it yet. "I've been so preoccupied since I got your note or I would have said something sooner. Plus, I don't know enough about baseball to really appreciate what you did, but Naomi said—"

Heath laughed. "I had the feeling she'd see the nuances at work. Chase Montoya wasn't too happy with me that I didn't put him in, but I thought it was a good time to send a message to the guys about what I expect from them. I'm not going to manage like a player anymore."

"You rewarded hard work." She could understand that much. "But it seemed like a risky time to test out a new approach."

"If not then, when?" He pulled out a folded sheet of paper from the thigh pocket of his shorts. "I was looking at these quotes you gave me before the game and there was one about success not preparing you for failure."

"I remember it." She studied him more carefully, beginning to see there was more at work here than just him lobbying for more time together.

"It made me think about how much I've learned to trust my instincts." He set the paper on a low side table. "That worked well as a player. Not so much as a manager. Or in relationships."

He'd thought about her today, during the most crucial game of his managing career. That alone would have touched her. But the fact that he seemed to want to make her happy gave her heart palpitations.

His thigh loomed so close. His big hand rested on his knee, and she thought about how it would feel to place her palm inside his.

"So you changed how you managed." She was starting to see the significance of what he'd done today by keeping in the relief pitcher.

Yes, it had been about baseball. But it represented a deeper shift in thinking. An openness to new ideas.

"Yes." He moved the hand closest to her, stretching that arm out along the back of her seat, without really touching her. "Not that I see myself as ever turning into a really hard-core, old-school tough guy or anything. But I'm not going to just blindly follow my instincts. I'm going to question everything, study traditional strategy and see where I can improve. More important, I'm not going to just assume that I can't make things work with you on a long-term basis because of my job."

Behind her, Heath's hand came to rest on her braid where it snaked along the seat. She could feel the gentle tug against her scalp as he slid his fingers very lightly up and down the woven center.

Her heart stuck in her throat, and her skin hummed with pleasurable shivers.

"Long-term?" Her breathless voice didn't sound like it belonged to her.

"I screwed up a marriage." He slid under the braid to cup her shoulder in one hand. "That doesn't mean I will always mess up relationships. I know how to dig in and work harder."

He used the tail of her braid like a paintbrush to trace patterns along her bare arm. Had he leaned closer? Amber couldn't quite breathe. Either that, or she was holding her breath waiting for him to kiss her.

"I would like that," she managed, hypnotized by the promise in his dark eyes. "In fact, I really want to be around to see you dig in and work hard."

His hand stilled in the middle of the mesmerizing patterns he'd been making along her arm.

"Are you sure?"

"Completely sure."

"Because this is one instance where overthinking could be a good thing."

Closing the gap between them, she edged over that last inch on the seat until her thigh brushed his and her hip bumped him.

"I've already thought about it enough." She stroked his cheek with shaky fingers, hardly daring to believe she might have shared her heart with a man who wanted to take really good care of it. "While I'm glad you're trying to be more analytical sometimes, you have to know that other times, I'd very much like you to trust your instincts."

A feral grin quirked his lips as he banged on the roof of the limo. Instantly, the driver set the vehicle in motion.

"In that case, we're going to a little beach house I know." He was already pulling the band out of her braid to free her hair.

"Not Nantucket?" They still had two games to play on the west coast.

"No, a little place on Catalina Island." Gently, he slid one strap of her tank top off her shoulder. "It's far away from everyone and everything."

Amber relaxed into his touch, her skin coming alive everywhere he stroked.

"You don't think the team will mind?"

"I don't care who thinks what." He kissed her bare collarbone as the limo picked up speed. "I called the Aces' owner and told him I'm not dancing to his tune anymore. He's not going to be breathing down my neck until at least next year. And as for the rest of the guys, a little worry about the new regime will do them good tonight."

Amber would have Heath all to herself, just like that first night in Nantucket when he helped her see the depth of passion that lurked inside her.

"I like the new regime," she observed, tugging at the neckline of her shirt in an effort to be free of any clothes in the way of Heath's hot, persuasive mouth. "In fact, I've come to a few of the same realizations about my own work, too."

"Really?"

"Management's been breathing down my neck quite a bit, too." She hadn't thought about it in quite those terms, but the metaphor was apt. "I've been running so hard to keep my job for the past six months that I haven't really thought about if it's making me happy anymore. And as much as I love the work, it's too much."

He frowned, shifting back from her as if to gauge her expression. "You're thinking about leaving the book reviewing business?"

"I can look for another outlet for my reviews. Or find something else for my unique skill set. There must be jobs available somewhere for a book geek."

"Maybe," he began, shifting closer again, "you could look for a job that you could do from anywhere. In case, you know, you felt like doing some traveling in the near future." He kissed a line from her cheek to her ear and down her neck, inciting shivers.

"I'll admit, I like flying first-class." She tipped her head, enjoying the way sensations chased down her spine.

"Then I'm going to show you the time of your life during the course of eighty-one road games."

"That's a lot of travel." Days full of endless possibilities by Heath's side.

"There's going to be a lot of time in hotels, just you and me." He laid her all the way down on the seat, his body half covering hers. "I hope you don't get bored seeing me all the time."

"And I hope you don't get tired of me telling you how to run your team when I don't know anything about baseball." She stared up at him, her lover turned lifetime love, and felt more complete than she'd ever been in her whole life.

He grinned as his hips settled against hers.

"I don't know how we'll do with the team, but I'm going to have a winning streak where you're concerned," he promised. "You wait and see."

* * * * *

We hope you enjoyed reading this special collection from Harlequin® books.

If you liked reading these stories, then you will love **Harlequin® Blaze®** books!

You like it hot! **Harlequin Blaze** stories sizzle with strong heroines and irresistible heroes playing the game of modern love and lust. They're fun, sexy and always steamy.

Enjoy four *new* stories from **Harlequin Blaze** every month!

Available wherever books and ebooks are sold.

HARLEQUIN®

Blaze®

Red-Hot Reads

www.Harlequin.com

COMING NEXT MONTH FROM
HARLEQUIN

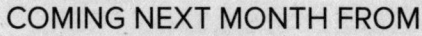

Available February 17, 2015

#835 SEARCH AND SEDUCE
Uniformly Hot!
by Sara Jane Stone
This time, Amy Benton is writing the rules: no strings, no promises and definitely no soldiers. Once she sees gorgeous pararescue jumper Mark Rhodes shirtless, though, she just may break every one...

#836 UNDER THE SURFACE
SEALs of Fortune
by Kira Sinclair
Former SEAL Jackson Duchane is searching for a sunken ship full of gold. Business rival Loralei Lancaster is determined to beat him to it. The race is on—if they can stay out of bed long enough to find the treasure.

#837 ANYWHERE WITH YOU
Made in Montana
by Debbi Rawlins
Stuntman and all-around bad boy Ben Wolf is only visiting Blackfoot Falls for a few days. But Deputy Grace Hendrix makes him want to get in trouble with the law...in a whole new way!

#838 PULLED UNDER
Pleasure Before Business
by Kelli Ireland
When Harper Banks barged into his club, Levi Walsh was ready to dress her down...all the way to her lacy lingerie. Until she tells him she's an IRS investigator—and she's closing his business!

YOU CAN FIND MORE INFORMATION ON UPCOMING HARLEQUIN® TITLES, FREE EXCERPTS AND MORE AT WWW.HARLEQUIN.COM.

SPECIAL EXCERPT FROM

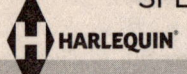

Mark had been her husband's best friend. Was it wrong to want more from him than a shoulder to cry on?

Read on for a sneak preview of
SEARCH AND SEDUCE,
a UNIFORMLY HOT! novel
by Sara Jane Stone.

"In those first few months, I made a cup of cocoa every night. Then I'd sit here and email you."

"You stopped sending memories of Darren," Mark said. "About six months ago."

"You noticed." Amy lowered the mug, a line of hot chocolate on her upper lip.

His gaze locked on her mouth. He wanted to lean forward and kiss her lips clean.

She shrugged. "I guess I was done living in the past. It was a good idea, though. It helped me find my way through it all."

He stared at their joined hands. "Must have been, if you started a new list."

Her fingers pressed against his skin. "This one's different."

"I know." He felt her drawing closer.

"I'm writing the rules this time." Her eyes lit with excitement. Unable to look away, Mark saw the moment desire rose up to meet her newfound joy.

He withdrew his hand. "I should go."

Mark pushed back from the table and stood. But Amy followed, stepping close, invading his space. Her hands rose, and before he could move away, he felt her palms touch his face.

He froze, not daring to move. He didn't even blink, just stared down at her. Her gaze narrowed in on his lips, her body shifting closer. Rising on to her tiptoes, she touched her lips to his.

Mark closed his eyes, his hands forming tight fists at his sides. He felt her tongue touch his lower lip as if asking for more. Unable to hold back, he gave in, opening his mouth to her kiss, deepening it, making it clear that this kiss was not tied to an offering of friendship and comfort.

Amy's hands moved over his jaw, running up through his hair. Pulling his mouth tightly against hers. He groaned. She tasted like chocolate—sweet and delicious. He wanted more, so damn much more.

Her fingers ran down the front of his shirt, moving lower and lower. His body hardened, ready and wanting.

He reached for her wrist, gently drawing her away. Then he leaned closer, his lips touching her ear, allowing her to hear the low growl of need in his voice. "Let me know when you've written your rules."

Don't miss
SEARCH AND SEDUCE by Sara Jane Stone,
available March 2015 wherever
Harlequin® Blaze® books and ebooks are sold.

www.Harlequin.com

Copyright © 2015 by Sarah Tormey

Love the Harlequin book you just read?

Your opinion matters.

Review this book on your favorite book site, review site, blog or your own social media properties and share your opinion with other readers!

Be sure to connect with us at:
Harlequin.com/Newsletters
Facebook.com/HarlequinBooks
Twitter.com/HarlequinBooks

JUST CAN'T GET ENOUGH?

Join our social communities and talk to us online.

You will have access to the latest news on upcoming titles and special promotions, but most importantly, you can talk to other fans about your favorite Harlequin reads.

Harlequin.com/Community

Facebook.com/HarlequinBooks

Twitter.com/HarlequinBooks

Pinterest.com/HarlequinBooks

HARLEQUIN®
A Romance FOR EVERY MOOD™

Stay up-to-date on all your romance-reading news with the *Harlequin Shopping Guide*, featuring bestselling authors, exciting new miniseries, books to watch and more!

The newest issue will be delivered right to you with our compliments! There are 4 each year.

Signing up is easy.

EMAIL
ShoppingGuide@Harlequin.ca

WRITE TO US
HARLEQUIN BOOKS
Attention: Customer Service Department
P.O. Box 9057, Buffalo, NY 14269-9057

OR PHONE
1-800-873-8635 in the United States
1-888-343-9777 in Canada

Please allow 4-6 weeks for delivery of the first issue by mail.